The Folklore of Devon

The Folklore of Devon

MARK NORMAN

UNIVERSITY
of
EXETER
PRESS

First published in 2023 by
University of Exeter Press
Reed Hall, Streatham Drive
Exeter EX4 4QR
UK

www.exeterpress.co.uk

British Library Cataloguing in Publication Data
A catalogue record for this book is available from the British Library.

https://doi.org/10.47788/YGMP5465

ISBN 978-1-80413-036-0 Hardback
ISBN 978-1-80413-037-7 ePub
ISBN 978-1-80413-038-4 PDF

Typeset in Chennai, India by S4Carlisle Publishing Services

Illustrations by Rhianna Wynter
Cover image: David Wyatt, *Ghost Road at Leigh Bridge*

Contents

Introduction 1

1. Folklore Collection in Devon 5

2. Stories from the Moors 18

3. The Calendar Year 38

4. Farming and the Weather 63

5. The Devil in Devon 82

6. Fairies in Devon 101

7. Some Devon Hauntings 121

8. The Black Dog 146

9. Witchcraft 161

10. Modern Folklore 180

Notes 192

Bibliography 208

Index 219

Introduction

The term 'folklore', coined in 1846 in a letter to the literary magazine *The Athenaeum* by antiquarian William Thoms,[1] refers to the collected beliefs, customs and traditions of any community. It is a compound term, which was originally hyphenated before combining into the form we recognize now. The second half of the term, 'lore', has as its root the Old English word *lār*, meaning 'instruction'. And so folklore is, quite literally, the beliefs of the people.

Of course, 'the people' and even the word 'community' are quite nebulous. How big is a community? The influential folklorist from University of California, Berkeley, Alan Dundes (1934–2005) described a folk group as 'any group of people whatsoever who share at least one common factor'.[2] Put simply, a community in this case is more than one. Where two people share a belief, so folklore may be created.

It was while reading Ronald M. James's excellent book *The Folklore of Cornwall*, published by the University of Exeter Press in 2018, that it suddenly became very apparent that a long time had passed since a similar volume examining the county of Devon in detail had emerged. There are of course books which make mention of folklore in Devon, but these tend to be coffee table books: short and easy reads with attractive glossy covers and containing a number of local tales, usually focusing heavily on the paranormal and the 'unexplained'.

Some of these are extremely good. But they do not usually provide any real analysis of the content, nor do they offer anything new. In the best story-telling traditions, they are usually a re-presentation of stories which have been told many times before. They are primarily aimed at a tourist market, and as such they have a tendency to suffer from the problems associated with 'guidebook folklore', where legends are retold and embellished based on information which has already been misrepresented many times before. It is a fate which befell some of the finest of Devon's folklore collectors and is an issue explored within this book, notably in Chapter Five on 'The Devil in Devon'.

The most recent title that is considered really important in terms of the preservation of custom and tradition across Devon is the namesake of this volume, *The Folklore of Devon*, written by Ralph Whitlock and published in 1977. It benefitted from being edited by the late Dr Venetia Newall, a notable Anglo-American folklore scholar whose document archives are now available to consult at Crediton Library in Devon, thanks to their preservation by the Folklore Library and Archive (the index to the collection can be consulted on the website at www.folklorelibrary.com). Whitlock (1914–1995) was a prolific author as well as being a farmer and conservationist. As such, he had a deep and rich understanding of the land and of the traditions associated with it, and his folklore collecting and writing reflected an interest that went beyond his home county of Wiltshire. In many ways, this volume can be considered as an expansion of and update to the ethos of Whitlock's smaller book, albeit with a slightly differing selection of subject matter.

Being longer in form, this new *Folklore of Devon* does not suffer to the same extent from the constraint that Ralph Whitlock found himself under, of trying to include as much information as possible without being able to expand upon it as much as he desired. I have taken the opportunity to draw on folkloric parallels across both time and geographical space in order to compare and contrast examples. That being said, in truth it remains possible only to scratch the surface: a volume of this size and more would be needed for each of the subjects my chapters cover, in order to record even a good part of the traditional past of the county.

In laying out the chapter structure of this book I have endeavoured to reflect at least in part the division of stories originally presented by Whitlock in his 1977 work. In places, the chapters in this volume are broken down further and some new subject areas are added. Most significantly, the last chapter explores 'Modern Folklore'.

It has long been the case that custom and superstition is seen as being confined to the uneducated rural classes or the peasantry. This was certainly the case propagated by the Victorian and Edwardian upper-class gentlemen who spent much of their time collecting and commenting on such things (and often bowdlerizing and misrepresenting the material), and who considered these views to be rather crass and beneath their status. Sir John Bowring, writing on the subject of the folklore of the county in a very early volume of the Devonshire Association *Transactions*, declared, for example: 'I am afraid the credulity and ignorance of our peasantry will not be deemed very creditable to the Devonian reputation, though they afford materials for amusing and instructive speculations.'[3]

Nothing could be further from the truth, of course, as interest in such superstitions can only be said to have boosted the county's appeal. Moreover, the placing of the peasantry as sole arbiters of local folklore is also misguided. After all, those upper-class Victorian collectors interacted with the subject themselves and in doing so created new traditions; and the same can be said for their own elite forebears and those who followed them. The final chapter of this book aims to show how this constant reinvention continues, even and perhaps especially in our global, technological modern world.

The world has changed remarkably since William Thoms put pen to paper to suggest a new word for the outdated terminology 'popular antiquities'. Some of us might live in a small village community or be part of a small social group, but across the planet a little over fifty per cent of us are also now part of a global community—that is, the community of internet users. Estimates at the start of 2021 suggest that there are now 4.2 billion live web pages on the internet,[4] using between them in excess of 40 zettabytes (40 trillion gigabytes) of data.[5] This gives us unprecedented access to information about cultures around the globe in a split-second.

However, there is a pervading misconception that something cannot be considered as folklore if it is not old. Yet this is manifestly not the case. In a TED talk given in 2015,[6] Dr Lynne S. McNeill, Associate Professor of Folklore at Utah State University and co-founder of the Digital Folklore Project, described the internet as 'the world's largest unintentional folklore archive'.

Folklore is surrounding us every day, whether online in the form of the latest amusing cat-based meme or whenever we see someone avoid walking under a ladder or saluting a magpie. But despite the sheer volume of folklore available to us, now more than ever it goes unrecorded. The internet might be, as Dr McNeill suggests, a repository of folklore, but how and by whom is it curated? We will explore this further in the final chapter.

Between the mid and late twentieth century, folklore arguably fell out of favour as a subject worthy of more serious study, at least in the United Kingdom where universities all but phased out courses that included it. It is only recently, in 2019, that we have seen the reintroduction of one Master's-level course in folklore.[7] However, folklore as an area of broader interest has seen something of a resurgence in the twenty-first century. This is in no small part thanks to the internet and social media, with projects such as Folklore Thursday on Twitter and my own *Folklore Podcast* engaging thousands of interested participants each week. In fact, despite the presence of learned organizations such as The Folklore Society, which was founded in 1878, it is more often those not affiliated with institutions of study whom we must thank for the majority of fieldwork and collecting of folklore traditions, beliefs and stories.

I am grateful to the University of Exeter Press for agreeing with me, on my first communication with them, that this volume was necessary. Also to Rhianna Wynter who has drawn the chapter headings and other line art for this book; my wife Tracey who not only wields the red pen so effectively on my manuscript drafts but also puts up with my frequent declarations of, 'Oh, this is really interesting…' from the other side of the office, while she is trying to write her own books; and most importantly, to all of the folklore collectors past, present and future, for allowing us all to understand the world around us just a little bit better.

Mark Norman

Devon

January 2023

CHAPTER ONE

Folklore Collection in Devon

There is a misapprehension that Devon is especially rich in folklore and custom. It is of course rich in these things, but it is not *especially* so when compared to other areas. Every county in the United Kingdom and every country beyond is equally full of superstition, tradition and custom, both ancient and modern. How much has been recorded and presented, how this was done and how much remains—these are where the distinctions lie. Devon is fortunate to have been home to some excellent collectors of folklore and many of them are profiled in this chapter. The Victorians and Edwardians are of particular note as prolific collectors of diverse curiosities, providing impetus for those who followed—well into the second half of the twentieth century. Some are more prominent than others, but all had a vital role to play in the recording of folklore in the county, and this book draws on their work throughout.

Devon is also extremely lucky to have such good records as those kept by the Devonshire Association, whose *Reports and Transactions* have been presenting them since the second half of the nineteenth century. This continues today through the role of 'Recorder of Folklore' in the Association, of which I am the latest in a long line. I make no apologies for drawing extensively from these records in certain chapters—this is probably the most valuable collection of folklore that the county holds to this day, and it is thus with the Devonshire Association that we begin.

The Devonshire Association

The Devonshire Association was founded in 1862 by the self-trained geologist and educator William Pengelly, FRS. Although born in Cornwall, Pengelly is more associated with Devon thanks to his archaeological excavations in the county, especially those at Kent's Cavern near Torquay which led to his providing irrefutable evidence that early humans lived alongside extinct animals such as the woolly mammoth.[1]

Pengelly first came up with the idea of forming a society dedicated to the arts and sciences in Devon while walking along Millbay Road in Plymouth with two friends—Charles Spence Bate and Reverend W. Harpley. His thinking was to model the organization after the British Association for the Advancement of Science (founded in 1831 and now known simply as the British Science Association). At first, those to whom he suggested the idea were rather sceptical about its success. Zoologist Spence Bate, for example, wrote to Pengelly in April of 1862:

> My dear Pengelly.—The scheme had better vegetate a little longer. I see nothing but failure shining brightly. You can call the meeting, if you like, for Plymouth at two or three o'clock, but I fear the Devonshire Association will be made up of Plymouth members, and what a farce it would be to have our first meeting in Exeter and no Exeter men there. It is your baby, and my advice is that you nurse it still a little. But whenever it is ready to be weaned, I shall be happy to assist you in getting it to run.[2]

As it happened, the first meeting, which took place in Exeter later that same year, was a resounding success. The Association's original statement of objective was laid out as follows: 'To give a stronger impulse and a more systematic direction to scientific enquiry, to promote the intercourse of those who cultivate science, literature and art in different parts of Devonshire, with one another and with others; and to obtain a more general attention to the objects of science, especially in relation to this County.'[3]

The first president of this fledgling group, Sir John Bowring, would also write on aspects of folklore, although not without some social commentary, as we saw in the Introduction. It was in 1876 that the first report of the Folklore Committee was read out, at that year's annual meeting at Ashburton, by Richard John King. Many of the subsequent Recorders of Folklore for the Devonshire Association would figure large in the collecting of material across the county.

Key Folklore Collectors

While not exhaustive, this chapter records those with a significant part to play in the collecting and preservation of folklore material in the county of Devon. To avoid any speculation on their relative importance, they are simply listed in chronological order by birth year.

There are plenty of other recurring names to be found in the material published within volumes such as the *Report and Transactions of the Devonshire Association* and *Devon and Cornwall Notes and Queries*, but it seems most may be classed only as correspondents or witnesses.

For the rest of this chapter we will record some of those who had a significant part to play in the collecting and preservation of folklore material in the county of Devon. The role of some may be seen as much greater than that of others, but to avoid any speculation on such ranking, they are listed simply in chronological order.

Anna Eliza Bray (1790–1883)

Despite a prodigious output during a long life, sadly very little of any merit has been written to celebrate the work of Mrs Bray (as she tends to be known in her folklore authoring). Born Anna Eliza Kempe in Surrey on Christmas Day, 1790, she would go on to become one of the very few female antiquarians of the nineteenth century.

Twice married, in February of 1818 Anna Eliza wed her first husband Charles Alfred Stothard, the son of painter Thomas Stothard. Thomas was elected a full member of the Royal Academy in 1794 and had eleven children with his wife Rebecca, although only six survived past infancy. Of these, Robert would also become a respected painter and Charles an antiquarian illustrator.

Three years after the marriage, in 1821, Charles died from a head injury sustained while working on his book *The Monumental Effigies of Great Britain*.[4] This took place at St Andrew's Church in Bere Ferrers, where he had erected a ladder to examine more closely a monument that he was drawing. Charles fell from the ladder and did not recover from his injuries. Anna Eliza would go on to ensure that the book was completed, enlisting the help of her brother Alfred John Kempe. It was published in 1832.[5]

Sometime the following year, Anna Eliza wed for a second time.[6] Her husband was Edward Atkyns Bray, vicar of the Devon town of Tavistock. It was from this point that Mrs Bray began to publish her works, as well as others such as those of her husband whose sermons and poetry she edited after his death. She wrote many historical novels, which were released between the years 1826 and 1874. The protagonists in some of these were drawn from families of note in the South West such as the Courtenays and the Fitz family of her hometown, about whom there is some well-known local lore.[7]

Mrs Bray collected and recorded her own versions of many local legends and traditions, which were published in the three-volume *A Description of the Part of Devonshire Bordering on the Tamar and the Tavy* in 1836. Later editions of the book would be known by the shorter title *The Borders of the Tamar and the Tavy*. The work takes an interesting format, being made up of a series of letters which Mrs Bray wrote to Robert Southey. He was Poet Laureate at the time of their correspondence and Mrs Bray would send him long missives detailing the traditions and superstitions to be found in the area in which she lived.

The Borders of the Tamar and the Tavy enjoyed a long life and is still a valuable work to this day. In 1879, Mrs Bray re-edited the work down into two volumes and also used it as a reference to form the basis of a book of stories for younger readers. This title, *A Peep at the Pixies, or Legends of the West*, first came out in 1854, almost twenty years after the original.[8]

Despite not often being in the best of health, Anna Eliza Bray lived into her nineties. She made provision on her death for the body of illustrations produced by her first husband to be given to the British Museum, where they may still be found, and she herself left behind an important legacy of folklore collecting which is a valuable record of her area at the time. Her papers, including much of her correspondence as well as her notes and manuscripts, are kept mainly at West Sussex Record Office.[9]

Richard John King (1818–1879)

King was an important voice in folklore during the nineteenth century, but not a publicly well-known one as much of his contribution was made anonymously.[10] His family was one of the oldest in Devon. His father, also called Richard, owned Bigadon House. This country house near Buckfast was, it turned out, heavily mortgaged and when Richard inherited it the finances were in such a poor state that everything had to be sold, including what was one of the finest private library collections in the country.[11] Leaving this behind, King moved to 'The Limes', a property in East Street in the mid-Devon town of Crediton.

It was quite late in his life that Richard King joined the Devonshire Association, in 1874, but he quickly moved into the office of President the following year. At the same meeting he read a paper on Devon folklore and then in 1876 he delivered the very first report of the Folklore Committee, which would continue to report almost every year thereafter.

Well before this time though, King was acknowledged as being an expert in the history, customs and folklore of the West of England.[12] Aside from his often unnamed contributions to the Devonshire Association, *Notes and Queries* and many other periodicals, he published some important larger works which were attributed to him. In 1856, *The Forest of Dartmoor and Its Borders* came out. This should have been a precursor to a more substantial work on the history of the county, but sadly that never materialized.

Another notable set of works was his *Handbooks to the Cathedrals of England and Wales*, which was published by John Murray in London between 1862 and 1867 as a series of six books. It is most fitting, therefore, that after his death on 10 March 1879, the Reverend Prebendary Smith worked hard to ensure the installation of a memorial stained-glass window in the Lady Chapel of the parish church in Crediton.

Sabine Baring-Gould (1834–1924)

Probably the best-known name in the field of folklore in Devon is that of the antiquarian Anglican priest, the Reverend Sabine Baring-Gould. This is certainly helped by his prodigious output of some thirty-eight novels, two hundred short stories and numerous non-fiction works including the sixteen-volume *Lives of the Saints*. His bibliography extends to over 1,200 known works,[13] and is being added to on a frequent basis as more documents are discovered. This is on top of his clergy life and his work collecting folk songs and tunes from around the West Country, the latter of which was considered by Baring-Gould to be the key achievement of his life.[14]

Baring-Gould was born in Exeter, the first son of Edward Baring-Gould who was Deputy Lieutenant of Devon at the time. Edward was lord of the manor of Lew Trenchard, a village in West Devon with a manor recorded as far back as the Domesday Book.[15] The building which currently stands in the village, and which belonged to Edward Baring-Gould, was built in the seventeenth century but was remodelled significantly by Sabine during his time there.

Because of the amount of time that the family spent travelling, Sabine Baring-Gould's education was undertaken in the first instance primarily by tutors employed by the family. He was, however, successful in gaining entrance to Cambridge University where he gained both a Bachelor and a Master of Arts qualification.[16] After a period of teaching he was ordained into the church in 1864.

Four years later, Baring-Gould was married somewhat controversially to Grace Taylor, who was the daughter of a mill-hand. The vicar to whom Baring-Gould was acting as curate, John Sharp, supported the match by sending Grace to live with his own relatives in York for two years prior to the wedding, in order to allow her to learn the manners required of a member of the middle classes in the nineteenth century. The couple remained married for forty-eight years until Grace's death, having fifteen children.

It was in 1872 that Sabine Baring-Gould inherited the estates and took up residency in Lewtrenchard Manor, and in 1881 when the position became available, he was able to appoint himself as the parson for the parish as well as acting as squire. This now gave Baring-Gould a settled base from which to work and travel in order to undertake his folk song collecting. Between 1889 and 1891 four volumes of these songs were published in what would become a classic series: *Songs and Ballads of the West*.[17] A later collaboration with the eminent folk song collector Cecil Sharp led to the creation of the book *English Folk Songs for Schools* in 1907, a title which would remain in use for some sixty years.

In the Prologue to folk song expert Martin Graebe's book *As I Walked Out*, Sabine Baring-Gould's granddaughter Dr Merriol Almond notes how ballad scholar Albert Barron Friedman once described her grandfather as 'a lousy editor of ballads'.[18] The criticism has certainly been made by many people, perhaps unfairly, that Baring-Gould bowdlerized too much of the material that he collected, because it was considered to be bawdy, and therefore that it does not provide a true reflection of the songs that were being sung in Devon. But Dr Almond goes on to note that Baring-Gould was not censoring material because of some clerical whim or attitude; rather he was ensuring that the songs he was collecting were able to be performed and sung as widely as possible.

In 1914, Baring-Gould deposited all of his notebooks, unedited versions of the words that he had collected and other folk song materials at the Public Library in Plymouth. So, far from destroying the original versions of songs that were performed, he was in fact ensuring that future generations were able to consult them. In 1998, further folk song manuscripts from Baring-Gould's library were discovered amongst the collections at the National Trust's Killerton House property. These are now deposited in the Devon Heritage Centre where they may be examined.[19]

Baring-Gould also collected and recorded folklore more widely, publishing both more general books such as *The Book of Were-Wolves* in 1865, which is still frequently cited in other works on the subject, and local studies such as *A Book of the West* (1899) and *Devonshire Characters and Strange Events* (1908).

The landscape and residents of Dartmoor provided another popular topic for Baring-Gould's writings, with titles such as *A Book of Dartmoor* coming out at the turn of the twentieth century in 1900. He had a particular interest in archaeology and was responsible for organizing the first properly undertaken excavation of the hut circles at Grimspound in 1893.[20] This, along with the later examinations of the same site, was instrumental in the forming of the section of the Devonshire Association responsible for the study of Dartmoor.

As with many of the other key folklore collectors examined in this chapter, Sabine Baring-Gould held key positions within the Devonshire Association. Although he never acted formally on the Folklore Committee, he was a regular contributor to their early reports and he held the position of President of the Association for the year 1896.

Lady Radford (1856?–1937)

Emma Louisa, later Lady Radford was part of a family who came from the mid-Devon village of Oakford, near Tiverton. Her father Daniel, a Justice of the Peace, was an active member of the Devonshire Association and Emma joined also in 1888, remaining a member until her death in 1937. She was the first woman to hold the position of President, being elected in 1928.[21] This was not the only prominent position she attained; she was also the first Devon woman to be elected as a Fellow of the Society of Antiquaries in London.

As an antiquarian, Lady Radford was a collector more of objects than of folklore per se, but she held the position of Recorder for the Folklore Committee from 1911 until 1917 and often contributed notes herself. She is arguably best known for finding the Tavistock Charter in the Public Records Office and producing an edited and annotated version, the publication of which brought it back into the public eye after it had been languishing in an overlooked state.

Two of the children of Lady Radford and her husband George Haynes Radford (the pair were first cousins) also held positions within the Devonshire Association. Cecily, an amateur archaeologist, served on the council from 1920 until 1965 and shared the position of Recorder of Ancient Monuments for the county with her uncle Ralegh. Ursula Mary was elected President of the Association in 1955.

The noted collector Sabine Baring-Gould (see above) was a very good friend of Daniel Radford, and the first volume of the former's *Reminiscences* is dedicated to him.

Richard Pearse Chope (1862–1938)

Coming from a family of merchants who settled in the North Devon town of Bideford in the sixteenth century, Chope was born in the family farmhouse in that area, Farford. Excelling at mathematics and with a first-class degree in the subject from Cambridge University behind him, Chope took a position at the Patent Office where he rose to the rank of Deputy Examiner and Principal of Abridgements and, at the same time, also ran the printing branch of his section, which was known as 'Chope's Branch'.[22]

Chope was interested in all aspects of Devon's history but he concentrated on folklore and was the Recorder for the Devonshire Association from 1925 until 1936. He is particularly acknowledged as having been the foremost authority on the speech and dialect of the county. His book *The Dialect of Hartland* was published for the English Dialect Society in 1891; as well as providing an extensive glossary of dialect terms from that area, it also presented a section on folklore.

Charles Hey Laycock (1879–1943)

The son of a wealthy Huddersfield family (his father William was a Justice of the Peace), Laycock embodies the stereotype of an Edwardian gentleman of the middle classes, having used his fortunate position to devote his life to the role of an antiquary, collecting both artefacts and knowledge on rural life and practices in Devon. He was educated at the prestigious Merton College in Oxford, which also counts Lord Randolph Churchill and poet T.S. Eliot amongst its alumni.

Known both in Oxford and in society generally as Charles H., back at home in Devon he was simply Charlie Laycock, a countryman who sang traditional songs and spoke in dialect. In both of these areas, Laycock made significant contributions to repositories of knowledge. He wrote on many topics for a variety of scholarly journals in his time, but in particular his understanding of folk matters can be seen in the papers that he submitted to the Devonshire Association. Having joined the organization in 1905, Laycock presented papers on local wit and humour and folk music and, crucially, edited reports on verbal provincialisms from 1929 until his death. The dialect collections at the

Devonshire Association are vast, unique and of vital importance to the region. Laycock also acted as Recorder of Folklore from 1938 until his death.

Laycock's Devon home was Mearsdon Manor in the Dartmoor village of Moretonhampstead, where he lived from 1910 until his death in 1943. As a folk singer he collected not only the music itself, but also a large number of instruments. Laycock was predominantly interested in stringed keyboards, and his collection included harpsichord, clavichord and spinet. But his main passion for collecting and preservation revolved around the traditional items one might find in a Devon farmhouse. Laycock amassed so many artefacts during his life that at one point he needed to enlarge the back of his Cross Street home in order to provide space for storage and display. He moved into

the small extension he had built on the back of the property, choosing to house his collection in the main building.

Charles Laycock possessed a determination to preserve the look and feel of the county's rural heritage, and this has ultimately been of huge benefit in modern times. He wrote about his wishes in this area:

> I should like to point out the desirability of acquiring and preserving at least one typical example of the old Devon farm-house, with its furniture and utensils intact, before it is too late and they have all been swept away and forgotten. Or if this could not be conveniently done, the desirability of erecting on some suitable spot ... a 'life-size' model in lath and plaster, or better still in cob, of a typical old farm-house, complete with its furniture and household utensils, as they appeared up to about fifty years ago.[23]

In 1936, no doubt mindful of this aim, Laycock began to present articles from his collection to the Torquay Natural History Society. These were kept together with other similar pieces which had been donated by Marjory Eckett Fielden, a Torquay resident who also contributed snippets of folklore to the Devonshire Association, and who wrote the book *Dartmoor My Dartmoor and Other Poems* in 1932. Together, these items formed the start of what was to become the culturally important Devon Folk Collection.

Laycock made provision that, upon his death, the contents of his Moretonhampstead home should go to the Torquay Natural History Society along with a bequest of £10,000 to be used for the construction of a permanent display of the items. This can now be viewed at Torquay Museum in the shape of the Old Devon Farmhouse gallery, a life-sized reconstruction of a Devon farmhouse from 1860. A few traces of Laycock's time living in Moretonhampstead remain: pot hangers from his collection are still affixed to the hanging bar over the fire and the seventeenth-century panelling that he installed is mostly present in the dining room, albeit sadly with a doorway now cut through the middle of it by a recent owner.[24]

Theo Brown (1914–1993)

Theo Brown has arguably contributed more to the collection and discussion of folklore across Devon than any other person either detailed in this chapter or elsewhere. Her archives, housed at the University of Exeter, are vast and wide-ranging and although accessed from time to time, currently do nothing near as much as they could to continue to enrich the subject.

Theo (baptized with the name Jean Marion Pryce) was born in Wales, although she lived in Devon for virtually her entire life. Her mother had sadly died at her birth. Her father, a Welsh scholar who held a high position at the British Museum, found himself unable to care for her and so placed her into an orphanage when she was very small. She was there for two years before being adopted by the Langford Brown family, who lived at Kingskerswell. Mrs Dorothy Brown, unable to have a child with her husband, a Devon squire, had advertised in *The Times* newspaper her desire to adopt, and after the usual procedures, the infant Theo was delivered to Mrs Brown in the Ladies' First Class Waiting Room at Paddington Station.[25]

The large country house, Barton Hall, at which the Langford Browns resided had been built by Theo's adoptive father. Here, Theo was educated by governesses. Her somewhat draconian mother, while allowing attendance at school, forbade Theo from taking any examinations and so she did not even achieve a School Certificate. In later life her lack of formal qualifications troubled Theo, despite her obvious intelligence and expertise. Music and art, however, were permissible to Mrs Brown and so Theo was for a time able to study at the Westminster School of Art.[26] She favoured working in wood and produced a number of woodcuts with folkloric themes during her life.

It may be that Theo's lifelong interest in folklore, and especially that of the county of Devon, was first kindled sitting around the dinner table at Barton Hall. She records a number of stories which were related by her father including his supposed encounter with a spectral Black Dog, a subject which was to become her main focus of interest later in life (see Chapter Eight). But it was a chance encounter in a railway station tearoom in Exeter which was to shape Theo's life and solidify her interest in the study of folklore.

That meeting, which took place in 1945, was with William Francis Jackson Knight, an English classical scholar known in particular for his work on the subject of Virgil. After teaching for a number of years in Oxfordshire, followed by some temporary work at the University of St Andrews, Jackson Knight had relocated to Exeter when offered a position as an Assistant Lecturer in Classics at what is now Exeter University, and was then the University College of South West England.

W.F. Jackson Knight himself had a strong interest in folklore, perhaps partly due to his adoption of spiritualism partway through his career, which had a somewhat detrimental effect on his reputation. In 1945, he headed up the Folklore Section of the Devonshire Association, having taken over from Charles Laycock (see above), and was to hand over the reins to Theo Brown in 1951. She went on to serve in this position for longer than any other member of the Association before or since.

After serving with the Women's Royal Naval Service, Theo lived for a while in a caravan from which she would strike out across the county visiting other collectors, gathering stories or viewing interesting locations. The family caravan had, in fact, been taken most years to the Postbridge area of Dartmoor for holidays and this undoubtedly influenced the concentrated collecting of information from that village, which ultimately led to the publication of *Tales of a Dartmoor Village* in 1961. W.F. Jackson Knight described the small book as 'important beyond its length'.[27]

Theo published two books in her own right, *The Fate of the Dead* in 1979 and *Devon Ghosts* in 1982, but she also contributed numerous articles to journals and other publications, and acted as an editor for other works. She was also instrumental in the organization of one of a series of small conferences at the University of Exeter, where she held a position as an Honorary Research Fellow.

Repositories of Information

Artefacts and ephemera relating to the folklore of the county of Devon may, naturally, be found scattered throughout the region, with most of the museums exhibiting items of interest as well as holding books and papers away from the public gaze. There are two significant collections of written and illustrated materials in the county that provide an invaluable resource for study of the subject.

The Devon and Exeter Institution is located on Cathedral Green in the city of Exeter, at the heart of the region. It was founded in 1813, citing its original aim as 'to promote the general diffusion of Science, Literature and the Arts, and for illustrating the Natural and Civic History in the County of Devon, and the History of the City of Exeter'.[28] The institution operates from a medieval building which was once used by the Courtenay family as a town house in the seventeenth century. In 1814, after the inception of the Devon and Exeter Institution, the interior was remodelled to create two large Georgian rooms. One of these housed the Institution's library and the other served as a museum until 1868, when the exhibits were removed and relocated across the city to create the start of the holdings of the Royal Albert Memorial Museum.

The library has since been much extended and houses books, newspapers and other periodicals; pamphlets, maps and artwork; and illustrations of all types. The collections range from fifteenth-century examples to the present day.

The West Country Studies Library was originally opened in 1975, bringing together the items held under the banner of 'Local Studies' at the old Exeter

City Library and at the Devon County Library. It operated as part of the central library service until 2012, when it was relocated and joined with the Devon Record Office to form what is now Devon Archives and Local Studies—a part of the South West Heritage Trust. Holdings number approximately 45,000 published works and 27,000 illustrations,[29] as well as parish cuttings files and other items. At its height in the late twentieth century, the West Country Studies Library was also responsible for publishing small books of folkloric interest.

Having begun by acknowledging the vital work undertaken by some of the key collectors of folklore across Devon over the last two centuries, in the remainder of this book we move on to examine the main themes which run through Devon's customs, traditions and beliefs, and look at how they compare with broader examples of folklore in the rest of the United Kingdom.

CHAPTER TWO

Stories from the Moors

The county of Devon has a total geographical area of some 2,589 square miles. Of this, a not insignificant sixteen per cent is taken up by land given over to national parks. To the north of the county lies Exmoor. Spanning the Devon–Somerset border, some twenty-nine per cent of its total area of 267 square miles lies on the Devon side. Further to the south is the larger and wilder landscape of Dartmoor. Covering twenty miles in a north–south direction and the same east to west, its total area of 368 square miles makes its size roughly equivalent with that of London.[1]

Both of these areas of moorland bear the evidence of habitation from early times, having been settled at least as far back as the Mesolithic period around 7,000 years ago. With humans having inhabited and worked these lands for so long, it is no surprise that we find many folkloric stories attached to the moors. While most of these find parallels across the rest of the county and beyond and will be explored in more subject-specific chapters dealing with fairies, witchcraft and the like later in this book, there are plenty that have firm roots in the moors themselves.

Moorland Characters

There are a number of notable characters associated with both Exmoor and Dartmoor. Some of these we can confidently say were real people whose histories were correctly recorded, whereas others have something of a more legendary status. While not primarily associated with the collection of folklore, like those figures mentioned in the first chapter, two women in particular were instrumental in working with and preserving information about the moors, and the traditions on the land there.

Hope Bourne

If there was ever a modern-day character living hand to mouth in the manner of the wise women of past times, then Hope Bourne was that figure. Hope was a well-known advocate for Exmoor life, as a countrywoman who understood its intricacies well. Born in Oxford in 1918, she moved with her mother to the North Devon town of Hartland when she was very young. Hope's mother was widowed and earned her income as a school headmistress, but passed away when Hope was in her thirties. Soon falling into debt, having no income of her own and with no qualifications since leaving school at age fourteen, Hope took the dramatic step to live purely from the land. She was to do so for virtually the rest of her life.

Hope moved from Hartland to Exmoor, where she found places to live in primitive moor buildings, and later an old caravan. She grew vegetables, collected old wood for fuel and hunted animals for meat. Any money that she did need was earned through helping farmers look after their livestock. She would regularly walk up to twenty miles a day across the moors, keeping a journal of her observations and drawing and painting the flora and fauna. Living in this way, she naturally drew together a massive collection of first-hand knowledge of the moors, which led to a series of books and a regular column in a local newspaper, the *West Somerset Free Press*. When she died in August 2010 at the age of ninety-one (proving what a hardy woman she was), she left some 2,000 documents and pieces of art, and 700 books, to the Exmoor Society—which now form a valuable and important archive.[2]

Beatrice Chase

If we were looking for a similar figure to Hope Bourne but on Dartmoor, then many people would probably suggest Beatrice Chase. Born Olive Katherine Parr in Middlesex in 1874, she moved to Venton near Widecombe-in-the-Moor with her mother after contracting tuberculosis in her late twenties. Parr wrote many books set on Dartmoor under the pen name of Beatrice Chase, and these works became very popular for their representation of the area and the people who lived and worked on it. As Hope Bourne did with Exmoor, so Beatrice Chase became an advocate for this moor too, working hard for its preservation. It is also generally understood that she was responsible for beginning a certain tradition which is still carried on to this day.

Not far from Beatrice Chase's home at Venton, Swallerton Gate is home to a roadside grave usually marked on maps as 'Jay's Grave'. Here are said to be interred the remains of Mary Jay, more commonly known as Kitty. She was a poorhouse orphan in the nineteenth century who found work at a farm at Manaton. The story tells that aged around sixteen, the son of the farm owners became enamoured of Kitty and she ended up falling pregnant. The difference in class between the two was unacceptable to the lad's parents and they turned Kitty away from the farm. Knowing that she would be unable to find other employment in the area and unwilling to return to the poorhouse, the girl is said to have hanged herself in one of the barns. In keeping with custom, given the suicide, the body could not be laid in a church grave and so had to be buried at a crossroads, in order to keep the restless spirit from returning.

It is difficult to say for certain how much of the story of Kitty Jay (if any) is based on historical fact. The story of the maid or servant who falls pregnant by an employer or other figure of a higher status is a very common one in folklore and accounts for a number of alleged hauntings in properties all over the country.[3] The local belief on Dartmoor at one time was that the grave did not in fact contain human remains at all, but only a pile of animal bones. And so at some point, possibly around the year 1860, a local farmer named James Bryant opened the grave and found inside a human skull and a collection of bones. These were examined and the skull was pronounced to be that of a young female.[4] Bryant reinterred the bones in a wooden box and rebuilt the grave to the form that stands on the site today.

Beatrice Chase is said to have started the tradition of leaving flowers on the grave,[5] which were originally placed in a jam jar that stood on top of the mound. She would do this unobtrusively and so, not knowing who was responsible, locals began to say that it was 'the pixies' who left them there. The custom seemed to naturally take root and so, after Beatrice died in 1955, flowers still continued to appear in the jar or on the grass. Now, Jay's Grave has become a site for modern-day contemporary assemblages and anyone passing by will most likely see coins, badges, flowers, arrangements of small stones and a plethora of other offerings left by visitors to the site.

Beatrice is also partly responsible for the revival of the famous Widecombe Fair. In the 1930s, this had become a very small affair, mostly just allowing local farmers to buy and sell sheep. Chase sent a telegram to the British Broadcasting Corporation (BBC) and managed to get the fair mentioned on the *Ten O'Clock News*.[6] For this she used the hook of the folk song 'Uncle Tom Cobley', which was played on the broadcast, and which leads us to the first of the moor stories featuring a more legendary character, yet still most probably based on a real-life person.

Tom Cobley

Although it is not irrefutable, it is likely that Tom Cobley and the other men who asked to borrow a mare from Tom Pearce, as described in the popular folk song 'Widecombe Fair', are based on real people who lived in the mid-Devon area. We find them all listed in the first verse of the common version of the song:

> Tom Pearce. Tom Pearce, lend me your grey mare,
> All along, down along, out along lee,
> For I want for to go to Widdecombe [*sic*] Fair,
> Wi' Bill Brewer, Jan Stewer, Peter Gurney, Peter Davy, Dan'l
>   Whiddon,
> Harry Hawk, old Uncle Tom Cobley and all, old Uncle Tom
>   Cobley and all.

The song relates how the men all get onto the grey mare and set off for Widecombe, but before they arrive the horse becomes sick and subsequently dies. Tom sets out to search for them when they do not return home and, finding the dead horse, sits and laments its passing. The final verses tell how, on cold moorland nights, the bright white ghost of the mare appears, with a groaning noise coming from 'Tom Pearce's old mare in her rattling bones'.

The Widecombe and District History Group undertook research into the names of the characters and were able to trace most of them to families who lived and worked in the areas around the villages of Sticklepath and Spreyton in the early nineteenth century. Spreyton is certainly the location most commonly associated with Cobley in modern times, with its sixteenth-century public house bearing the name Tom Cobley Tavern. A sign here suggests that the characters in the song set off for the fair from that place in 1802, which was noted by the History Group as the earliest reference to the names that they were able to find.[7] As we shall see elsewhere in this book, however, we should be mindful of the difficulties in confirming the origin of public house names, and claims made by them for links to historic events. We cannot discount the claim in this case, but neither can it be proven.

There is a grave in Spreyton churchyard which bears the name Tom Cobley. The date of death given on this stone is 11 January 1844, but locally it is said that this is the nephew of the Tom Cobley who is portrayed in the song. He is recorded to have died in 1794 and lived at nearby Colebrooke. There seems to be something of a difference of opinion over the character of Tom Cobley Senior. It is said around the Spreyton area that he had a disagreement with his nephew and made no provision for him in his will. However, the Reverend Sabine Baring-Gould notes:

> The original Uncle Tom Cobley lived in a house near Yeoford Junction, in the Parish of Spreyton. His will was signed on January 20, 1787, and was proved on March 14, 1794. He was a genial old bachelor. Mr Samuel Peach, his oldest relation living, tells me, 'My great-uncle, who succeeded him, with whom I lived for some years, died in 1843, over eighty years of age; he married, but left no children'.[8]

Would a 'genial old bachelor' be the sort of person to cut a member of the family from his will? It is possible, but the two seem a little at odds.

Like the character of Tom Cobley, the song 'Widecombe Fair' is itself somewhat contested. Probably one of the best-known of all Devon folk songs, and something that comes to mind first for many when asked about Devon folklore, its point of origin is unknown. It was originally thought to have emerged somewhere in the early nineteenth century, but in fact it exists in many much older variations found all over the country. Historian Todd Gray suggests that the earliest version of the tune, known as 'Old Cobley', can be traced to the city of Exeter in 1761 where it was used to accompany a satirical ballad commentating on the Parliamentary election of that year.[9] This predates the first iterations of Widecombe Fair as a cattle market by some hundred years.[10]

The song came to prominence and became forever associated with the village fair at Widecombe when Baring-Gould published it in the classic *Songs of the West*. What is generally less known is that Baring-Gould did not just have one set of words for the song. There was another version which he collected and which did not get put into the final book.

The commonly sung tune and chorus were collected by Baring-Gould from Henry Westaway, a farmer who kept 100 acres at Priestacott Farm near Belstone, after the two were introduced in 1888. Westaway was sixty-four at the time. However, the words published in *Songs of the West* were those sent to Baring-Gould by William Collier, a Plymouth wine merchant. It is these that have gone down in history.

In 1951, folk song collector Peter Kennedy went to Belstone and collected some songs from two of Henry Westaway's sons. They told an anecdote about the original collecting, saying that Baring-Gould treated their father very well and they thought that he had deliberately got him drunk in order to collect 'Widecombe Fair'. Unfortunately, the words collected by Baring-Gould from Henry Westaway no longer survive, but the chorus as sung by his sons does, and it is very likely that the verses sung by their father were similar. Their version has the lyrics as:

> Tom Pearce, Tom Pearce, lend me thy grey mare
> Right-fol-lol-li-dol, diddle-i-do
> That I may ride out to Widdicombe Fair
> With Will Lewer, Jan Brewer, Harry Hawkins, Hugh Davey,
> Philly Wigpot, George Parsley, Dick Wilson
> Tom Cobleigh and all, here is Uncle Tom Cobleigh and all.[11]

The variation in spelling of Tom Cobley's surname is still often found and the two are now almost interchangeable.

Widecombe Fair and Mythology

There is a theory, proposed by Theo Brown, which suggests that the Widecombe Fair song is not local at all, but probably travelled here with German tinners who came to work the mines on Dartmoor—the same people who are sometimes erroneously said to have brought the symbol of the three hares joined at the ears, commonly and incorrectly named 'Tinner's Rabbits'.

Looking to Germanic folklore we find the symbol of the 'Schimmelreiter', a ghost of which the literal translation is 'rider on the white horse'. In reference to horses, the term 'grey' is often used for those that appear white—hence the 'grey mare' of the song. Both in England and in Germany it is said to be a bad omen to meet a white horse.

The Germanic Schimmelreiter is described as an emissary from the underworld,[12] which implies that the grey horse was a spirit guide—a psychopomp who would lead the souls of the dead to their resting place. If this was the case, then when the song's lyrics relate

> So Tom Pearce's old mare, her took sick and died.
> All along, down along, out along lee,
> And Tom he sat down on a stone, and he cried

then he is not, in fact, lamenting the horse's death, but rather weeping for the souls who will now end up in purgatory, because they cannot be transported to the Otherworld.

At first glance, this theory seems a little far-fetched; there are after all what seem like stronger connections closer to home, in the hobby horses of the Mari Lwyd in Wales and Pen Glaz in Cornwall. However, there are a couple of tentative clues which might be seen to support the Germanic origin idea. One collected verse of the song contains the words 'And how did you know it was Tommy's Grey Mare? ... / 'Cos one foot was shod, and the t'others was bare.'

If the theory is correct, then this couplet could allude to the fact that a number of German deities rode on three-legged horses, such as the death-goddess Hel. Such creatures are also connected with the Wild Hunt, which in turn has links with the Dartmoor location of Wistman's Wood.

Another hint is found in the following nursery rhyme:

> Widdicote, woddicote, over-cote hang,
> Nothing so broad and nothing so lang,
> As widdicote, woddicote, over-cote hang.[13]

'Widdicote', which is sometimes connected with Widecombe, is a Devonshire word meaning 'sky'. In terms of the Otherworld, this is the usual direction in which you would hope to be transported!

While the principle of Occam's Razor tells us that the song 'Widecombe Fair' is most likely about a number of moorland characters who probably existed in the nineteenth century, we should never overlook the other vague possibilities of more deep-rooted meaning. You never know where they might lead.

The Doone Family

In 1869, the author Richard Doddridge (R.D.) Blackmore published the book with which Exmoor is probably most frequently connected even today,

Lorna Doone. Born in the village of Longworth in the Vale of the White Horse, Blackmore spent much of his early childhood visiting the moor upon which he would end up setting his most enduring novel.

Set in the late seventeenth century, the novel follows the story of John Ridd, whose father—a local farmer—was murdered by the Doones, a noble family who had fallen from grace and were living as outlaws. John falls in love with a girl from the Doone family, Lorna, who is the granddaughter of Sir Ensor, the lord of the Doone clan. After Ensor's death his heir Carver, who has always planned to marry Lorna, pursues her, but the Ridds harbour her at the family farm. After the death of King Charles II, the Doones side with the Duke of Monmouth in his challenge for the throne and the plan for Carver to marry Lorna is sidelined.

Following a number of events which lead to John Ridd's capture and eventual pardoning with a title, the action centres on the Exmoor communities' wish to rid the area of the Doones, and John's part in this.

R.D. Blackmore is generally considered to be, as was his contemporary Thomas Hardy, particularly proficient at reflecting the landscape and people about which he was writing, and any traditions and customs which took place there. While the character of John Ridd is most definitely fictitious, to what extent are the Doones based on historical people and events? This is a question that has been long debated. It was at one time suggested that they were wholly invented, but there also appears to be evidence to the contrary. As early as 1903, F. J. Snell noted in *A Book of Exmoor* that

> long before Blackmore had written a syllable of his romance, there was in existence a well-established tradition concerning the Doones. ... In 1862 Dr Collyns completed and gave the world his *Chase of the Wild Red Deer*, in which he quotes from a West Country guide-book the assertion that Exmoor was formerly the headquarters of a set of freebooters, the Doones, who were supposed to have arisen during the confusion caused by the Civil Wars.[14]

As we will come to see during our examination of folklore surrounding the Devil in Chapter Five, one must be wary of information recorded in old guidebooks, but in this case it appears to be accurate. The Reverend John Frederick Chanter, who published a paper on Blackmore and the Doones in 1903, is recognized as having named Doone Valley on Exmoor as such,[15] and in fact there are a number of place names on the moor which have arisen from the novel itself. Blackmore's father owned a book compiled by Matthew Mundy, the Perpetual Curate of Lynton, which contained three Exmoor legends that he had heard in 1833 from Ursula Johnson. One of these concerned the Doone family specifically, the second another family in the area and the last a highwayman named Tom Faggus. All of these would find a place in the novel, suggesting that even though this book was not broadly published, it was familiar to Blackmore.

Faggus, who in the novel receives a pardon from the King, was a blacksmith from North Devon. The Old Smithy in North Molton is generally agreed to be the location of his workplace. He became caught up in a legal case with a well-known and rich Devon family, the Bampfyldes, and after this turned to the role of the highwayman as a way of making ends meet. Tales about him relate that he was something of a Robin Hood figure, only robbing wealthy travellers and using no violence. He was said to have remained free for so long because of the intelligence of his horse Winnie, who would respond to a whistle from Faggus when he needed help.

A gun which is said to have been Tom Faggus's is on display at the Museum of Barnstaple and North Devon.[16] This is not the only gun in existence which can be connected with *Lorna Doone*; there is another which was allegedly fired directly at the Doones. Although its location is not certain, photographs of the weapon are said to exist. 'One night while they were attacking Yenworthy Farm,' the legend goes, 'the Doones were fired at by an old woman wielding a duck-gun. The raiders retreated, leaving a trail of blood which could be followed for several miles towards Badgeworthy.'[17]

This was the second of the legends recorded by Mundy and is the one that appears to have the strongest physical evidence attached. But the best-known of the legends is probably the third, which tells how the Doones attacked a farmhouse at Exford, which was empty apart from a child and a maid. The servant took shelter in the large oven of the house, from where she heard the Doones murder the child, saying, 'If anyone asks who killed thee; Tell 'em 'twas the Doones of Badgeworthy.' This story can be found described in a number of guidebooks and popular magazines of the nineteenth century in various forms, including two in which the child is also eaten.[18] It is possible that this legend had been based either upon a raid on a farm at Badgery in which the farmer's wife hid in a barrel of feathers and the son in a chimney, the farmer and the other labourers having been killed when investigating a commotion outside; or one reported to have taken place at Parsonage Farm, Oare, where a child was killed by stabbing and the fate of its mother is uncertain. This latter example had the name of the Doones attached to it at some point, and it is interesting to note that Blackmore's grandfather was rector at Oare and the family farmed Parsonage Farm.[19] The location figures heavily in *Lorna Doone*.

A lack of documentary evidence makes it difficult to ensure historical accuracy surrounding the Doone family. There is evidence to suggest that the nature of some of the events described is accurate, but no evidence to ascribe a name to them. And while there were existing legends about the Doone family in the area at the time that Blackmore published *Lorna Doone*, they are nothing more than legend. It is probable that in many cases the ascribing of names to events has happened later, in the same way that names are sometimes retro-fitted to locations to reflect something that took place there. Looked at as a whole, the folklore is a conflation of many aspects of truth which may never be fully unpicked.

The Gubbins Family

Moving back from Exmoor to Dartmoor once again, we find another notorious family who have appeared in fiction, although once again doubts do arise over the actual historical facts. The Gubbins family lived around Lydford at the time of the English Civil War and are written of as highwaymen, robbers, beggars and sheep-stealers. Anna Eliza Bray (see Chapter One) included them in one of her historical fictions, *Warleigh*, and Charles Kingsley mentions them in *Westward Ho!*:

> Now I am sorry to say, for the honor of my country, that it was by no means a safe thing in those days to travel from Plymouth to the north of Devon; because, to get to your journey's end, unless you were minded to make a circuit of many miles, you must needs pass through the territory of a foreign and hostile potentate, who had many times ravaged the dominions, and defeated the forces of her Majesty Queen Elizabeth, and was named (behind his back at least) the King of the Gubbings. 'So now I dare call them,' says Fuller, 'secured by distance, which one of more valor durst not do to their face, for fear their fury fall upon him. Yet hitherto have I met with none who could render a reason of their name. We call the shavings of fish (which are little worth) gubbings; and sure it is that they are sensible that the word importeth shame and disgrace.[20]

The 'Fuller' referred to by Kingsley in this quote is Thomas Fuller, author of *The History of the Worthies of England* which was published posthumously in

1662. He notes that they lived outside of either ecclesiastical or civil rule, in cotts (a kind of rough shed), and had over time incestuously and greatly multiplied. Their line was said by Fuller to have begun in the fifteenth century when two women carrying children out of wedlock hid themselves in the location, where they were found by some local men who took advantage of them themselves.

Fuller's story of the Gubbins clan was not without criticism, however. Edward Gibson, in his enlarging and revision of *Camden's Brittania*, originally published in 1695, says that Fuller was mistaken in calling what he termed 'a village nam'd the Gubbins' heathen.[21] A few years later, the Reverend Thomas Cox suggested that the image of the Gubbins as barbarians was falsely painted for Fuller by someone in the local area who held a grudge against them.[22] It may simply be the case that a collective of people living in abject poverty, in what amounted to nothing more than caves or crude dwellings in the middle of nowhere, made local people who lived more conventionally nervous. Such people would have been seen as 'other' in exactly the same way that healers or wise women were in the early modern period. Patricia Milton, writing in 2006, also puts forward the suggestion that such rumours of a wild tribe might have provided ideas for writers in the nineteenth century who were searching for local folk tales to add interest to the newly emerging tourist literature market (see Chapter Five).[23]

The leader of the Gubbins clan was Roger Rowle, and his name is still found attached to a pool at one end of Lydford Gorge, suggesting that the memory of their deeds was strong enough at least to remain in the landscape which they inhabited. Mrs Bray portrayed Rowle as again something of a Robin Hood figure, not unlike the reputation held by Tom Faggus further north in Doone country, but historical records don't seem to imply he was particularly kind to anyone, downtrodden or otherwise, and so we might see this as something of a romanticized fictionalization of his true character. This was, after all, the style of many of Mrs Bray's historical fictions.

Baring-Gould, writing in his *Book of Dartmoor* in 1900, was of the opinion that there was still some vestige of the Gubbins tribe remaining at Lydford, but his only evidence for this was the fact that magistrates in the area had dealt with other people living rough and stealing sheep on the periphery of the moor.[24] Arguably, this was a problem that easily arose in any remote area and would hardly prove that the Gubbins line was still going some two centuries or more after Fuller's first mention of them. As suggested by some, it is highly likely that it was their lifestyle (and in particular their inbreeding) which caused the Gubbins to die out. There were some stories suggesting that the clan were converted to a Christian way of life by Jesuit priests who hid in Lydford Gorge to avoid capture by Cromwell's soldiers. These, however, probably have more to do with the church laying a claim to the tale and using it as a mechanism to promote a God-fearing way of life than any kind of historical attribution. There certainly seems to be no written evidence to support the claim. Folklore is often taken up and adopted by religious establishments for this purpose and forms the basis of many morality tales.

Other Moorland Tales

Water

It isn't only the people who live or work on the moor that feature heavily in folk tradition. Sometimes, aspects of the landscape itself can also be seen to take on an identity of sorts.

Dartmoor takes its name from the main river which flows through it, the Dart. The 1182 name of 'Dertemora' translates as 'Moor in the Dart valley'.[25] More accurately, the Dart is made up of two rivers which later join to form one whole. The West Dart rises close to Flat Tor and the East Dart begins close to Whitehorse Hill. The two come together at Dartmeet, probably one of the most popular tourist spots on the whole of the moor and certainly a very picturesque one.

One well-known folk tale of Dartmoor tells how a young farmhand from Rowbrook, Jan Coo, hears his name being called from somewhere down by the Dart. Thinking someone is in trouble, he rushes to tell the other farmworkers and together they search the area but find nothing. The next night, the same thing happens again. This time the workers stay at the farm and listen. After a while, they conclude that it is the pixies out on the moor sporting with them. To engage with them would be foolhardy and so they go back to the farm and lock the door.

Winter turns to spring and things continue as normal. Then, one day, Jan is returning home across the moor with a friend named Abel when he again hears a voice calling his name. Jan sends Abel back to the farm while he goes to investigate the voice. Abel can still hear the voice all the way to the farm, but as soon as he opens the door it ceases. Taking a mug of tea, he tells the labourers what has happened. They say that once Jan returns, then they will know for certain whether it was the pixies or something else that was calling from the river. But time passes and Jan does not return. Becoming concerned, they venture down to the Dart with ropes and lanterns, but Jan is nowhere to be found. One man still blames the pixies and says that it will be a year until they see Jan again. But another disagrees and says that it was the river calling for Jan, and that he will never return now. And he never does.

It is certainly true that the river Dart might be said to 'cry'. At least, the sound of water rushing through the valley carried on the wind does take on an eerie quality. All over the world we find traditions relating to river spirits and goddesses, and most major watercourses were said to have them at one time. We still see evidence of this in the landscape now: Coventina's Well in Scotland is a striking example.

It has long been said that the Dart claims a soul every year. While this belief is seen as superstitious, maybe stemming from the old ideas of river deities and sacrifice, it is based very much on the natural qualities of the landscape and the law of averages. Dartmoor writer William Crossing noted that the Dart was prone to sudden flooding and had a particularly fast current, meaning that there was at least one drowning reported nearly every year.[26] He also speculated that this fast flow of water gave rise to the river's name. This tale of the claiming of a life each year led to a rhyming couplet still often repeated in the area, in some variation of the original: 'River of Dart, oh, river of Dart! Every year thou claimest a heart.'

The Dart is certainly not the only river to carry such a superstition. The idea of rivers requiring one or more souls each year is an international one, and prevalent all over the United Kingdom. Many of the rivers have their own rhymes also, such as the river Don in Sheffield: 'The shelving, slimy river Dun, / Each year a daughter or a son'.[27]

Also in Devon, the River Tamar is said to demand one life each year.[28] The Tamar is thought by many to be named from a prehistoric term meaning 'dark flowing', also the origin of the River Thames. More local legend names the river for the nymph Tamara, an etymology taken by some to hint at a connection with the water deity and a need for sacrifice. In this legend, while Tamara was walking on Dartmoor one day she met two giants, named Tavy and Torridge. Both wanted Tamara's affections but she would not allow either of them near her. After some time, Tamara's father came looking for her and seeing what was going on, put both of the giants into a trance. This angered his daughter who refused to leave with him, and so he turned her into a spring, which then formed the Tamar. When they later woke and discovered what had happened, the two giants both sought magical aid and had themselves turned into rivers to try and meet with Tamara, in her new guise as the Tamar. The Devon rivers of the Tavy and Torridge came about because of this.

This story was popularized by Robert Hunt in his book *Popular Romances of the West of England* (1865) but, writing in 1838, the engineer Davies Gilbert acknowledges that it is a 'pretty vulgar fiction', which seems to suggest a native fantasy story.[29]

It is not only running water which has superstition attached to it on the moors; still water most certainly runs deep if you consider the number of 'bottomless pool' stories which abound. One such relates to Pinkworthy (or sometimes Pinkery) Pond on Exmoor. Local folklore says that it has no bottom and is filled with the 'Devil's water'. The story tells that a local farmer drowned in the pond in 1906 and his body was never seen again, although his ghost can still be sighted walking the shores around the pool.

It is quite obvious of course that most stories of bottomless waters came about by way of a warning to stop children and others from straying too close to their edges, especially when the pond in question is remote and hence there are unlikely to be many people around to affect a rescue. The same is true of Crazywell Pool on Dartmoor (again there are alternative spellings), which legend not only says is bottomless but also should not be passed at night, because to do so would risk hearing a voice foretelling the next person in the parish to die.[30] Crazywell is not in fact a pool at all, but rather the water-filled remains of tin-mining excavations whose depth has been measured at just fifteen feet.[31]

The actual events behind Pinkworthy's legend also dismiss the bottomless idea, as you would expect. The formation of Pinkworthy was down to a Mr Knight who, it was recorded in the *Taunton Courier* of 1818, paid a sum of £50,000 to purchase 10,000 acres of the Forest of Exmoor that had been put on sale by the Crown. Knight was to undertake many works on Exmoor, including the formation of good-quality roads, and looked to make an income back from his purchase via mining and farming. He was to bring in shepherds from Scotland to look after his flocks and miners from over the border in Cornwall, and from Wales, where the necessary skills lay. For general labour, as was often the case in the nineteenth century, he used an Irish workforce. Part of their building work has remained in the landscape with the now rather racially troubling name 'Paddy's Fence',[32] although that seems to have now fallen out of general use.

Knight had Pinkworthy dug as a reservoir which was originally some seven acres in size, although the remains of it now are much smaller than this. His original plan was to construct a canal between the site and Simonsbath, presumably to aid in the removal of resources from the moor, but this never came to fruition due to the difficult terrain and high cost.

The dating of the drowned farmer in the legend of the Pinkworthy haunting is erroneous. Snell notes in his 1903 book on Exmoor that the man, whose name was Gammon, had committed suicide 'a few years ago'.[33] The man had been trying unsuccessfully to court a barmaid and in his distress rode off and threw himself into the pond. It is true that his body was not seen again, at least for some time. This led to an operation to dredge and then empty Pinkworthy in order to retrieve it, a spectacle which apparently attracted a large audience, all of whom would have witnessed the fact that the pond had a bottom!

Supernatural animals

Some moorland tales have much more of a fantastical edge to them. A tale from the western fringe of Dartmoor relates how there was once a fairy ring which grew in an area of meadowland where, on certain nights, a black hen could be sighted with her young. Nobody ever saw where they came from, or where they disappeared to, but some who got close enough said that the hen had bright red eyes.

The vicar of the parish nearby was known by his parishioners to have an occult library and to be unusually knowledgeable in the dark arts. (This is a trope which is found in a few places across the county and has some basis in the actual parsons who performed exorcisms and other similar services. It is explored in more detail in Chapter Seven on 'Devon Hauntings'.) One Sunday while the vicar was preaching the service, one of the staff at his house found a large book open on the vicar's study table and, in an effort to ascertain what it was about, began to read passages from it. Almost at once, the same black hen and chicks walked into the study and, as the sky darkened outside, began growing to the size of cattle and more. In the church the vicar became aware of what was happening back in his study, and ran home before he had even completed the service. Entering the study and seeing the unusual sight before him, the vicar grabbed a sack of rice from the corner of the room and threw a handful to the floor. The hen and the chicks immediately began pecking at the treat before them, affording the vicar enough time to access his book and reverse the spell the servant had inadvertently cast.

Those with an interest in vampire lore will know that the scattering of rice or other grain is one method of protection against the undead; it acts as a distraction, as they are compelled to stop what they are doing and count the husks. We see the rice in this story being used slightly differently, but still as a distraction technique. Elsewhere on Dartmoor, seed might be used for divination purposes. On Valentine's Eve, for example, it was common for boys and girls to go to the church porch at 12.30pm and, as the clock struck, to run home while scattering hempseed. As they did so, they would recite a rhyme such as:

> Hempseed I sow, hempseed I sow
> (S)he that will my true love be
> Come rake this hemp seed after me[34]

The spirit of their intended partner was then said to appear and rake up the seeds. The fact that both boys and girls undertook this exercise distinguishes the Devon ritual from similar plant- or seed-based love divination practices in other areas, which were generally only undertaken by girls wanting to find their future husband.

Some moorland stories stand apart as being real curiosities, unique to the extent that it is very difficult to find logical links to other examples within the folklore records.

There is a strange legend of ghostly pigs attached to the area of Dartmoor around Merripit Hill, about a mile out of the village of Postbridge. It was recorded in writing by an elderly resident of the village, Elizabeth Warne, in 1951 and given to Theo Brown when she was researching the folklore of Postbridge. The story tells that at particular times of the year, the ghosts of a sow and her litter of piglets can be seen making their way from Merripit to Cator Gate. As they walk, the piglets can be heard to say to the sow: 'Starvin', starvin'.'

The mother reassures them that food can be found at their destination: 'Cator Gate, Cator Gate. / Dead hoss, dead hoss, dead hoss.'

However, when they reach Cator Gate they find that they are too late, and that the carcass of the horse which was going to sustain them has already gone, with only the skeleton and hide left. At this, the piglets begin to cry: 'Skin an' bone, skin an' bone.'

The sow tells the litter to leave the carcass as it is—'Let 'un lie, let 'un lie'—and they all return to Merripit Hill, where they vanish into the air.[35]

It is difficult to ascertain where this story might come from because, although it has elements which can be found in other tales, it really makes no sense as a legend that has remained in circulation because there is no notable event attached. There are certainly traditions to be found of other ghostly pigs, in Devon and further afield. One tells that the ghost of the notorious Judge Jeffreys haunts the castle and surrounding area at Lydford in the form of a black pig, but there is no obvious reason for this either. Sabine Baring-Gould wrote on the subject of animals used as foundation sacrifices. This practice emerged from older rituals of sacrifice in early Christian times, he said, with the significance being that a building would only stand firm if the foundations were laid in blood. It was also believed that the first burial in a churchyard must watch over all of the other dead, and so an animal was often interred for this purpose. Ghostly apparitions of these foundation sacrifices were known as Church Grims, and Baring-Gould notes that in his own home parish around the time of the 1830s the church was said to be haunted by 'two white sows yoked together with a silver chain'.[36]

Neither of these other hauntings seem to suggest any connection with the Merripit pigs. There are Scandinavian examples of ghostly pigs in the landscape, such as the Glosen, but these are more monstrous spirits and very different to the Merripit example, which has no interaction with humans.

What stands out as most interesting in the Merripit story is the very rhythmic sound of the words 'spoken' by the pigs. If you speak them out loud, they have a very definite repeating pattern. This is similar to the tradition of a Black Dog apparition at Belle Hole in Lincolnshire, recorded by the folklorist Ethel Rudkin, which was said to run circles around a district nurse saying, 'Put me in yer pocket, put me in yer pocket.'[37] One theory related to this story suggests that the pattern of speech comes from the sound of a passing train which was carried on the wind; the rhythm when spoken aloud is very like the sound of wheels passing over track fishplates. The legend of the Merripit pigs was said to have taken place around 200 years before the story was recorded, which would place it in the mid-eighteenth century. This is too early for any rail workings (and indeed there were none in this area). However, the area around Merripit was regularly mined from the medieval period, and both Vitifer and Golden Dagger mines are not too far distant. Could it be that the sound of mine workings played the same part as the railway might have done at Belle Hole?

Intriguingly, there is more both locally and further afield that seems to tie into the image of the dead horse and the rhythmic speech of the pigs. Folk song collector Sam Richards collected a chant from children at Meshaw School, not far from the southern edge of Exmoor, which is strangely similar. It was said to have arisen after the discovery of a dead horse, belonging to a John Ley in Meshaw Wood, and was constructed to sound a little like the cry of a pigeon.

> Dead 'oss, Dead 'oss
> Whose whose? whose whose?
> John Ley's, John Ley's
> Where to? where to?
> Meshaw 'Ood, Meshaw 'Ood[38]

There is little to connect the rhyme with the spectral pig story, but the patterns are evident between the two. Remarkably, a closer connection is found right at the other end of the country in Shetland, where there is a legend telling of a Finn who has lost his horse. Because the Finns were said to know the corvid tongue, he discovers both that his horse has died and where it is from a conversation between two crows.

1: 'Dead horse! Dead horse!'
2: 'Whaar pairt? Whaar pairt?'
1: 'Upo da Neep, upo da Neep'
2: 'Is he fat? Is he fat?'
1: 'Aa spick, aa spick'[39]

Death on the moor

In these days before modern transport made things much easier, many items would have to be carried across the moors from parish to parish. A split flat stone at the foot of Yar Tor on Dartmoor, known as the coffin stone, was a place where men carrying a coffin across the moor for burial could lay it down and take a rest. Similar stones may be found on the edges of such routes, now known generally as 'corpse roads', all over the United Kingdom. Inclement weather could make trips such as this very difficult at certain times of the year.

A story is told of a man caught in bad snowy weather on Dartmoor who came upon an isolated farm. Seeing smoke rising from the chimney, he knocked at the door seeking shelter and was taken in by the farmer and his elderly mother. The couple stabled the man's horse and provided him with both food and accommodation.

The night was bitterly cold and yet the farmer gave up his bed for the man. In the corner of the bedroom was a large chest, about which the mother had been rather noncommittal when questioned. Unable to sleep for the cold, the man decided to satisfy his curiosity and crossed to the chest, lifting the lid to peer inside. Horrified, he discovered a dead body within. He returned to bed and spent the rest of the night on edge, expecting to be murdered at any moment by the gang upon whom he thought he may have stumbled.

At breakfast the following morning, in a calmer state, the man admitted that he had opened the chest, and asked about the corpse.

'Bless your heart, your honour, 'tis nothing at all,' the farmer said. ''Tis only Fayther.' He went on to explain that the snow had prevented their passage to Tavistock with the farmer for burial and so, 'Mother put 'un in the old box and salted 'un in. Mother's a fine hand at salting 'un in.'

Hearing this, the man politely declined to have any of the home-cured bacon which he was offered for breakfast, worried that it might be a piece of the wrong salted meat.

This folk tale reads with the format of a modern urban legend. It has just the right quirkiness and humorous content and yet is based on enough truth that it could just have happened. It is certainly true that bodies were transported across the moor for burial as described above, and also true that bad weather prevented the normal operation of many things—not only transporting bodies but also burying those that had been moved to the church, as the frozen ground would be too hard to dig. This particular tale is ascribed to a variety of places apart from this traditional example of the farmhouse.

Mrs Bray suggests that it took place at a pub at Moretonhampstead, while S.H. Burton, the author of *Devon Villages*, places it at the Warren House Inn. As this is not too far out of Moretonhampstead, Burton may have drawn the assumption from the writing of Mrs Bray, as the Warren House is the best-known pub in that area of the moor.

It should be no surprise that the remoteness and solitude of living and working the moors in Devon have led to such a range of superstitious beliefs, traditions and stories. While modern living has led to them being engaged with differently these days (and this is something that will be explored further in Chapter Ten), we do still find new tales being recorded today. One prime example is the repeated sightings and sometimes photographs of what is generally termed the 'Beast of Exmoor'—a wild big cat or a number of such animals, which are thought by many to have lived on the moors since the 1970s, when the Dangerous Wild Animals Act (1976) led to such creatures being released from private collections. Whether their descendants are still living in the wild is a subject of continued speculation to this day.

CHAPTER THREE

The Calendar Year

The cycle of the year is very important to any culture, and was especially so in past days when agriculture had a much greater impact on people's working lives. Nowhere is this more true than in a county like Devon, where so many people's livelihoods relied (and still do to a certain extent) on the working of the land. It is in an environment such as this that customs and traditions emerge which relate directly to the passing of the year.

Calendar customs are those traditions which take place regularly at fixed times of the year, or on particular dates. If the precise date is not fixed, then they may be considered to be movable customs.[1] Calendar customs are usually very particular to a country (on a macro level) or to a certain region of a country such as Devon (on a micro level) and therefore they may be considered as part of the intrinsic cultural make-up of that place. Any country may have many hundreds or thousands of calendar customs, even on a macro level, and they may be connected to very many different things, such as historical events, important figures, religious beliefs or working practices. As such, we can only hope to consider some of them in the course of this chapter.

Understanding and working with nature was of great importance to our ancestors. It is a vital part of what we might term the 'old ways'—that is, (especially) pre-Christian beliefs. When looking at these old religions or belief systems, people are usually very quick to throw the catch-all term 'pagan' at them. This can be very unhelpful as the term means different things to different people from a cultural perspective, and is often applied incorrectly.

It is very difficult to succinctly define a concept as broad as paganism. However, a useful summary might be something like: 'a non-dogmatic, polytheistic following of an individual interpretation of the Divine. It may be considered to be a species-wide ancestral religion which venerates nature and the spirit of place. Paganism views the cycle of the year as a model for individual growth and renewal on a spiritual level.'[2]

These influences can be seen in many of the customs which take place during the calendar year in Devon, from the start of the new year to its end.

The New Year

Ralph Whitlock points out in his 1977 book *The Folklore of Devon* that it is important to remember that dates for New Year events (and subsequently all other calendrical practices) moved in 1753 after the British calendar was changed.[3] In September of 1752, the country moved from the Julian calendar to the Gregorian, which had already been adopted by most of Europe. This move corrected an error in calculating the solar year from Julius Caesar's original calendar which meant that the date of Easter was moving away from the spring equinox at the rate of one day every 128 years.[4]

This alteration led to well-established calendar customs moving from their traditional placement, with inevitable resistance to the changes. Such resistance would come in no small part from the confusion of trying to work out exactly when some events should happen. This is summed up neatly in an advertisement of the new dates for fairs to be held in the town of Charlbury:

> The FAIR formerly held on the 29th Day of September, will be holden on the 10th day of October. The fair formerly held on St Thomas's Day [21 December] will be holden on the first Day of January. Lent Fair will be holden on the second Friday in Lent. The Fair formerly held on the second Friday in May, will be holden on the second Friday after Old May Day, unless when the 12th of May falls on a Friday, then to be holden on the Friday next following; and so to be continued, unless any of the above days falls on a Sunday, and then to be held on the Monday following.[5]

Many folk in Devon and elsewhere stuck to the original days for celebrations for as long as possible, such as with 'Old Christmas Eve', before gradually the eleven days were added back in and most celebrations crept to the dates that we know of now.

New Year, like other important calendrical events all over the world, is often used as a time for divination—to try and ascertain whether one will become wealthy in the year to come, or perhaps whether love will come one's way. A famous New Year tradition in Germanic countries is to divine the future using drops of molten lead poured into water, where they harden. The resulting shape may tell you something about the year ahead. The practice is called molybdomancy, taken from the Greek word *molybdos*, meaning lead. It may have taken place in old farmhouses across Devon at one time.

Another divination practice which certainly did take place in Devon at New Year was the act of sitting under a sprig of holly with a Bible. With eyes closed, the sitter would open the Bible at a random place and the revealed chapter would be read aloud. The content of the chapter was said to be an indication of the year ahead.

Turning times were always important in trying to bring about good fortune. Wassailing is one well-known example of this, where good and bountiful crops are encouraged for the later harvest time. The word 'wassail' is generally considered to come from the Anglo-Saxon words *waes hael*, which was a toast to good health, although there is another school of thought which places the origin in the Norse *ves heill*, which translates as 'be healthy'.[6] In either case, the meaning is the same. The ceremony, in which offerings and prayers are made to the spirits of the apple trees, is generally accompanied by much shouting and beating of pans and other metal containers. In times when shotguns were commonplace, a volley would often be fired.

Devon tithe maps from the nineteenth century show how large areas of the county were given over to orchards.[7] Most of these would have seen wassail celebrations take place at traditional times around New Year. Toast would be attached to the trees and ale would be poured over the roots to encourage the crops. The noise was there to scare off demons. As the celebrants worked their way around the orchard, a traditional wassail song would be sung or recited. There are a number of variations of this, but they all run along similar lines. Whitlock cites:

> Old Apple Tree, Old Apple Tree,
> We wassail thee and hope that thou wilt bear;

For the Lord doth know where we shall be
Till apples come another year.
For to bear well and to bloom well,
So merry let us be;
Let every man take off his hat and shout to thee,
Old Apple Tree, Old Apple Tree,
We wassail thee and hope that thou wilt bear
Hat fulls,
Cap fulls,
Three bushel bag fulls,
And a little heap under the stairs.[8]

Although most were similar to this, there are a couple of more unusual versions. One from Kingsbridge is interesting because it threatens the tree with harm if the harvest fails:

Apple-tree, apple-tree,
Bear good fruit,
Or down with your top
And up with your root.[9]

This seems to match with a report from the British Consul at Seoul which was noted in Volume Two of *Devon Notes and Queries* in 1900.[10] It refers to a Japanese fruit tree custom which took place on the last day of the year. Two men would visit the orchard. One would climb a tree while the other stayed at the bottom holding an axe. The man on the ground would ask the tree if it was going to bear good fruit in the coming year, suggesting that it would be cut down if it did not. The man at the top of the tree would answer, 'I will bear well'. The acting out of this little scene would ensure the success of the crop.

Another interesting variant is a song sung by the wassailers themselves, bemoaning the fact that they are working hard while the farm owners stay at home, and celebrating not so much the apples as the cider which they desire from them. It was published in the *Western Morning News* in 1931:

Here come us poor 'Wassailers' a'tridding in the mire
While master and mistress be sitting round the fire
Telling of cider and what they could sell
If apples would grow and bountifully swell

Chorus:
Hug a lug, hug a lug, white bread and brown,
Who's the best dame in all of the town?
She who taps cider of the old-fashioned kind
And gives them poor 'Wassailers' so much as they mind,
Hats full, caps full, bushel, bushel bags full,
Hats full, caps full, bushel, bushel bags full,
Hip, hip, hurrah! Us will pepper the trees,
And bring on the apples and keep off disease.

Here's to the master, a two-gallon man,
Who always gets 'tiddly' whenever he can;
And here's to the mistress when mister's not in,
Who goes to the cupboard and brings out the gin.

Chorus.[11]

The song pokes light-hearted fun at the employers of the men who would have sung it; they would of course been out of work altogether if the crops were not successful.

As the number of orchards declined over the years, so the ceremony gradually died away, but it has seen a resurgence recently. Some of these modern wassails are down to folk groups or recreationists, while others happen at orchards which are still in use. Sandford Orchards near Crediton, for example, hold an annual wassail which keeps the tradition alive, provides entertainment in the form of folk dance and mumming, and of course acts as good publicity for the business.

While the main ceremony itself has survived, this is not true of one interesting custom which often took place afterwards. The men would return to the farmhouse after the wassail and find that they were locked out by the women inside. They would not be allowed back in until they had correctly guessed what was turning on the spit. This was inevitably an object which would not normally be expected to be placed there, and which would be given as a prize to whomever guessed it. Many people thought at one time that if this last part of the tradition did not take place, then the trees would certainly not fruit.

There was once a tradition among farmers around the mid-Devon area of Crediton that in order to ensure good fortune for the year, a robin should be shot on 6 January (Old Christmas Day). This idea does not seem to have been present in other places. It may have some obscure connection to the tradition of the Wren Boys, who would capture a wren and mount it on a stick as part of a parade of celebration. This was most prolific in Ireland, although it was and is found elsewhere (a fake wren is used in modern times)—but this one is associated with St Stephen's Day (26 December). There is a traditional couplet which connects the two birds: 'Robin Redbreast and Jenny Wren / Are God Almighty's cock and hen'.

What seems odd about the Crediton tradition is that it is normally considered to be unlucky to bring about the death of a robin. Should one die in your hand, it could have even more serious repercussions. One story told that a boy who had this happen suffered forever afterwards with a hand that shook.

Another strong New Year tradition in Devon, also found country-wide, was that of 'First Footing'. All the lights in the house would be put out and the door and windows opened on the last stroke of midnight, as the New Year came into being. The first person to visit the house would be an indicator of the times to follow. If they were dark, then they would bring good fortune. A light-haired or pale-skinned visitor would bring bad luck.

It is not known for certain why darker people were considered to be more lucky, and in fact Simpson and Roud acknowledge that in different areas of the country, good luck was ascribed to either dark-haired or fair people.[12] If the visitor brought a gift, then the nature of this might also indicate the year to come. A lump of coal was common (signifying warmth). A coin would be a natural choice, for wealth. It was usual, of course, for the first visitor to be pre-arranged rather than actually left to fate.

Traditions in February

2 February is Candlemas, also once known as The Wives' Feast and marking what was said to have been the fortieth day after the birth of Christ. It is a date which used to hold far more significance for us than it does today. This was once the date that marked the end of the Christmas season, and superstition still tells us that any Christmas decorations that are not taken down by Twelfth Night should be left in place until Candlemas Day and then be removed. On Dartmoor, not removing all the greenery in this way was thought to tempt a death in the household in the year to come. The seventeenth-century English poet and clergyman Robert Herrick referenced the tradition in his 'Ceremonies for Candlemas Eve'.[13] A similar risk was ascribed to bringing snowdrops into the house before this date. In fact, there were quite a number of other portents of death associated with Candlemas, probably because of its leading into the time of rebirth with the coming of spring.

Candlemas, drawing some of its Christian elements from the earlier festival of light which marked the middle of winter, literally became the mass of the candles. All the candles that were going to be used in the church over the coming year would be brought in and a blessing would be said over them. The folklore reports of the Devonshire Association note a contribution by Mrs M.A. Terrell, who recorded that if a candle dripped at one side when carried into the church at this celebration, then it was foretelling a death of someone close in the next twelve months.[14] Many houses would burn a candle in each window on 2 February to ensure good luck.

February was traditionally said to be a good time for sowing certain crops. J. Manley Hawker, a resident of the North Devon village of Berrynarbor, recalled in 1883 that an employee born on the edge of Exmoor had told him 'when the

parson begins to read Genesis it's time to sow black oats'.[15] This was due to this particular crop being hardy and therefore able to withstand the frost which would probably still form overnight at this time of year. Richard Pearce Chope associates this saying with the festival of Septuagesima seven days before Easter.[16]

February's other popular date of celebration is Valentine's Day, on the fourteenth of the month. Many complain of this now being a commercialized marketing ploy by greetings card companies and the like, and in fact this idea was being voiced as far back as the middle of the nineteenth century, when Robert Chambers wrote in his *Book of Days* that it was 'a much degenerated festival, the only observance of any note consisting merely of the sending of jocular anonymous letters to parties whom one wishes to quiz, and this confined very much to the humbler classes.'[17]

We have already seen in Chapter Two how hempseed would be scattered on the eve of this day to try and divine one's intended partner. Important calendar dates (whether long established or more recent) often had divination customs attached to them. If a girl wanted to know if she would be wed in the coming year, then she should look through the keyhole of her front door on Valentine's eve. If she caught sight of a hen and cock together, then the answer was yes. If she wanted to know who the groom would be, then she should write the letters of the alphabet on pieces of paper and float them in a bowl of water. After this, she should place a pair of shoes in front of the bowl in the shape of a T and recite a verse:

> I place my shoes like the letter T
> In hopes my true love I shall see
> In his apparel and his array
> As he is now and every day

The shoes would need to be moved three times after this, and then the following morning some of the letters in the bowl would be found face up, signifying the initials of the man.

A less convoluted method was to sleep with yarrow under the pillow. The next day, the first man seen after leaving the house would be the girl's betrothed. If, however, you were not looking to get married then the key was in the same flower which featured at Candlemas above—the snowdrop. Pick one before 14 February and you would stay single for the rest of the year.

At one time, Valentine's Day was also used as a time to give a gift in preparation for the Easter period, when it was the custom to wear something new on Easter Day. Often, a girl would select a young man to gift her a pair of gloves for the occasion, and use Valentine's to suggest that if he did so, then it would be looked on favourably in the future. Mrs Bray recorded a traditional approach that girls would use:

> Good morrow, Valentine, I go to-day
> To wear for you what you must pay,
> A pair of gloves next Easter-Day.[18]

We will move on to look at the traditions around Easter weekend shortly, but first we pass through the traditional fasting period of Lent—and that means first we need to use up all of our best foods in a period of feasting, so that they do not go to waste!

Shrovetide

The most prominent remnant of celebrations at Shrovetide, still practiced today, is the making of pancakes. This is the food we most associate with Shrove Tuesday, but it is only one of many that are traditionally eaten all over the world at this time.

The stereotypical act of tossing pancakes was a part of the old Shrove Tuesday celebrations, and Mrs Bray records that this time was treated as a holiday by farmers, who ensured that their staff had plenty of pancakes. Everyone would gather around the fire and would have to toss their pancake before eating it. She notes that those who were not so skilled at this would still be told to eat theirs, even if they failed to catch it and it fell into the fire, much to everyone's amusement.[19]

Not everybody was fortunate enough to have plenty of food to feast on. Being at the opposite end of the year to harvest time, the early season was a difficult one for many—one reason agricultural labourers benefitted from their employers on Shrove Tuesday. Poverty from the seventeenth to the nineteenth centuries being particularly bad, the custom of 'Shroving' developed, where people would go door to door in an effort to beg for food or ingredients. This generally took place either the night before, or on the morning of Shrove Tuesday.

In Devon, Shroving was also commonly known as 'Lent-crocking' and there is some confusion around this custom—seen by some to be the practice of begging for food at doors, and by others as the throwing of crockery sherds. This latter aspect took place as a punishment meted out to people who refused to give anything to the caller, and might be seen as similar to the modern Halloween 'Trick or Treat' concept.

The former, the traditional visiting of houses to ask for food at Shrovetide, was the custom known in Devon as either Lent-crocking or Shroving. Various songs were recited at the door, such as this example from Bridestowe, near Okehampton:

> Lean crock, give a pancake,
> Or a fritter, for my labour,
> Or a dish of flour, or a piece of bread,
> Or what you please to render.
> I see, by the latch,
> There's something to catch;
> I see, by the string,
> There's a good dame within.
> Trap, trapping throw,
> Give me my mumps, and I'll be go[20]

The phrase 'trap, trapping[,] throw' probably refers to the callers walking up to the door on tiptoe to avoid detection; another variant of the rhyme from the same area uses 'Trepy, Trapy, Tro'. The English Folk Dance and Song Society note a version in more modern English which can be seen to directly relate to these older variants:

> Tip, tip, toe
> Please to give us a penny
> And away we'll go[21]

This refers to the separate tiptoeing custom where children would march around the village in pairs collecting money. At Gittisham, this is recorded as having been organized by the school, with all the money being taken back there to be divided up by the headmistress.[22] The Gittisham ritual still continues to this day, being organized by village mothers for the children and culminating with tea in the village hall.[23]

The punishment for householders who did not give food was originally the throwing of stones at the door.

> Give a cake, for I've none;
> At the door goes a stone,
> Come give, and I'm gone.[24]

After battering the door, the caller would run away, sometimes pursued by the homeowner. If they were caught, they would be taken back to the house where they would have to undergo a punishment of their own, known as 'roasting the shoe'. An old shoe would be hung over the fire and the person responsible for throwing the stones would have to keep it spinning, meaning that the shoe was not the only thing to be roasted.

Throwing stones was replaced in some cases by throwing sherds of pottery. It may be that the confusion over the custom of Lent-crocking came about because people misinterpreted the meaning of 'crock', thinking it referred not to a cake, but to throwing crocks, or crockery pieces. Where the throwing of sherds is the main element of the custom, then it was generally known in Devon as 'Lent-sherd night', 'Drowing of cloam' ('cloam' being the term for clay or earthenware pots, and 'drowing' being Devonshire Dialect for 'throwing') or 'Dappy-door night'. This last term is probably derived again from the Devonshire dialect, where to 'dap' means to hit.[25]

There is definitely more joking and pranking carried out in these versions of the Shrove Tuesday traditions. The vicar of Ilfracombe, John Mill Chanter, records in his book *Wanderings in North Devon* examples of people tying long strings to the handles of front doors so that, when they were answered, the culprits could yank the door out of the owner's hands.[26] This trick certainly makes sense when noting that it was the 'Dappy-door night' name that was used in this town.

Mothering Sunday

In the United Kingdom, Mothering Sunday takes place on the fourth Sunday of Lent and finds its origins in the Roman Catholic processional custom of mid-Lent Sunday. At this time, worshippers from the outskirts of parishes would make their way to their 'Mother Church' for a religious service that was followed by much eating, drinking and merriment.[27] The day was also once known as Refreshment Day, recounting the story of the Feeding of the Five Thousand. Being almost halfway through the period of Lent, this celebration permits the enjoyment of food, which would have been withheld during the rest of the run-up to Easter.

It became traditional into the seventeenth century for servants and other young workers to be granted permission to visit their parents to celebrate Mothering Sunday. The Tiverton-based folklore collector Sarah Hewett described the food that would be prepared the day before by the mother, in advance of her children arriving: 'Of course, the *mothering-cake* is her chief care. It is big and rich, and must be well baked, sugared and ornamented with fanciful designs. The dinner on Sunday consists of a hind quarter of lamb with mint sauce, a well-boiled suet pudding, seakale, and cauliflower, wheat furmity, with home-made wines.'[28]

In some cases, the daughter of the family who was away in service would make the cake rather than the mother, with the ingredients being provided by the mistress of the house where she was employed. The better opinion the mistress had of the girl, the better the ingredients given would be, which would have been a good incentive to be a hard worker. This celebration also gave the girl an opportunity to demonstrate her cooking skills to the family. One old Devon recipe for the mothering-cake, which was a simnel cake, used six squares of pastry to make a cube-shaped receptacle to hold all the fruit and peel ingredients. The method for cooking this notes that the pastry lid should be held in place using a 'cock crimp' rather than a 'hen crimp'. This means that the lid should be crimped clockwise rather than anticlockwise. The same nomenclature is found over the border in relation to pasties, which must be crimped in order to be described as 'Cornish', with a 'hen pasty' being made by a right-handed baker and a 'cock pasty' by a left-handed one.[29]

Easter Traditions

In his *Reminiscences of Exeter Fifty Years Since*, writer James Cossins recalls a custom occurring after the Maundy Thursday service had taken place at the cathedral, where coins were given out to the children:

> distributed by the vergers, standing at the door under the north tower; the exit being the entrance near Southernhay, giving the alert ones time to come round again. The confusion and noise was so great, the vergers were desired to throw the pence in the yard for a general scramble, which excited much amusement to lookers-on. This custom ceased many years since.[30]

Coin scrambles were common in Devon but were more associated with fairs. Many of these still take place each year around the county. Traditionally, coins that had been heated until red-hot were thrown by the wealthy, who took delight on seeing the discomfort suffered by the poorer members of the community trying to collect them. Most modern versions are aimed more at an entertainment for children and the coins are generally no longer heated, although at Honiton Hot Pennies Day, which takes place on the first Tuesday after 19 July, they are still warmed.[31]

Cossins says that the coins referred to in this custom were known as 'Peter's Pence', but this does not seem to make sense. 'Peter's Pence' was a term given to a levy of one penny that was once applied to each household, with the money being sent to Rome to support the Pope.[32] Later this became a voluntary contribution given to the Catholic Church to support charities as decreed by the Holy See, although recent questions have been asked over what percentage of this money is actually finding its way to the charities in question. Exeter Cathedral is Anglican and so Cossins's reference to 'Peter's Pence' seems misplaced. It is possible that it came about because the cathedral is dedicated to St Peter and so the coins are named in the same way, though describing something different. The same may be true of a sixteenth-century oak chest which is said to be a receptacle for 'Peter's Pence', found in the Anglican church at Combe Martin on the North Devon coast. This church is dedicated to Saint Peter ad Vincula, meaning 'Peter in Chains'. This church dedication is very rare, with some old books on the village of Combe Martin stating that the only other example is the chapel at the Tower of London. In fact, there are a few other examples found in Wales, Chichester, Warwickshire and Stockton-on-Tees, amongst others.

Following on from Maundy Thursday, Good Friday is probably most often associated with the hot cross bun, now eaten all over the world on this day. Many people probably learned to play the recorder at school using the sung nursery rhyme named after this bun. The musical rhyme started life as a street cry used by confectionery sellers. It was first recorded in the 1733 edition of *Poor Robin's Almanac* as 'Good Friday comes this month, the old woman runs. With one or two a penny, hot cross-buns'.[33] There have been many variations of this rhyme recorded over the years. William Crossing noted a Devon version when collecting folk rhymes across the county:

> Hot cross buns, hot cross buns,
> One a penny, two a penny, hot cross buns;
> Smoking hot, piping hot,
> Just come out of the baker's shop;
> One a penny poker, two a penny tongs,
> Three a penny fire-shovel, hot cross buns.[34]

At one time in Devon, house visiting for hot cross buns took place on Good Friday in a similar fashion to Lent-crocking, although it was not as common at Easter time.

A number of superstitions arose regarding the baking and use of buns on Good Friday, some of which were contradictory. Some held that it was impossible to bake bread at all on this date, because the water needed to mix the dough would turn into blood in memory of Christ's crucifixion.[35] Other folklore said that bread baked on Good Friday would keep for a whole year without going mouldy. The former superstition probably arose from efforts by church clergy to try and keep the day holy, and so to attempt to dissuade people from working. The latter belief led to the hot cross bun being associated with a number of folk medicine cures.

Sarah Hewett recorded the belief that grating a hardened, stale hot cross bun into a powder which was then mixed with cold water and drunk acted as a cure for diarrhoea.[36] This curative is very similar to ones found elsewhere in the world claiming that bread baked on Good Friday and kept for a year will treat stomach complaints if ground into water. Hot cross buns would normally have been baked fresh on the morning of Good Friday in times past. All of this comes together in a tradition from Hartland which used a larger round cake baked on Good Friday, also for stomach problems. The cake was made from unleavened Lent bread, which ties in with the more global ideas surrounding Good Friday bread.

The manner of preserving the hot cross buns for the year was to harden them in the oven and then hang them from the rafters of the house. In some areas of Devon they were used for treating cattle as well as human ailments.

A whole raft of superstitions pertaining to good or bad luck depending on which tasks are undertaken on Good Friday are recorded, from planting crops and weaning children (good things) to washing clothes and killing pigs (bad things, unless you were the pig, which would not die if the attempt was made on this day).

As the day of Christ's resurrection, Easter Sunday is naturally a day of celebration for those of the Christian faith. A letter written in 1892 preserves a rhyme from this day suggesting that everyone should rise early on this morning as Christ did:

> Get up, my men, I give you warning
> The sun will rise soon, this Easter morning.
> Shame to the man that lies abed
> When Christ so early rose from the dead,
> And sees not the sun drive away night's gloom
> On the morning that Jesus arose from the tomb.[37]

The letter was penned by the Reverend J.B. Hughes and collected by the Reverend Sabine Baring-Gould.

The sun also figured in other Easter Sunday folklore. Richard Chope describes in his article on movable festivals in the *Report and Transactions of the Devonshire Association* how in Devon the sun was believed to dance in the sky on Easter Sunday in celebration of Christ's resurrection. He quotes a piece from *Devon and Cornwall Notes and Queries* where one Thomas Corney and Mary Wilkey had ventured out to try and observe the phenomenon.[38] Thomas professed to witnessing it, but Mary could not. After asking her repeatedly, and with her still not being able to see it, Thomas declared that the 'devil must have shut your eyes' because he could see it plainly.

Thomas is probably playing a trick on Mary in this account, and it is unlikely that he would be the only person to do such a thing. The idea of the sun dancing on Easter Sunday is not one that comes purely from Devon, but in fact was recorded all over the country as an event which people tried to witness. We must remember that you could not observe the movement by looking directly at the sun, as this would be dangerous and could damage your eyesight. Therefore, people would look into a pond, a well or some other container of water and watch the reflection. Agitation on the surface of the water would make it look as if the sun were moving. It is quite possible that the whole idea came about from one person once telling another the story, and once their audience was staring into the water, unscrupulously knocking the container or otherwise causing the surface of the water to move. The strength of religious belief or superstition would have done the rest.

What does seem to have been ascribed only to Devon is the observation of the sun on Easter Sunday to look for an image of a lamb in its middle, most likely as reference to the 'Lamb of God'. William Henderson records that this took place on Dartmoor: 'Devonshire maidens get up to see the sun rise on Easter morning ... Poor women in the neighbourhood of Dartmoor have told me that they used, as girls, to go out in parties at sunrise to see the Lamb in the sun, and look at it through a darkened glass, and some always declared that they saw it.'[39]

There are a few important points that we should note from this short quote. Firstly, although the author has been told the story by one group of women on Dartmoor, he has extrapolated it to suggest that 'Devonshire maidens' do this generally. There is no evidence in other sources to confirm this, and the event might only have been performed by this one group. This shows how one story can easily be later interpreted as common practice, hence generating folklore. Secondly, Henderson says that he was told this story by 'poor women', which contains the frequent underlying suggestion by higher-class writers and collectors in the nineteenth century that superstitious, rural people believed fervently in notions which were ridiculous to the educated. Finally, if this was a tradition only followed by this one group, as is highly possible, and they were using a piece of smoked glass or similar, it is quite likely that they were observing a flaw in the glass projected onto the disc of the sun in the background. The fact that 'some always declared that they saw it' (my italics) would seem to back this up.

The remaining days of the Easter period commonly saw village or town fairs and revels staged, with food stalls, rides, music and theatrical performance commonplace. A curious revel took place on Easter Monday in the grounds of Torre Abbey. The festivities here would close with a ceremony of the 'ducking of the Lord Mayor'. This character was not the actual town mayor but rather a stand-in drawn from the working classes and elevated to the position for the revel, acting as a 'mock mayor'. Many communities would elect such a pretend official at celebrations during the year, with this person acting as a wry commentary on actual authority figures,[40] and allowing the townsfolk to air their frustrations in a relatively harmless way.

In his 1912 guide to Torre Abbey, Watkin speculated that the custom is connected with Hoke Day, one of two days on which financial liabilities would be due or, later, tithes would be payable.[41] He believed the ritual to be a remembrance of the bailiffs ensuring that people paid the sums that were due, stating that Hoke Day was on the same day as the revel—Easter Monday. Unfortunately, Watkin has his dates confused with this theory, as Hock-Tide was actually later than this, being the Monday and Tuesday following the second Sunday after Easter.[42]

May Day

Between the customs at Easter and the Whitsun and Ascension Tide traditions to which we will turn in a moment lies the bank holiday of May Day. May customs are generally associated with flowers and greenery, with the first of the month being known in many Devon towns and villages as Garland Day. Processions through the streets with poles and other items decked with flowers were common. Also frequently in use at this time of year, although now only remaining very sporadically across the county, is the maypole. This decorated pole with its hanging ribbons would have been a feature of many a village green and revel in Devon, and along with its associated dances is certainly one of the most quintessential representations of the festivities which usher in the month. The origins of the maypole are not known for certain; some claim it has Roman roots but there is little hard evidence for this. The first firm references come from the fourteenth century,[43] becoming more widespread in parish accounts from the fifteenth century onwards. Chaucer referenced a pole which used to be found at the church of St Andrew Undershaft in London, an example so well known in its day that the name of the church actually derives from the shaft of the pole, which was set up opposite the building every year.

The image of primary school children weaving around one another, plaiting the ribbons that they hold, is one readily associated with the maypole. In fact, the addition of the ribbons is a very late one which became well established during the revivals of the Victorian and Edwardian periods. Prior to this, choreography took the form of a circle dance with the pole in the centre. Another variation found at Moretonhampstead replaced the pole with a 'Dancing Tree', making use of a massive elm tree that used to stand in the centre of the village and which supported a platform large enough for musicians and dancers.[44] The tree was well known in Devon, having appeared in R.D. Blackmore's novel *Christowell* in 1885 with chapter 15 named after it.[45]

In Tavistock, a pyramid of greenery and flowers was built which was then worn by a man who would dance as part of the May procession. This was a local version of the traditional 'Jack-in-the-Green', which derived from chimney sweeps' May Day celebrations.[46] Tavistock named theirs 'Jack-in-the-Bush'.

A rhyme recorded in Gloucestershire and likely elsewhere that was sung by children as they danced around the maypole was employed in Devon for a slightly different use.

> Round the Maypole, trit-trit-trot!
> See what a Maypole we have got;
> Fine and gay, trip away,
> Happy is our new May-day[47]

In Devon this was sung as part of the local tradition of May Dolls, which were made on 30 April and taken door to door on May Day where they would be shown to the occupants for a small price, not unlike the 'Penny for the Guy' traditions later in the year. The custom is recorded as having taken place in the parishes of Tor and Upton,[48] and acknowledged as happening elsewhere in Devon too. Girls would dress their dolls in their finest clothes and lay them in a cardboard box, which would be decorated with flowers and greens either obtained from the garden or from willing locals. The box would be covered with a piece of material and taken 'visiting' around the parish, being unveiled for householders who were willing to pay a small price to have a look. Money was generally collected in a bag and shared equally between the children, who would go round in a group. This equitable distribution of collected money is similar to that seen in the Gittisham 'Tip Tip Toe' ritual discussed above.

Girls also used to leave the house early on 1 May to wash their faces in the dew, as it was said to have magical properties on this day that would ensure a good complexion for the year. Some thought that it would also remove spots and freckles. Conversely, it was considered unlucky to buy a broom or to wash your blankets in May.

Another May Day rhyme collected in Torquay describes other customs on subsequent days:

> The first of May is May-pole day,
> The second of May is ducking-day,
> The third of May is kissing-day![49]

Ducking Day may have originated in the practice of punishing the village scold in the pond, later becoming a date where it was acceptable to throw water at passers-by. In Kingsbridge, things were taken a stage further with the local fire engine being employed to make use of its hose for the purpose.

The Exeter Assize records for June 1894 contain details of a case brought to trial against two boys, William John Luscombe (thirteen) and Samuel George Hine (sixteen) for the manslaughter of Dr Alfred Hughes Twining at Loddiswell during Ducking Day celebrations. The boys were part of a group who threw water over a fence into the road below. Dr Twining and another man, Dr Hellier, were being driven along the road in a carriage. The falling water frightened the horse, causing it to hit a fence. A second lot of water made the horse bolt, overturning the carriage. Dr Twining suffered an ankle injury when thrown from the carriage which led to his leg being amputated. He did not survive the operation. Luscombe was found not guilty and Hine was bailed for a sum of £5 of his own funds and £5 surety from his father.

Kissing Day described a custom which needs no further elaboration. Unrecorded in the rhyme above but appearing in variants elsewhere in Devon was Sting-Nettle Day, when children would run around the village attempting to sting each other with nettle fronds.

Ascension and Whitsun

Some believe that the term Whitsun is derived from the word 'wit', meaning understanding, and that this refers to a time of being filled with the knowledge of the Holy Spirit. If this were the case then the term would have come into use during the transition between the old and new religions.

The accepted derivation is that the name comes from a contraction of 'White Sunday', probably because people baptized on this day would wear white garments. Some old folklore seems to bear this out, as there are records of girls attending church wearing white and carrying garlands of wildflowers. Interestingly, Plymouth once associated another colour with this time, as Whit Sunday in that city was Scarlet Day. In this case, the colour does not come from any religious aspect, but rather from the fact that the mayor and corporation would attend the church services in scarlet dress robes.

In some areas, Whitsun weekend was the time appointed for 'Beating the Bounds'. This is a custom which still takes place to this day in many rural parishes, despite modern surveying techniques making it unnecessary from a practical point of view. Beating the Bounds was a method employed to ensure that the locations of the parish boundary markers would not be forgotten. The boys of the parish would be taken on a journey around the periphery, the boundary stones or landmarks of importance would be checked, and then the boys would be beaten. In extreme cases they would be held upside down over the stone and bounced headfirst upon it. By this method, it was made certain that they did not forget the location of that part of the boundary. At the village of Belstone, the oldest member of the parish would be the one to invert the youngest who was taking part.

The custom still takes place on Whit Monday at Bridestow (although obviously without the associated beating), for instance, where it happens once every seven years. This perambulation was so well known for the refreshments which were laid on after the ceremony, consisting of a wagonload of baked goods, that it became known as 'Beating the Buns'. Food was also involved in the Okehampton Beating, which took place on Ascension Day and was known locally as Spurling Day. Quantities of apples and nuts would be thrown into miry places on the route, causing the boys to scramble to pick them up.[50]

A mire was also the location of a boundary dispute between the parishes of Farway, Honiton, Sidbury and Gittisham. Legend tells that the argument was settled by Isabel de Forz, the 8th Countess of Devon, when she removed her ring and threw it into the mire, declaring the boundary to be where it landed.[51] The location is today called 'Ring in the Mire'. The countess is also said to have been responsible for the supply of water to Tiverton via the town leat, and a medieval water-bailing custom, which features many similar elements to Beating the Bounds, is carried out there every seven years.

The importance of water can also be seen in the practice of visiting holy wells in the county. It was believed that water from wells that were said to have curative powers was particularly effective at certain times of the year. This might be the feast day of the saint associated with the well, or a religious festival such as Easter or Whitsun. In North Devon this belief was linked with Ascension Day, and water from wells in North Molton and Hatherleigh was collected in the morning for that purpose.[52] In the case of the latter well, there was also a custom of dropping a pin into the water and making a wish. The idea of the wishing well is common, and the use of pins is probably taken from beliefs that dropping a pin into the water at certain holy wells could be used for divination. The custom of well dressing (the decoration of the well with elaborate designs and pictures constructed from flowers) is also often linked with this time of year.

One of the South West's three remaining established hobby horse customs takes place in the Devon village of Combe Martin on Ascension Day. 'The Hunting of the Earl of Rone' sees a party of village men dressed as grenadiers capture a fugitive figure, masked and dressed in sackcloth, in the woods before parading him through the street seated backwards on a donkey. At intervals, the captive is 'shot' by the grenadiers and resurrected by the hobby horse, before reaching the sea where an effigy is thrown into the water.[53] The ceremony is said to represent the capture of Hugh O'Neill, Earl of Tyrone, who fled from Ireland during the 'Flight of the Earls' in 1607, although much of the claimed history is flawed. 'The Hunting of the Earl of Rone' was banned by the church in 1837 after a local man fell from the steps of a cottage and broke his neck, but in 1978 was recreated in the form in which it still takes place today.

In many parts of Devon, Whitsun celebrations finished on the Tuesday with fairs or similar community gatherings. A ram roast was held for many years at Kingsteignton, whereas in Paignton one notable custom was the making of a giant plum pudding. The Paignton Pudding is claimed to have originated in 1295 as a token payment in recognition of the granting of a charter for the town. A white-pot or bag pudding was made annually at first, later being made every fifty years when it was divided between the poor, before lapsing into obscurity prior to a nineteenth-century revival.

While this claim remains difficult to substantiate for certain, there is no doubt that the tradition predates the revival in 1819, when a pudding weighing 900 pounds was boiled for the annual fair. Thomas Westcote notes of Paignton in his *View of Devonshire* in 1630: 'I must tell you … of the huge and costly white-pot there made of late; some term it a bag pudding. In former ages it was an annual action, and of that greatness that it is incredible to the bearer: but thence it hath the addition of white-pot, and called Paignton White-Pot.'[54]

Despite having been in the brewing copper of the local inn for four days, the massive 1819 pudding was apparently still raw on the inside when cut. Another attempt was made in 1859 to celebrate the coming of the railway to Paignton. This time the pudding, which weighed a ton and a half, was constructed in the shape of a pyramid, baked in sections which were joined together later.

This pudding was supposed to be divided up to thank all the labourers who had built the railway, and their families. It was driven through the town as part of a big procession, with a band, wagons of bread, meat and cider, and finally the giant dessert in a wagon pulled by eight horses. Unfortunately, what was intended to be a celebratory meal turned into a riot when an estimated 18,000 people turned up, all wanting a piece of the pudding.[55]

Midsummer's Day

Due to its being a solstice holiday, the celebration of Midsummer on 24 June is an important date connected with many and various older religions, and we find customs associated with it all over the world.

In areas such as Devon that are rich in agriculture, weather conditions on Midsummer's Day were steeped in superstition. If the weather was good, then it would be a very fruitful growing season. Midsummer in Devon may also be connected with divinatory practices, which are often linked to calendrical celebrations in terms of their folklore. Crazywell Pool, below Cramber Tor on Dartmoor, is one such place. Here, it was said that anyone who looked into the waters of the pool on Midsummer's Eve would see the likeness of the next parishioner who was going to die (see Chapter Two).

There is an interesting modern version of this story—undoubtedly apocryphal as it contains the usual elements of an urban legend. Two motor-cyclists were said to have been told the story of Crazywell in the pub one night, and a bet was made that they would be too afraid to visit the pool on Midsummer's Eve and try it for themselves. The bet, of course, was accepted. Because of the distance to get there, they went on the motorbike rather than walking. They arrived at the pool and looked in but, of course, they only saw their own reflections. On the way home to claim their prize, the bike veered from the road and both men were killed. The pool, it seems, had been quite accurate.[56]

Another divination practice at Hatherleigh, this time connected with marriage, was described by a servant girl born there in 1855 and who stayed in the area for the next twenty years.[57] She told how some of the village men would assemble in the church porch on Midsummer's Eve and watch the spirits of living neighbours, which became visible at midnight. All of these spirits would be identified as they entered the church. Those that came out again would be married in the next twelve months. Conversely, any that did not emerge would die during the same period, as would any men who fell asleep there.

The foretelling deaths aspect of this custom is certainly not just a local one, and we find it in a similar form in many other counties. A better-known version actually takes place on St Mark's Eve (Midsummer is St John's Eve) and it is likely that the two have been conflated over time, as is often the case with folklore traditions. Other divinations for finding love and similar, which are said to take place at Midsummer, are also sometimes associated with other times of the year, such as the use of hemp seeds discussed elsewhere in this book.

Harvest

As one of the most important times of the year in an agricultural county such as Devon, there is a plethora of custom and tradition associated with the annual harvests. This is considered in detail in the next chapter, which looks at farming and its associated superstitions.

All Hallows and Bonfire Night

How the modern celebration of Halloween has developed is a rather controversial subject for many. There is an argument that modern Halloween is imposed onto the ancient holiday of Samhain, which was three days of feasting beginning on 31 October. All Hallows used to fall on different dates. At one point it was celebrated in May and then moved to 1 November. It is essentially a church festival relating to purgatory and intercession or intervention with those in the afterlife. All Souls became a taboo celebration when prayers for the dead were outlawed at the time of the Reformation, and now we might look upon Halloween as a Roman Catholic holiday which was revived in the twentieth century as a result of Americanization.

The way in which Trick or Treat operates now is specifically an American incursion, but going house to house for food is a much older underlying tradition with links to medieval Christianity and the custom of souling and the soul cake. This would be baked in the home, made from currants and spices, in the form of a biscuit with a cross on the top, not unlike the Good Friday bun but with the cross symbolizing the memory of family members who had died and were in purgatory. Visitors to the door would ask, 'A soul cake, a soul cake', or sing a song. Householders would give the poor a soul cake (a treat) and in exchange the visitor would perform the trick of trying to relieve the suffering of loved ones in purgatory through prayer.

Halloween in Devon was a good time for divination, because of the belief that it was easier to commune with spirits at this time. A girl who wanted to know the identity of her future husband would sit in front of a mirror brushing her hair, while holding an apple in her other hand. As she ate the apple, the image of her intended would appear in the mirror behind her shoulder.

Hazelnuts were often used, leading to Halloween also being known as Nutcrack Night. By throwing them into the fire and observing the results, girls would establish who would marry and how happy the marriages would be.

One custom in East Budleigh which took place on 1 November appears to have been unique to that town. This was 'halloaing for biscuits', where children clamoured for small cakes in a manner not unlike the penny toss seen at many fairs, and which was discussed earlier with reference to 'Peter's Pence'. Author 'Volo non Valeo' (the pen name of Maria Susannah Gibbons) observed this custom taking place three days later, on 4 November. She notes that the cakes had used to be thrown from the church porch at one time.[58] The change in location and calendar date were both due to the local vicar, who on the one hand decided that the custom was unsuitable for the church grounds while at the same time placing it on the Feast of All Saints, his church patron's festival date.

Some events associated with Halloween and Bonfire Night have been inter-changeable over the years. When children in Chulmleigh took their guy round on the evening of 5 November, they would carry turnip lanterns fashioned in a similar way to our modern carved pumpkins. Also in this town, and elsewhere in North Devon, it was not Guy Fawkes who was burned in effigy but local residents who were unscrupulous or poorly thought of—and this would take place outside their own house.

Fire has always played a big part in Bonfire Night traditions in Devon, and there used to be many torchlight processions. The carrying of flaming tar barrels is still undertaken in Ottery St Mary and is very famous, but there used to be many other events where lit barrels were rolled, including in Chulmleigh, Exeter, Torquay and at Ashburton where the barrels were carried and oil-soaked rags attached to a chain were swung by men running through the town.

The Ottery St Mary tar barrels are part of a wider day of activities for the town's carnival. This begins at the very early hour of 5.30am with the firing of rock cannons, which is repeated periodically throughout the day. A. Nelson Owen, who took part in this for many decades, recalled that 'probably 30 or more men owned cannons made for them by local blacksmiths. The gunpowder used to create the explosion was then known as rock-powder— used for blasting and readily available in some ironmongers' shops.'[59]

Christmas

Staying with Ottery St Mary, we note that this was most likely the last place in England to hear a traditional cry on Christmas morning from the town's night watchman. A bell would be rung three times, before the cry went out: 'At the Nativity of Christ our Lord, the angels did rejoice with one accord that Christians imitate them here on earth, and spend this day with joy and pious mirth.'[60] This would be followed by the giving of the time and weather condition, or any other status of the town.

As we saw at the beginning of this chapter, the change in calendar system caused some confusion in terms of traditional customs, with people gradually trying to ascribe them to the new dates, while those who refused to accept the change insisted on using the old ones. This has led to some beliefs being declared for both. For example, there was a superstitious belief that farm animals would kneel in devotion on Christmas Eve, but some reports say that this was on 24 December while others refer to Old Christmas Eve (4 January) as the only time that this would happen. Tozer, citing 'Christmas Eve' without specifying the date, notes the observation of one farmer who said that he saw two of his oldest oxen kneel in their stalls and 'make a cruel moan like Christian creatures'.[61]

One of the great Yule traditions observed in Devon on Christmas Eve was the burning of the Ashen Faggot, which would have taken place in most farmhouses and many domestic dwellings across the county. The methods observed in this tradition would have varied from family to family, but in essence the faggot was a substitute for the customary Yule Log. Ash twigs and small branches would be secured by as many withies as possible. The mass would be dragged into the house and thrown onto the fire. The burning through and snapping of each of the withies would have been the cue for a fresh round of cider.

The faggot was sometimes used for divination. In one version, each young person present would choose a bond securing the faggot. The chooser of the one which burned through first would be the first to marry in the new year. In another custom, nine withies were used to bind the faggot. Anyone who opted out of drinking the cider as the bond snapped would have to pay for the next nine drinks. Some faggots would be as long as eight feet and weight a couple of hundredweight.

The choice of ash was said to have originated as a commemoration of the first dressing of Jesus as a baby in swaddling, in front of a fire of ash which had been cut and lit by Joseph, who had selected it because of its ability to burn green. Ash has been considered a sacred tree since pre-Christian times and features in a wealth of plant lore, so it should be no surprise to see it used in this way at a later date.

In the same way that the old practices of beating children during the boundary perambulations could not take place today, one custom relating to the ashen faggot, recorded at Ashburton in the nineteenth century, sits firmly in the same camp: 'It was usual, when the fire was well lighted and the wood beginning to crack, to place the youngest child of the household on the faggot. The length of time the child stayed there was regarded by the old people as a sign of future bravery, or otherwise.'[62]

CHAPTER FOUR

Farming and the Weather

The South West of the United Kingdom is known by many as a rural spur, and even in modern times with increased transport links and the associated tourist industry that came with them, Devon is predominantly an agricultural county. Eighty per cent of Britain is still given over to farmland[1] and statistics published by the Department for Environment, Food and Rural Affairs (DEFRA) in March 2021 show that 1,789,000 hectares of land in the South West are farmed.[2] In Devon itself, according to mapping data generated by the BBC in 2017, enormous swathes of land are farmed with ninety-two per cent of Mid Devon and eighty-four per cent of the East being the highest proportions.[3]

With so much of the county set aside for this purpose and so many livelihoods dependent on the success of animal and crop production, it should be no
great surprise that historically we find many and varied folk beliefs attached to
the tasks of agricultural production—and, by association, to the prediction of
the favourable weather conditions required to undertake them. Even with the
advent of intensive farming techniques in the 1950s and increased industrial
processes, traditional sayings and customs have not died away completely. Many
farming families in Devon go back generations and such habits are not easily
removed from daily life. There are still plenty of smallholdings in the county
and, at sixty-eight hectares, the average farm size in the region is below that
of the country as a whole.[4] The county retains the largest mileage of natural
hedgerows in Britain because of this propensity for smaller-scale operations.[5]

In this chapter, we will note a number of these superstitious Devonian
beliefs, many of which are now quite obscure, and consider where in some
cases there could be valid science or meteorology involved which gave rise to
their construction.

The Weather

There can be few people unfamiliar with arguably the best-known proverbial
saying connected with the weather: 'Red sky at night, shepherd's delight / Red
sky in the morning, shepherd's warning.'

Probably less well known to many is the fact that the origin of the verse lies
in the Bible, in the Gospel of Saint Matthew: 'Jesus said, "When in evening, ye
say, it will be fair weather: For the sky is red. And in the morning, it will be
foul weather today; for the sky is red and lowering.["]'[6] This was used originally
by shepherds to help them to prepare for the next day's tasks, hence their
inclusion in the saying, although there are other variants replacing them with
sailors, for example.

Although people often consider these provincial verses to be nothing more
than 'old wives' tales', in many cases there is some truth behind them, in
the same way that folk remedies can be efficacious due to elements in their
recipe which science has later shown to be medically sound. The difficulty can
sometimes lie in working out which ones have that element of real-world logic
behind them, and which ones are pure fantasy. In Britain at least, the proverb
relating to red skies does have some reliability to it.

Red skies are created when high pressure in the atmosphere causes dust and
other particles to become trapped. This has the effect of scattering blue light
from the spectrum, leaving the red light behind to give the sky that hue. If this

happens when the sun is setting, then the high pressure is moving from the west, which increases the chances of the following day being dry. At sunrise, then it is an indicator that the high pressure front has already moved from the west to the east, and hence the fair weather that accompanied it has already passed overhead and is moving away. This increases the chances of poorer weather following behind it.

Because of its altitude and position, Dartmoor is known to have very changeable and often quite harsh weather. Mrs Bray made note of a humorous retreatment of the red sky proverb which was used to describe the climate in her hometown of Tavistock (being close to Dartmoor, it often enjoys the same inclement weather):

> The west wind always brings wet weather,
> The east wind wet and cold together,
> The south wind surely brings us rain,
> The north wind blows it back again.
>
> If the sun in red should set,
> The next day surely will be wet;
> If the sun should set in gray [sic],
> The next will be a rainy day.[7]

She does not unfortunately know the name of the wit responsible for the verse, but no doubt appreciated its accuracy!

Other verses and superstitions dealt with particular types of weather, and often the time when they could be expected.

Rain

One Devonshire rhyming couplet alluded specifically to the weather on a Friday: 'Friday and the week / Never aleek'.[8] 'Aleek' here is a dialect rendering of the word 'alike'. The context of this saying is therefore that it always rains on a Friday when other days of the week are generally dry, and vice versa. Another couplet looked at the rain on a Sunday as an indicator of the week to come: 'Rain Sunday before mass / Rain all the week, more or lass'.[9]

Sometimes one particular weather condition can lead to another; this is one of the constants which can allow meteorologists to make relatively accurate weather predictions from what is an inherently chaotic system. We may find this fact reflected in some of the traditional sayings which pass observation on Devon's weather. It was said, for example, that three successive frosty

mornings would bring rain. Another observation noted that 'when Cadbury Castle wears a cap, then Cadbury Tower' will be wet.[10] This undoubtedly related to cloud formation around the earthwork, which rises some 500 feet above sea level on what is otherwise a relatively flat plateau.

Although this is over the border in Somerset, it was recorded in the Devonshire Association *Transactions* along with another interesting note, stating that one could hear the rain crying before it arrived. There is unfortunately no other context listed for this idea, but it possibly refers to the sound of heavy rainfall being carried on the wind before the rain itself arrives, in particularly adverse conditions. Another contributor in a later volume offered another observation on the subject: that rain would be approaching if you could smell the earth.[11] This has sense behind it, as there can be a distinct smell associated with heavy rainfall.

Predicting rain can be quite important for agricultural workers, who might need to sow or harvest at particular times. The behaviour of animals was thought to offer clues. We are all familiar with the idea that cows lying down is a precursor to rain—in fact, according to the Met Office, sixty-one per cent of Brits believe it to be true.[12] Yet there is no scientific evidence for this at all; sometimes cows are just a bit tired. It was also said that rain was coming if the deer in the park at Powderham Castle, on the outskirts of Exeter, were near the railway. Again, there is no obvious reason for this. Aerial satellite images of the deer park do not suggest that there is more natural cover there than in any other part of the grounds, which have remained largely unchanged since the 1920s when that saying was recorded.

Horses, on the other hand, were said to stand with their hindquarters towards the hedges if wet weather was about to arrive. This does seem more sensible; if horses are able to sense any change in pressure which would indicate bad weather, then this would offer them at least some protection while still allowing them to see out into open land. Anecdotal evidence from many horse owners backs up the idea that horses can sense a storm.

The behaviour of many varieties of bird is also a good indicator of rain and would have fed into weather lore. Even as far back as 1900, folklore collector Sarah Hewett noted in her book of Devon folklore *Nummits and Crummits* some of the science between bird behaviour and weather prediction, as well as listing the relevant superstitions: 'When kine view the sky, stretching up their heads and snuffing the air, moist vapours are engendering, the cause of their doing so being their sensibility of the air's sudden alteration from dry to wet; and sudden rain will ensue, though at that time the sun may be shining brightly.'[13] 'Kine' is an old term for cattle.

Cats were said to be good animals at predicting rain. One old rhyme recorded in 1892 said 'If a cat sleeps on her brain / It's a sure sign of rain',[14] relating to the way that cats sometimes sleep curled up with their head upside down. Another piece of lore collected recently on a social media discussion forum recalled that a cat washing behind its ears was also said to be a sign of rain to come.

One obscure piece of Devon lore was described in 1885 by a washerwoman working in Great Torrington, who said that it was always wet when the assizes were being held, this being caused by the fact that they told so many lies there.[15] This draws on the idea that poor weather is reflective of misery in opposition to sunny, happy days; this can also be seen in another tradition which claimed that the weather would always be dull and overcast when someone was about to be executed.

On a lighter note, folklore collected from a user post on the Devonshire Dialect Facebook forum told that, talking of the weather in relation to the view of Lundy Island from the North Devon coast, a Mrs Gifford in Hartland would say:

> Lundy high, sign of dry
> Lundy plain, sign of rain
> If you can't see Lundy, it's raining already!

A similar saying is given about Ugborough Beacon in South Devon, Sidmouth Gap, the view of the moors from the A30 dual carriageway, and doubtless many other Devon landmarks.

Sunshine

While it was important to know when inclement weather was approaching, sunshine was also said to be an indicator of future weather and therefore was thought to give knowledge of whether crops would be strong or would fail. The weather at Christmas was believed to be related to that in May: 'Hours of sun on Christmas Day / So many frosts in month of May'.[16]

The sun shining on apple trees on Christmas Day was said to be an indicator of good crops to come later in the year. As we have already seen in Chapter Three, the wassailing ceremony was key to ensuring a good apple harvest in Devonian folklife. To ripen the apples, however, it was hoped that it would rain on St Swithin's Day (15 July). A woman in Torquay, sometime around 1925, who noted to her friend that the apples were getting red and would soon ripen after they had 'been christened', was asked when this would happen. Her reply was that 'St Swithin's christens the apples'.[17] This belief should be considered alongside the popular tradition that rain on St Swithin's Day meant that the following forty days would also be wet. This would be exactly what was needed to swell apples to a good size.

Another piece of Devon weather lore, this time connected with sunny weather, also appears to relate to a saint. This time, however, the connection is somewhat erroneous. A man in Hatherleigh sometime around the turn of the twentieth century was heard to remark on a particular hot and humid day that it was 'proper St Lawrence weather'.[18] The man concerned, when asked the explanation for this phrase, simply replied that it was hot and that St Lawrence was an idler. However, here St Lawrence is being confused with the folk figure of 'Lazy Lawrence' or 'Idle Laurence'. In this tale, which probably first appeared in print in a seventeenth-century chapbook,[19] and was extensively reprinted thereafter, Lawrence (who has been virtually motionless since birth) is given a red ring one day which has the power to put anyone he looks at into a deep sleep until the ring is removed. The story led over time to the figure of Lawrence becoming, as described by William Barnes, 'the patron or personification of laziness'.[20]

The appearance of a mock sun was said to be a foreshadowing of bad weather. A mock sun, sometimes known as a 'sun dog', is a patch of sunlight which appears approximately twenty-two degrees to the left or right of the sun (or sometimes both sides together). Known scientifically as a parhelion, the phenomenon occurs when sunlight refracts through clouds containing hexagonal ice crystals that have their flat sides parallel to the ground. The result is the appearance of something resembling a weaker second or third sun in the sky. The appearance of a sun dog in Exmouth on 21 July 1925 was described in a letter to the *Western Morning News* newspaper, along with the resulting prediction:

> We were engrossed in the phenomenon when a local fisherman politely volunteered to inform us, 'I don't like the look of 'im.' We were eager to know what ''im' was, and the fisherman answered, 'We calls 'im a sun-dog. We shall have rain or thunder and lightning before long'. And we did.[21]

The Night Sky

It was thought at one time in Devon that the weather could be forecast through study of the Milky Way. This belief was recorded back in the 1860s without any information to elaborate as to how this might be done. The only plausible suggestion, as the pattern of stars in the night sky does not change day to day, might be regarding the clarity of the galaxy arm itself, as conditions need to be very favourable to see it clearly. Even then, in the nineteenth century with far less light pollution, it would have been much easier to see the Milky Way on a clear night. The Milky Way is also said to have been known in Devon as 'rishe'. This is probably a contraction of 'rishlight', the dialect term for a rushlight which would be burned as a night light. A rush would be stripped of all its rind except for one line, which was then dipped repeatedly into tallow to form a thin candle. This burned with a very weak light and may relate either to the low light levels in that part of the sky, or possibly to the shape that the Milky Way forms across the heavens.

As our closest celestial body and one that has such a direct effect upon the Earth in various ways, the moon is a strong symbol in folklore. Naturally, we find that it has a bearing in terms of weather lore in Devon. A cook living in Chagford in the late nineteenth century quoted the saying: 'A Saturday moon / Comes seven years too soon'.[22] This refers to a month where all four changes of the moon took place on a Saturday. Where this was the case, it was believed that the weather would be especially bad and so it was hoped to not occur for another seven years. Another variant on this was connected with a new moon falling on a Saturday—the outcome is the same:

> 'A Saturday new moon
> If it comes once in seven years
> Comes too soon'[23]

As an aside, the way in which the new moon was observed could determine one's fortune, and also predict other things. It was unlucky to see the new moon through glass or over your left shoulder, whereas seeing it over the right shoulder brought good luck.

Whether the moon was in a waxing or waning state when apples were picked was believed to have a bearing on how well the fruit would store. Apples picked during a waning moon were said to rot quickly, whereas those picked when the moon was waxing would keep much better. It was even suggested that this was based on good science because of the influence the moon has on fluids. While it is the case that the gravitational pull is stronger during the new moon, the effect is not powerful enough to have a bearing on the storage of fruit. It is also not clear why another Devon superstition said that bacon must be cured when the moon was waxing. This was probably connected with a similar belief that if you killed a pig during the waning moon, then the pork would shrink if it was boiled or turn to fat if fried.

A general rule for planting, recorded at a meeting of the Bishopsteignton Women's Institute in 1956, was that anything that grew below ground should be planted during the moon's waning phase, and leaf vegetables and similar which grew above ground should be planted in the waxing phase.[24]

It is easy to think of these beliefs as mere superstitions of simple, rustic folk—as many of the collectors often did—but we should approach that idea with caution. Many of the suggestions have direct parallels going back to much earlier times. The links with the phases of the moon, for example, can all be found in the *Geoponica*, a tenth-century collection of Greek agricultural beliefs and practices dedicated to Emperor Constantine VII. This passage was translated into English in a 1933 journal article:

> Some ... advise that nothing should be planted while the moon is waning, but always while she is waxing. Others tell us to plant from the fourth to the eighteenth day of the moon; others again, only in the pre-lunar days, that is to say the first three days after the birth of the moon; yet others are of opinion that one should plant nothing from the tenth to the twentieth day, lest her light should be buried with the plants. But the exact doctrine and the best concerning the above observations is this: plant when the moon is under the earth and cut timber when she is above it.[25]

Traditions of the moon have certainly been observed for a long time.

Miscellaneous Weather Lore

The period between 19 and 21 March was thought by some to indicate the weather that could be expected for three key events later in the agricultural year: sowing, the early harvest and the late harvest respectively. On the last of these March dates it was also said that the direction of the wind would be that which would prevail for the summer. A variety of local rhymes recorded weather predictions based on the direction of the wind, and many of them are contradictory, as folklore so often is when we look at a number of examples for comparison. For example, Sarah Hewett offers both

> When the wind is in the north, hail comes forth,
> When the wind is in the west, look for a wet blast;
> When the wind is in the south, the weather will be fresh
>   and good,
> When the wind is in the east, cold and snow comes most[26]

and then on the next page

> When the wind is in the west,
> Then the weather's always best.[27]

Possibly, the difference can be accounted for by setting fire to some leather goods, as another verse suggests that this can have a meteorological effect: 'Burn some leather: / Change the weather.'[28]

On Exmoor, at least according to a letter in the *Western Morning News* newspaper, it is the sport which the Devil decides to undertake which will tell you what conditions to expect:

> There is a local legend which is extraordinarily accurate, that when the mists roll down the Foreland from Exmoor into the sea, it is Old Nick going a-fishing, and it will rain. When it rolls in from the sea and up over the Moor, it is the old gentleman going a-hunting, and it will be fine. Sometimes Old Nick gets stuck halfway up, immovable, and the weather-wise prophets scratch their heads and refuse to be drawn.[29]

Farming

> Out of work in to bed
> Out of bed in to work[30]

This description of his life by an Exmoor farmer in 1935 summarizes neatly what a hard job farming was, and indeed still is. By no means restricted to working Monday to Friday, nine to five, farmers would be out in all weathers and at all hours to tend to their animals or look after their crops. The success or failure of a farm depends on many variables, some of which are completely out of the hands of the farmworkers, and if things did not go well it could spell ruin for the farmer and disaster for the local community. Farmers would therefore take all the help they could get, from divine intervention to superstitious assistance, and from reading the weather to supernatural healing.

Surprisingly, we are still discovering some of the old superstitions and practices related to working with the land and the chaotic and unpredictable nature of growing. For example, until fairly recently it seemed that the concept of the goodman's croft, where one corner of a field was left uncultivated as an offering to appease the fairies or other spirits, to ensure that they left the rest of the crop alone, was found only in the north. However, we now know of anecdotal evidence recorded by folklorist Steve Patterson which suggests that this also happened in Cornwall, much closer to home.

While we cannot say with certainty that the practice also stretched into Devon, we do know that there was other folklore connected solely with fields. One old custom undertaken in the county was to bury three living puppies in the corner of a field in order to prevent particular weeds from growing.[31] The corners of a field have long been seen as important when looking to ensure good crops. Once again, we see links in the *Geoponica* from many hundreds of years ago, which lists various ways of ridding a field of weeds, including planting rose-laurel in the four corners and middle, and also using the same locations to bury potsherds on which have been drawn chalk images of Heracles strangling a lion.[32] The Book of Leviticus made reference (19:9) to farmers leaving the corners of their fields unharvested, in order that the poor of a parish may have an opportunity to gather food.

The right time to sow crops in the fields was obviously important to give them the best chance of success and took account of a number of factors relating to the weather, soil condition and temperature. Particular crops are best sown at particular times, and this was reflected in a number of proverbs which linked their planting to certain annual Devon fairs. This pinned the time on something easier to remember than the calendar date itself, as these fairs took place at the same time every year. Thus, for example, it was said to be unwise to plant kidney beans until after Georgenympton (modern spelling: George Nympton) Revel.

Until the Second World War, the Revel was held on the first Wednesday that followed the last Sunday in April. Botanist and plant folklore expert Roy Vickery believes that this probably associated it with the feast of St George, which takes place on 23 April, and that would seem to make sense considering the village's name. He notes that this puts it in line with other similar bean planting traditions in Devon and over the border in Somerset, occurring from that date up until 6 May, which was known in the latter county as Kidney Bean Day.[33]

Honiton Fair was also used as a marker; it was the date by which swedes should have been singled. Honiton's fair dates from 1221 when it was granted a charter. The fair is one of the remaining celebrations in Devon that still preserves the custom of carrying a glove on a pole to mark the beginning of the event. This takes place on the first Tuesday after 19 July and is followed by a coin scramble, such as those previously discussed.

Where there were repeated problems with the same area of land, then often some kind of supernatural reason was sought to explain it and in extreme cases this led to the land being turned over to another use. Often, a local person who was thought of as a witch would be scapegoated for having bewitched the field (this is dealt with more fully in Chapter Nine). This appears to have been the case with a field opposite Hayne Park near Tiverton. At some time near the beginning of the nineteenth century, an argument broke out between two farm labourers while the corn was being harvested. One man threw a hook at the other, which resulted in the man struck being killed. When the same thing happened again the next year, labourers refused to work the field again, thinking it bewitched. The land was turned over to wilderness, and oak trees were planted on it.

This story might have been lost to obscurity were it not for the fact that in 1963 the owner of the land decided to fell the trees and turn the land back over to crops. After all the trees had been cut down, they were logged using a circular saw. At some point during this process the saw blade shattered and one of the pieces struck and killed an onlooker. This makes for an intriguing postscript which might almost put this story in the category of urban myth. The incident does not seem to have been reported in the local press as far as can be ascertained. Interestingly, the victim in this incident was said to have been a man named 'Batten' which, although not unknown as a surname in the area, is also the term given to a piece of sawn timber. For now, this story must remain unsubstantiated.

In past times, most practical farming work was seen as very much the domain of the male, and in some areas women were said to bring agricultural ill fortune, such as at Bishops Nympton where it was recorded that they must never go near earth which had been freshly turned. We cannot help but note the irony of this when women have always been instrumental in the production of food; never more so than at wartime. During the First World War, 23,000 women worked full-time in the Women's Land Army (commonly known as the Land Girls) and this increased almost tenfold to over 200,000 during World War Two.[34] Their work certainly included ploughing.

Another Devon verse remarked on how having too many women or pigs around was ruinous:

> More women than men
> More pigs than ten
> A man will get rich
> When the Devil gets blen [blind][35]

There were some roles given to women during harvest time in Devon. One custom told that the final load of hay from the harvest should be driven out of the field and back by a woman. If she was able to do this without the cart grazing the gatepost as it went through, then she was crowned as 'missus' of the hayfield for the following year.

Another task made sure that women had the opportunity for a little fun as part of the harvest celebrations. It relates to the custom of 'Crying the Neck', where handfuls of ears from the last wheat to be cut are plaited into the shape of a corn dolly or other decoration. These tokens were quite large in size, quoted in one account given by farmer Tom Dobb of West Down as needing to be 'big's your hand wrist'.[36] After a ceremony in the field, where the 'neck' had been held aloft and a cry and much cheering had taken place, then it needed to be kept dry while being transported into the farmhouse—where it would hang until being replaced by a new one at the next harvest. If the neck became wet, then the bearer would not be allowed to have anything to drink for the rest of the evening's festivities. The women of the house would be responsible for trying to affect this by throwing water over the man carrying the neck. Farmer Dobb notes in his old account how he had been soaked on many occasions, but had previously handed the neck off to someone else to smuggle in, while he acted as a diversion.

This account from West Down is mirrored all over the county in different variations, some without the water element and some taking place predominantly in the field. The important aspects of crying and the neck being hung until the next year to ensure a good crop are generally consistent. In some cases the neck would be ploughed back into the ground the following spring, symbolically returning to the land that which was taken from it. If the origins of this custom do come from early nature religions, as many believe, then this symbolic offering makes good sense. As with much old custom which appears to be 'pagan', Mrs Bray links 'Crying the Neck' with Druidic practices, but there is no evidence as to why this should be the case.

Animals

The growing of crops was, and is, only one part of Devon's agricultural practices. The rearing of livestock plays a big part in farming in the region, with data from agricultural census returns in 2004 and 2006 showing that roughly two-thirds of farms were solely or partly concerned with this area.[37] With that in mind, we will examine some folklore connected with the various animals generally kept on Devon farms.

Poultry

Back on 5 March 1877, the wife of an agricultural labourer based at Torrington made mention of the fact that poultry should not be 'set' (upon their eggs) before dinner. If they were, it was said to be more likely that their eggs would hatch as male birds, whereas hens who were set later would produce more female chicks. This was obviously preferable if looking to make an income from the provision of eggs before birds were later used for meat. It was also recorded at South Molton that it was considered to be unlucky to pick daffodils from the garden when setting poultry.[38] This is not the only example of garden flowers being folklorically linked with poultry in Devon.

It was unwise to bring a gift of primroses to a poultry farmer, unless you had access to a lot of them. It was believed that the number of chickens reared in a year would equate to the number of primroses brought into the house, so a visitor should never turn up with a small bunch. Similarly, the number of goslings hatched and reared was believed to be governed by the number of wild daffodils which came into the house in the first bunch of the season.

When hens were set, then traditionally it was considered wise to set them on thirteen eggs on the thirteenth day of the month. This seems to be an unusual choice when the number is generally thought to be unlucky. Possibly the two occurrences of the number together offset the ill fortune.

Even today, modern folklore and belief examines good times to set poultry. The (American) calendar website *Almanac.com* revisits the previously explored ideas relating to moon cycles to provide an astrological method of finding good setting times, noting among other calculations that chicks 'born under a waxing Moon, in the fruitful signs of Cancer, Scorpio and Pisces are healthier and mature faster'.[39]

Eggs could be used as a form of divination known as oomancy, deriving from the Greek words for 'egg' and 'divination'. At Hatherleigh, according to a servant girl who worked there, unmarried women should break a hen's egg into a glass at noon precisely on Midsummer's Day. The contents of the glass should be studied carefully because in them the woman would see either the face of her future husband, or something resembling his position. In one case, the girl told that a friend of hers had seen 'a mansion in the egg, which showed that she would marry a rich man'.[40]

Divination could be used *on* the eggs as well, in order to ascertain the sex of the chick that would emerge. Even as recently as 1960, this was seen taking place in the manner of pendulum divining. A needle was tied to a length of wool and hung over the egg. If the egg was fertile then the needle would move, otherwise it would remain still. A circular movement would indicate a hen whereas if the needle described a cross, then the egg contained a cockerel.

On Dartmoor, cock-birds were often known as stags or masters, and the cruel sport of cock fighting was popular at one time. There used to be a pub at Sherwell called 'The Cockler's Peep' in recognition of the sport—cockler being the old name for someone who bred cocks. Various superstitions surrounded the birds, such as it being unlucky to hear one crowing at midnight. Some form of misfortune or even death was said to surely follow.

If a cock crowed at your door, however, this was a sign of news to come, or a visitor from a great distance. There was also the saying 'Every cock will crow on its own dunghill', which essentially means people are comfortable on their own home territory.

Sheep

Grazing sheep are one of the most common sights of the Devon countryside, from hardy breeds on the heights of Exmoor and Dartmoor to lowland flocks widely distributed around the county. Devon, in fact, makes up approximately one-fifth of the English sheep population on farms.[41] And yet there is much less associated with the animal in terms of folklore than we find with other farm creatures.

'Wether' is the term used for a castrated ram, and one old Devon folk tale explains how this came to be associated with a pair of prehistoric stone circles to the north of Postbridge on Dartmoor, now known as 'Grey Wethers'. The story, which also shows the feeling local residents sometimes have for 'incomers' who hold contradictory views or make complaints, centres around a farmer who had relocated to Dartmoor from elsewhere. One day, the man visited the market held at Tavistock, where he passed criticism on the quality of the sheep on sale there. The local farmers were not best pleased by this and so, when everyone stopped at the Warren House Inn in the middle of the moor for drinks on the way home, they made sure that the man had more than enough cider. Once he was suitably intoxicated, the local farmers took him onto the moor to see a flock of exceptionally high-quality sheep which they offered up for sale. There was a heavy mist, but the man could just make out a formation of shapes in the distance. He agreed that they looked very good and that he would therefore buy them. The next day, on going back to the site, he discovered that he had paid for forty-nine stones.

The story is, of course, undoubtedly apocryphal and is more a commentary on those who move into the area and think that they know better than others.

Sheep-shearing was an important occasion and usually took place in June. Margaret Baker notes that, once again, there is a connection here between the practice and the phases of the moon, as it was thought that if it was done 'at the moon's increase' then this would enhance the bulk of the wool.[42] Shearing time could be a community affair in much the same way as harvest was later in the year, with people coming together to help in return for good food and a party once the work was done. Miss A.M. Trump described such an event in an unpublished essay from 1938 recalling the memories of her grandmother. Both

ladies were part of a well-established farming family in the Broadclyst area of
Exeter.

> At sheep-shearing parties the young men of the farms would go
> from one farm to another to shear the sheep. Hard-working days
> those, but the young men were tough, for later the ladies would
> arrive and sheep-shearing were followed by dancing evenings and
> youngsters would shear all day and dance half the night.[43]

At the end of the day's work the men would change out of the white
shearing suits common in Devon and dress for the evening's feast. An effective
local method of cleaning the lanolin and other grease from their hands was
to wash them in a bucket of water which contained flowering wild mint.
This was not only good for degreasing but it also removed the smell of the
fleece. Traditional local food served at sheep-shearing feasts included squab
pie (mutton with layers of apple and onion in shortcrust pastry) and junket (a
dessert made of sweetened milk and rennet which is known from the nursery
rhyme in some places as curds and whey). In some areas of Devon, a portion
of the Christmas pudding was kept back in December and then served at the
shearing.

Ruth St Leger-Gordon comments on the ram roast traditionally held
at Holne and makes the suggestion that this relates to some sort of 'ancient
blood-sacrifice'.[44] This originally took place on May Day when all of the young
village men would catch a ram on the open moor and then tie it to a standing
stone, where it would be slaughtered and then spit-roasted. The custom died
away in this form in the nineteenth century and was moved to 6 July, when a
ram would be dressed with flowers and then roasted.

We need to be wary of ascribing the ideas of ancient sacrifice to this event
where there is no evidence to do so. While a sacrificial link is possible, the
notion has something in common with the ideas that led Mrs Bray to believe
that old legends were all 'Druidic', and the Victorian guidebooks to misuse
folklore for tourists. For more on this, see Chapter Five.

Unless the custom was wholly constructed based on folkloric motifs, one
plausible alternative origin might lie in an observation made by the Reverend
Sabine Baring-Gould concerning the sacrifice of a sheep to the pixies to cure
sickness in cattle, which was believed to be of supernatural origin.

This was done in 1879 by a farmer on West Dartmoor, with the reported
result that the animals began to recover soon afterwards and did not become ill
again. Baring-Gould later wrote on the subject again. It is unclear whether the

second report refers to the same incident or another one that occurred for the same reason, as the dates are a few years apart.

> In or about 1883 a man whose name was J- S-, in Meavy parish, a farmer who had come from North Devon, performed a curious rite that shall be described in the words of the Rev. W.A.G. Gray, then Vicar of Meavy. ... 'Soon after his arrival in the parish, as I believe not infrequently happens with an entire change of pasture, he lost a good many cattle and sheep, and told me that he accordingly took a sheep up to the top of Calisham Tor and killed it there to propitiate the evil influences which were destroying his flocks and herds. And the offering had the desired effect—he had lost no more cattle.'[45]

We are undoubtedly all familiar with the idea of the 'black sheep of the family', marking someone or something out as bad or rebellious in comparison to others, but traditional belief in Devon surrounding the black sheep in a flock is contradictory. One recorded saying with regard to them was 'If your flock begins to blacken / Your luck begins to slacken',[46] but elsewhere it was said that the black lamb in a flock was lucky. This was particularly true if it was the first of the season. With regard to luck, it was also important that you should see the first lamb of the year before hearing it, and that it should be looking at you when you did. If these criteria were not met, ill fortune would follow. Burning onion skins would also bring bad luck to your flock.

When selling sheep in Devon, it used to be good practice to return one coin to the buyer when the transaction was complete. This was 'luck money' and the same also held true for the sale of cattle.

Cows

The dairy industry has always formed a large part of the make-up of farms in Devon, and hence the keeping of cattle for milk and for meat has always been a significant area of farming in the region. There is therefore much folklore to be found around the protection of herds to maximize their potential.

It was once the custom on farms around the Great Torrington area to keep a billy-goat in the field with a herd of cows. Some farmers would tie a small log to the animal, because goats are prone to try and break out of enclosures and this would prevent the creature from being able to get through small gaps in the hedge. The superstitious belief was that keeping the goat with the cows would stop the latter from 'stratting'—that is, birthing stillborn calves. Originally this was thought to happen if the cows had been bewitched. Another belief in the north of Devon was that a calf born with a rose shape on the front of its withers would die young.

Poor milk yield could bring financial difficulty to a dairy farm very quickly and so the health of female cattle was of great importance. Farmers used to believe that hedgehogs (often called 'vuzz-pigs' in old Devonshire dialect) were a great threat to their milk herd. It was thought that as the cows lay down, the hedgehogs would come along and steal milk from them, causing red milk in the cattle. The folk remedy for this was to milk the animal through the spring of a set of sheep-shears. An alternative if shears were not available was a door key, which at the time usually had a large loop on the top through which the milk could pass.

Mammitis (now called mastitis) was known in Devon as 'udder-ill' and was usually cured by striking the udder. One old method was to allow a mole to die in the hand and then hit the udder with it. This was also said to be effective on humans. A later cure was to use a stone, which was certainly easier to obtain than a live mole. This had to be used in a particular way:

> the right udder was struck with the left hand, and the left udder with the right ... then, illustrating the method on the palm of his hand, he said it would be three times obliquely, then three times across (St Andrew's Cross), then three times across the two arms of the cross.[47]

It was important not to milk a cow out onto the ground, as this would cause the animal to go dry. They were also said to yield less if cobwebs were swept away—maybe this was a belief generated by those responsible for cleaning! Shod cows were said to give better milk than unshod ones, and there are folk cures for animals that have problems with their feet. A condition where there is tenderness between the parts of the cloven foot used to be called 'kebbit' or 'kebble' in Devon. It is probably what now tends to be diagnosed as 'Foul-in-the-Foot'. This was said to be treated by cutting the square of turf where the cow trod with the problem foot and lifting it. This would then be hung from a hawthorn tree in one version, or turned upside down and reset in the ground in another. As the turf rotted, so the problem would clear.

It was said to be unlucky to sharpen a knife on Sunday if you kept cattle, as you would soon find problems in the herd if you did. The cattle would also die if the farmer burned anything green. Charmers were often used to treat infections in animals, and one farmer reported in the second half of the twentieth century that a charmer had successfully cured his bullocks of ringworm … via the telephone.[48]

An intriguing old piece of folklore surrounds the butchering of cattle for beef, and a particular cut which was known in Devon as the 'Judas Steak'. This was said by some to have been the best steak from a bullock, with lean and even fat running all the way around it and prime-quality meat. There is no definite idea as to where this name came from, but one possibility is that if the meat was particularly good, then it would have been very rich in colour and hence the name relates to the traditional iconography of the biblical Judas with red hair.

Confusingly, it seems that in the Torrington area the name was also used, but the opposite was true; that is, the meat was particularly poor. The steak would look good on the surface but underneath it would consist mainly of hidden bone. In other words, as a joint of meat it presented as a traitor, again like the biblical Judas.

In 1974, folklorist Theo Brown overheard a conversation in a Devon pub about a traitorous animal which she termed the 'Judas Ram'. She recorded the conversation between the two men from memory later:

> Funny thing about that firm. You see, there was this old ram. Why? Well, 'twas a slaughterhouse in Devon, and it seems the sheep don't like going to slaughter. They're nervous-like. So, what they does, they have a ram, see? It belongs to the place and it leads the sheep into the slaughter—and they all go quiet. Saves a lot of bother. Well now, there was this old ram, a black one (no, no special reason) and it had been around the place for years and led hundreds of sheep in to slaughter. But long last they decided he was too old for the job and his time had come. So the boss, he says put the old ram in to slaughter, along o' the rest. But the men said no—he was a pet and they wouldn't see 'un killed. The boss he said 'Nonsense. You treat he same as rest.' But, d'you know? The men threatened to come out on strike first, so the boss gave in—and the old ram was put out to grass for the rest of his natural. All in the papers, 'twas![49]

CHAPTER FIVE

The Devil in Devon

You don't have to look far in Devon to find traces of legendary visitations by the Devil in the landscape. Of course, these don't just stop at the county borders, and across the whole country (and many others in the world too) you will come across mentions of the Devil in place names and geographical features. From his Arse (the name of a show cave in Derbyshire) to his Elbow (a hairpin bend in both Scotland and the Isle of Man, but found elsewhere too), 'Old Nick' really does get around.

One must exercise extreme caution to avoid jumping to conclusions when looking for historical clues within folkloric place names. As can be seen in the example of the naming of public houses in Chapter Eight, what looks like an obvious connection may be something else entirely.

This problem tends to come about because people have a desire to look for evidence of longevity in the history of names, customs and practices. Often, particularly with religious or social groups, they do this in order to try and evidence a long-established and traditional past where one may not in fact exist. Ethan Doyle White points out how this happened with reference to the idea that Druids from Iron Age times were responsible for the construction of megaliths.[1] This idea took hold in the eighteenth century, and was propagated by the clergyman antiquarian William Stukeley. It was at this point that a number of our stone circles became known as 'Druidic' (and in some cases were even renamed as such) despite the lack of actual evidence to back the idea up. In fact, the 'Druidic megalith' concept was simply replacing a line of previous ideas for the origin of these structures where the actual details of their construction and purpose were long since lost.

In fact, this is a problem we find also associated with some of the Devon folklore collectors of the past (see Chapter One). This does not necessarily devalue the collecting they did, the significance of which we already know, but it means rather that we should exercise some caution in interpretation. Anna Bray, for example, was somewhat influenced by her antiquarian husband, the Reverend Edward Bray, who favoured the prevalent viewpoint of the time of ascribing Druidic overtones to natural geology.

It was in the nineteenth century that these misunderstandings became exacerbated, with the emerging interest in folklore as a discipline and the work undertaken by Victorian collectors and commentators on the area. In their excitement to bring together material on the beliefs of our ancestors—as collected stories, individual interpretations and artefacts for the flourishing private museum sector—these antiquarians failed to grasp that folk beliefs and stories are mutable, fluid things, reacting to cultural shifts and changes all the time. Instead, they took the approach that things 'were ever thus', and even now some of their ideas have stayed with us.

Folklorist Jeremy Harte points out that many of the origin stories which led to the Devil being referred to in the landscape are simply reworking older tales where giants were the ones responsible:

In the earliest accounts, it is they who dig the ditches, hurl the stones and leap from crag to crag to leave their footprints impressed into the solid rock. Monuments such as these are proportional to their vast bodies, and so when the Devil inherits their oversized mantle, he also has to be imagined on a vast scale.[2]

While there are obvious religious connotations to many Devil stories, this idea of a giant Lucifer striding through the landscape hints at an alternative, and rather more comedic view. These are the stories where the Devil, the Prince of Darkness, the Evil One, is outwitted by the straw-chewing rustic or the humble villager, or where he is found doing something amusing or very out of character.

Bridges

Approximately six miles from the Exmoor town of Dulverton is found Tarr Steps, a seventeen-span clapper bridge crossing the River Barle. Now a scheduled monument, Tarr Steps is the longest and oldest example of a clapper (a bridge constructed by laying slabs across piles of stones) in the country. The actual age of the bridge is not known for certain. Officially, it is ascribed as medieval but potentially dates back much further.

Legend here tells that the bridge was constructed by the Devil for his own use, and that no mortal was permitted to use it to cross the river.[3] It was said that a black cat which wandered across the bridge vanished halfway with just a puff of smoke left behind. Of course, the locals would not stand for this and so the local vicar, armed with a cross, stepped across the slabs. After much arguing and waving of the holy symbol, the Devil backed down and agreed to allow others to walk over the bridge … on the understanding that he could use it as a spot to sunbathe whenever he liked.

We see here a fusion of the religious element of Devil-based folklore (the power of the holy symbol over evil) with the comedic aspects of Devilish folk tales (the idea of him lying sunning himself). There is an interesting secondary piece of humour in this story also, albeit one which does not seem commonly told. One person commenting on an internet blog post about the steps recalled that on a school trip to Tarr Steps in the 1980s, they were told that it was built by the Devil out of burned biscuits that he discarded into the river.[4]

Stories associated with bridges are found often in folklore, not least because of the long-held belief that most supernatural threats are not able to cross running water. We find so many examples of structures named 'Devil's Bridge' that there is a category for them in the Aarne–Thompson–Uther (ATU) Index for folk tale types (number 1191).

The most common variety of Devil's Bridge story is one involving a pact or contract with the Devil. In these stories, the Devil agrees to build a bridge over a particular span in return for the soul of the first mortal to cross the bridge once it is completed. The Devil is, of course, fooled at the end of the exercise when an animal of some kind (usually a dog) is enticed over the crossing before any human sets foot on it.

This trope does not seem to come up anywhere in Devon with relation to bridges, although we do find a Devil's Bridge located on Dartmoor, close to Princetown. In this case, there is no longer a bridge at the site, a part of the main road which crosses the moor from east to west. The bridge itself was removed in 1964 as part of a safety scheme which also eased the treacherous S-bend that the road used to take here—known as Devil's Elbow, which we have already learned is a common landscape name across the country. Not far from this site we also find reference to Devil's Gully. All of this would seem to suggest that some kind of major event once took place here to account for so many Devil references. However, we have noted previously that caution is in order when examining these sorts of names. In this case, it appears that the name comes not from any nefarious or religious symbolism, but rather from the fact that the bridge was originally built by a workman whose nickname was 'Devil'.[5] Unfortunately, history does not record why he held this moniker.

The battle between Church and Devil can also be found in the legendary origins of the Long Bridge in the North Devon town of Bideford. Spanning the River Torridge at a length of 677 feet, this is one of the longest medieval bridges in England. Although it is likely that a wooden bridge stood on the site from the thirteenth century, the stone bridge was established a century later. Legend says that this came about thanks to some divine intervention. Originally, the site for the Long Bridge was intended to be half a mile or so upstream of the current location, but every time stones were placed into the river to form foundations, the Devil would throw them further downstream. The solution was said to have been presented to the parish priest of the town, Richard Gurney, in a vision one night from the Virgin Mary, who told him to build on the stones where they had been tossed, as the footing here was firm.

Charles Kingsley notes the story in chapter 12 of his famous book, *Westward Ho!*

> All do not know how, when it began to be built some half mile higher up, hands invisible carried the stones down stream each night to the present site; until Sir Richard Gurney, parson of the parish, going to bed one night in sore perplexity and fear of the evil spirit who seemed so busy in his sheepfold, beheld a vision of an angel, who bade build the bridge where he himself had so kindly transported the materials; for there alone was sure foundation amid the broad sheet of shifting sand. All do not know how Bishop Grandison of Exeter proclaimed throughout his diocese indulgences, benedictions, and 'participation in all spiritual blessings forever,' to all who would promote the bridging of that dangerous ford; and so, consulting alike the interests of their souls and of their bodies, 'make the best of both worlds.'[6]

We see from this quote the confirmation from the Bishop of Exeter, who essentially stated that it was down to God's intercession that the bridge had been built. *The Worthies of Devon* mentions that the bishop noted that there was a rock on which part of the bridge was built 'whose greatness argued its being in that place to be only the work of God'.[7]

Interestingly, this is not the only piece of folklore connected with Bideford Long Bridge, although the Devil does not feature in the other tales. It has been long thought by many that the twenty-four arches which form the base of the bridge are of different widths due to the wealth of the people who funded their construction. There is no recorded evidence for this story to be found, and it is more likely to be down to the location of the natural footings which acted as foundation points.

There are many bridges in Devon that are said to be haunted, as you might expect, but New Bridge over the River Teign in the south of the county is unusual in that it is said to be haunted by the Devil. There seems to be no sensible explanation in terms of folklore for why this might be the case. It is not for any of the sorts of reasons which we have already examined, nor is the bridge a particularly significant piece of ancient architecture such that its coming about could only have been thanks to supernatural forces. It is relatively modern, having been constructed in 1845. The only clue comes with the fact that the Devil is supposed to haunt this location under his ancient local name of Dewer, suggesting the story has been ascribed to the bridge for reasons unknown by borrowing from more well-established Devil folklore on nearby Dartmoor.

Dewer and Guidebook Folklore

It is generally related that Dewer is a Celtic term for the Devil and that on Dartmoor he is considered to be the leader of the Wild Hunt, careening across the moor on windswept nights with his pack of demonic Wisht Hounds in his search for souls (see Chapter Eight). It is said that the oft-visited Dartmoor crag, the Dewerstone, is one of the locations haunted by Dewer and his phantom hounds. Unfortunately both this and most of the other Devil stories we find on Dartmoor owe more to the folklorist's role in creating the guidebook literature of Victorian times, as rail links saw the area becoming a tourist honeypot, than to any sort of long-established tradition. It is a problem not too far removed from the 'Druidic megaliths' issue mentioned earlier.

Folklore collector Richard King (discussed in Chapter One) probably did more to embed the image of the Devil on Dartmoor than any stories from our ancient past. He was commissioned to write the first edition of John Murray's *Handbook for Travellers in Devon and Cornwall* in 1856, published as the continued expansion of the rail network made travel to remote places such as the moor less difficult. King took pains to ensure that his interest in the burgeoning field of folklore was woven together with the romantic stories of Dartmoor, and by doing so sowed the seeds of a crop of 'traditional' stories which are not as old as many people now believe.[8]

In the case of the Dewerstone, we can see from different publications for which King wrote that he tended to recycle stories that he had probably been told by local inhabitants—the phraseology being similar in each publication.

There was already an existing story regarding the Dewerstone and the Devil in the local area, surrounding the belief that after a heavy snowfall one year, a trail of footprints was discovered leading to the top of the stone. One of these was from a human foot and the other was said to resemble a cloven hoof. Tradition told that the Devil was said to lure men to their deaths from the top of the Dewerstone. What King was to do in his writings was combine this story with reports of a Black Dog from the nearby valley and tether all of this to the concept of the Wild Hunt, led in some versions by Dewer himself, using the poorly evidenced links with Druidry explored above. The result is that, even now, the whole folkloric tangle is what is commonly told about the area, particularly to tourists:

> The Dewerstone is a large granite outcrop over 100 metres high and its name derives from 'Old Dewer', the local term for the Devil. The legends say that he used to terrorize the moor at night with his pack of Wisht Hounds (from Wistman's Wood) and drive poor travellers to their deaths off the top of the Dewerstone.[9]

The image of the cloven hoof is one that we naturally associate with the Devil, and we find it in various forms in folklore across the county. This might be in the form of footprints on the ground, or alternatively as a means of identifying the beast in our midst.

The Devil's Footprints

The best-known story of the Devil's footprints appearing in Devon is one for which the press coined the phrase 'The Great Devon Mystery'. Overnight between 8 and 9 February of 1855, a line of cloven prints appeared in the heavy snow the county had been experiencing. Reports say that this line was continuous and ran for anywhere between forty and a hundred miles, crossing obstructions such as rooftops and walls.

It was not long before this remarkable event was being discussed in the local press. A letter from an anonymous correspondent signing themselves 'Spectator' in the *Exeter and Plymouth Gazette* said:

> Sir, Thursday night, the 8th of February, was marked by a heavy fall of snow, followed by rain and boisterous wind from the east, and in the morning, frost.
>
> The return of day-light revealed the ramblings of some most busy and mysterious animal, endowed with the power of ubiquity, as its foot-prints were to be seen in all sorts of unaccountable places—on the tops of houses, narrow walls, in gardens and court yards, enclosed by high walls and palings, as well as in the open fields. The creature seems to have frolicked about through Exmouth, Littleham, Lympstone, Woodbury, Topsham, Starcross, Teignmouth etc etc.
>
> There is hardly a garden in Lympstone where his foot-prints are not observable, and in this parish he seems to have gambolled about with inexpressible activity. Its tracks appear more like that of a biped than a quadruped, and the steps are generally eight inches in advance of each other, though in some cases twelve or fourteen, and are alternate like the steps of a man, being close enough to be included between two parallel lines six inches apart.
>
> The impression of the foot closely resembles that of a donkey's shoe, and measures from an inch and a half to (in some cases) two inches and a half across, here and there appearing as if the foot was cleft, but in the generality of its steps the impression of the shoe was continuous and perfect; in the centre the snow remains entire, merely showing the outer crust of the foot, which, therefore, must have been convex.
>
> The creature seems to have advanced to the doors of several houses, and then to have retraced its steps, but no one is able to explain the mystery; the poor are full of superstition, and consider it little short of a visit from old Satan or some of his imps.[10]

The last sentence of this letter is very much reflective of the period, as we have seen many times already, with the blame for any superstitious ideas being levelled at the poor—the implication being that they are uneducated. However, we have no evidence to determine the social status of the author of this letter. In a period of history full of Christian morality, why would they suggest that only the poor would consider this a visit from the Devil? Why remain anonymous in writing this letter in the first place? Were the tracks a hoax, and was the correspondent involved and drawing attention to them so that the story gained traction?

The only known documents from the time that directly relate to the case of the 'Devil's Footprints' were not found until the middle of the twentieth century. They belonged to the Reverend Henry Thomas Ellacombe, vicar of Clyst St George, which was one of the parishes through which the footprints ran. Ellacombe, who was an expert on church bells and even invented

an apparatus which allowed one person to ring all the bells in a tower arrangement, owned an extensive collection of documents, most of which are now held in Bristol Archives. Ellacombe's papers on the footprints included items of personal correspondence, a letter written to the *Illustrated London News* marked 'not for publication' and what appeared to be tracings of the prints. This newspaper would go on to bring the case to national prominence.

Over the years there have been many theories put forward to explain how such a long line of tracks could have been made. Many of these hypothesize that animals were responsible—potentially different types or numerous of the same species. Historian Mike Dash, an authority on the case, believes that there are probably a number of different explanations for different sets of the prints, and that they all come together to form a whole.

One particularly unusual theory was offered by the author Geoffrey Household, a British thriller novelist who lived between 1900 and 1988 and edited a 1985 booklet on the subject of the Footprints. In line perhaps with his style of writing, Household suggested that an experimental balloon released from Devonport dockyards was responsible, with shackles on trailing mooring ropes leaving the impressions as they hit the ground. Household even cites a source for this, a Major Carter, who said that his grandfather worked at the dockyards at the time of the incident and that the escape of the balloon was hushed up because of the number of properties that it had damaged.

We are perhaps more familiar with military balloons being put forward as the explanation for sightings of unidentified flying objects, and there are a number of potential problems with the idea that one is responsible for the 'Devil's Footprints'. The track was described as being relatively uniform; it would be unlikely for the balloon ropes to be able to lay such a consistent trail. Why would the balloon travel at ground level and then rise over a building before descending on the other side again? There were also reports of the tracks going up to the doors of houses and then retracing their steps before carrying on. If these reports are correct, it would certainly discount the random path a balloon would take.

Most people view the story of the Devil leaving a trail of footprints across a large part of Devon in the mid-nineteenth century as an isolated curio. In fact, however, there have been other examples ... and the Devon one was not the first. Fifteen years before, on 14 March 1840, the *Times* newspaper had carried a report on a similar example, albeit on a smaller scale. Similar sets of tracks have been reported over the years in different locations around the world.

As recently as 2009, the mystery returned to the county of Devon. On 5 March of that year, a single-line track of cloven hoofprints appeared overnight in the freshly fallen snow in the back garden of 76-year-old Jill Wade of Woolfardisworthy. These prints were much bigger, at some five inches long. This time, of course, a proper record was able to be made and the prints were both photographed and filmed. It is likely that these were formed by an animal such as a rabbit or hare, but having partially melted in the snow they definitely resemble cloven hooves. A simple online search will turn up plenty of examples of the photographs. A new article written by Brian V. Ridout in 2021 provides convincing evidence that the original tracks of the 'Great Devon Mystery' were also formed from melting animal prints.[11]

The other stories regarding the Devil's feet are the ones where they give away his identity. You would think that after being caught out once or twice, he would grow wise to this problem—but I suppose it is difficult to find shoes in the correct size (or shape)! In some stories the Devil has a single foot that is cloven, and in others it is both that are spotted. This disparity is also reflected in the different versions of the explanation for the tracks at the Dewerstone. In the original version of this story it is just the Devil walking in a part-human part-beast form, which accounts for the two different sorts of footprint. Later, once the stories of the Devil, the Hunt and the luring of people over the edge of the Dewerstone become enmeshed, then the footprints symbolize a cloven-footed Devil leading a human to their fate.

Author J.R.W. Coxhead cites the single hoof as being the Devil's undoing in the famous Dartmoor legend of the formation of the rocky structure known as Branscombe's Loaf. In short, Walter Bronescombe (who was Bishop of Exeter from 1258 to 1280) is riding across the moor towards Sourton with his chaplain. Becoming tired and hungry on what is an arduous journey, the bishop turns to his attendant and notes how Christ was tempted in the wilderness by Satan who offered him bread made from stones, and how he was so hungry that he thought he would be unable to turn down the same offer if it was made to him now.

Of course, at this point a swarthy moorman appears as if from nowhere and offers the pair bread and cheese. The only payment he requests is that the bishop doff his hat and call him master. Coxhead describes what happens next:

> The bishop was just about to remove his hat and address the man in a tone of entreaty and by the title of master, when the chaplain noticed that the swarthy stranger possessed one cloven hoof very similar to that of a goat. He instantly cried out to God for protection, and drew the bishop's attention to the foot in question.[12]

The Devil of course disappears, and the bread and cheese turn to stone which forms the outcrop of rock. This is one of a number of similar stories explaining rock formations across the county.

The Devil and Gambling

The Devil is caught out in a similar fashion at nearby Widecombe-in-the-Moor, in one of the variants of the stories used to explain the great storm that damaged the Church of St Pancras on 21 October 1638. It was on this date that the church appears to have been struck by ball lightning during an afternoon service, killing four and injuring sixty. The event is recounted on a set of wooden boards to be found in the foyer of the building to this day.

In the most common version of the legend attached to this storm, the Devil is riding to Widecombe to claim the soul of Jan Reynolds, a local gambler who had made a pact with him in return for good fortune. If Jan was ever caught asleep in church, then his soul could be taken. On the day in question he falls asleep during the service, with a pack of cards in his hand. The cards are important to the end of the story and so feature in other versions, such as one where the Devil is claiming the souls of four people playing cards during the sermon.

The Devil stops on the way to the church to ask directions. One location stated for this interaction is at the Tavistock Inn at Poundsgate, where in one version the protagonist is named as Bobby Read, although Jan Reynolds is the usual suspect. The landlady is about to offer to act as a guide for the Devil (who is in disguise, of course) when she notices a cloven hoof, as well as noting that the beer he drinks hisses as he swallows it, and so she sends him on his way.

When he finally arrives at the church, the Devil ties his horse to one of the pinnacles of the tower before snatching Jan Reynolds from the midst of the congregation, causing all the associated destruction which was in truth the result of bad weather. As they ride off across the sky, the horse pulls down the pinnacle, which ends up in the churchyard below. The playing cards now become important in the various versions of the tale. Passing over Birch Tor, the four aces from the pack of cards fall to the ground, where they account for four medieval field enclosures visible from the modern road, past the Warren House Inn, which are in the rough shape of card suits.

We may find other examples in Devon of stories where the Devil makes an appearance because of the use of playing cards. This should be no great surprise, such stories having been constructed frequently during the morally upstanding Victorian era in order to warn people away from vices such as gambling, or by members of the church in order to remind people that they should be paying attention to the sermon while at service on a Sunday.

One legend attached to Lustleigh Church uses a combination of elements found both in the story from Widecombe and also in folkloric tales where an animal is sacrificed in place of a human, such as those earlier in the chapter relating to new bridges. In this story, a man enters Lustleigh Church with a pack of playing cards in his pocket, and is confronted by the Devil, who threatens to take the man for this misdemeanour unless another sacrifice can be made instead. Running from the church, the man scoops up a cat walking through the churchyard and kills it, satisfying the Devil who disappears 'to a blue fire and brimstone accompaniment'.[13]

In his original book on Devon folklore, Ralph Whitlock also relates a story of the Devil visiting a group of men playing cards at the Railway Inn in the town of Topsham.[14] The Devil grabs the hand of one of the men as he is bending down to retrieve a card from the floor. A struggle breaks out, with the rest of the gang trying to pull the man free. They eventually do so, but in the aftermath of the fight and the Devil leaving, the corner of the building collapses. The collapse of part of a building is not unknown in Devon folklore. As part of its recorded route across the county plotted by Barbara Carbonell, the spectral Black Dog of Torrington was said to pass by the school in Morchard Bishop. As it did so, the corner of the wall surrounding the schoolyard could be heard to collapse, although the structure was always complete and sound when examined.

Whitlock also notes the slate formation of Ragged Dick at the Valley of the Rocks in Lynton, which was said to have been formed when the Devil caught seven men dancing on a Sunday, turning them into the landmark. This is a common trope found all over the country and usually associated with stone circles, which are often said to be comprised of people turned to stone for this or other transgressions. The Merry Maidens circle over the border in Cornwall and the Nine Ladies stone circle in Derbyshire are two well-known examples. Also in Cornwall, The Hurlers stone circle is said to be made up of men turned to stone for playing a game of hurling on a Sunday. They serve as further lessons on the consequences of breaking the rules of the Sabbath.

The Devil and the Church

Naturally, there are stories in which the Devil attempts to prevent churches from being built, and these are often associated with locations where the position of the church is somewhat unusual. One of the most famous and picturesque examples is the Church of St Michel de Rupe, which sits atop Brent Tor four miles to the north of Tavistock.

This building, the 'Church of Saint Michael of the Rock' in its translated form, dates from the thirteenth century and is unusual in its positioning in such an inaccessible place. It is only used for a limited number of services now, with a newer church in the village below the tor being the more usual location for worship. The legend says that the original intent was for the church to be built at the base of the tor, but that every morning the builders would find that during the night the Devil had moved all the materials to the summit in an effort to stop the construction. Eventually the authorities relented and decided they would just go ahead and build at the top.

This story certainly isn't unique. In Devon there are other examples to be found at Buckfastleigh Church, which was said to have been built at the top of a flight of 196 steps in an attempt to stop the Devil interfering with its construction, and at Honiton where the Church of St Michael was built atop a hill for the same reason. We find other parallels outside the county too. Lincolnshire folklorist Ethel Rudkin recalled the same story with regards to Dorrington and similar is said of the Church of St Bartholomew's in Gloucester. This twelfth-century building is located at the top of Churchdown Hill, which is also known locally as Chosen Hill. Some relate this name to the Devil legend and the site being subsequently 'chosen', but there seems little evidence for this. Interestingly Churchdown comes from the Celtic word *crouco*, meaning hill, and the Old English word *dūn*, also meaning hill. So, in fact, the church is built on 'Hill Hill Hill'![15]

The legend is a very common one. There are plentiful other examples both within and outside the county. At Brent Tor, on completion of the building, the story ends with St Michael, to whom the church is dedicated, throwing the Devil down the hill and pitching a large rock after him. The rock can still be found at the base of the tor.

Devil Stones

Significant or unusual rocks and stones which seem out of place are ripe for explanatory folk stories. The Devil is frequently said to be responsible, or had some part to play. In many cases, the centrepiece of the story in reality will be a glacial erratic. These are stones which were transported by a glacier many years ago, remaining in their current position at the end of the ice age, when the glaciers melted. This is the reason their geological make-up does not necessarily match that of their surroundings, and why old stories ascribe supernatural conditions to their transportation.

An erratic on the village green at Shebbear, near Holsworthy, is probably one of the most famous to be associated with the Devil, because of a long-running calendar custom associated with it. Every 5 November, as an alternative to the more usual Bonfire Night celebrations, the Devil's Stone is turned over, in order that the village will not suffer misfortune for the next twelve months. This turning is undertaken by the village bell-ringers, using crowbars to invert the six-foot by four-foot rock, having first been to the church and rung a discordant peal of bells.

Records do not indicate when this tradition first began. It does not seem to be mentioned prior to the twentieth century, suggesting that it was possibly a late Victorian construction, like so much of today's purported 'ancient practice'. Indeed, there is a theory which suggests that the stone may be a Druidic or pagan altar, but no evidence can be discovered to substantiate this idea, placing it alongside the thoughts expressed by Ethan Doyle White with which we opened this chapter.

There is not just one folkloric reason for the Devil being associated with the stone at Shebbear; in fact there are a whole plethora of them. One tale suggests that St Michael dropped the stone on the Devil—a similar story to that at Brent Tor Church, only this time it was when the Devil was expelled from heaven. This act trapped the Devil under the stone, meaning he had to dig his way out. This is said to take him a year, hence the annual turning of the stone to rebury him. Another story ties in with the concept of the Devil preventing churches from being built, which we have already explored. In this tale, the stone is one which was quarried for building the foundations of nearby Hanscott Church, but was moved by the Devil to its position in Shebbear. Every time the local builders took it back, it would end up in Shebbear again. This version of the story, however, gives us no explanation as to why the stone should be turned now, and hence it is more likely that someone just appended this common trope at a later date.

Other versions of the story include the Devil throwing the stone at the church and missing, the Devil dropping it from his pocket and the Devil using it as a seat (the annual turning being done to make sure that he does not get too comfortable and end up staying on it).

Author Tina Gaydon records another story, stating that the Devil dropped the stone when he died of the cold at Northlew.[16] This seems to be the only reference to this particular idea and probably conflates the story of the Devil Stone with another which has that ending—surrounding a stone quoit on the peak of Heltor, near the Dartmoor town of Moretonhampstead. This is one of the many that were believed to have been thrown by the Devil. In this case, unusually, the Devil was said to be fighting with King Arthur. Having been resoundingly beaten by the king, so the story goes, the Devil retired to the West Devon village of Northlew where he expired from the cold.

Northlew is located on a hilltop and is relatively exposed to the elements. The story of the Devil dying of the cold there is now a very widespread one, and features in tourist literature about the area. It is generally thought to have been mostly a commentary on the inhospitable nature of the location, probably from those in neighbouring parishes. But there is a far more compelling idea, albeit somewhat tentative, which does in fact connect Northlew with the town of Shebbear, which is some twenty-five minutes distant by car. That comes in the form of a link with the long since discontinued local practice of the 'stag hunt'.

The inverted commas around this term are to indicate that this is not a hunt chasing down an actual stag. The 'stag hunt' was a custom carried out in many areas of Devon where an outcast in a community (often an adulterer or, taking place in less understanding times, a homosexual) was chased through the streets by a crowd of baying men dressed as hunters. Sometimes the person being hunted was represented by another person playing the part, in which case they wore horns in the manner of a cuckold, but often the party would go to the house of the actual person and drive them out.

The last 'stag hunts' seem to have taken place just before the outbreak of the First World War, with Northlew being one of the locations. The legend of the Devil dying at Northlew says that he is buried under the village cross (or a large stone, depending on the account). In an article on the custom of the 'stag hunt' for the journal *Folklore*, Theo Brown records the notes on this from a small booklet on Northlew written by a previous rector of the village:

> The old legend tells the tale that the Devil died of a cold caught on Sourton Moor and was buried under the Village Cross. The Devil by some was said to have been a stag which was hunted again and again and was called 'The Devil', and which died one hard winter in the village square. Others say that the devil was a Cornish cock or 'stag', called 'The Devil', which was brought to fight the North Lew cock and died in a mysterious way.[17]

In her journal article, Theo Brown notes that in 1974 she was given information that seemed to relate to a 'stag hunt' which had taken place in the area.

The lover of a married woman was tracked down to where he was hiding in a pub at Shebbear (now called the Devil's Stone Inn, but which used to be named The New Inn), from where he was driven out. The party chased him all the way to Northlew where the results of this brutal custom evidently took their toll and the man died—inevitably from heart failure but possibly exacerbated by the cold conditions. It is suggested that he was buried under the Village Cross. Brown notes that 'he was said to be the Devil'.[18] She obviously doesn't mean this in the ecclesiastical sense. So here we have all the ingredients for a potential truth that ties the story together: the 'Devil', the stag, death and the cold. It is a tantalizing possibility.

Romancing the Devil

The Devil's involvement with humanity in Devon isn't just limited to geology, of course. That would be rather a narrow scope of interest! We also find examples of the classic motif of the Devil in disguise as a handsome man, such as was expanded upon by the author John Updike in his novel *The Witches of Eastwick*—in which the antagonist Daryl Van Horne is an obvious metaphor for something demonic, if not the Devil himself.

An example of this trope comes from the Bridgerule area of North Devon, where it was said a woman lived with her beautiful, and single, daughter. One night an impressive-looking carriage, pulled by four horses, arrived at their cottage and a stereotypical 'tall, dark and handsome' man alighted and began talking to the young girl, who quickly became very enamoured of him. The man stayed for a little while before leaving, returning the next night, when he stayed for longer. At the end of the evening this time, he asked the girl to promise to leave with him in the carriage the next night, after which they would be married.

The girl was very taken with the stranger and agreed to the request, but her mother was suspicious and so went to visit the local vicar, to whom she told the story of the rapid courtship. The vicar agreed that all was not right, and suspected that four jet-black horses such as those owned by the visitor could only be pulling the Devil himself. He gave the old woman a candle, instructing her to light it when he turned up the next night and to tell the man to wait until it had burned out before leaving with her daughter.

With thanks, the woman returned home and explained the conversation to her daughter, who agreed to do as the vicar suggested. The next night, when the man arrived, the daughter asked him to wait until she had changed into better clothes before leaving, getting the man to agree to give her the time it would take the candle to burn out. As soon as he did so, the old woman blew out the candle and ran to the vicar at Bridgerule who quickly bricked it up in the church wall. Sabine Baring-Gould noted on more than one occasion that a candle was said to still be immured in the chancel wall here.[19]

On learning that he had been outwitted, the easily fooled Devil rode away furiously in his carriage. Upon reaching Affaland Moor, the whole vehicle plunged into a bog in a flash of blue flames. In his study of the motif of the phantom coach, Edward Waring has noted that a number of the stories include the vehicle disappearing into a stretch of water. He took this to come from a pre-Christian belief about a wagon which collected souls. It would make sense for the Devil's return to the underworld to follow a similar psychopompic route.

When a folkloric tale features such a strong motif, there is often more than one version to be found. A very similar story emerges elsewhere in North Devon, known in some sources as 'The Marwood Legend'. The first part of the tale is very similar, only with the girl concerned (named Molly in this case) going to Barnstaple Fair in order to try and find a suitor. It is disclosed that Barnstaple Fair is also a favourite haunt of the Devil. He duly appears on the scene and begins courting Molly at her house, but always disappears in the evening before the lamps are lit. The conclusion of the story, essentially the same but with some variations, is related by J.R.W. Coxhead in his 1959 book *Devon Traditions and Fairy Tales*:

> One stormy night a frightful noise was heard as though a number of men were threshing with heavy flails on the roof of the farmhouse. The farmer and his servants made every effort to discover the cause of the turmoil but without success. Eventually, they entered Molly's room on the top floor of the house, and to their great consternation they found the terrified girl wedged between her bed and the wall in such a manner that nobody was able to go near her, or help her, in her unfortunate plight.
>
> The farmer gathered together ten men, and in spite of all their combined efforts they were unable to release the poor maiden from the powerful spell that enfolded her. Twelve parsons then endeavoured to rescue her from the satanic enchantment, but all to no avail. At last, the farmer sent a message to the learned and venerable Rector of Ashford, asking him to come as swiftly as possible to thwart the power of the demon. The pious priest quickly arrived on the scene, and being a great scholar soon outwitted the prince of darkness.[20]

The rector goes on to employ the same candle trick, placing it in a box in the wall of Marwood Church.

Although found in more than one Devon location, the story is much more widespread (and much older) than that. In Norse mythology, two of the Norns—representative of the Fates—bless a child lying in a cradle with two candles burning next to it with good fortune, but the third, who has been treated poorly, curses it: 'The child shall live no longer than these candles burn'. The other two sisters put out the candles and give them to the child's mother, telling her to take good care of them.

It is possible that all of these stories stem from the ancient practice of the placing of foundation sacrifices in buildings. In *Strange Survivals*, Baring-Gould gives examples of buildings where cauldrons and bones were found within the walls. In Romania, stonemasons were said to try and catch the shadow of a passing pedestrian and wall it into a building. When it became illegal to use sacrifices in buildings, a symbolic equivalent was sought out instead. Sometimes this was an egg, representing life, and sometimes a candle was burned in the place of a sacrifice. Baring-Gould notes, 'At Heliopolis, till the reign of Amasis, three men were daily sacrificed; but when Amasis expelled the Hyksos kings, he abolished these human offerings, and ordered that in their place three candles should be burned daily on the altar.'[21] There is certainly some continuity suggested in these accounts.

The Devil and Blight

In terms of the cycle of nature, most people are familiar with the concept of the Devil spoiling blackberries in late September. British folklore states that Michaelmas Day, 29 September, is the last day on which blackberries should be picked, because this is the time at which the Devil spits on them (or worse) and spoils them. The date is also sometimes known as 'Devil Spit Day'. In Devon, the date given seems to vary from this norm. There are different dates offered depending on the source, but they generally tend to be a few days earlier.[22]

In a similar way, the Devil is also associated in the county with the spoiling of apple blossom at the other end of the year. Volume 27 of the *Transactions of the Devonshire Association* notes that in the Taw Valley area it was said that dates around 19–21 May were St Frankin's Days, also known as 'Francimass'. An unusually late frost on these days would do much damage to the apple blossoms. The associated story revolves around a brewer called Frankan who makes a deal with the Devil to give him his soul, in return for the Devil sending frost to ruin the apple crop, because sales of cider were outstripping his own beer sales.

There are many versions of this story across the county. It is probable that it comes from an earlier attribution of the apple tree blighting to the Devil and St Dunstan, also known as a brewer of beer. His feast day is 19 May, and the three days leading up to it were known as St Dunstan's Days.

As we have demonstrated, many of the stories related to the Devil have a much later construction than imagined—but when they do originate earlier, then they can often be traced a long way back and come from endless variations of alternative stories. Such is the complexity of most areas of folklore in Devon and beyond.

CHAPTER SIX

Fairies in Devon

The concept of the fairy, pixie or other small sprite is a particularly ancient one which is found all over the world. As a symbol to be interpreted, the concept of the fairy is especially pliant. All folklore develops meaning when seen in a cultural context, and the long history of fairies means that the way in which their stories are read has changed often over the centuries. Some of today's unidentified flying object (UFO) abduction reports have many things in common with older stories of being led astray, or removed from our own world, by the fairies.

Theories on the origins of the fairies abound. One in particular was found among writings on the subject in Devon, but was popular everywhere, even well into the twentieth century. That was the idea that they were some form of folk memory of a prehistoric race. Archaeologist Leslie Grinsell OBE explained this in a paper which he delivered to the Folklore Society in 1937:

> The enormous barrows and megalithic monuments erected during the Neolithic and Bronze Ages bespeak a very strong cult of the dead, so strong that it has even been said that the prehistoric races spent the best part of their lives erecting tombs for their dead, and it is almost only these tombs that have survived to the present day. It seems most likely that the cult in question was one of ancestor-worship.
>
> As soon as the dead were buried in their barrows, the latter would come to be regarded as the haunts of the spirits of the dead. As time went on it is possible that these ancestral spirits became less ghostlike and more fairylike, until the mounds in which they dwelt became known as fairy-mounds.[1]

A parallel theory, which was common in the nineteenth century but has certainly been around for longer, is that when we think of fairies we are actually remembering in some time-worn way a prehistoric race of pygmies who lived alongside humans. Writing back in the 1950s, for instance, Coxhead suggested that it was 'considered to be very probable by many authorities on Devon folklore' that stories of the pixies come from the Bronze Age Iberian people who lived on Dartmoor three centuries or more ago, and about whom the early Iron Age people carried many superstitions.[2]

It might be tempting to consider this alongside the fact that the pixie (the most common form of the little people in Devon) is generally described as 'pygsy' in older dialect. However, both of these folk memory theories have been essentially discredited as having nothing but circumstantial evidence to back them up.

Many counties draw distinctions between terms such as fairy, pixie or elf, but in Devon they tend to be interchangeable. Both here and over the border in Cornwall the most prolific 'pixie' was often spoken as 'piskey' due to the West Country dialect's tendency to transpose pairs of letters from the order found in standard English, much as the latter does from its Old English equivalents. This can still be heard today in the county (people 'aksing' a question is a very common one) but the term piskey is now mostly relegated to tourist postcards and lucky charms in gift shops.

Belief in the fae folk was particularly strong in the South West and hence there are many mentions of reported sightings, or fairy mischief, in old writings about the county. Victorian folklore collectors would as usual put this down to the county being in a rural backwater, full of 'uneducated peasantry', but it is kinder to focus on the fact that the nature of the landscape here and the work done on it meant that a far higher percentage of people had a natural affinity with the countryside.

The pixies can turn up in some surprising places in Devon. For example, the first published version of the classic children's nursery tale 'The Three Little Pigs' comes from Dartmoor in 1853, although the story itself is probably much older in an unrecorded form. In this version, the pigs are pixies and the villain of the piece is a fox rather than a wolf. With the latter having become extinct in Britain sometime around the reign of Henry VII and fox hunting being a common pursuit in Devon at the time, it probably made more sense to follow the trope of the fox as a trickster, which was established with the publication of the medieval literary fable cycle *Reynard the Fox*. All of the elements of the fairy tale as we now know them were present in the Dartmoor pixie version.

> There was once a fox who, prowling by night in search of prey, came unexpectedly on a colony of pixies. Each pixy had a separate house. The first he came to was a wooden house.
>
> 'Let me in, let me in,' said the fox.
>
> 'I won't,' was the pixy's answer; 'and the door is fastened.'
>
> Upon this the fox climbed to the top of the house; and having pawed it down, made a meal of the unfortunate pixy. The next was a 'stonen' house.
>
> 'Let me in,' said the fox.
>
> 'The door is fastened,' answered the pixy.
>
> Again was the house pulled down, and its inmate eaten.
>
> The third was an iron house. The fox again craved admittance, and was again refused.
>
> 'But I bring you good news,' said the fox.
>
> 'No, no,' replied the pixy; 'I know what you want; you shall not come in here to-night.'[3]

It is interesting to note here that the house of the third pixy is made of iron—a substance which traditionally wards off the fae rather than offering protection *to* them against another threat.

The story continues in the same manner as the traditional version, with the fox trying to tempt the pixy to a field of turnips early in the morning, but being outwitted by the pixy who arrives early. Also present is the fair, with the pixy climbing into a crock which he has obtained there and rolling down the hill to evade the fox. The story then concludes in a slightly different manner to the demise of the wolf:

> The fox returned the next morning; and finding the door open went in, when he caught the pixy in bed, put him in a box, and locked him in.
>
> 'Let me out,' said the pixy, 'and I will tell you a wonderful secret.'
>
> The fox was after a time persuaded to lift the cover; and the pixy, coming out, threw such a charm upon him that he was compelled to enter the box in his turn; and there he died.[4]

Common Motifs

There are certain stories connected with the fairies which occur time and again and for which there are often regional versions. One of the most common of these is generally known either as 'The Fairy Ointment' or 'The Fairy Midwife'. The tale tells of a human woman working as a midwife who is approached by a stranger, often on a wild and stormy night, and offered a good rate of pay to attend a birth. In some versions the pregnant woman is described as a princess or similar; sometimes it is a local girl who was previously thought to have died. The midwife is given an ointment which she is told she must put on the baby's eyes after the birth. However, she either accidentally or deliberately also ends up with ointment on her own eyes, which it transpires allows her to see the stranger and others as fairies. She is taken home and paid, and the fae are unaware of what has happened until she later sees the stranger in the market and asks after the mother and child. Realizing what has happened, he either blinds her or puts out whichever eye she put the ointment in.

In the Devon variant, the woman is a nurse who comes from Tavistock and accidentally returns home with the fairy ointment in her pocket. She puts the liquid in her left eye out of curiosity for what it is, and this is the eye that the fairy king ends up blinding.

In some stories concerning the fairies, the creatures are used to deliver a moral message—a common theme found not only with these characters but across folklore more widely. This concept became particularly prevalent during the nineteenth century. This is the point at which we see fairies transformed by the Victorians into diminutive, winged flower folk, the versions so commonly used in children's stories and cartoons in modern times. But it is also a point where the moral compass of the time period is applied to many stories, converting them into warnings of what will happen to those who do not follow righteous, God-fearing ways. One theory on the origin of the fairies which failed to gain as much traction as some others emerged from the Christian Church and suggested that they were the souls of children who had died before being baptized, or were stillborn, and therefore were trapped in Limbo. This argument is further weakened philosophically by the fact that the Catholic Church now refutes the concept of *limbus infantium* and children being held accountable for original sin or the sins of their ancestors.

Remaining in the town of Tavistock for a moment, Anna Eliza Bray recorded a tale concerning two female servants who found that if they left a bucket of clean water in the 'chimney corner' (a recess containing seating next to the open fire) before retiring for the night, then a gratitude of silver would be waiting for them in the morning. All was well until one night when they forgot to leave the bucket in place:

> the pixies came rustling indignantly into their room. The girls woke up and heard what was going on; one of them thought they should get up immediately and set the hearth in order, but the other yawned lazily and said they should not stir themselves, not for all the pixies in Devon. Well the hard-working girl got up, and filled the bucket, where a handful of silver pennies were found waiting for her the next morning; but the lazy one was afflicted with a lameness in her leg, and this lasted for seven years.[5]

The moral in this story is simple and not too serious, discouraging the act of being slovenly. Other stories have more severe consequences, with fairies visiting the human world to show what might happen to those who do not lead a righteous life. A story collected in 1932 told that both the father and grandfather of a woman from Widecombe-in-the-Moor used to see fairies nearby at Buckland in the dusk. Her grandfather in particular was highly religious and believed that they were sent to Earth from Hell as a warning to drunks, gamblers and so on about the nature of their punishment in the afterlife.[6] His description of them as having heads like balls of fire and long legs might easily refer to the phosphorescent balls of light seen in marshy areas and known in folklore as 'will-o'-the-wisps'. These used to be thought of as a form of pixie or sprite responsible for leading unwary travellers away from a path. We will return to this later in the chapter.

The idea of leaving something for the fairies to ensure either their help or as protection against any potential mischief was found throughout Devon. When gathering wild mushrooms, for example, it was customary to leave one behind for the fairies. Offerings of dishes of milk or cream were common, with bread and alcohol such as ale or cider also frequently used. Poet John Milton describes this as early as 1645 in his pastoral poem 'L'Allegro':

> And he by friar's lanthorn led,
> Tells how the drudging goblin sweat,
> To earn his cream-bowl duly set,
> When in one night, ere glimpse of morn,
> His shadowy flail hath thresh'd the corn,
> That ten day-labourers could not end[7]

Fairies in Devon were often happy to help with work in return for such offerings, in the same way as brownies or house spirits in other areas of the country. At a cottage in the village of Belstone, near Okehampton, they were rewarded with honey, cream and a basin of water. For this, the fairies would work the loom overnight, producing yards of cloth. Caution needed to be exercised in the way that thanks was given out, however. It was unwise to thank them directly, or to be found to be watching their activity. While rewards should not be scrimped over, a balance needed to be struck and they should not be too valuable. Giving new clothes as a reward would cause the fairies to leave to enjoy their gift—an idea which was taken by author J.K. Rowling and incorporated into her *Harry Potter* stories, where Dobby the House Elf is set free by being given a sock.

> A washerwoman was one morning greatly surprised, on coming down stairs, to find all her clothes neatly washed and folded. She watched the next evening, and observed a pixy in the act of performing this kind office for her; but she was ragged and mean in appearance, and Betty's gratitude was sufficiently great to induce her to prepare a yellow petticoat and a red cap for the obliging pixy. She placed them, accordingly, by the side of the basin of water, and watched for the result. The pixy, after putting them on, disappeared through the window, apparently in great delight. But Betty was ever afterwards obliged to wash all her clothes herself.[8]

If you pried too closely into the affairs of the fairies, you could suffer for it in the same way. The Devonian family of Sokespitch who lived near Topsham were said to have a barrel of ale in their cellar which had kept providing drinks for many years without running dry. A local saying in the area, given to describe a favourable undertaking, was 'It is going on like Sokespitch's cann.'[9] Unfortunately, one day a maid became too curious as to why the barrel never ran dry and so removed the bung to look inside. There was nothing to be seen but cobwebs, but the vessel never produced ale again because she had offended the pixies who had provided it.

A farmer living on the north of Dartmoor was fortunate to find that the pixies had decided to help with the threshing of his wheat. He found them one day in his barn and watched them for some time, marvelling at how efficient they were and how they didn't even seem to raise a sweat. But his presence was noticed and the pixies all turned and ran. One, while rushing for the exit, tripped and fell and the farmer managed to catch it and put it into a lanthorn,

where it lived for some time before the farmer inadvertently left the door open and it escaped.

Long after belief in the fairies was said to have died away, both those working the land and those travelling across it still reported sightings. A peat-cutter at Ponsworthy told in the 1930s that he still regularly saw pixies in the dusk. He said that they looked like white ladies dancing along.[10] The landscape here is not dissimilar to that at Buckland and so this is possibly another description of something like the decaying plant matter that causes 'will-o'-the wisps'.

In Devon, and elsewhere, this phenomena was also sometimes referred to as an appearance of 'Jack o' th' Lantern' and was linked to the fairy realm long before the character's association with Halloween. In most cases he was a source of concern in the same way as other interpretations of bog lights, being thought responsible for leading people from their path and into danger. Sometimes though, his help was called upon in order to light a traveller's way. Lady Rosalind Northcote recorded a verse towards the end of the nineteenth century which was used in Devon as an invocation to call up the spirit of Jack to provide help: 'Jack o' the Lantern, Jan of the Lub, / Light me home and I'll give you a crub.'[11] A 'crub' here means a crumb; that is, some food as recompense for service.

Fairy Descriptions

Most people have a stereotypical view of what the fairies look like. Aside from the gossamer wings which we know are a later addition,[12] in many cases the image probably looks like a miniature version of a normal human being, dressed in clothes the colour of which may well suggest the natural environment in which they generally live. We can turn to tradition to see how this matches up with the way the fairy folk are thought to look in Devon, but also to a number of alleged eyewitness accounts which have been recorded over time.

In his chapter on pixies and fairies in *The Folklore of Devon*, Ralph Whitlock noted that in Devon pixies 'are often rather ugly little men, almost invariably dressed in rags'.[13] Indeed, one story tells of a woman who was returning home on the northern side of Dartmoor in the dark. She had three children with her—two walking along and a third whom she was carrying—but when she got home she noticed that one had gone missing on the way. A search party of local people immediately went out and discovered the missing boy under an oak tree that was known to be popular with the pixies. He described being led away by 'two large bundles of rags'[14] which had disappeared as the lights of the crowd were seen approaching.

Devonian poet and journalist Elias Tozer suggested that not all pixies were ugly as described by Whitlock, but rather that their appearance varied: 'Some are pretty and graceful; others are quaint and uncouth—diminutive Hunchbacks in fact. They delight in solitary places, and disport themselves in pathless woods, on hills, in vales, and on the banks of rivers, their dress being invariably green.'[15]

How do any of the recorded eyewitness accounts from the county fit with the traditional beliefs we have already noted? One which took place at the end of the nineteenth century, but was noted some thirty or so years later, seems to follow many stereotypes:

> I saw the pixie under an overhanging boulder close to Shaugh Bridge (on the southern edge of Dartmoor) in the afternoon. I cannot say more definitely as to the time, but I remember running in to my mother after an afternoon walk and saying I had seen a pixie—and being laughed at. This was in 1897.
>
> It was like a little wizened man about (as far as I can remember) 18 inches or possibly 2 feet high, but I incline to the lesser height. It had a little pointed hat, slightly curved to the front, a doublet, and little short knicker things. My impression is of some contrasting colours, but I cannot remember now what colours, though I think they were blue and red. Its face was brown and wrinkled and wizened. I saw it for a moment and it vanished. It was under the boulder when I looked, and then vanished.[16]

An informant from St Marychurch in 1935 reported having seen pixies at the marshland in that area. She described them as looking like the moon rising out of the marsh, being so frightening that she ran all the way home. It is highly likely that this is another instance of phosphorescent marsh gas being super-stitiously interpreted. Interestingly, the informant stated how that night she dreamed about the pixies pinching her legs. It was local belief that if maidser-vants or other workers were not judged hard-working enough by the pixies, then they would pinch them

Not all eyewitness reports of sightings are from as long ago. A woman living near Yeoford in 1975 believed that fairies quite often came to the edge of a stream close to her bungalow to dance. She said that they were slim, about two feet tall and wearing green. She saw them frequently and her presence did not seem to stop them from going about their business. In the previous decade, while giving a talk on the fairy folk, folklore author and collector Ruth

St Leger-Gordon was told by a lady in the audience that she had seen four on
the outskirts of Widecombe-in-the-Moor. She described archetypal clothing of
doublet and hose, and a pointed cap. Sightings are still recorded even into the
present century. For a chapter in the recent book *Magical Folk: British and Irish
Fairies 500 AD to the Present*, my co-author and I collected an example from the
Dartmoor village of Chagford, where a resident observed a bright light sitting
on the top of a pile of potato peelings in a kitchen bin in a dark cottage. She
says that she knew it to be a fairy.[17]

As recently as 2016 there was an alleged pixie sighting with two eyewit-
nesses, which seems to share some similarities with the Shaugh Bridge sighting
in 1897. It took place in gardens at Heathercombe, close to the Dartmoor
village of Manaton, and the sighting was made by a mother and daughter
(Claire). The couple had been walking around a sculpture trail in the gardens,
which were open to the public as part of an annual open gardens scheme.
They had retired to a small ornamental garden next to the café. This paved
area contained figures of fairies and small animals and various plants. Claire
noticed the figure sitting on the end of a log. She described it as a pixie, sitting
with its knees tucked up, wearing brown clothes and with brown skin. The
skin colour is a match with the Shaugh Bridge example, as was the style of
clothes reported. The colouring seems reminiscent of the earthy, environ-
mental colours often associated with fairies. Claire commented on the sighting
to her mother, who confirmed that she had also seen it.[18]

Fairy Culture

We have already established that some of the fairy folk like to work and help
human folk out, usually for a certain reward or other benefit. In most other
cases, there is little crossover between the world of the fairies and the world of
humans. Or at least, it is seen to be better that way. Where the two do intersect
in folklore, it usually comes off better for the fairies than it does for us.

Food features prominently in the fairy culture of Devon, as does music,
dance and partying. The account from Yeoford above mentioned the bank of
the stream as a gathering place for dancing, but there are also examples of
more formal fairy fairs and parties.

The Blackdown Hills, which form a border between Devon and Somerset,
are often said to be the site of one of the most significant fairy fairs in the
county. Here, the fairies gathered to trade in goods and food and drink, as
well as to party. However, an error of interpretation in the original textual
reference for this event may have misplaced it, and it is more likely that this

fairy gathering should actually be located over the border in Somerset. This first reference comes from the book *Pandemonium, or the Devil's Cloister*, written in 1684 by English author Richard Bovet, a staunch anti-Catholic who often drew parallels between that religion and witchcraft. The 'ninth relation' of the book is titled *A Relation of the Apparition of Fairies, their seeming to keep a Fair, and what happened to a certain man that endeavoured to put himself amongst them,* and reads:

> The place near which they most ordinarily shewed themselves, was on the side of a Hill, named Black-down, between the Parishes of Pittminster, and Chestonford, not many miles from Tanton: Those that have had occasion to Travel that way, have frequently seen them there, appearing like Men and Women of a stature, generally, near the smaller size of Men; their habits used to be of red, blew, or green, according to the old way of Country Garb, with high crown'd hats. One time about 50 years since, a person (living at Comb St. Nicholas, a Parish lying on one side of that hill, near Chard) was riding towards his home that way; and saw just before him, on the side of the hill a great company of People, that seemed to him like Country Folks, Assembled, as at a Fair; there was all sorts of Commodities to his appearance, as at our ordinary Fairs; Pewterers, Shoe-makers, Pedlars, with all kind of Trinkets, Fruit, and drinking Booths; he could not remember any thing which he had usually seen at Fairs, but what he saw there.[19]

It is clear that 'Tanton' is an archaic form of the town name of Taunton and therefore, looking at the rest of this description, Bovet is actually referring to Blagdon Hill rather than the Blackdown Hills, which are a little further to the south-east.

It was generally considered to be dangerous to attempt to approach a gathering of fairies, especially if they were feasting or dancing. In line with more general fairy folklore an errant wayfarer could become captured by them, forced to dance at the very least until sunrise. Partaking in fairy food was also unwise as it could, it was said, lead to one becoming trapped in the fairy world.[20]

There are however stories which relate to fairy food in a more mundane and day-to-day way. William Crossing relates a tale of a ploughman who has been working the land since dawn and by breakfast time is quite hungry. His ploughing takes him to an old granite standing stone in the field, from beneath which he can hear voices. Stopping to listen, he hears one of the voices declare that the oven is hot.

> 'Bake me a cake, then,' instantly cried the hungry ploughman, in whose mind the very mention of an oven had conjured up thoughts of appetising cheer; 'Bake me a cake, then.' He continued the furrow to the end of the field, when, turning his plough, he set out on his return journey. When he approached the rock, what was his surprise and delight at seeing, placed on its surface, a nice cake, smoking hot. He knew at once that this was the work of the obliging little pixies, who evidently had a resort under the rock, and who had taken pity upon his hunger, and provided him with a morning meal.[21]

It is unsurprising that the actual location of this story is not named. Much like the story of the midwife who anoints her eye with ointment and is able to see into the fairy world, the story which Crossing relates is not just found in Devon but is rather a local variant of a much more prevalent fairy motif, known generally as 'The Cake in the Furrow'. In its usual form, a ploughman or other labourer is rewarded with food from the fairies because he has repaired something of theirs. Although Crossing's version does away with this element, the rest is fairly similar to the standard story told.

Arguably the earliest reference to the fairies baking in the open in this way comes from Robert Kirk in 1691, who states that 'they are sometimes heard to bake bread … within the little hillocks where they most haunt'.[22] But the story is found in other countries, notably Norway and Denmark, which may hint at its having travelled to Britain at some early point. In most of these versions the repair of a tool is involved, but the variant without this, often termed 'The Fairies' Gift', is widespread across Europe.[23]

Lady Rosalind Northcote recorded other versions of the story from the Exeter area. She cites two very similar examples in the journal *Folklore* in 1900,[24] one which ends favourably in the manner of 'The Fairies' Gift' (at least for one party) and one less so. In the latter, a plough-boy picks up a pixies' oven unearthed while tilling a field and breaks it, declaring that the pixies will bake no more bread. He was said to straightaway be attacked by unseen forces and was pinched black and blue. He had to retire home to bed and could not open his eyes for some days after the incident. In the version with the more favourable conclusion, the oven only required a nail to repair it and so the ploughman does so and is rewarded by the pixies leaving him a mug of cider in the field. He offers some to the disrespectful plough-boy and the lad is then attacked by the pixies in the same manner as before when he refuses to drink it.

The modern fairy sighting recorded at Chagford and mentioned earlier in this chapter is not the only time that the fairies have been seen in that locale. Sarah Hewett records the story of a man who was driving (this would refer to a horse and carriage rather than a motor vehicle) towards Chagford at night when he heard the ringing of bells.[25] As the hour was so late, this seemed strange so he stopped to investigate. He became aware of thousands of small lights in the meadow and could see that the field was full of fairies, dancing and playing music. He observed them from a distance for some time before the crow of a rooster came and the whole sight disappeared from view, the meadow falling into darkness.

It used to be said by the residents of Chagford that the sound of music and dance could often be heard on the wind from the surrounding countryside. The English composer Thomas Wood once heard what he believed was fairy music while holidaying on Dartmoor in 1921. He recorded the event in his autobiography *True Thomas*, as part of a discussion of the various paranormal events that had occurred during his life.[26] Wood was working on a music score somewhere on the moor (he does not specify where) when he heard a voice calling the name 'Tommy'. He notes that people knew better than to use that contraction of his name. The weather was very clear and he could see nothing through his field glasses.

The next day, Wood returned to the same spot. Again, he was working on his music score when he heard faint music on the air. Having discounted the source as being from anyone enjoying a picnic—nobody was visible through his field glasses and portable radios were not in use at this time—he concluded that the ethereal music was not human in origin, and wrote down the musical notation for what he heard as best as he could. The music still exists today, and renditions of it can be heard online.[27]

Fairies in the Landscape

there was once an old lady who planted an amazing flower garden and her tulips were so beautiful, that the fairies chose their flower cups as cradles for their tiny babies. They say the fairies were so grateful to the old lady for her amazing tulips, that they presented the blooms with bright colours and a delicate fragrance. Sadly, after the old lady passed away, the beautiful garden was destroyed

by the new harsh owner and, to revenge themselves on him, the
fairies took away the smell of the tulips.[28]

This Devon folk tale is used to explain why tulips have a much subtler scent
than many other flowers, but it also presents a picture of fairies in the landscape
that is far more reminiscent of the Victorian flower fairy image, or a Disney
cartoon, than the descriptions we have explored above.

To search for evidence of the areas of the county where fairies were
considered to dwell, we might look to place names. As mentioned above,
however, this must be done cautiously—place names can often change over
time through the distortion of language, or they can have stories retrospec-
tively mapped onto them. Many people assume, for example, that the public
house in the village of Black Dog, called the 'Black Dog Inn' is named for that
particular aspect of folklore (explored in Chapter Eight), whereas the name
actually comes from the fact that a previous landlord had a favoured pet hunting
dog which was black. The pub had previously been known by an unconnected
name until he changed it.

The hamlet of Fairy Cross might thus be seen as having a strong connection
with the fairies, particularly as the location in the area of Alwington has two
fine recently constructed bus shelters flanking the main road that look like they
would make fine homes for any fairy family. There is, however, little evidence
in the folklore record to connect stories of fairies with this area. Other areas of
Devon have much stronger links.

Not far from Challacombe on Exmoor is a craggy combe known as Pixy
Rocks. It lies a short distance from Bratton Down, which was an area much
associated with pixy-leading in the past. A similar area on Dartmoor, known
as the Pixies' House or Pixies' Cave, was recorded by William Crossing in
his *Tales of the Dartmoor Pixies*. The narrow opening, through which a person
may just squeeze, had been attributed this way by many earlier writers, but
Crossing expanded on the beliefs about the place in more detail, describing
the interior of the fissure. Once inside, a narrow passage turned to the left
and led down into a cave which Crossing describes romantically as 'a small
grotto'.[29] In fact, the space was capable of housing several people and was used
in the time of the Civil War for this purpose to great effect. A member of the
Elford family, who lived in nearby Tavistock, retreated to the space in order to
conceal himself from Cromwell's men.[30] John Elford was Lord of the Manor
and a member of the Long Parliament, but his own views began to diverge
from Cromwell's. Elford got wind that Cromwell had sent troops to find him

and so exiled himself at Sheepstor, an act which likely ensured this particular Pixie House was marked strongly on the map. The name of the nearby town of Yelverton is a modern corruption of Elford-town.[31]

A similarly named location at Chudleigh Rocks is now listed as a scheduled monument (number 1010740) by Historic England. Pixies' Hole has also been known as Pixies' House, and the hollow inside the rocks associated with its diminutive occupants was called Pixies' Parlour. There is much archaeological evidence to suggest that the cave system was used for domestic purposes in the past. Excavations in 1823 uncovered animal remains as well as charcoal, pottery and flint tools. Archaeology from the 1940s suggested possible habitation by the Romans here, and more modern digging in the 1970s evidenced a rudimentary hearth as well as flint deposits dated to the Later Upper Palaeolithic.[32] When we consider that stone and flint tools such as these were, in earlier times before the benefits of scientific study revealed them for what they actually are, thought to be elf-shot (tiny arrowheads made by elves, pixies and the like) it is not difficult to imagine how the caves at Chudleigh Rocks became associated with fairy dwellings.

Chudleigh resident Mary Jones notes that in July of 1840 a fete was held at the Pixies' Parlour for the Honourable Mr Clifford. The decorations were of a theme suitable for the folklore of the location:

> the splendid cavern was illuminated by a number of fairy lanterns, whose twinkling lights were most enchanting; the interior was also decorated with laurel and oak branches, interspersed with choice flowers. The visitors were accommodated with rustic seats and also a plentiful supply of viands and rich delicacies, on rustic tables erected for the purpose. A Glee of Lord Mornington's was sung, 'Here in cool grot and mossy cell, where rural Fays and Fairies dwell.'[33]

Guests at the event were met and directed by someone dressed in green, sporting artificial wings, representing Ariel. Such an event could have done nothing but strengthen associations with the fairies at the Pixies' Parlour.

Another consistency in the recording of information about the fairies at Sheepstor and Chudleigh is Mrs Bray, who discusses both of them in her writings. She even fictionalized the Elford story in her novel *Warleigh*, published in 1834. Bray was also responsible for noting that a rock that used to stand on

Dartmoor, known as Belfry Rock or Church Rock, was associated with the fairy folk, such that it became known locally as Pixies' Church:

> many old persons declared that ever since they could remember, if you placed your ear close to the rock on a Sunday, you could hear a small tinkling sound, resembling the church bells at Tavistock, and usually at the very time they were ringing to warn the good people of that town for the morning service. It was said, likewise, that the same sound could be heard when the bells of Tavistock chimed, as they always did at four, and eight, and twelve o'clock.[34]

It seems clear from this description that the position of the rock was such that it acted as a natural echo chamber for the nearby Tavistock Church, with the romantic notion of the pixie bells being overlaid. Sadly, the rock was dynamited some time ago in order to make use of the stone elsewhere, and so the phenomenon can no longer be experienced.

One recent development to fairy folklore within the landscape is the clandestine adding of small wooden doors to trees to make them resemble a fairy dwelling place. These appear to have originated in America in 1993,[35] and have since grown in popularity. Although good fun and a nice way of keeping the ideas of fairy occupancy alive, the practice can be environmentally troubling, particularly when holes are made in trees for the purpose of installing a door, or materials are used which are harmful to the trees or the animals that live within them. In 2016, estate managers at Dartington Hall in South Devon used social media to try and discourage whoever was adding fairy doors to their trees, because of the detrimental effects on bat populations from the types of materials used. A previous spate of fairy door installations over the border in woodland at Crewkerne, Somerset had escalated to the point where 200 doors were discovered and they all had to be removed. Similar concerns have been voiced around the hammering of coins into tree trunks for luck and the tying of strips of cloth, known as clooties, onto trees as a charm.

Fairies as Scapegoats: Pixy-Leading and Changelings

> A man or woman walks on familiar ground, crossing a field, say, when they become disorientated and unaccountably lose their way. This experience might be explained by any number of factors: darkness, freak neurological events, intoxicants, atmospheric

conditions, etc. However, in Britain, or at least in parts of Britain, the experience was traditionally blamed on supernatural entities.[36]

In Devon, where reports of this were common, people who inexplicably lost their way on a route that they knew well, or who were lured from a path, described themselves as being pixy-led, using the spelling of the word pixie popularized by Mrs Bray in her writings.

An interesting account of a case of pixy-leading at Torrington in North Devon was reported in the *Western Daily Mercury* newspaper on 6 June 1890. It includes within its summary all the relevant aspects of any pixy-leading case. The incident happened to one of a group of men who were working in woodland a few miles outside of Torrington, ripping bark from the trees. At the end of the work day, one of the group members separated from the others in order to fetch a tool he had left elsewhere in the wood. The man described how a strange feeling came over him and how he heard laughter from all around him.

This took place at around 5.30pm and by 7pm his wife was growing concerned that he had not returned home, especially as she met one of the other men by chance and he believed that the men had all left at the same time. By 10pm she went to the woods herself, where she met her husband, very wet, coming the other way. He explained to her that he had been pixy-led, escaping after crawling away, falling into a stream and at that point realizing where he was. The report continued:

> 'You girt fule, why didden 'ee turn your pockets inside out?' was all the comfort he received from his better half; 'then you would have been able to come away tu wance.' The man firmly believes in pixies, and what strengthens his belief is the fact that a tailor named Short was 'pixy-led' in the same wood some years before, and remained under their spell until morning. It may be said the man was drunk, but it can be proved on the best authority that no intoxicating liquor was drunk that day by any of the party.[37]

There are some similarities between this story, told in a newspaper as a factual account, and the folk tale of Jan Coo discussed in Chapter Two.

Turning your pockets inside out was the most common protection against pixy-leading, but in general it was the act of reversing clothing that was important. Other people have reversed coats or jackets, or aprons and shawls in the case of women. There is no definitive reason given for why this somewhat strange act would counter fairy magic. Mrs Bray suggested that it was because fairies liked everything to be neat and ordered and so would instantly be repelled by clothing that was in disarray, but provided no evidence to back this up. As mentioned above, there is a link between clothing and pixies whereby gifting clothing to them will free them from service. But again, there is no evidence to link these two aspects.

One piece of obscure belief collected from Princetown said that in order to ward off trouble from the pixies when driving a carriage in the fog, one should reverse the carriage lamps.[38] The same belief states that you should tie a handkerchief over the eyes and ears of the horse as well—a practice which sounds more likely to invite trouble than to repel it, albeit more physical than supernatural.

The ideas around pixy-leading and the Irish concept of the stray sod were taken up and used in the children's fantasy series *The Spiderwick Chronicles* by Tony DiTerlizzi and Holly Black, which tell the story of a group of children who move into the Spiderwick Estate and discover a fairy world there. The stray sod is discussed in one of the accompanying books, *Arthur Spiderwick's Field Guide to the Fantastical World Around You*. In this version, it is suggested that the stray sod is a subspecies of the pixie which, if trodden on, causes one to lose their sense of direction. In real-world lore, the stray sod refers rather to a patch of ground which has been enchanted by fairies. Stepping on it causes the same problem.

In terms of scapegoating, it is likely that being pixy-led was used as an excuse by people for a variety of issues. One is, naturally, as an excuse for spending rather too long in the pub and ending up lost, or in a ditch, on one's way home. While the story of the bark strippers states that no alcohol was drunk, this might only be applied to the daytime hours. It is reasonable to suggest that the pixy-led individual might have made a trip to a nearby tavern for a few hours, returned to the woods to collect his things, and then suffered at the hands of poor coordination. Tozer made this suggestion in his observations on superstition in the second half of *Devonshire and other original poems* back in 1873, describing how a farmer or labourer who had partaken in one cup of cider too many would be led a 'purty dance' by the pixies on his way home because of their dislike of 'over-drinking'. In these cases a supernatural entity in whom many held a firm belief proved a useful source on which to lay the blame.

We might also consider a case of pixy-leading from early in the nineteenth century, with a rather clever solution provided for prevention. There was a clergyman, Tanner, who had two adjoining benefices situated between the towns of Crediton and South Molton. Every year, Tanner would hold a tithe-audit at his property which all the farmers would attend, having to cross some quite wild moorland areas to get there. It became an ongoing problem that, although the farmers would be able to navigate the moor quite well in the morning, they invariably became pixy-led on their way back and usually spent the night wandering the moor looking for the right track home. As the audit took place around Christmas, this was obviously quite problematic. A deputation of locals sought help from a wise woman in Exeter, who was known as a good charmer. She was able to provide a solution to the problem which proved equally effective as her cures for toothache. She instructed the farmers that, on reaching the edge of the moor, they should remove their clothes, place them in a pile on the ground and sit on them for no less than thirty-five minutes (longer if the weather allowed). As soon as they felt the fug from the pixies lifting, they could dress and proceed on their way. By this course of action, the supernatural effects of the pixies no longer caused an issue, and nor did the effects of the clergyman's generous cider provision.

It is quite probable that the fairies also provided a suitable scapegoat for someone who should have known the land very well and simply became lost, though not necessarily drunk—many of the pixy-leading stories take place at night and often in fog. Not every case, however, is as clear-cut.

In the autumn of 1980, a widow named Mrs Stevens suffered an effect which would superstitiously be termed pixy-leading. She would, each day, traverse a field between the bungalow in which she lived and the farm occupied by her son and his family. There was an obvious path between the two, thanks to the daily trips, but she still became lost there one evening and ended up doing a few circuits of the field. She didn't respond to suggestions that she was pixy-led when they were made to her.[39] We do not know the age of Mrs Stevens but we can assume that, if her husband had died and her son had a family, then she was probably of more advancing years. It is possible that she just suffered from some natural confusion.

Another area where fairies are scapegoated is in the stories of changelings, where the fairies are said to take away healthy babies from their cribs and replace them with sickly ones. When we look at changeling stories generally, we can see that they are a remarkably troubling area of folklore. More often than not, the fairies are being used to explain some mental or physical affliction which a child has developed as it has grown up—the parents being unable to accept it. Equally as worrying is that in modern interpretations, most of these children are being suggested as autistic; this is most certainly not true and should be questioned at every opportunity. While there may have been some autistic children who were said to be changelings, there were plenty of other reasons why someone might have this term attached to them.

In Devon, there are few changeling stories compared to some other areas. Probably the best-known, cited by Ralph Whitlock in his original *The Folklore of Devon*, is that of a Tavistock woman whose child is taken by fairies and replaced while she is hanging out washing in the garden. The story ultimately has a happy ending, with the fairies being so pleased with the way the woman has raised their offspring as her own that they eventually return the human child, who enjoys good fortune thereafter. This is undoubtedly a morality tale designed to warn against the dangers of leaving children unattended, but which was retold by Mrs Bray with her usual vigour.

There was also a woman who lived in Totnes in South Devon in the middle of the nineteenth century who was said by everyone to be a fairy, but this seems to be purely because she looked like one. Whether this was physically or in her mode of dress is unclear, but the story seems quite apt when we consider that, in modern times, Totnes is Devon's equivalent to Glastonbury—with an above-average percentage of people who follow more 'new age' practices. She would have been quite at home there.

The tradition that suggests fairies steal horses at night and ride them hard on the moors is probably also a form of scapegoating. It is likely that these stories find their origin amongst the smuggling community, used to explain why the horses they might have 'borrowed' from local owners overnight in order to move their goods were so exhausted and dishevelled in the morning. Snell suggests in his *Book of Exmoor* (1903) that the presence of smugglers also explains the stories of fairies ascribed to certain other locations.[40] This would certainly be the case in more malicious tales, such as the example which he quotes to back this idea up, regarding Comer's Gate: 'Some of the country people 'tis said, fear to pass this spot after dark, having no desire to make the acquaintance of a race noted for its caprice, and wielding, as they suppose, supernatural power.'[41]

CHAPTER SEVEN

Some Devon Hauntings

Devon is the most haunted county in the United Kingdom. But then again so is Cornwall, or Somerset, or Yorkshire. Devon is also home to the most haunted pub in the United Kingdom. Unless it is in Cornwall, or Somerset, or Yorkshire. It all depends on the book you are reading, or the website that came up on your recent internet search. These claims are all put forward by the same sort of guidebook literature which often connects Druidical history with megaliths (see Chapter Five) or suggests that particular customs have 'pagan origins' (see Chapter Three).

It is, of course, impossible to quantify which county is 'the most haunted' or which pub has the most ghosts. In the case of the former there are no records which draw together the number of legends, accounts or vague traditions of hauntings in one place for comparison. In the case of the latter, we would first need to prove the existence of the said ghosts and nobody has yet done so.

In the field of folklore, proof of existence is irrelevant. The study of folklore does not set out to prove the existence of anything from a scientific perspective. That is the role of other disciplines. Folklorists are interested in why people tell the stories that they do, how those stories relate to place, how they transmit and form variants, and other social history interactions. From the outset, therefore, it is important to note that this chapter will not be

121

looking for 'evidence' of ghosts in the hauntings discussed, but will examine common themes in the ghost stories of the county of Devon. It may not be the most haunted county, but there are plenty to choose from. The approach here will be to draw on some of the well-established tales, or those with complex narratives, in order to highlight the common themes and draw comparison elsewhere.

Conjuring Parsons

We begin with the tale of a haunted rectory—not quite on the scale of the infamous Borley (also described as 'the most haunted house in England'!) but certainly of much interest.

Luffincott Rectory was to be found in the parish of that name, approximately six miles to the south of Holsworthy. The parish is a tiny place, with a population of just forty-five recorded in the 2001 census data.[1] It was intended to be the home of the serving vicar of St James's Church (a building declared redundant in 1975) and sat half a mile to its east.

Key to the story of Luffincott is the Reverend Franke Parker, who served as rector there for around forty-five years from the year 1835. He was far from poor, as many men of the cloth were at that time. He farmed the glebe and kept a good number of staff both working the land and serving at the rectory. He seems to have treated them well and used to give the traditional harvest home celebration for his farmworkers at the glebe each year. His strong financial position allowed Rev. Parker to rebuild and then subsequently enlarge Luffincott Rectory.[2]

Parker died a bachelor in the early 1880s and his body was buried outside the east window of the church. According to the Reverend Norman McGee, writing in 1959, 'He is said to have been very happy at Luffincott, and the saying goes that he was wont to express a wish that no successor should ever dispossess him of what he had come to regard as his own.'[3]

After Reverend Parker's death other vicars came and went until the arrival of the Reverend Thomas Warde Browne, a fairly stout man with a small pointed beard. He was known for wearing the broad-brimmed hat traditional for priests of the time and had a notable way of walking with his head down, due to being partly paralysed.[4] He was far more impoverished than the preceding Reverend Parker and chose to live with no staff.

At some point around the year 1901, Reverend Browne was sitting down to his evening meal in the rectory, on his own as usual and reading a book as he ate. Glancing up, he saw what he later described as the ghost of Franke Parker standing before him (although he didn't identify him as such at the time). If the story as related by McGee is to be believed, Reverend Browne was so terrified by this that he upped and left the rectory immediately, fleeing to the nearby village of Clawton where he had previously held the position of curate and seeking sanctuary from the farmer with whom he had lived when there. He was never to return to Luffincott Rectory again and he would not allow any of his possessions to be retrieved. Even his half-finished meal remained on the table.

Browne was to remain in his tenure for another two years, but he continued to live at Clawton. Some sources say that he was taken to the church each Sunday by his landlord in a pony and trap, but most note that he walked the four-and-a-half miles each way in his cassock. If this is the case, it would have been quite a feat for someone described as partially paralysed. Between delivering the morning service and evensong, he would eat his lunch in the church porch.

Luffincott Rectory naturally developed a reputation for its haunting over time. Local residents decided that if Reverend Browne did not want all of the possessions that he had abandoned there, then they should not go to waste, and they gradually removed them. People began to break the windows of the property in order to gain access and stay the night there. The building fell into a poor state of repair until it finally burned down. Whether this was accidental or a deliberate act remains an open question.

Some did not believe that there was anything remotely supernatural about Luffincott. In a newspaper clipping which I believe to be from the 1960s but which is otherwise unsourced,[5] the case is discussed by a gentleman named Frederick Lyle. He was thirteen at the time of the incident and recalls that Browne was a 'very timid and easily frightened man'. Lyle suggests that the night on which he fled the rectory was in fact the only night that Browne ever stayed there.

The incident took place, according to Lyle, not when Reverend Browne was eating his meal, but when he was in bed. The ghost was, according to him, nothing more than a couple of local lads who draped themselves in a white sheet and crept into his bedroom. The easily frightened parson was so terrified that he fled the building without even getting dressed. Lyle believed the whole story of the ghost probably came from Franke Parker's request just before his death that they should 'bury me six feet deep so that I should never rise again'.[6]

This sounds like a somewhat dramatic request, but we should consider it alongside the suggestion put forward by some that Reverend Parker was a 'conjuring parson'.

We find the figure of the conjuring parson in many places within English folklore, but the idea is particularly strong in Devon. These were men who blurred the boundaries between Christian preacher and folk magician. Some were believed to have magical libraries and the ability to perform acts of astrology, divination or even more fantastical feats. In actuality, we should consider these men as exorcists at least, as they were often called upon to 'lay down' or banish restless spirits.

> The ghost-laying parsons of folklore usually acted in groups of nine or twelve, were trained at Oxford University, and were preferably learned in Latin, Greek, Hebrew and Arabic. Parsons might banish a spirit to a magic circle, otherwise known as a 'gallitrap' or 'Lob's pound'. These might be invisible or marked out with bands of iron taken from barrels (owing to the belief that spirits cannot pass iron). A clergyman could protect himself from harm by being in the presence of a pregnant woman or a baby, since it was believed that spirits could not harm the innocent. A spirit could also be banished by throwing consecrated graveyard earth, which was believed to absorb the bodies of the dead and was therefore 'doubly potent'.[7]

Contrary to Young's suggestion in the above quote, when we look at folklore across the country more generally, we can see that Oxford was not the only university at which the conjuring parson might be trained. They certainly had to be learned, but some such as John Rudall of Launceston were educated at Cambridge.[8] However, in Devon, Oxford was the preferred institution. There may be a couple of reasons for this. One could be down to close ties between Oxford and Exeter. The Bodleian Library had been established by an Exeter-born scholar and led to the formation of an Oxford college named after the city. The other may be simply because there are other significant folk ghosts in the county who were banished by Oxford men, after those from Cambridge had failed.

Such was the case with the ghost of 'Mr Lyde' at Sidmouth, the penitential spirit of a man who was rumoured to have murdered his uncle, a spirit which was laid to rest by Mr George Cornish of Pascombe (an Oxford scholar) after six Cambridge-educated ministers had failed.

Returning to Luffincott, the Reverend J.G.M. Scott, writing in 1960 in response to a published article about the case, notes that he was told by a female parishioner that her grandmother used to speak of Reverend Franke Parker's 'conjuring' reputation:

> They used to say that he could turn himself into a lion or a snake or a wolf; and once he stopped in the middle of his sermon at Luffincott and rushed off home because he said that his maids back in the Rectory were looking at his Books and he knew it and must go back and stop them.[9]

The reputation of practising magical acts as well as Christian ones was ascribed to some members of the clergy not because they actually had this arcane knowledge, but because they were easily the most educated person in the surrounding area, or because they were especially eccentric. While Parker was not considered the latter, he was incumbent for a long time and this suggests that he was probably good at what he did. But the story of the books is not unique and should be recognized as a variation on the story of 'The Sorcerer's Apprentice'. It is also not the only version of the claim to be found in Devon.

In the journal *Folklore* for 1954, Sir W.R. Halliday notes the same story being related to him by Rev. C.E. Gover about William Gimmingham, Rector of Bratton Fleming between 1820 and 1837: 'One story about him is that while he was in church his maids got hold of his books of magic with the result that they were infested with crowds of fowls which the rector spirited away.'[10]

Another story about Gimmingham told that he once saw a man outside his house stealing his vegetables, and so he cast a spell on him rendering him unable to move until the vicar reversed it. In the case of Gimmingham it was possibly his eccentricity which led to his reputation. He was said to leave his church during services if he became bored in order to smoke a pipe in the churchyard, and that his pet dog (which was large and black but not spectral!) would often go to church with him. He also left a handwritten note in the parish marriage register, which was witnessed by two other people, stating that in a time of drought he had prophesied that it would rain within twenty-four hours. Which it did.[11]

Secret Rooms and Tunnels

Ghost stories often contain details that are stated as factual but in actuality are common elements found across folklore. This is especially true when they are delivered repeatedly as historic fact, sometimes with physical evidence which would seem to corroborate them—until such time as you delve a little more deeply into the background.

Chambercombe Manor, in Ilfracombe on the North Devon coast, offers up such a story. It has featured on television more than once because of its hauntings and is sometimes used for paranormal investigations even now because of its ghostly reputation. Thought to have been built in the eleventh century, the manor was in the possession of the Champernon family for some 400 years until there was nobody left to inherit the property. It then passed between various high-status families before ending up in the possession of the Crown after its owner at the time—the Duke of Suffolk—was executed for treason in 1554.[12]

There are vague references to Lady Jane Grey, daughter of Suffolk, being one of the ghosts said to haunt the property. But the best-established tale concerns a space next to the room that bears her name (because she had slept in it when once staying at the property).

Author Keith Poole notes that the Gorges family of the area sold all their lands at some time towards the end of the sixteenth century, with the vicar of Ilfracombe becoming trustee.[13] The land was rented out in sections, called 'ropers', to farmers in the area, one of whom ended up with Chambercombe which was a farm at the time. In 1885, while attempting to repair a leak in the roof, the man noticed from his viewpoint at the top of the ladder what seemed to be the outline of an old bricked-up window, which was not easily visible when at ground level. This prompted him to investigate more closely the corresponding area inside the property, and in so doing he noticed faint marks on the wall between the Lady Jane Grey Room and the next room along. He broke through the wall, and a small secret chamber was discovered. It had evidently been created between the two larger rooms at some point. In the long-sealed room were the remains of wall tapestries and some old furniture including a four-poster bed. And behind the drapes of the bed was found a skeleton, laid out on the mattress.

At this point, things become very complicated in terms of the story because a number of different variants exist. The most common tells that the skeleton belonged to a girl named Kate Oatway, the daughter of a notorious wrecker, William, and his wife Ellen who lived in the manor in the seventeenth century. In some versions, William unwittingly wrecked the boat on which Kate was travelling and carried her body back to the manor through a smugglers' tunnel said to run from Hele beach to his home. Full of remorse, the couple strangely decided to brick the body up in the secret room. Other versions say that Kate was walled-up because she threatened to tell the authorities about her father's illicit activities. And in yet more, the body belongs to a wealthy Spanish woman who was aboard the wrecked craft.

There are even variations in the details surrounding the uncovering of the room. Some, such as Poole above, date this as 1855. Others say that it was in 1865. In one obscure monograph about the story, C.H. Warwick puts it much earlier still, suggesting that it was in 1738, just thirty years after the body was hidden, that the tenants of the property found the skeleton. Warwick suggests that these tenants, the Vye family, were responsible for ensuring that Kate Oatway's remains were interred next to her mother in the graveyard at Ilfracombe Parish Church.[14]

The secret chamber is, of course, now seen as a prime spot for alleged ghostly activity, although visitors to the manor report sightings of different apparitions all around the property. Rather than the stories all relating to one specific ghost, the concealed skeleton acts as a springboard for many different experiences. This central tale, irrespective of who the skeleton might have been, contains two particular tropes found in other folkloric tales: the secret room and the legendary tunnel.

Where an alleged tunnel features prominently in a folk tale, there is usually little or nothing to substantiate it. On occasion, scant evidence of something which might resemble the start of a tunnel leads to the idea being put forward. Such is probably the case with Chambercombe Manor. Here a tunnel from the manor to Hele beach where the association with smuggling is placed would have been virtually impossible to construct at the time the stories are set. The distance between the two is somewhere in the region of a mile and a quarter, and there are at least three watercourses which would pass over the top. Local historian John Moore suggests another alternative for the tunnel story here:

> At Chambercombe, part of what appears to have been a chimney breast, contains a curious hidden vertical shaft, with an iron ladder, leading up into the roof. The shaft is filled to ground level but it is said that early in the 20th century it led down into a tunnel, blocked after some 20–30 paces. The shaft's stones are unfaced and it would have been useless for hiding smuggled goods, there being barely enough room to climb the rungs. If not just an architectural accident, capitalised by the addition of a ladder, then it may have once led to a priest hole … Many old houses have hiding places that were made in times of religious persecution. Perhaps the shaft led to a priest hole in the roof, or underground. If there really was a tunnel, it could have been a route leading to the nearby stream, some 40–50m away, where a small ravine 3–4m deep provides good cover for escape.[15]

Moore's final point also refutes the idea of a long smugglers' tunnel. It would be impossible to escape if followed into a long tunnel, and hence smugglers would prefer to work in the open air where they could easily bolt if spotted.

A similarly impossible tunnel in terms of construction is rumoured to exist in South Devon, joining two properties that each contain ghost stories. This is the tunnel said to run between Torre Abbey and the nearby

St Michael's Chapel in Torquay. In this case the non-existent tunnel would have to run for half a mile and include a vertical section that had been bored through limestone.

It has been suggested by many that the chapel, built in the thirteenth or fourteenth century, once belonged to Torre Abbey, but there does not seem to be any evidence in the Abbey records to substantiate this claim; it only starts to appear in later sources after the medieval period. The abbey itself, founded in 1196, is considered the best example of a medieval monastery preserved in Devon to this day.

A medieval tithe barn stands in the abbey grounds. Originally used to store the produce obtained from the payment of rentals, the building housed somewhat different contents at the end of the sixteenth century, leading to it becoming known as The Spanish Barn. In 1588, Sir Francis Drake captured a Spanish ship, the *Capitana*, taking all 397 crew prisoner.[16] The fiancée of one of these crew members was also on board, and refused to be separated so dressed herself as a sailor and was taken ashore with the others. For two weeks, all the prisoners were kept in terrible conditions in the tithe barn at the abbey. The woman died of a chill during her incarceration and her ghost is now said to wander the area of the barn, mourning for her lost lover.

St Michael's Chapel is found at the very top of Chapel Hill, a tor formed of the limestone which would have made any tunnel impossible. It is not particularly accessible and certainly not an obvious place to build such a structure. Religious buildings on the tops of hills are often dedicated to St Michael (see the example at Brent Tor in Chapter Five), although in this case there is also some uncertainty as to the original name, recorded as 'St Marie's' by John Speed on his sixteenth-century map of the county.[17] J.T. White, in his history of Torquay, suggests that the name St Marie's originates erroneously from a map published towards the end of the reign of King Henry VIII.[18]

Similar uncertainty surrounds the construction and its original purpose. The bedrock from which the foundation was cut can be seen in the chapel interior in a quite worn state, suggesting that no other flooring was laid over it. It is possible that the original use might not have been for group worship at all. Certainly, the story of the haunting features a hermit very prominently and it may have been some sort of home or retreat early in its life, although White lists a whole range of possible uses, noting that all of them can only be conjecture.[19]

During a massive storm one night, says the story, at a time unknown, a ship was wrecked on the coast near Torre Abbey, with all souls being lost— except for one man who was taken to the monastery, where the monks cared for him until he returned to health. In thanks for being saved, it is said that the man built St Michael's Chapel, living there in seclusion and praying for sailors during times of bad weather.

Three hundred years later, a young man arrives at St Michael's on a quest for knowledge. He rests there for a while, falling asleep and dreaming that inside the chapel he meets an old man with white hair who tells him that one day he will be grateful to the builder of the place.

Later, having stayed in the area, the man falls in love with a local girl and the pair often sit outside the chapel, discussing the strange vision the man once had there and more besides. Eventually, the man has to go to sea and says that he will be away for three years. The girl promises to visit the chapel each year on the day of his leaving, but on the third visit she has become concerned because he is still absent. The weather is dreadful and she does not reach the chapel until after dark, but the lamp there is lit. On her arrival she finds a man whom she recognizes as the one from her lover's dream—the hermit who originally constructed the building. He tells her that her lover is in danger on a boat and escorts her to the shore, where they find an unconscious body on the beach. They take him ashore where he eventually recovers and proves to be the missing man.

We might recognize some elements here that connect vaguely with parts of the Chambercombe wrecking tale, but there is no link with smuggling and, in fact, nothing to suggest why a mysterious tunnel should ever have been thought to exist between Torre Abbey and St Michael's Chapel.

Staying in the Torquay area, we might note that the prehistoric cave system known as Kent's Cavern has a legend of tunnels that run for such a distance that they emerge in the county of Kent, said to account for the name. In fact, the cave was originally known as Kent's Hole Close, as shown on a deed from 1659.[20] The derivation of 'Kent' has never been substantiated, but is likely to stem from a personal name. A local rhyme is said to tell of a dog that became lost in the cave system:

> And he went
> And he went
> Until he come out
> In the county of Kent

The story relates that when the dog finally emerges at the other end of the tunnels, in Kent, it has lost all its fur, which was pulled out by pixies who lived under the earth.

It is of course fanciful to suggest that an intact tunnel system actually crossed the whole country. The feature of the dog losing its fur is interesting, however, as it seems to have a parallel in a story about a piper and his dog recorded by Donald A. Mackenzie in 1917. The tale was said to take place in another mythic underground passage between Edinburgh Castle and Holyrood Palace in Scotland:

> In days of long ago the underground passage was used by soldiers when the enemies of the King of Scotland invaded the kingdom and laid siege to Edinburgh Castle, his chief stronghold. The soldiers could leave the castle and fall upon the besiegers from behind, and through it reinforcements could be sent to the castle. When, however, the spirit called Great-Hand began to haunt the tunnel, it could not be used any longer, for every man who entered it perished in the darkness.
>
> The piper was a brave man, and he resolved to explore the tunnel with his dog. 'I shall play my bagpipe all the way through,' he said to his friends, 'and you can follow the sound of the piping above the ground.'
>
> There is a cave below the castle which leads to the tunnel, and the piper entered it one morning, playing a merry tune. His faithful dog followed him. The people heard the sound of the bagpipe as they walked down High Street, listening intently, but when they reached the spot which is called the 'Heart of Midlothian' the piping stopped abruptly, as if the pipes had been torn suddenly from the piper's hands. The piper was never seen again, but his dog, without a hair on its body, came running out of the cave below the castle.[21]

Sometimes tunnels really do exist, but even then the history ascribed to them may be somewhat debatable. A tunnel cut through the rock to access the Ness beach at Shaldon is even described as 'an original Smugglers tunnel' on the official *Visit South Devon* website,[22] although it does then go on to admit that while some people believe the tunnel was constructed for this purpose, others suggest that it was created by the owners of Ness House, which is not too far away, in order to provide them with a route to the beach. It is more probable, considering the location of an old lime kiln very close to the entrance of the tunnel on the land side, that it was used for ease of bringing ashore lime for burning, and for shipping other goods out from the area.

Another interesting location with genuine tunnels is the King's Arms public house in Winkleigh. This venue is said to be haunted too, boasting two alleged ghosts known by the local clientele as George and Cecilia. The tunnels in question run out from the bottom of a thirty-foot well, now capped in glass and under the floor of the dining room—the site of the old courtyard. One heads to the north-west and the other in the direction of the church. It would be easy to speculate on stories of illicit goods being moved from one building to the other, maybe by a corrupt rector or one complicit in nefarious deeds. But sadly, both tunnels stop abruptly after a distance of fifteen or twenty feet. A 2002 exploration by a local group of cave and mine enthusiasts concluded that these were probably test adits for mining,[23] so it might be reasonable to speculate that they were dug by enterprising residents trying to make money, unbeknown to the royal tax inspectors many years ago—especially as silver deposits have been found close to the site.

To return to the idea of the secret room, we find a number of these scattered through other properties in Devon. At least one other example seems to have also come with the discovery of a skeleton.

Powderham Castle is a fortified manor house with a history stretching back at least to the Domesday Book. It is the seat of the Courtenay family, having passed to them in the dowry of Margaret de Bohun in 1325 when she married Hugh de Courtenay, the son of the first Earl of Devon. It was here in the nineteenth century, while undertaking structural work to put in a new staircase, that the owners found a locked oak door on the ground floor. Behind the door was concealed a small room with no windows. In the room was a bedstead and on this was a skeleton.[24] Nothing in the room gave any further clue, either to who the remains belonged to or how they came to be locked in the room. Other sources suggest that this renovation work took place in the Guard Tower and that the remains were found after workmen discovered that one of the walls was hollow, rather than behind a door. In this version, the bones belonged to a mother and a baby and, despite being given a proper burial, their ghosts still haunt the property because they had been bricked up alive.

The Courtenay family themselves should be considered the source closest to actual events, as owners of the property, as far as any 'facts' can be ascertained. In a 2005 interview for *TES Magazine* Lord Devon admitted that his grandfather was responsible for creating some of the ghost stories recorded about Powderham Castle. This was something that he did to entertain his grandchildren. However, he does go on to discuss the skeleton: 'in the mid-19th century, during renovations, the skeleton of an unidentified woman and child were discovered hidden under the floorboards'.[25]

The castle has another reported ghost, which again takes a form found frequently in folkloric hauntings—the 'Grey Lady'. In this example, the ghost is said to appear when a member of the family is ill. Many accounts have a tendency to exaggerate this to say that the ghost appears when the head of the family is about to die (we will return to the concept of the family portent shortly). In a recent interview, however, the current Earl of Devonshire clarified that appearances were said to coincide with illness and furthermore, rather than being a bad omen, the ghost had actually been a comfort to his young son:

> there's one wonderful tale of the grey lady, who walks across the top of the big staircase whenever a member of the family is particularly ill—she's always introduced as the caring one, who's there to look out for us. Jack [the Earl's son] always used to come into our room to get into bed, and one night he didn't. And when we asked him why not, he said, 'The grey lady put me into bed last night and tucked me in.' He was never scared of ghosts again.[26]

Depending on the version of the remains that you accept, different possibilities might exist for the use of the sealed room. In the case of the mother and child, a story of a servant becoming pregnant at the hands of a titled householder would sit well and accounts for a number of other ghost stories. Or if the bones belonged to just one person, one possibility could be interment in the room due to a particularly contagious or unpleasant disease that needed to be kept secret.

In her 1982 book on ghosts in the county, Theo Brown mentions a story she was given by someone who used to live in Devon. It refers to Weare Giffard Hall, a Grade I-listed building rebuilt in the fifteenth century for the Fortescue family, and does not seem to appear in any other sources or literature:

> in the Hall there is said to be a room in the upper floor which has been bricked up. A young woman had a certain disease (not specified) and in accordance with custom the room with her in it was 'eliminated'. Recently a visitor took a dog to this floor, and the animal on coming to the door of the room appeared panic-stricken and ran away, looking back frequently as though there was someone there.[27]

There are two other ghosts which have been more widely recorded at Weare Giffard. One is just a vague reference to a disembodied voice that can be heard to shout 'get you gone' at visitors to the property. The other is reported to be the spirit of Sir Walter Giffard (d. 1243). Stories say that this ghost walks the path between the gatehouse of the hall and Weare Giffard Church, in search of his wife.[28] The reason for this search is evident upon visiting the church itself, where a stone effigy of Sir Walter can be seen in a niche in the wall. This carving used to lie alongside that of his wife Lady Alice de St George, but the two were separated in the nineteenth century when they were moved in order to clear space for the installation of a new organ. It may be many centuries since Sir Walter Giffard died but if his ghost does roam the grounds, it is spurred by a much more recent event.

An equally interesting-sounding property used to stand in the village of Branscombe, a place also known for its links with smuggling. The Clergy House was a Tudor building that was pulled down in the nineteenth century due to being structurally unsound. This place offers a whole raft of stories about hiding spots and underground chambers. Little seems to exist of any substance, but a vague and intriguing reference from a book published in 1901 on the subject of secret rooms in buildings suggests that locals used to say there was a whole other house concealed under the foundations of the Clergy House.[29]

One nearby Tudor property which does survive to the present day is Bovey House at Beer. This was the medieval seat of the Walrond family, although a substantial house had existed at this spot from a much earlier period with the Saxons having built on the site of a Roman fort here. Once again, there are a number of concealed spaces to be found. During roof repairs a small partitioned area was found, containing a chair. Outside, thirty feet down a well from which the house once obtained its main water supply, a further recess is large enough to hide two people.

Before converting to its current use as a hotel, Bovey House was owned by Lord Clinton, who was resident at the time of the roof repairs. It is said that when he was told about the partitioned room in the roof, he instructed that the chair be removed and the space sealed off—but when this was done, the house was plagued with various poltergeist activity, which stopped once the chair was put back.[30]

Poltergeists

While there is an absolute plethora of ghost stories across the county, poltergeist cases are somewhat scarcer. These are the events characterized not by sightings of a spirit, but by physical and audible manifestations such as objects being moved around, taps or bangs on the walls, floors of a property with no apparent source and other similar effects. These phenomena are what led to the term poltergeist being taken up into common usage—an apt description from the original German word, translating as 'noisy spirit'.

We should recognize that there are two distinct categories of ghost story, as I have described elsewhere.[31] The first of these is the alleged personal sighting or experience, generally a relatively recent event which can be backed up with names, possible other witnesses and more exact times and dates. The second type is what I prefer to term the 'folk ghost'—a more legendary type of story which probably derives from a retelling of previous events, an existing belief onto which other historical events are mapped, or something more mythical. The folk ghost is, in most cases, not generally examined as something which actually existed in the form described by the story. There is, naturally, an occasional overlap between the two, with the latter type being the one more usually worked on by the folklorist.

The fact that poltergeist cases are far rarer as a folkloric trope than 'ghosts that walk abroad' would account for the perceived low number of examples in Devon. There may, of course, be many events which might be seen as representative of a poltergeist case but which have never been recorded. For example, a friend who used to live in a cottage in the Devon village of Newton St Cyres told me, one day when I was visiting, of some unusual things he had witnessed in the building which had the hallmarks of physical poltergeist phenomena. But they were never told in such a way that they would be passed on, by request, and so will not enter into any kind of historical record. As a side note, I do wonder whether the cottage is the same one referred to in the story of a Black Dog apparition that was said to walk upright in the village, where a murder had previously taken place (see Chapter Eight). It is a tantalizing link, but there is no point of reference that allows the two to be connected. Of course, if I stated that they were linked, then that would enter into the record and after some repetition, would become established. That's how folklore works!

One of the most definitive, and at the time controversial, records of alleged poltergeist manifestation in Devon took place in Sampford Peverall in East Devon, for a prolonged period of time from 1810. In July of the previous year, the owner of the property—Mr Talley—rented it out to John Chave and his wife. Mrs Chave's brother, aged around twenty, also lived with the couple at this address. The family were well established in the area and John Chave ran a not unsubstantial shop in the village. The Chaves therefore also had staff living at the property: two maids, one elderly and one aged around thirteen, an apprentice and a cooper who worked from the shed there.

Seemingly supernatural activity began in the house in April 1810, in the form of loud banging both at night and during the day. This seemed to have some agency to it. When people in the house stamped their feet, for example, the unseen banging would respond in a like fashion only even louder. These noises continued for the next five weeks, after which activity escalated further and the two maids, along with two other women, experienced physical attacks from unseen hands which left them with various injuries.

The case started to receive much local attention, with many people visiting the property. Amongst these was the Reverend Charles Caleb Colton from the town of Tiverton, who published two pamphlets on the happenings. In the first he describes some of the violence:

> The blows given differ in violence: at times, they can be compared to nothing but a very strong man striking with the greatest force he is master of, with a closed fist on the bed. They leave a great soreness, and visible marks; I saw a swelling at least as big as a turkey's egg on the cheek of Anne Mills; she voluntarily made oath that she was alone in the bed when she received the blow that caused that protuberance, from some invisible hand. [32]

Colton goes on to describe some of the other physical manifestations which accompanied these attacks, including when the women were given an attempt at protection, and events were sometimes witnessed by others:

> I have seen a sword, when placed in the hands of some of these women, repeatedly and violently wrested out of them, after the space of a few minutes, and thrown with a very loud noise sometimes into the middle of the room, sometimes still more violently against the wall. This sword I have heard it take up, and with it beat the bed; by its shaking the handle in a particular manner, I have been aware of its taking it up. I have placed a large folio greek [sic] testament, weighing about 8 or 9 pounds, on the bed, it has been repeatedly thrown into the centre of the room ... I have often heard the curtains of the bed most violently agitated, accompanied with a loud and almost indescribable motion of the ring; on one occasion there was from the moon, a sufficient degree of light to see this motion, and at the same

time clearly to ascertain that the cause, whatever it might be, was something invisible.[33]

Colton's views held little sway with the editor of the *Taunton Courier* newspaper, a Mr Marriott. Colton had originally intended to publish his findings through letters to the newspaper, until he realized that they were too substantial. The newspaper did publish on the subject of the Sampford Peverall haunting, but with this leader:

> The Taunton Courier of Thursday contains the following pleasant account of this precious piece of imposition. The Editor, in his next paper, it is hoped, will be able to inform the public the precise amount of the 'very considerable sum of money' which the Reverend Mr. Colton has pledged himself to bestow on the poor of his parish, whenever the affair shall have been proved to have originated in human agency. This promise must not be forgotten—It may be useful for the Editor to know, that in various places on the coast, it has been no uncommon practice for smugglers to give out that certain houses have been haunted by evil spirits—and it really might be of some service, in the elucidation of the affair, if the Excise Officer was to take a peep into that same 'hollow depth' about which the owner knows nothing—Did not the Ghost amuse himself in terrifying the females who sleep in the house, one should not object so much to his taste in refusing to appear when male visitors were there; but if his gallantry be disputable, his prudence must be allowed to be unquestionable,—a quality not always discoverable in these grim visitors.[34]

There was much toing and froing between the vicar and the editor, which became increasingly acrimonious and led to Colton publishing a second pamphlet in September of 1810 to enlarge further on his discoveries.

Marriott's somewhat scathing commentary does include a couple of interesting points of note. He refers to a 'very considerable sum of money' which Colton had offered to pay if anyone could prove that the supernatural activity was happening thanks to human hands. This sum was never claimed, despite the disruption apparently continuing for three years or more: 'in defiance of a reward of two hundred and fifty pounds, to be given to any one who can produce such information as may lead to a discovery'.[35]

The second point of interest is Marriott's mention of the fact that ghost stories were often the invention of smugglers, who used them to keep people away from areas where they were moving or concealing goods, for example. There are certainly many instances around the coasts of Devon where stories more than likely arose for this reason. Marriott refers to a 'hollow depth about which the owner knows nothing'. In fact, a previous tenant of the property named Mr Bellamy had been involved in smuggling and had dug a deep hole under the floor of the sitting room in order to conceal goods. [36]

Poltergeist cases tend to centre around teenagers, in particular girls. Indeed, central to this case appears to be a maid of thirteen named Sally Case. But was she the focal point for an actual set of supernatural activities, or something more locally constructed? We can never know the answer for certain, but in his account of the case Reverend Sabine Baring-Gould states that he believes there was a rational cause:

> There can, I think, be little doubt that it was not Mr. Chave, but the servant-maids who managed the whole series of phenomena. These knockings could easily be transmitted through boards, and the curtains tossed about, and books and candlesticks flung across the room, by having horsehair attached to them. That is the true secret of the Poltergeist manifestations in England, France, and Germany. [37]

He does not state what the motivation for doing so might be, or any evidence for what he says is the 'true secret' of other poltergeist cases.

Ghosts as Portents

One final category of ghosts worthy of consideration is that of the portentous spirit whose appearance is said to presage death. The idea is a common one to be found all over the country. At Leeds Castle in Kent, for example, a spectral Black Dog was said to appear, foretelling ill fortune or worse for the occupants at that time. We will see in the next chapter how this idea was ascribed to the Baskerville family in Devon by Sir Arthur Conan Doyle, who drew on the tale for his Sherlock Holmes novel *The Hound of the Baskervilles*.

While the Baskerville fetch was an invented one, other families in Devon were said to play host to some form of ghost or other haunting manifestation which foretold doom. One is attributed to the Pine-Coffin family in the form of a ringing bell. Portledge Manor, near Bideford, was in the hands of the

Coffin family for over 900 years. The family is a long-established one in the county, and in 1671 Dorothy Coffin married Edward Pine. Two generations later, their grandson the Reverend John Pine sought an Act of Parliament to assume the name and family arms of the Coffins in order to ensure that the Coffin family remained linked with Portledge.

In 1868, while staying at Portledge Manor, the Crosse family were woken at midnight on an unspecified date by what sounded like a church bell ringing nearby. Thinking this odd, they questioned neighbours about it the next day. The neighbours informed them that the bell only sounded to foretell a death in the Pine-Coffin family. It is said that it came to light later that a Pine-Coffin family member had indeed died overseas in India at this time.

There is admittedly a lack of other obvious recorded examples of bells being heard just before deaths in the family. However, the linking of ringing bells with death is quite an obvious one, encapsulated in the famous quote from John Donne:

> Perchance he for whom this bell tolls may be so ill, as that he knows not it tolls for him; and perchance I may think myself so much better than I am, as that they who are about me, and see my state, may have caused it to toll for me, and I know not that … never send to know for whom the bell tolls; it tolls for thee.[38]

Another common type of ghost said to appear as an omen of death is the White Lady, and we find one at what is often called one of the most haunted places in Devon (though we have already seen how impossible it is to substantiate such a claim), Berry Pomeroy Castle. Now in a ruined state, the original outer castle defences were built in the fifteenth century by the Pomeroy family. Later, the Seymour family added a mansion inside these, which began on quite a small scale but was much extended with the aim of establishing a building to rival any other Elizabethan palace. Unfortunately, the Seymours' funds did not match their ambitions and by 1700 the castle had been abandoned and left to deteriorate.

Depending on which story you listen to, the ghost of the White Lady at Berry Pomeroy might be the daughter of a previous owner who, because she was wicked in life, has been condemned to walk the grounds eternally as penance. Or alternatively, the White Lady could be the ghost of Margaret Pomeroy, who was said to have been a victim of sibling rivalry. More beautiful than her sister Eleanor, and in love with a man whom Eleanor wanted, Margaret was supposed to have been locked in one of the towers and left to starve.

The problem with these and other ghost stories attached to Berry Pomeroy—such as the tale of the two Pomeroy brothers who rode their horses from the castle ramparts and jumped into the gorge rather than hand over the castle in defeat to attackers, and whose screams can still be heard carried on the wind—is that there is very little recorded history to substantiate any of them.

With its ruinous Gothic splendour and imposing grounds, Berry Pomeroy Castle was ripe for the kind of guidebook tourism we explored in Chapter Five. The White Lady, like so many other folkloric characters, came to prominence in the Victorian era. Physician Sir Walter Farquhar (1739–1819) was a well-respected man who treated high-profile clients of his time such as the Prince of Wales and Prime Minister William Pitt. In his memoirs, published some time after his death at the end of the nineteenth century, Farquhar is said to have written about how he had been sent for by the steward of the castle to visit his wife, who was very ill.[39] While waiting to attend to the patient, he says that he saw a woman dressed in white enter the room in some distress. She crossed the room, walked partway up a staircase, turned and looked at Sir Walter and then disappeared. The next day, Sir Walter mentioned the apparition to the steward who became very agitated, explaining that the White Lady was the family's omen of death. The steward's wife, who had been recovering, is said to have taken a turn for the worse within a few hours and subsequently died.

There were certainly local stories of ghosts relating to Berry Pomeroy Castle at the time of Sir Walter's visit, but nothing of huge public prominence. It is possible that Sir Walter retold one of these local stories in his memoirs, where it was seized upon and publicized, with the site being a draw for tourism. Certainly, the stories have become conflated and confused over time, with the aspects of the White Lady sometimes being ascribed to a 'Blue Lady', which is in fact a separate story. The whole pantheon of stories at Berry Pomeroy, with a lack of historical evidence to back them up, have taken on legendary status and are now—as in Victorian times—very much a guidebook collection.

There is another very well-known story of a Devon family spirit omen which has been similarly treated over the years, and will prove interesting to deconstruct to bring this chapter to a close. That is the story of the White Bird of the Oxenhams, a legend oft told but only with its bare bones and without all the historical detail (and sometimes conjecture) that can be ascribed to it.

In short, the story centres around the Oxenham family, who were from South Zeal, and spans many generations. A white, or sometimes white-breasted, bird was often reported as appearing to members of the family shortly before their death. Described sometimes as a dove, other times as a thrush or a ring ouzel, the earliest example is probably from 1618 when Grace Oxenham saw the bird above her sick bed. There is no documentation for this account, other than a mention in other sources,[40] and the first well-recorded version comes from 1635.

This version relates to Grace's grandson John Oxenham, a man who was said to exhibit the common Oxenham trait of piety. When John became ill, says Richard Cotton in his account for the Devonshire Association, 'there appeared the likeness of a bird with a white breast, hovering over him'.[41] The word 'likeness' here is probably the earliest suggestion that the Oxenham bird is not a living creature.

Anna Bray heard of the bird appearing to John Oxenham from a source published in 1638 (three years after John died) and recorded it in her *Traditions &c of Devon*. After another similar period of time, in 1641, a twenty-page tract on the incident was published anonymously. Two copies are known to remain of this, one being held in the British Museum and the other in the Bodleian Library. Possibly, it is this document which led to Daniel and Samuel Lysons recording the event in their *Magna Brittanica*, a topographical survey of several counties of the United Kingdom published between 1806 and 1822.[42] According to the 1641 tract, John Oxenham was in the company of two local men, Robert Woodley and Humphry King, who told the story of the appearance to the parish minister under questioning later.

Also in the company of others was the next member of the family to see the bird, Thomazine, who was the wife of James Oxenham, John's younger brother. Witnesses Elizabeth Frost and Joan Tooker were questioned by the minister. The tract takes pains to emphasize the good character of these women, no doubt adding credence to the story.

Further deaths occurred following a sighting of the bird, whereas other family members who were ill and did not see the bird appeared to recover. The fact that one of the deaths was of a baby raises an interesting question as to who was able to see the bird. With the baby unable to give the report, the suggestion is that the witnesses must have also been able to see it.

Although the Oxenham family were based mostly in the South Zeal area, probably having first settled at South Tawton where Historic England has a listing for 'Oxenham Manor' and the village pub is called 'The Oxenham Arms', the white bird appears to the branch of the family who settled at the nearby village of Zeal Monachorum, according to many reports. Zeal was originally written as Sale, Sele or Zele, from the Old English *sealh* or 'sallow-tree'. The later affixing of the Latin *Monachorum* ('of the monks') refers to the fact that the manor there was given to Buckfast Abbey in 1018 by King Cnut.[43]

Other versions of the legend place the family members concerned at South Zeal, meaning that there is a lot of historic confusion here to unpick. The registers of Zeal Monachorum do not contain any entries for the Oxenham family. South Tawton registers, which encompass South Zeal, do contain James and John, but do not mention Thomazine (or the alternative spelling Thomasine), or Rebecca—another family member to sight the bird before passing away.

Another mystery exists in that the 1641 tract states that surviving family members recorded the appearances of the bird on a monument placed in the church with the bishop's approval. This stone was said to have been produced by a tomb maker named Edward Marshall in Fleet Street, London. But is there any evidence for this either?

In 1645, a clerk to the Privy Council in London, James Howell, published the book *Familiar Letters* detailing his travels around Europe. In this book, Howell tells how he once visited the Fleet Street shop and while there, how he saw a large marble which he found curious. He wrote the inscription down from memory in his letter:

> Here lies John Oxenham a goodly young man, in whose Chamber, as he was struggling with the pangs of death, a Bird with a White-brest was seen fluttering about his Bed, and so vanish'd. Here lies also Mary Oxenham the sister of the said John, who died the next day, and the same Apparition was seen in the Room ...
>
> Here lies hard by James Oxenham, the son of the said John, who died a child in his cradle a little after, and such a Bird was seen fluttering about his head, a little before he expir'd, which vanish'd afterwards. Here lies Elizabeth Oxenham, the Mother of the said John, who died 16 years since, when such as Bird with a White-Brest was seen about her Bed before her death.[44]

The names and circumstances recorded by Howell vary from the details recorded in the original tract, and Howell does state that he is writing from memory. Further, he states that the marble listed names of local worthies who had witnessed the events. But we must note that the majority of Howells' letters were written while he was incarcerated in Fleet Prison in the 1640s. They are generally considered now to be a fictional invention—that is, written to record interesting events rather than as actual letters designed to be sent to the person to whom they were addressed. It is therefore probable that Howell never actually saw a monument, but rather said that he had in order to add embellishment to a story he might have read about, or heard second-hand.

Did the marble ever, in fact, exist at all? If it did, then it never reached the church for which it was supposedly intended. There is no local evidence of the witnesses whose names were inscribed upon it, and it was not unknown for the authors of ballads and chapbooks to invent witnesses to give their stories veracity.

In 1791, a collection of the writings of Sir William Pole was published, aiming to be a survey of the county of Devon at the time. In this publication, undertaken by Sir John Pole based on his father Sir William's original writing, the entry on the Oxenhams reads:

> Oxenham, the land of Wm Oxenham, the father of John, the grand-father of Will, father of another John, grandfather of James, whose tombstone respects a strange wonder of this family, that at their deaths were still seen a bird with a white brest, which fluttering for a while about their beds suddenly vanish away.[45]

However, it is likely that this entry, which is vastly extended from the original, was constructed by Sir John after his having read either the tract or Howell's letter, or both; the original as written by Sir William simply referred to 'Oxenham, the land of Wm Oxenham'.

After a period with no sightings, there are two more accounts from the eighteenth century which run along similar lines. After this, it would not be surprising if the move from more superstitious to more enlightened thinking brought an end to the reports, but this is not the case. An account published in an 1875 book called *Glimpses of the Supernatural*, by the Reverend Frederick George Lee, is interesting because at the time of writing the witness was still living and was able to confirm the details, backed up by a member of the Oxenham family with the authority to do so. While this is no guarantee of accuracy (or indeed truth) it does at least make the details more credible than in the early tales, where there is little or no evidence.

The story was told to the Reverend Lee by another man of the cloth, the Reverend Henry Nutcombe Oxenham, who was the head of the family at the time. The entry in the book was quite brief, but Richard W. Cotton recorded a

much more detailed account in the Reverend Henry's own words, in his article
in the *Report and Transactions of the Devonshire Association*:

> Shortly before the death of my late uncle, GN Oxenham ... who
> was then the head of the family, this occurred: His only surviving
> daughter, now Mrs Thomas Peter, but then unmarried, and living
> at home, and a friend of my aunt's, Miss Roberts, who happened
> to be staying in the house, but was no relation, and had never
> heard of the family tradition, were sitting in the dining-room,
> immediately under his bedroom, about a week before his death,
> which took place on 15th December, 1873, when their attention
> was roused by a shouting outside the window. On looking out they
> observed a white bird—which might have been a pigeon, but if
> so, was an unusually large one—perched on the thorn-tree outside
> the windows, and it remained there for several minutes, in spite of
> some workmen on the opposite side of the road throwing their hats
> at it, in the vain attempt to drive it away. Miss Roberts mentioned
> this to my aunt at the time, though not of course attaching any
> special significance to it, and my aunt (since deceased) repeated it
> to me soon after my uncle's death. Neither did my cousin, though
> aware of the family tradition, think of it at the time. Miss Roberts
> we have lost sight of for some years, and do not even know if she is
> still living; but Mrs Thomas Peter confirms in every particular the
> accuracy of the statement.[46]

Another interesting record exists concerning Richard Oxenham, who died
on 23 August 1844, at his home in Penzance. There does not seem to be any
appearance of the bird connected with him, but he was a bachelor and lived
alone. The only person with him when he passed away was his sister, Mrs
Oddy, so she would have been the only witness able to report anything had it
happened, and she did not. We do not know, however, whether she was necessarily aware of the legend, just because she was a member of the family. But
there is an interesting event relating to her death in 1861. A relative of the
family told that Mrs Oddy's daughter had spoken of the fact that on the night
before Mrs Oddy died, birds were flapping and hopping on the windowsill
outside her bedroom window. A curious coincidence.

The belief that birds hovering around a house, resting on a windowsill or
tapping on the glass is a portent of death was found in many places, including
Devon. The Oxenhams are not alone in having a particular bird. The Arundel

family of Wardour Castle in Wiltshire, for example, had a pair of owls who appeared on the battlements as a portent.

What actually took place in the case of the White Bird of the Oxenhams is open to debate. It seems plausible to suggest that the six early sightings were genuine and, in a period where beliefs in witchcraft and the like were at their height, were easily taken to be more supernatural than they actually were. This probably led to later stories, some fabrications, some misreporting and specu-lation, all adding to the canon until it became impossible to separate truth from fiction, and thus a legend was born.

CHAPTER EIGHT

The Black Dog

Sightings of ghostly Black Dogs are a worldwide phenomenon, but are most prevalent in the United Kingdom, where virtually every variation may be found. The earliest recorded report in this country is probably that cited in the *Anglo-Saxon Chronicle*, dated from 1127,[1] although this refers more specifically to the concept of the Wild Hunt, as we shall see shortly. Despite this timeframe of almost a thousand years, most people's knowledge of the motif probably extends no further than arguably the best-loved of the Sherlock Holmes novels, the Devon-based *Hound of the Baskervilles*. In this chapter, we will use the novel as a springboard to explore the folklore that informed its central premise.

> I sprang to my feet, my inert hand grasping my pistol, my mind paralysed by the dreadful shape which had sprung out upon us from the shadows of the fog. A hound it was, an enormous coal-black hound, but not such a hound as mortal eyes have ever seen. Fire burst from its open mouth, its eyes glowed with a smouldering glare, its muzzles and hackles and dewlap were outlined in flickering flame. Never in the delirious dream of a disordered brain could anything more savage, more appalling, more hellish be

conceived than that dark form and savage face which broke upon us out of the wall of fog.[2]

These words formed the cliffhanger to the penultimate part of the story when it was first serialized at the turn of the twentieth century. There can be no doubt that in writing the novel, Doyle drew on many aspects of folklore surrounding the Black Dog, and certainly much of this came from the county of Devon.

Of course, *The Hound of the Baskervilles* is a work of fiction and we must allow for artistic licence, both from the characters within the tale and from Conan Doyle outside it. Holmes comments many times that Watson uses just this mechanism in his own recording of their cases, and we can see that in play in the quote above. He describes fire coming from the dog's mouth, and yet when the creature is shot and shown to be a flesh and blood animal, there is no mention of this aspect—though an explanation is given for the 'flickering flame' in the form of phosphorous paint.

Sir Arthur Conan Doyle takes similar liberties with the folklore. The Baskerville creature is atypical in chasing the head of the house to his death— no other portent of death does this, most just appearing like the White Bird of the Oxenhams examined in the previous chapter.

The story's use of phosphorous directly relates to the Victorian and Edwardian practice of hoaxing ghosts, where people would dress up in often elaborate costumes to hide on the streets at night and terrify unsuspecting passers-by. This 'hobby' undoubtedly led to the escalation of the figure of Springheeled Jack in British folklore. Costumes would often include parts coated in phosphorous paint, and the technique was often also used in stage plays at the time for the rendering of characters such as the ghost of Hamlet's father.

We know, and have explored elsewhere in this book, that there was a two-way interaction between folkloric legends and smuggling. Some of our folklore sprang from stories invented by smugglers to keep people away from the places in which they were operating, but at the same time those smugglers also drew on pre-existing folklore when coming up with stories. The situation was very much 'chicken and egg', and it can be difficult to separate the two. It is more than likely that smugglers used (and invented) stories of portentous Black Dogs in coastal areas, and this led to the more demonic Shuck or Barguest type of dog that is dominant around the East Anglia coast and on the Fens. Smugglers also employed glowing paint, as shown in one Devon example at Kingskerswell. Here they used a hearse, which had been painted with luminous paint, as a vehicle to move contraband inland from the coast. Drawing on stories of phantom coaches, they padded the horse's feet so they could not be heard, as well as painting them too. Leaving the head unpainted would allow the horse to look headless from a distance.[3]

In his book *The Life of Sir Arthur Conan Doyle*, John Dickson Carr tells that in March of 1901 Doyle was in poor health and went to stay for four days at a hotel in Cromer, being accompanied on the trip by his friend, the journalist Bertram Fletcher Robinson.[4] As the weekend weather was inclement, they sat in the sitting room at the hotel and Fletcher Robinson told Doyle a number of stories from Dartmoor, as his family lived just on the fringes of the moor at Ipplepen. Doyle's imagination was fired by one particular legend of a spectral hound and thus it was not long afterwards, on 2 April, that Doyle travelled down to stay at Princetown and explore the moor for himself. Much of the surrounding area would end up represented in the novel. Dartmoor Prison obviously features largely, and Grimpen Mire in the story was to stand in for the actual location of Fox Tor.

While in the South West, Doyle inevitably went to stay with the Robinsons for a time. He was collected from the station by the Robinsons' coachman, a man named Harry Baskerville, whose family were said to have owned two local manors in their more affluent past. He would also drive Doyle around the moor so that he could visit some of the sites he had been previously told about. While we know some of the places Doyle went to, what has never been certain is the particular Black Dog story which was told to him on that afternoon in Cromer.

There are a number of Black Dog stories which pepper the Dartmoor area, but many of them are too sparse in detail to have provided the inspiration on their own. There are some though which are more significant, and any one (or more) of them could be candidates.

One is the story of Lady Mary Howard of Tavistock. Living at Fitzford House in the town in the seventeenth century, the daughter of Sir John Fitz who was much disliked, she is said (without basis) to have murdered her four husbands. Her penitential ghost was rumoured to have to make a nightly trip from her family home to Okehampton Castle, where it had to pick a blade of grass from the castle mound before returning home. In some versions of the story she does this in the form of a hound, while in others she rides in a phantom carriage of bones led by a black hound with one eye in the middle of its forehead.

Anna Bray notes in her letters to Robert Southey that there had been a common saying amongst the upper classes in Tavistock in years past, when attending a party and deciding not to stay too long: 'Come, it is growing late, let us begone, or we shall meet Lady Howard as she starts from Fitz-ford.'[5]

At Bridestowe, there was a hollow oak tree which the ghost would pass on its nightly journey. It bore the name of 'Lady Howard's Oak', although Arthur H. Norway noted in 1911 that it had been lost in winter floods two years earlier.[6] It was said to be bad luck to accept a lift from Lady Howard if she stopped her coach and offered one.

Another story which might have been related to Doyle is that of the Demon of Spreyton, a poltergeist-type case which afflicted the Furze family in 1682. However, the image of the Black Dog forms a very minor part of this tale, being one of a number of forms which the shapeshifting spirit was said to take.

The two main sources of inspiration from the Dartmoor area would appear to be the ghostly hunting dogs known in the area as Wisht Hounds or Yeth Hounds (the regional naming of what is essentially the Wild Hunt motif), and the story of the notorious Squire Richard Cabell of Buckfastleigh. These two stories are also linked.

The Wild Hunt, sometimes known by the Raging Host or other similar titles, is a piece of folk mythology well known across much of Europe, although its form varies slightly in each area. In spite of these regional variations the fundamental aspects of the myth remain the same: a group of phantom huntsmen, on horses and accompanied by hounds, rampaging across the land or the sky in search of their quarry. The leader of the pack tends to vary based upon local tradition, or by local character—so for example, King Arthur was installed as one leader in the Middle Ages, and in Devon we find that Sir Francis Drake is often ascribed to the role.

Later, Christian influences were applied to the mythology, as with many older traditions, and so we find the Devil as Hunt leader, seeking out the souls of evil sinners or unbaptized children. Ghostly dogs are often seen as diabolic (in some countries such as Scandinavia, nearly always so) and often the Devil appears in this form. In fact, the earliest recorded reference in the United Kingdom links the symbolism of the Black Dog with that of the Wild Hunt. This can be found in the Peterborough copy of the *Anglo-Saxon Chronicle* from 1154. There are many translations of the phrase in question, one being: 'several persons saw and heard many huntsmen hunting. The hunters were swarthy, and huge, and ugly; and their hounds were all swarthy, and broad-eyed, and ugly. And they rode on swarthy horses, and swarthy bucks.'[7] The word 'swarthy' in this translation means 'black'.

On Dartmoor, the ancient Wistman's Wood is traditionally said to be a common hunting ground for the Wisht Hounds. Like the branches of the trees themselves, unfortunately, the folklore here is somewhat tangled. There is no obvious etymology for the name Wistman's Wood, but Jeremy Harte makes the valid point that as woods were generally named after their owners, something like 'the wood of a man called Westman' is probable.[8] As we saw in our examination of the Devil in Chapter Five, however, leaps of faith to ascribe more significance to a mythic past were very common; Anna Bray and her husband preferred the idea that it was the Wood of the Wise Men and hence carried a Druidic origin. For instance: '[the wild hunt] was originally the connection of the hunter with the spirit of the beast being hunted, a theme that goes back to Palaeolithic shamanistic times, but which became christianised into the devil hunting for human souls.'[9]

This is exacerbated by the supposition that the Saxons thought of this place as the home of Odin and his Wild Hunt.

Stories told that the hunt would set off from the wood at midnight, with the Devil riding a headless black horse, and chase victims towards the Dewerstone. We have already explored the troubling origins of this location in the chapter on the Devil himself.

Arguably the piece of local Black Dog legend which would most likely have added to Doyle's plotting of *The Hound of the Baskervilles* is that of Squire Richard Cabell—the link to the Wild Hunt being that because of his wicked nature, they came for his soul at the end of his life. The dedication in the novel has been changed many times over the years, but in the original one to Fletcher Robinson, Doyle states that he took his inspiration from the story that Robinson told him.[10]

It is important to address the story of Richard Cabell from a perspective of historical accuracy versus folklore. It is a rare case where the latter has taken hold so strongly that the former is at risk of being lost altogether. The coffee table anthologies of Devon ghosts and legends, written for exactly the same market in modern times as in the Victorian era—tourists—will constantly retell the story of the 'evil Cabell' and his unusual grave.

The grave in question is one of the few surviving 'penthouse' tombs in the country. Located outside the south door of Buckfastleigh Church, which was almost completely destroyed by fire in an act of vandalism in 1992, Cabell's remains lie in an altar tomb. A heavy stone was said to have been placed on his head. Over this was built a small structure with a pointed roof; a wide iron grille was placed in the wall facing the church and on the opposite side a strong wooden door with a keyhole. Folklore tells us that all this was done in order to keep the wicked squire in place and stop him rising from the grave to continue to terrorize the town. Local children used to say that if you walked around the tomb a number of times (either three, seven or thirteen, depending on the source) and then put your finger into the keyhole of the door, either Squire Cabell or the Devil would bite the end of it.

Richard Cabell lived at nearby Brook Manor, which still stands to this day and is privately owned. In one of the two different versions of the legend that tells of his wickedness, related by the Reverend Sabine Baring-Gould, Cabell was chased across Dartmoor by Black Dogs, being hunted to death for his soul.[11] The alternative story says that as he lay in his deathbed at the manor, the black Wisht Hounds approached the window, howling.

Interestingly, neither of these appears to be the legend related to Cabell, which was then related to Doyle. Susan Cabell Djabri, a descendant of the squire, records that

> [a]ccording to Robinson, Richard Cabell of Brook Manor, believing his wife to have been unfaithful to him, drove her out of the house and across the moor. When he caught up with her, he stabbed her to death with his hunting knife, but her faithful hound turned on him and tore out his throat before they both fell dead. The ghostly hound was still supposed to prowl Dartmoor, reappearing to each successive generation.[12]

There are certainly elements in all of this mirrored in the story of Hugo de Baskerville in Doyle's novel. It is likely that the author also drew upon the Black Dog legends of Norfolk when staying in Cromer, where Fletcher Robinson first told his stories, as in that area the Shuck or Barguest type of spectral dog most definitely leans more heavily towards the hell-hound apparently witnessed by Holmes and Watson before its more earthly nature is discovered.

With regards to the actual story of Richard Cabell, some digging is necessary in order to establish where his evil reputation came from. There were at least three men named Richard Cabell who were resident at Brook Manor in the period in question. The man who is probably the source of the legends was baptized in 1622 and married Elizabeth Fowell, daughter of the MP for Ashburton, in 1655. A year after their marriage he undertook significant building work at Brook Manor, demonstrating their place and position among the landowners of the area. The hearth tax lists for 1674, after his death, show that his widow was living in the largest house in the area, with a total of twenty-two hearths.[13]

It is possible that this wealth was partly the reason for locals feeling animosity towards the family, particularly as they were not established in the area from past generations and had taken over various properties as landlords. There are rumours that he kept mistresses at a nearby house, Hawson Court, although there is no documentary evidence for this. There is, however, evidence of religious persecution associated with this Richard Cabell, against Nonconformist worshippers, and in particular one John Syms who was removed from the parish in 1660 when the previous vicar, the well-known poet Robert Herrick, returned.[14]

Herrick had been vicar of Dean Combe, near Buckfastleigh, from 1629 until 1647 when, as the Civil War was on the verge of beginning, he was forced back to his family home in London for refusing to support the Covenant for Reformation. Syms was to take his place until the restoration of King Charles II in 1660, when Herrick's support for the monarch was rewarded with his re-establishing as vicar. He remained in the position until his death seventeen years later.

A story of a Black Dog haunting can be found attached to this parish. This concerns the ghost of a weaver named Thomas Knowles who lived in a cottage at Dean Combe. He was well known in the area for his expert handiwork, and so it was that upon his death his spirit continued to sit at the loom in the upstairs room of the cottage every day, the rattling of his weaving clearly audible to the rest of the family on the floor below.

Knowles's son Phillip became increasingly annoyed at this situation, presumably because he should have inherited his father's business and the old man had other ideas! Phillip went to fetch the local vicar of the parish, who duly came to the cottage and summoned the spirit of the weaver downstairs. As the ghost of Thomas Knowles descended the stairs, the vicar threw a handful of earth which he had brought from his churchyard into the weaver's face. At this, the human form vanished and was replaced with the spirit of a large black hound. This animal was led by the vicar to a nearby pool in the woods, where he furnished it with a nutshell and commanded it to empty the pool and not return to the cottage until the task was finished.

There is no specific date given for this tale, but it is generally said to be within the seventeenth century. For a large part of this period, Robert Herrick was in position at Dean Prior, so perhaps he is the very vicar who was sent for to deal with the unquiet weaver.

We can see in this story a number of common folkloric elements—the endless task of a ghost that cannot rest, or as a penance for ill deeds, for instance, which was also ascribed to Lady Howard above. Similarly, the ghost of William de Tracy, one of the murderers of Thomas Becket, is said to haunt the sands at Woolacombe in North Devon where he is condemned to weave

ropes out of sand. Every time he is close to finishing, a black dog carrying a ball of fire in its mouth appears and burns through the rope, so he must begin again.

The spirit of Black Vaughan was enclosed in a snuff box and committed to a pool. Moreover, the spirit of an old mayor of Okehampton was famously put to work emptying a pool with a sieve. Elsewhere, another claim on the origin of the Baskerville hound is made in the county of Herefordshire. Dr Maurice Campbell, a noted expert in heart disease and the surgery to treat it, was also an active member of the Sherlock Holmes Club and wrote a paper proposing that the Black Dog of Hergest was a strong influence on the novel's central story.[15]

Hergest Court was owned by a family named Vaughan, who were related by marriage to the family on the adjoining estate—the Baskervilles. Although the Baskerville name is present, there is little else in the story of the Hergest creature which has commonality with that other version. The dog is associated with Sir Thomas Vaughan, killed at the Battle of Banbury in 1469, and who was known locally as 'Black' Vaughan because, as with the legend of Richard Cabell, he was much disliked for his attitude and behaviour. According to some versions of his legend he had been accompanied in life by a demon dog, and it would be sighted before a death in the Vaughan family. His troublesome ghost was reduced in size by the local clergy in an act of 'reading down' until it could be enclosed in a snuff box, which was buried in the bottom of Hergest Pool with a large stone on top.

Pools and bodies of water are another common element of many stories. The spirit of an old mayor of Okehampton was famously put to work emptying a pool with a sieve. This is the legend of Benjamin Gayer, who was elected mayor of the town five times in the seventeenth century. Folklore collector Ruth St Leger-Gordon suggests that he was mapped onto the legend in much the same way as Lady Howard was misrepresented and inserted into hers.[16] Gayer was accused of stealing sheep from Dartmoor, the very place where he held rights to keep both cattle and sheep himself. It was for this crime that the locals gave him the punishment of emptying Cranmere Pool on the moor, but the legend tells that he used the skin of one of the sheep to line the sieve and hence completed what should have been an impossible task in three hours. So annoyed were the townsfolk that they hanged the mayor at the location that later became known as Hangingstone Hill, and then committed his spirit to weave ropes from the sand in the bottom of the pool. Again, more repetition of the same folkloric themes.

In these sorts of folk tales the central character is often one who was disliked or resented by the surrounding community. This might be because they enjoyed high status or wealth. Or it might have been because they exhibited special skills or intellect. This was the case with Knowles the Weaver, for example.

Returning to the story of Richard Cabell, we have already seen that he possessed wealth and power in the area. It is also interesting to note that he had ownership of the town's mills, which caused much unrest. There are traditionally supernatural associations with the mill itself because of the seemingly magical nature of the machinery and the process by which it worked, and this extended to the miller as well. As I have explored elsewhere, the early image of the miller in folklore is always as a crook or a villain.[17] Here these same views undoubtedly add to the somewhat undeserved reputation of Richard Cabell.

It is clear that there is much fabrication surrounding the Cabell story. Nothing appears in print about it before the nineteenth century. This might suggest that it was another invention of the tourism-driven folklore writers. But also, there was a known problem with body snatching at this time from the graveyard at Buckfastleigh, and so the legend may have been created in a similar way to the ghost stories invented by smugglers—in this case to keep the resurrectionists from the area. The version of the Cabell legend told to Sir Arthur Conan Doyle by Bertram Fletcher Robinson must also have been fabricated. The squire could not have murdered his wife as described because, as we have seen from the fact that she was assessed for the hearth tax, she survived him by a period of fourteen years.

There is an interesting modern postscript to the Cabell history which also features ghostly Black Dogs, but in a different way. This was related in 1981 by a Mrs M. Moore who was living at Hawson Court, the property where oral tradition related that Richard Cabell kept his mistresses. Mrs Moore was not especially well versed with any of the legends; she had not read *Hound of the Baskervilles* and did not know that Cabell was supposed to have pursued village women with his hunting dogs, or been chased down at his death by demonic ones. But her strange experience in the house was recorded in the *Report and Transactions of the Devonshire Association* a couple of years later.

> A few months ago, last summer (1981), I awoke in the middle of the night and saw three black dogs passing from left to right in the air, about two feet from the ceiling, at the far end of my bedroom. They were totally black, medium-sized hunting dogs with pointed noses. They were not quite in line and overlapped one another— but appeared identical. I saw all three heads, but the rest of the middle one was indistinct. I can see them quite clearly in my memory—but on the night I am describing I felt they were present in the room. I have not felt their presence since.
>
> I was aware of them only from the centre of the room. Then I ceased to see them, I saw them stationary as a silhouette in the centre of the far window (parallel with it) for what seemed several seconds. I felt them to be ominous, not protective, unfortunately, and was worried by the memory of them the following morning. I can offer no reason, but I dread seeing them again![18]

In 2012, the BBC modern-day adaption of the Holmes stories, *Sherlock*, took on the Baskerville story. The episode, written by co-creator Mark Gatiss and titled 'The Hounds of Baskerville', kept many of the elements of the original but revealed the hound to be an image brought on by the use of mind-altering drugs, with 'Baskerville' being a military research base. Some sequences were shot at the popular Dartmoor site of Hound Tor which, as the name suggests, has canine connections of its own—although it is far less likely to have been as much an inspiration for the original novel the popular or tourist press would have you believe.

A large granite tor in the parish of Manaton, Hound Tor was recorded in the Domesday Book in 1086 as 'Hundatora'. In 1240, when King Henry III instructed the Sheriff of Devon to organize a perambulation of the Royal Forest of Dartmoor to record its bounds, the location was marked down as 'Hundetorre'. Many people believe 'Hunde' to mean 'Hound', but no evidence exists as to why this might be the case. William Crossing, the well-known writer on Dartmoor and its stories, notes that the term could equally be derived from another word whose significance has since been lost. There are many other instances where this is the case and only the sound of the word remains in place today.[19]

Dartmoor legend tells that the rocks of Hound Tor are the pack of dogs who belonged to the hunter Bowerman, turned to stone along with their master (the nearby Bowerman's Nose outcrop) after having run through the centre of a coven of witches at work on the moor. Many people, in writing about Hound Tor, have made claims of ghostly dogs in the vicinity, but without anything substantive to back them up. In fact, there are very few Black Dog stories relating to this area.

In 1965, a resident of the village of Hemyock in the Blackdown Hills, close to the Devon/Somerset border, recorded an experience her daughter had at Hound Tor for Somerset folklore collector Ruth L. Tongue:

> My daughter used to ride (everywhere). She went everywhere on the Moor. One evening she came back and said: 'I was up by the Tor and suddenly a huge black dog came out of the rocks. The pony didn't like it, but I thought he was lost, so I called him, and he followed all the way home, about ten yards off. Just as I got off at our yard he disappeared. I was looking right at him. He was huge.'[20]

There are many stories of Black Dogs accompanying pedestrians. The default position of many people when considering the image of the Black Dog is that it is evil, or an omen of some kind. This is due to the propensity of journalists and others in the media to always draw associations with the 'hound of hell' trope when referencing the subject, because it is naturally more sensational and exciting— and likely to sell newspapers! In fact, analysing my own archives of over a thousand examples from across the country, it is clear that the balance falls in favour of neutral or protective animals over portentous ones, when the subject is taken as a whole. Often, animals walking alongside the witness seem to have friendly or protective intent, or are merely offering the natural companionship of a living creature.

Such a story was told on Dartmoor in the days when the disused mines which now scatter the moor were being worked. A man from the village of South Zeal named Otto Osbourne was a miner at Vitifer on the high moor, not far from Postbridge. Although the distance between the two is only a little over half an hour by modern transport, it would have taken much longer to travel the thirteen and a half miles in the years when the mine was active. (The story is undated but Vitifer closed in 1925, well before motorized travel was commonplace in the area.) For this reason, Osbourne would stay in a makeshift shack at the mine during the week but travel home across the moor on a Saturday evening, returning early on the Monday morning. Lighting his way with his lamp, the miner would often feel that he was being accompanied by a black dog on the journey. Sometimes it would be ahead, and sometimes follow on behind, but in either case it would disappear completely at the end of the journey. Osbourne was apparently not the only miner to report such a phenomenon.[21]

Vitifer is not far from the Warren House Inn, which at 434 metres above sea level is the highest public house in the South of England. Maybe the dog that Otto Osbourne believed accompanied him across the moor is the same one reported to Theo Brown in a private letter dated July 1960, and held in her archives:

> about 35 years ago [making the date of this event around 1925, the year that Vitifer closed] my father was passing the Warren House Inn about 12.30am on his pony when all of a sudden he seen [sic] this big black curly dog, running alongside him. It was black and it stood about 3 feet tall. He tried to touch it but could not just get near it. It followed him about 300 yards and then it vanished.

It is certainly curious that these two stories coexist so closely, as there are no other sightings recorded in the area to speak of. There are no spectral hounds associated with the Warren House, although it does have plenty of other folkloric associations, such as the (debatable) claim that the fire in the grate has burned continuously since 1845, or even longer if one can believe that the smouldering peat was carried across from the grate in the original pub on the opposite side of the road. The sign on the Warren House also depicts the famous motif of three hares chasing each other in a circle, with each hare sharing an ear with the next so that only three ears are visible. This is both a reference to the many rabbit warrens that used to exist in this area and which were a major source of food for the miners and others, and also to the assay mark of the Vitifer tin mine.[22]

Many still refer to this symbol as the 'Tinner's Rabbits', believing that it was an emblem used and associated with the Dartmoor tin mining community. This is not the case, as the symbol has much older roots, with the earliest known example probably being the one painted on the ceiling of the Magao caves near the town of Dunhuang in China.[23] Its actual meaning is not known for certain, but suggestions that it is symbolic of the cycle of life and rebirth seem sensible considering that the hare is representative of resurrection in Chinese mythology.

The misattribution of the symbol to Dartmoor tinners was probably brought to prominence by Lady Sylvia Sayer, a long-time chairperson of the Dartmoor Preservation Association and tireless campaigner for conservation and environment issues on the moor. Sayer had strong connections with the history of Dartmoor, being the granddaughter of Robert Burnard who had undertaken the first serious excavations of ancient monuments such as Grimspound alongside the Reverend Sabine Baring-Gould. In 1987 she wrote:

> The Fifteenth century was a particularly prosperous time for Dartmoor tinners, and by way of a thank-offering they enlarged and rebuilt some of the moorland churches. Widecombe church is a fine example, and there you can see the tinners' emblem carved on a roof-boss—three rabbits sharing ears.[24]

It may be that Lady Sayer, when she says 'tinners' emblem', actually means a tin assay mark, and simply mistook the hares for rabbits. But this is probably the point at which the link was first made and, if she was simply misunderstood due to her phrasing, then the idea took hold locally.

The Dartmoor correspondent who tried to touch the dog he saw is not alone in his efforts. There are other stories in which the person involved is unable to feel the physical presence of the animal that appears to be right in front of them. In 1972, Cecil Williamson, recognized as one of the founders of modern British witchcraft as well as being responsible for amassing much of the collection housed by the Museum of Witchcraft and Magic in Boscastle, Cornwall, visited the churchyard at Buckfastleigh where Richard Cabell's tomb is to be found. While there, Williamson says that he saw a dog which he described as being quite substantial-looking, but which when he tried to touch it, proved not to be. His hand passed straight through the animal's body.[25]

Returning to the idea of the dog acting in a protective manner, as was believed to be the case by the miner Otto Osbourne as he travelled to and from Vitifer, an interesting story was recorded in personal correspondence to Theo Brown when she was actively collecting this folklore at the height of her work in the twentieth century. The account was provided to her by an eminent academic, Professor John F.D. Shrewsbury, the author of *A History of Bubonic Plague in the British Isles* and Professor of Bacteriology at the University of Birmingham from 1937 until 1963. He wrote to Theo the year after leaving academia, with a family story.

> My mother was not free from country superstitions although she was a devoutly God-fearing woman, with a firm faith in her God and a strong belief in the efficacy of prayer ... One moonlight summer night, as a girl of sixteen or seventeen, she found herself in circumstances which necessitated a walk—if I remember rightly—from Sampford Courtenay to Okehampton. At one particular stage of the walk—which I think passed through a belt of woodland—she became very frightened for some reason that I cannot now remember, and in her fear prayed that she might have some companion to protect her. Very soon a large black dog appeared from the wood and paced quietly by her side until she was entering the outskirts of Okehampton.[26]

This account, we must assume, had been relayed at some point by the mother to her son, who was a man used to dealing with facts and data in his professional career. Nothing in the account suggests that the son has manipulated it to make it fit his naturally rational mind. What makes this particularly interesting, therefore, is that it is an experience which is far from unique. There are examples from all over the country where the dog appears in a similar way, acting as a protector to a woman out on her own, or a weak man at risk of being robbed or similar.

Lincolnshire-based folklore collector Ethel Rudkin collected many Black Dog stories from her area and published a number of them in an article for the

Folklore Society journal *Folklore* in 1938. She cites an example of the trope in her writing:

> Years ago, when Crosby and Scunthorpe were both villages, Mrs. D.'s mother had gone from old Crosby to do some shopping at Scunthorpe. She was returning, and noticed that a very large dog was walking behind her; this was a strange dog to her, one she had never seen before. Presently she passed some Irish labourers, and she heard them say what they would do to the lone woman if 'that (something) dog hadn't been with her.' She arrived home safely and called to her husband to come and see this fine animal, but they couldn't find it anywhere—it had completely vanished.[27]

A similar story is found at Stoney Middleton in Derbyshire, recorded in notes by folklorist Jeremy Harte as being reported in 1973, where a Methodist minister is protected from unsavoury characters by a dog who walks with him and acts as a guardian.[28] Other versions repeat around the country.

Of course, it is far from uncommon in folklore to see similar stories embedded in different areas. As we saw in Chapter Six, the tale of the Tavistock midwife who abuses the fairy ointment is not confined to Devon but is a common one from much further afield. The difference in that case is that the story is more obviously a folk tale—literally a fairy story, in fact. In the case of the mother of Professor Shrewsbury and many others, the stories have been told or noted down within living memory. Does this make them genuine experiences that were recorded as seen? Or is something else at play, with an experience constructed by an unconscious drawing upon much older folklore? These are questions to which there is no definite answer, but which demonstrate the power of folklore and its influence on everyone's lives, whether they realize it or not.

CHAPTER NINE

Witchcraft

If you carry out a simple internet search for the subject 'Witchcraft in Devon', then the first two pages of results at the very least will be dominated by one topic: the Bideford Witches.[1] These three women, Temperance Lloyd, Susannah Edwards and Mary Trembles, were among the last to be tried and executed for the alleged crime of witchcraft in the United Kingdom, having been hanged in 1682. A memorial plaque to the three is now present at the ruins of Exeter Castle in Northernhay Gardens. In 2014, a bid was made by hundreds of modern practitioners of witchcraft to have a retrospective pardon issued to the women,[2] who were undoubtedly victims of circumstance in a period of history where being poor and destitute was the default position for many. Similar cases have been made for others executed for the same crime across the country and beyond.

Lloyd, Edwards and Trembles were undoubtedly unremarkable characters and we would not comment upon them today at all if it were not for the sad fact of the timing of their deaths. Without that, they would be lost to history as so many others are. Miles of print have been dedicated over the years to their case, while so much more remains largely unexplored. In this chapter, we look to the more obscure records to try and establish the common themes found amongst stories of witchcraft in Devon.

The topic of witchcraft probably suffers from the application of stereotypes more than any other examined, in terms of its folklore. Some of these stereotypes have their roots in old practices, such as the idea of the witch riding a broomstick. While the first recorded image of this is found in a marginal illustration in the 1451 edition of *Le champion des dames*,[3] the use of the besom probably comes from a mix of earlier land-based fertility rituals. Other stereotypes are much more modern. The idea of the witch having green skin is known of no earlier than 1939, when the colour was employed in Margaret Hamilton's make-up design for the Wicked Witch of the West.[4] At the time of the witch trials, green was associated with the fairy realm, but not with the accused witches themselves. Other popular images of the 'hag' having a hook nose and missing teeth also come from cinematic representation, first appearing two years before *The Wizard of Oz* in the 1937 Disney animated feature *Snow White and the Seven Dwarfs*.[5] Medieval woodcuts, covers of tracts and chapbooks, and contemporary book illustrations invariably show a representation of a normal-looking, if sometimes dishevelled woman.

Some of these stereotypes make an appearance outside the sphere of fictional representation. In 1984, a planning application was lodged in the St Thomas area of Exeter for the construction of two new houses. One of the recorded objections from local residents came from a lady who described herself as a 'white witch'. Her own house had a large roof window which she had added, she said, to enable her to fly out on her broomstick, and the new houses would block her flight path. The objector also stated that she had learned her skills from her mother, and that she was training her daughter to continue the art.[6]

The concept of 'white' and 'black' witches is an outdated one today, but was in common use across Devon to describe the tasks that those practising witchcraft undertook. Ruth St Leger-Gordon summarized them in her work on Dartmoor witchcraft, but the descriptions hold true for the whole county:

> (1) The reputed ability to ill-wish, or curse, or over-look with the evil-eye which is Black Witchcraft.
>
> (2) A genuine and natural gift of healing, 'blessing' or 'charming' away certain minor ailments, an ability which is the wholly beneficent 'White Witchcraft'.[7]

The phraseology of this quote is notable. The use of witchcraft to do harm is 'reputed', whereas the healing abilities of those who do good with the practice is 'genuine'. This bias played out in actual events. Farmers and those in need of medical help would rely on and believed in the efficacy of the work done by charmers and those using folk medicine, whereas trials against alleged witches for maleficium, cursing and the like were often dismissed by judges or laughed out of court. Even the judge in the trial of the Bideford Witches is reported by some to have wanted to move to acquittal, but did not purely because of the strength of public feeling against them.

Overlooking

The idea of using magic to bewitch someone or something, to cause ill fortune or poor health, was identified in Devon, according to Lady Rosalind Northcote amongst others, as 'overlooking'.[8] She uses by way of example the story of two neighbours close to where she lived who had a long-standing argument, telling how sometimes when they were both outside, one of the women looked at the other in 'such a way' that her knees trembled and she had to go indoors and 'have a cry'. Northcote notes that for days after this happened, the overlooked neighbour was in discomfort and bent double.[9]

One could argue in this case that one of the women must have been particularly weak and susceptible to the idea of being overlooked and the other, purely by the way that she stared at her, was able to play on this fear and cause extreme upset, with the resultant physical condition being psychosomatic and brought on through distress. The case of the Luffincott Rectory haunting described in Chapter Seven seemed to centre on just this idea of distress through timidity.

Another case from the nineteenth century might either show how older superstitious beliefs began to be challenged as the more enlightened twentieth century approached, or could equally serve to demonstrate how strong the default superstitious position was for some.

The case in question comes from the Probate Courts in Barnstaple in 1886, where the will of a retired farmer was challenged on the grounds that he was of unsound mind when he made it. The farmer had always enjoyed a good relationship with his children but this had deteriorated in the years leading up to his death. In 1883, when he developed eczema on his hand, the farmer came to believe that overlooking by some of his children was responsible. The man sought assistance from the White Witch of Exeter for his condition. The witch confirmed that the man had been overlooked by two people. One, he said, was a member of the farmer's family, and the other lived nearby. The witch went on to note that one of the two would be found out because she would come running three times to the farmer's house; the other, he described as 'a crab'.

The farmer relayed this to one of his sons, saying that he believed that his daughter Ellen was the one described as 'a crab' because she was deformed. He had also seen one of his other daughters come running to the house three times, and so decided that she was the other responsible for the overlooking. The farmer told the same information to a number of other people, who were called as witnesses in the court. These people confirmed that the farmer seemed to be in full control of his mind, and the judge eventually ruled that the two sides (presumably the daughters who had probably been cut out of the will and the sons who had not) would have to reach a compromise.[10]

It appears that the superstitious farmer held a belief which was then verified by an 'authority' figure—in this case, the White Witch. He was then able to fit the things he saw to that case to substantiate it. The deformity of the daughter Ellen is not noted, so we can only speculate that it was either something that affected her movement, or an abnormality about the shape of the fingers or hands. But what is notable is that the man accused one of his other daughters because he had seen her running to the house three times, even though the witch had described the person as 'living nearby'; he had specifically said that one was a member of the family, not both. Thus the farmer seems to have twisted his observations to fit his belief.

The White Witch of Exeter

The White Witch of Exeter features in many such cases. As his involvement can be seen spanning a period of over a hundred years, it is most likely the case that as one man left the job, another took his place in an effort to continue the business. Probably the best-known was a man named Snow who is cited by name in many cases. He seems to have received visitors at his house in Exeter but also travelled to other places for consultation. E.H. Young notes that he would visit Okehampton market once a week until around 1890.[11] Snow might have replaced a man called Tuckett (the dates are uncertain) who was noted to have visited the Bell Inn at Parkham to work, having come from Exeter to carry out his trade there.[12]

To what extent the role the White Witch played was genuine and to what extent it involved something more underhand probably depended upon the person who held the position. Certainly, some were skilled at healing and employed herbal remedies which have since been shown to have beneficial effects. Others might have been a little more fraudulent in their claims. Sometimes, not much effort was needed, when it was easy to exploit the beliefs of the client. On many occasions the advice of the witch was sought purely to confirm that a particular person was responsible for a perceived case of overlooking. It would be straightforward to just perform a few simple rituals before agreeing that the name given was indeed correct. It is easy to see how accusations in a community could escalate in such cases.

Tuckett seems to have been considered an imposter, at least according to an anecdote recorded by the Devonshire Association.[13] This told how the man employed a servant in full livery who would answer the door to visitors, conducting them into a waiting room. Here, the man would politely engage the client in conversation, allowing him to ascertain the nature of the visit. Once he was sure as to the reason the client was there, the servant would ring to summon Tuckett. It was alleged that the pattern of bell pulls would inform the witch as to the nature of the visit, which he could then use as a conversation opener, thus proving his skills before he had even started the consultation. No evidence to back up this claim of fraud was provided in the report.

Around the same time, the Exeter White Witch visited a couple in Ashburton, solving their case through a very clever use of language. The couple who sought help had been ill for some time. Although the illness was not serious, none of the cures tried had seemed to work and the couple were starting to believe that they had been overlooked. The witch, upon arrival, examined the couple and immediately agreed that they had been bewitched. He gave them some charms which had to be recited at particular times, and finished by informing them that within twenty-four hours the person responsible for their overlooking would come and beg their pardon.

After following the witch's instructions, the couple went to bed at their usual time—they retired early at around nine in the evening. A little while later a woman who lived nearby came to the house. She had been working late in the fields but knew that the couple were ill and called on the way home to enquire after them. Her knocking on the door roused the husband who shouted down from the bedroom window. The visiting woman saw that the couple had gone to bed and so took her leave, saying 'Oh, I beg your pardon' for waking them. And thus the witch's prediction was proven.

When other residents learned of this the next day, they became very abusive towards the neighbour and the situation could have escalated but for the threat of police involvement. The man and wife who thought themselves overlooked made a very quick recovery from their illness thereafter.[14]

Magical Protection and Apotropaic Charms

One of the best ways of protecting against magic in times of great super-stition was naturally to use magic oneself. This was often done at the advice of someone such as the White Witch, but also sometimes took place through the concealment of objects in the property to ward off evil. Many of these concealed objects or markings, termed apotropaic from the Greek term 'to ward off', are unearthed during renovations of old properties today.

In Devon, animal hearts were often used as a protective object. A couple from South Devon who believed themselves overlooked travelled to Exeter for a consultation and were told to purchase a bullock's heart when they returned home. This they had to place in their fire to burn at midnight, having first ensured that all entrances into their home were secured. While the heart burned, according to the Exeter witch, the woman responsible for the overlooking would come to the house and try to get in, but if the couple were successful in keeping her out until the heart had been completely consumed in the flames, then the spell would be broken. The couple did as they were instructed and reported that events panned out exactly as described, with their fortune improving from that day on.

More often than not, the advice was to stick pins into a heart before concealing it in one's property. The magic that was said to take place in this case was the heart of the person who wished ill on you being pierced in the same manner, ultimately leading to death if the spell was not reversed. A Mr Chown, recorded as being cooper in the parish of Clyst Honiton, had a number of houses which he rented out. On one becoming vacant in 1877, some building work was undertaken to prepare for a new tenant, during which a pig's heart stuck with thorns was found in the chimney. It was said to be the third such example uncovered in the area around that time.[15]

Around a century later, in 1975, a similar discovery was made at Luppitt by workers who were replacing a thatched roof. A calf's heart was found in a bag, nailed to the chimney and stuck with pins and thorns. The farmer who owned the property was wary of the discovery and consulted his local vicar for advice. The priest went to the church with two helpers and offered prayers before visiting the house, performing an exorcism on the heart and then burning it.[16] This action seems to demonstrate a lack of understanding of the traditions behind these offerings as it essentially served to destroy what was a positive charm seeking to protect from harm, allowing a route in for evil forces if viewed from the same superstitious perspective.

Pins were also used in other ways, aside from sticking them into a heart. At Narracombe Farm in Ilsington, while stripping whitewash from a beam across the hearth in the kitchen, a quantity of pins, broken needles and broken knife blades were discovered stuck into the cracks of the wood. Blades were thought to deter negativity, but it was also generally recognized that iron kept witches at bay in the same way that it did fairies.

Lady Northcote records the story of how a woman who used to collect old iron and sell it to a former blacksmith was accused of being a witch, and how that same iron was used to keep her out of his forge, on the advice of others. They told the man that he must find a place where she had put her foot inside the forge and then hammer a nail into the track that she had left. He did so and from that point on she would stop outside the forge but not come in, calling for him to come to her instead. After a while, he apparently took the nail out and she began entering the forge once again.[17]

The advice the smith was given comes from folklore about the use of a 'maiden nail' to stop a witch. A maiden nail is one which has been freshly made by a smith from bar-iron and has never been used or been allowed to touch the ground. Beliefs surrounding the use of the maiden nail state that you could either hammer it into the threshold of the witch's door, which would prevent them from being able to cross it, or drive it into the spot where the witch had placed their foot, which would remove their powers for the day. These methods were noted as having been used at Kenton near Exeter in the late nineteenth century.[18] The story told by Lady Northcote seems to be a conflation of these two pieces of lore.

An example of the belief in pinning a witch through a footprint appeared in a very strange place in 1924—an advertisement in *The Times* newspaper. The anecdote was told of a Mrs Dovell who had previously owned a farm near the top of Countisbury Hill, called Huxtable's.

> One day Jem Smith, of the Blue Bull, spied her going into church, and drove a peg into the impression her foot had made in the churchyard clay. The old lady was on her knees in church, and there she had to remain, it being impossible for her to rise until Jem had withdrawn the peg from the clay.[19]

There was a long-held belief in Devon and beyond that scratching a witch and drawing their blood would be effective in breaking whatever manner of overlooking they had cast on a person. While this could generally be done with any kind of pin, thorn or other sharp object, we do find some crossover in Devon between this and the belief in the power of the maiden nail.

A woman named 'Mother Butt' by her neighbours was thought to be a witch, and a number of people were very wary of her. She was the widow of a local farmer and worked in a tanyard, as did a 35-year-old man named Billy Gray. Gray would make accusations against the woman when he passed her, so she in turn would mutter under her breath, probably to play on his fears rather than put up with the abuse. After a while, Billy Gray came to believe that Mother Butts had overlooked him and so he decided to consult with a White Witch. He was advised to go to a blacksmith and make a long horseshoe nail, which he had to be careful to ensure did not touch the ground. This he should use to draw blood from the woman, which he did successfully from her wrist to her elbow—but the act reportedly made no difference to him. Mother Butt said later that she had no powers to overlook people, but that they were all generally very wary of her. The case seems to be a prime example of the effects of stereotyping and psychology.

Another example was recorded in *The Times* in 1930. It came from a letter written by the author Maria Callcott (1785–1842) to Sir Francis Palgrave. Born Francis Cohen in 1788, Palgrave was an archivist and historian and is considered to have been the founder of the Public Record Office. Callcott wrote to him about a witch scratching case in 1821, saying that it had happened about five years before her letter.

> A rich baker in Plymouth was condemned to pay five pounds sterling to a reputed witch as compensation money on the following account. The baker and his wife had several chubby children and one poor puny one. The little creature had, according to its Granny's opinion, been overlooked; and nothing but blood from the witch who had overlooked it could cure it. Accordingly, the lady of the Oven watched her opportunity; and when the witch next came for a loaf she flew upon her and, with certain Corking pins prepared for the purpose, she and her maid so tore the arms and neck of the poor old woman that she narrowly escaped with her life.[20]

The details of this case demonstrate how the fears of a community draw upon cultural themes relevant to them at that time, and how those fears can change over the course of history. At the time that this took place, belief in the power of a witch to overlook was still very strong. In an earlier period of history, the circumstances of the family with regards to the health of their children would very likely have been blamed on the fairies having taken one of them and replaced it with a sickly fairy changeling.

Pins, nails and other sharp objects were one of the important constituent parts of a witch bottle, concealed in many old properties as protection against supernatural attack by witches. Probably originating at some point in the seventeenth century, a bottle (usually stoneware but later also glass) would be filled with a combination of urine, iron pins, nails or thorns, human hair and varying other fragments. The bottle would be stoppered and then concealed under the floor or in the walls of the building, where it would remain often until being discovered during later building work.

In 1970, an example was discovered in a cottage in the Dartmoor village of Chagford. The property, which had been built in 1446, was being renovated and the bottle was found buried upside down under the old floor. The man who found it unfortunately removed the cork which caused a quantity of black liquid, with an apparently none-too-pleasant smell, to exit the bottle under pressure. Also found in the bottle were seventeen thorns and seven pins.

Belief in the efficacy of the witch bottle was still to be found in Devon in the nineteenth century. A shop owner in North Devon wrote to his local newspaper about an example he had come across first-hand. An old woman had entered his shop, requesting a new bottle and cork. She rejected the first one that the man offered her, saying that she could see that it had been washed out with water and she needed one which had never had anything in it. She went on to explain to the man that she had been 'witched' and that she was going to take the bottle home and fill it with needles and pins. She had previously done the same thing in another case with favourable effects. 'These pins and needles will then stick into the heart of the person who has witched me,' she said, 'and who is bound to appear in my presence'.[21]

A report of the discovery of a witch bottle carried in the *Exeter Gazette* of 4 May 1900 is particularly interesting because the bottle was not concealed in a house as usual, but was found during the reopening of a grave in the churchyard at Monkleigh. The grave, which was located close to the vestry door, was being dug by the sexton, who found the object at a depth of about a foot. The newspaper reported that the bottle contained an inky fluid, and that the cork was stuck with a large number of pins. These facts were later substantiated in a letter written by the vicar of the parish at the time, L. Coutier Bigg. The sexton did not discuss the find, and as soon as he could he buried it in line with the general procedure of replacing anything dug up when working on a grave. Some people passing by had the opportunity to examine the bottle before he was able to do this, which is most likely how the report came to appear in the newspaper.

In his letter, the vicar states that he believed the burying of the bottle was a counter-charm. His implication was that the bottle had been an object used to magically attack a living person and that they had buried it in the grave in order to transfer the spell to the dead body interred there instead. This was purely conjecture on the part of the vicar and seems to be a misinterpretation of the use of a witch bottle, which was always used for protection against attack, not as a malefic object in order to harm someone else.

This is not the only time that a container such as this appears to have been unearthed in a Devon churchyard. Five years earlier, W.T. Wellacott wrote from the vicarage at Bradworthy to the *Western Morning News* about a small jar found by workmen while preparing the path through the churchyard for a new layer of gravel. The jar was about eight feet from the church porch and buried with the top at a depth of around three inches. The contents of this container were again some thorns and pins. The vicar wrote to the newspaper to ask whether readers had any knowledge of how this jar might be connected to overlooking, and also whether the power of a witch could be destroyed by burying a jar like this in three different churchyards, as he believed.

What makes this letter particularly significant is the fact that the author, whether he realized it or not, appears to be referencing a known ritual from Devon involving the magical use of toads.

Toad Magic

Toads have a long association with witchcraft, both as mechanisms for casting spells and in roles as witch's familiars. In her 1900 collection of Devon folklore and superstition *Nummits and Crummits*, Sarah Hewett records a ritual for removing a witch's power, which is undoubtedly connected to the belief expressed by Rev. Wellacott in his letter to the newspaper.

> Take three small-necked stone jars: place in each the liver of a frog stuck full of new pins, and the heart of a toad stuck full of thorns from the holy thorn bush. Cork and seal each jar. Bury in three different churchyard paths seven inches from the surface and seven feet from the porch. While in the act of burying each jar, repeat the Lord's prayer backwards. As the hearts and livers decay so will the witch's power vanish. After performing this ceremony, no witch can have any power over the operator.[22]

The jar found at Bradworthy is certainly the right distance from the porch (give or take a few inches) and if a small jar, then also at the right sort of depth. The animal organs having decayed away, the pins and thorns left in the jar are representative of the nature of the ritual. It would certainly appear that Wellacott had some knowledge of the ritual involving the three jars, around the same sort of time that Hewett had obviously heard and collected it for her book.

Lady Northcote noted in her article 'Devonshire Folklore' that toads could be used to cause harm to others and also, if you knew how, as a means of divination. She cites one informant whose mother was familiar with a bedridden woman who kept toads in her bed with her in order to tell people's fortunes.[23] One visitor to the Rev. Franke Parker, who spent so many years living in the allegedly haunted Luffincott Rectory (see Chapter Seven), said that they had found him in bed one day surrounded by dead toads.[24] No explanation is given, sadly.

An old woman living at Axmouth named Charity Perry was also alleged to have kept toads. Perry is the subject of a couple of cases of overlooking in the area. One follows the standard routine of another member of the village believing that they have been overlooked and consulting a White Witch, who explains the way by which they will recover. Another man who used to live next door to Charity was said to be unable to keep his pig there because it was overlooked by the woman, who caused it to turn somersaults. A neighbour who looked after Charity while she was ill for a while (said to be connected to the White Witch's cure for overlooking) related that Perry dared her to look in a box she kept under her bed, and that when she did so she found that it was full of toads.

Another Devon widow who was said to be able to control toads was once observed secretly by her son at midnight. She removed a number of toads from a jar and put them on the ground, where they remained perfectly still until she laid a piece of straw in front of them. At this, they all followed her round the room. She apparently did three circuits with the animals, after which she told them to leave and do their work. The implication in the story is that they were responsible for the burning down of a haystack overnight, discovered by a neighbouring farmer when he went to work the next day.

Some believed that the toads themselves had the power of the 'evil eye' and that this could be exploited by a witch. This was said to be the case with a woman from Bishopsteignton who allegedly put a toad on the doorstep of a person to whom she wished ill. By this means, as soon as the person opened the door they would meet the gaze of the toad and so the magic would take effect.

Toads were not only used in connection with causing harm, but were also said to possess curative properties. One complaint in need of treatment that comes up often in old Devon records is the 'King's Evil'. This was the common name across Europe for *tuberculous lymphadenitis* or scrofula, a swelling of the lymph glands, which earned its nickname from the superstitious belief that the touch of a member of royalty could affect a cure. This was thought true until the end of the eighteenth century.[25]

The Rector of Manaton recorded that he had been told by an old man in his parish that King's Evil or any other type of sore could be cured using a toad. The part of the animal which corresponded with the part of the body where the ailment was to be found would be placed in a small bag and attached to the afflicted person. It was further noted that this cure was only effective if 'dry toads' were used rather than 'wet toads'. The meaning of 'dry' and 'wet' in this case has been lost over time. It may relate to the location in which the toad is found (such as close to a watercourse or pond) or it may relate to the breed of toad. Toads found underneath a sage bush were said to be most effective.[26] Another way of treating King's Evil with the help of a toad was by using a 'toad stone'. This was a stone which was believed to be found in the head of a toad and which acted as a poison antidote. The thinking behind this idea, first recorded by Pliny the Elder in the first century, was that because toads had poison glands in their skin, then they must naturally carry their own protection against it. The mythical toad stone was said to be this antidote.

An article on the subject of the toad stone presented in Sidmouth in 1873 referred to a description by the author Edward Fenton in the book *Notable Things*, of a stone found in the head of old and usually male toads.[27] Science has since shown that the object is actually the fossilized tooth of a species of fish from the Jurassic period, and completely unconnected to toads. The presentation in Sidmouth also exhibited a toad stone which had belonged to a Devon man called Blagdon. Although he did not believe himself that the object contained any power, he was constantly asked by others if they could borrow it, and so had to allow them so as not to cause offence. It would be worn around the neck so that the stone reached the wearer's stomach.[28]

Toads were also said to be kept by one of Devon's notorious witches, whose story we will now examine.

Case Study: Hannah Henley

A number of the beliefs associated with witchcraft in Devon historically can be tied together in the story of Hannah Henley, an alleged witch who lived in the parish of Membury in East Devon and who died in 1841. She had quite a reputation for causing ill—so much so, in fact, that it is likely that some of the stories about her have since been levelled against other characters who came later. It was said that nothing would grow on the ground where Hannah Henley lived and so the area of Membury where her cottage once stood was known as 'Witches Field'. This seems to have been a colloquial name for the area locally. An examination of the tithe apportionments for Membury recorded in 1844 show no such name attributed to any of the fields there. The name Henley is noted on the records, attached to a carpenter's shop and garden, but unlike all the other people listed there is no Christian name attached, which is curious in itself.

Hannah was by all accounts quite a clean and tidy person. Her small dwelling, which consisted of only two rooms, was always immaculate, as was she herself. She lived close to a farmer who was quite prosperous and she obtained most of what she needed by asking for charity from the farm. For a while, this was given happily but as the demands grew greater, so Hannah began to be turned away by the farm residents. This appears to be the point at which things started to go wrong for the farmer and his family, seemingly as a result of Hannah overlooking them.

Historian Tracey Norman points out in her pamphlet on the stories of some of Devon's witches that the refusal of charity features in many examples where people are said to be bewitched, following a model put forward by Keith Thomas in his important 1971 work *Religion and the Decline of Magic*.[29] The farmer's brother refused Hannah money, upon which she informed him that he would not live long enough to use it himself. The man is said to have died three weeks later. Similarly, the family's youngest child died after meeting with Hannah. The boy had been playing with a walnut shell which Hannah asked for, but the child's nurse refused him permission to pass it over. Hannah is said to have drawn a cross on the floor, with a circle around it, and then simply walked away. The child died four days later after becoming very ill, one symptom of which was spinning round and round and making himself dizzy.

A raft of trouble followed at the farm—all things quite common in reports of witches overlooking farmers and farmworkers in the county. Milk did not set, butter did not churn and bread failed to bake. Horses were taken ill after a request for barley made to one of the servants was refused, and sheep died of disease in large numbers. Things became very serious for the farmer and his family as their business fell into ruin. The man decided to follow the normal course of events for such stories and organized a consultation with a White Witch; not the Exeter one in this case but a man from over the border in Chard.

The White Witch came to stay at the farm in order to assess the situation the family found themselves in. After spending some time there, the man announced that Hannah Henley was the strongest witch he had ever come across. Following one of the methods discussed earlier in this chapter, the White Witch sent for six bullocks' hearts. Two of these he stuck with pins and the other four with new nails (akin to the maiden nails used to pin witches through their footprints). All of these hearts were hung in the large fireplace in the kitchen and allowed to slowly melt. The White Witch told that as the hearts melted, so would Hannah Henley's own. Indeed, Hannah did come to the farmhouse to beg for relief, but the farmer turned her away.

After almost a month at the farm, the White Witch was still working against Hannah. He secured a butt and had a quantity of nails driven into it, the whole thing then being taken to the top of the hill and rolled down. That afternoon, Hannah again came to the house, saying that she was dying. The following morning, Good Friday, at four o'clock, the White Witch visited Hannah's home and found her in a tree with a sheet wrapped around her. The tree was cut down as Hannah was too high to reach, and as it fell, so her body was thrown into a ditch. On examination, it was found that her flesh seemed to have been torn as if by nails or some other sharp object. The inside of her property was also covered in blood.

Some boxes next to Hannah's bed were subsequently opened. One was said to contain money and goods such as bread and sugar. Two smaller ones both apparently housed toads of different sizes.

The picture painted of Hannah Henley is one representative of standard witch stereotypes. She was said to have a large number of cats, which after her death local people tried to kill but could not (there is no elaboration as to why), and it was said that the dumplings she baked were mysteriously whiter than anyone else's. Her body was interred at a crossroads—the usual burial place for people whose manner of death led to a superstitious concern that they might return from the grave—and horses were said to spook at the spot afterwards.

Another farmer, who had to plough areas close to Hannah's hut at Boobhill, said that he used to tie 'bush brimble' on the gates to ward Hannah away.[30] 'Bush brimble' is a local Devon term for a bramble bush, the thorns of which would work similarly to the witch bottle or pierced heart methods. The local hunt said that they used to pursue Hannah through the area because she was able to turn herself into a hare. This, in a similar way to the proliferation of stories about the fairy ointment and the midwife (see Chapter Six), is a very common motif in Devon and beyond. Witches in hare form would be shot or otherwise injured, with the witch in human form sporting the same injuries later. A case was recorded at Rose Ash where a man named Webber had tried

and failed to shoot a hare on his property, until he was informed that if he cut up a sixpence and put that in the gun then the wound would be effective.

Folk Remedies

The common picture painted of witches in history tends to focus on the more macabre and dark elements: cases of cursing, overlooking and causing harm, and the associated accusations and trials that go with them. It is important to put the character of the witch into some historical perspective and recognize that this is only a small part of the picture. The wise woman or cunning man— an individual skilled in plant knowledge, healing and often other medical care such as midwifery—was a central part of the make-up of many rural communities. People of all classes and beliefs would consult them for help, although many would never admit to it. In Devon and the South West, they were sometimes known as 'wayside witches' after a term coined by Cecil Williamson, the founder of the witchcraft museum in Boscastle, Cornwall. The name is reflective both of their use of plants and materials found in the hedges and wider landscape, and their remote living conditions and place on the periphery both socially and geographically.

Although traditional cures and remedies were categorized by many past commentators as a habit of the rural, uneducated class who thrived on super-stition, and though many people still class these techniques as 'old wives' tales', science has shown that, in the case of plant use at the very least, many of them have merit. Substances such as the gel from snails (a traditional treatment for deafness) are used in modern times for ear conditions, for example.

There are countless charms and folk medicine recipes and treatments to be found in Devon, for hundreds of medical complaints. A substantial book could be produced on this subject alone. By way of example, we can examine just one frequently suffered condition for which remedies were sought from local healers: whooping cough.

Whooping cough is a bacterial disease which affects the lungs and respir-atory system, causing a very bad cough which can last for a number of weeks, a fact which led to its sometimes being called the '100-day cough'. The condition is highly contagious and relatively easily protected against now with a straight-forward vaccine. Before this was available, whooping cough could readily sweep through a community.

It was not uncommon in Devon for people to think that those who were taken ill were suffering from possession. This was highlighted in a case that came before the Court of Chancery in 1893 to determine a plantiff's medical condition, due to them having asked to be locked in a room and the key to be taken away because the Devil was after them. The judge in the case had noted that he had previous first-hand experience of people in the county thinking this way.[31] We therefore often find that cures for medical conditions run a gamut from those involving herbal treatment to more superstitious undertakings.

An example of the latter as a cure for whooping cough was collected in Exmouth in 1877 by a Miss Wright. It was suggested that the afflicted child should be taken out early in the morning, while there was still dew on the ground. A sleeping sheep should be located and driven away and the child should be laid face down on the spot where the sheep had been. Farmers' wives in the area apparently had so much faith in this cure that they would bring sheep into the farmyard overnight purely for this purpose.[32] Another example seems to have relied on advice from another person. The sufferer needed to stop a man in a cart being pulled by a white horse and ask him how to cure the cough. Simply following whatever advice was given was enough for the cure to be effective.

The transference of an affliction is a common treatment for many ailments in Devon. It can be seen often with wart charming, for example. Sometimes the wart would need to be rubbed with something, which was then buried or hung in a tree. As the object rotted away, so the wart also died. Some cures were undertaken by transferring the illness to an animal, in much the same way as the biblical story of the Miracle of the Gadarene Swine describes Jesus exorcizing demons from a man into a herd of pigs. One example for whooping cough was to take a hair from the head of the child suffering and place it between two slices of bread and butter, which should then be fed to a dog. There is possibly something in this cure which might have led to a psycho-somatic feeling of improvement at least. A dog will naturally cough when eating bread, due to its texture, thus seeming to demonstrate that the cough is moving from the child to the animal.

T. Cann Hughes reported to the Devonshire Association how his mother had been told, when she lived in the village of Bow around the 1820s or 1830s, to take her infant sister into three parishes in order to cure her whooping cough. The parishes named were Bow itself, North Tawton and Broad Nymet. There seems there was no suggestion of any action to take other than the travelling.[33] Some connection could possibly be made between this and the need to bury three jars in three different churchyards for the charm to dispel witchcraft, discussed in the section on toad magic above. Whatever the thinking behind it, the belief was obviously strong enough to carry forward, as an article titled 'Superstitious Parents' in the national press in 1906 noted that during a measles outbreak in Chittlehampton, parents had taken their children around three parishes in one day in order to cure them.[34]

In some examples, variations of these cures were combined. It was noted at Bridestowe that a child should be taken three days in a row into a field containing sheep and be sat in a spot from where a sheep had just stood up.[35] The same collector, L.M. Francis, had also heard that the sufferer should be given a piece of Good Friday bun for three days in a row. This seems to be utilizing a cure which was also suggested for stomach conditions (see Chapter Three) but with the three-day timeframe added. Many superstitions were interchangeable as required.

An unusual treatment noted by Richard Pearse Chope was to pass the child completely around the stomach of a donkey. The child should begin in a sitting position on the animal's back and then be rotated around.[36]

Although in the case of whooping cough most of the remedies seemed to rely purely on taking an action of some kind, there were examples where a herbal treatment was used—such as the one recorded in a letter from Miss A. Challis of Budleigh Salterton in 1951, who said that a certain cure for the condition was to 'take five green-slimed stones from a brook and boil them, pouring the liquid over the left shoulder'.[37]

Snails were also used as a medicinal treatment for the condition:

> Collect sufficient snails to half fill a 2-lb jam jar. It is preferable to collect these in the late evening after the snails have had time to crawl and clean themselves. Cover with about two tablespoonful of brown moist sugar. Replace lid and leave overnight in warm place. Next morning, there will be a golden coloured syrup in the jar; drain off syrup and strain through muslin. Bottle, taking care not to fill the bottles as the pressure generated may cause them to crack.[38]

A teaspoon of this mixture was given three times a day and was also apparently used with success to prevent children from catching the cough at times of outbreak. This example was recorded at Chudleigh Knighton but was also known elsewhere in Devon. Although most commonly known as an effective skin treatment now, there has been scientific study to show that, under laboratory conditions, the mucus from certain snails can treat respiratory conditions.[39]

Sometimes treatment came in the form of a charm. One such example was putting a long, hairy caterpillar into a small bag and wearing it around one's neck in the manner of the toad stone charm described earlier. Another combined a charm with the idea mentioned previously of the transference of disease to an animal. In this case a spider was placed in the charm bag, which was worn in the same way. When the spider died, then the affliction did too.

Charms were often accompanied by some form of religious text or spoken word, which was used in order to request divine help in its application. A very important example of this was discovered in the 1930s by Canon E.F. Hall, who lived at Leusdon on Dartmoor. Sometime around the 1930s he had spoken to a moorland woman who was said to be able to cure the King's Evil. She told him how she used the milk of a red cow, the wool of a black sheep and some hawthorn, which she used to stroke the patient before bandaging

them. Finally, the woman said that she 'makes the sign of the cross and I says IN
NUMNEY DUMNEY'.[40]

The woman is using a dialect pronunciation of the Latin 'In nomine Domini',
working her charm in the name of the Lord. What makes this story so
important, aside from the fact that the name and address of the woman is also
supplied along with the account, is that previously the earliest noted survival
of pre-Reformation liturgical Latin in remote Devon areas was in the seventeenth century. This example demonstrated that there were still pockets of use
existing three hundred years later than first thought.

CHAPTER TEN

Modern Folklore

In the first chapter of this book, we learned that the term 'folklore' as the compound word we use and recognize today was employed in 1846 by the British writer William John Thoms (1803–1885), a Fellow of the Society of Antiquaries and Deputy Librarian of the House of Lords Library. Thoms was also the founder of the journal *Notes and Queries* which has been published continuously since its inception in 1849, and which was designed as a scholarly forum where both academics and researchers who were not affiliated to a learned institution could offer information on a variety of topics related to history, folklore and the wider literary world. This often took place in the form of a question posed in one issue with subsequent answers in the following ones. In the late nineteenth century a number of similar publications began on a county level across the United Kingdom. Although most of these have now ceased, the volume for Devon and Cornwall is still published regularly, alongside its neighbour *Notes and Queries for Somerset and Dorset*.

Thoms introduced the term 'folklore' as a replacement for a number of others in use at the time, not least 'popular antiquities'.[1] Folklore in its simplest form relates to the beliefs (lore) of the people (folk), although the latter of these two terms has shifted a little in meaning over time. When first employed in the nineteenth century, the term folk was taken to mean uneducated, rural dwellers—frequently poor and often superstitious. For this reason, there is a common misconception that folklore as we view it now relates only to these old practices and traditions and has no real relevance to modern life. Not only is this far from the truth, but it also ironically opposes the work of Thoms himself, who was instrumental in discrediting what we now think of as survivals theory.

Put simply, survivals theory in terms of folklore 'promotes the extremely widespread assumption that all our superstitions and customs are thousands of years old, and ... can be used to support any view which is fashionable at the time, whether sun or moon worship, fertility, phallic symbols, female deities, or Freudian or Jungian psychology'.[2] It is often employed by groups or individuals who wish to legitimize their practices by claiming longevity from our ancestors.

Returning to the American folklorist Alan Dundes's refined description of 'folk' as 'any group of people whatsoever who share at least one common factor',[3] we can see that not only does this definition encompass any shared experience or belief, but it also applies to any number of people greater than one and suggests that the people in question may not only operate within the said beliefs or traditions, but may also be creators of it. This is especially relevant in terms of the internet and social media.

We find a similar irony in terms of online information as we do when we look at the work of William John Thoms to disprove ideas of longevity in myth and legend. The internet and social media platforms are widely responsible for propagating the ideas of survivals theory and this mistaken belief that all folklore must be old. And yet, the internet itself is creating folklore every second of every minute of every day.

In her TED talk folklorist Lynne S. McNeill described the internet as 'the world's largest unintentional folklore archive' because it is constantly providing a platform to record and preserve the way that people work within their cultural norms.[4] There are many places where this can be done through discussion, in Facebook groups such as Devon Folklore[5] or Devonshire Dialect[6] for example. Since the enforced lockdowns of the global Covid pandemic forced the majority of people to spend long periods in their own homes, there has also been a rise in lectures and presentations delivered online by organizations such as the Devonshire Association or Devon Heritage Centre, which cover topics of folkloric interest. Many of these are now archived for future use.

In terms of the creation of folklore by users, a prime example which many would not consider to be part of the area of study, but which absolutely is by definition, is the production and dissemination of internet memes. *Oxford Learner's Dictionaries* describe a meme as 'an idea that is passed from one member of society to another, not in the genes but often by people copying it', and an internet meme as 'an image, a video, a piece of text, etc. that is passed very quickly from one internet user to another, often with slight changes that make it humorous'.[7]

It is easy to see how this is simply an online variation on an age-old tradition; survivals theory, but in a sense that actually works! We might consider the internet meme to be the next step in a natural progression from the postcards we find available in most Devon gift shops, repurposing an old photograph of, for example, a particularly rustic-looking 'local' with a new caption, often written in pseudo-Devonshire dialect.

In the same talk referenced above, Lynne McNeill notes that by making or sharing an internet meme, a user is actively participating in the documentation and preservation of contemporary folk culture. This is because they are interacting with their own and wider shared cultural views in order to convey a message to others and make meaning in a humorous way. Although most examples are culturally broader, such as writing a short message in Impact font over a picture of Sean Bean from *The Lord of the Rings* or Gene Wilder portraying Willy Wonka in *Charlie and the Chocolate Factory*, there are always more local examples to be found. To make sense to others, these memes need to offer up cultural meaning and commentary through interplay with a recognizable local trope. In Devon, there are two obvious examples—agricultural machinery and cream teas.

Memes do not necessarily originate on a local level (in fact, it is often virtually impossible to find a distinct point of origin) but they are adopted in this way and make a comment on local views through the way they are captioned or manipulated.

One example is an image of a red tractor pulling a similarly coloured slurry tanker, on the back of which is seen the Coca-Cola logo, which has (in all likelihood) been photoshopped on. The image appears to have first been shared online sometime in 2008. Since then it has been reshared and altered many times, often to reflect on current culture. It has been claimed as a Devon joke, portraying a local variation of the famous Coca-Cola Christmas lorry used as an advertising campaign, and has been passed round social media for a number of years in this context around Christmas time. As a side note, since 2020 it has been repurposed as a social commentary on Britain leaving the European Union, with captions such as 'Since Brexit, the Coca Cola Christmas lorry is no longer as impressive in the UK'.[8]

There is a long-standing debate between Devon and the neighbouring county of Cornwall over the make-up of the 'cream tea', generally formed in modern times of one or more warmed scones cut in half and topped with strawberry jam and clotted cream. This debate centres mainly on which is the correct way of serving the scones—cream topped with jam, or jam first and then cream on top.

Recently, there has been speculation on the origin of the cream tea, which has proven to be an interesting demonstration on the way unreferenced information can be quickly spread online and embed itself as fact (another type of modern folklore which is usually linked with urban legends). In 2004, an anonymous article appeared on the BBC News website which made claims to the cream tea coming from Tavistock in the tenth century.

> Historians in Devon have unearthed evidence which they claim proves the traditional cream tea originated in the county some 1,000 years ago. Local historians have been studying ancient manuscripts as part of research leading up to next year's 900th anniversary of the granting of Tavistock's Royal Charter by King Henry I in 1105. After piecing together fragments of manuscripts, they have discovered that the monks of Tavistock's Benedictine Abbey could have created the famous dish to reward workers who helped to restore the building. The Abbey was established in the 10th Century, but was plundered and badly damaged by Vikings in 997 AD. The task of restoring the Abbey was undertaken by Ordulf, Earl of Devon whose father had been responsible for establishing the Abbey. Ordulf was helped by local workers who the monks fed with bread, clotted cream and strawberry preserves.[9]

There are a number of issues with this claim. While it is the case that the strawberry is mentioned in the leechbooks,[10] sugar did not arrive in England until a century later, and this was unrefined and very different to what we would now recognize as such. Consequently, the strawberry preserve would be similarly unrecognizable. The article also mentions the study of ancient manuscripts but does not name them, and no subsequent research has yet turned up a reference such as that described. It is probably the case that the original news piece, written coincidentally around the time that the Tavistock Food Festival was about to take place, is more of a talking point for advertising the festival and is somewhat liberal in its use of documented evidence. Since 2004, however, the article has been cited and recited and used many times as 'evidence' within Devon to show that their method of assembling a cream tea is correct—even though the news article makes no mention of what order the ingredients are placed on the bread or scone. Geographical origin, it seems, is sufficient to overlook this.

Friendly (and sometimes not-so-friendly) rivalry between Devon and Cornwall mostly centres on this last point. A Devon cream tea is made with the clotted cream being spread on the scone first, with the jam being placed on top. The reasoning behind this is generally explained by farmers using cream as a substitute for butter, which would naturally be spread before the preserve is added. Over the border in Cornwall, jam goes first followed by cream. As you might expect, the internet has been home not only to the historical debate on

the origin of the cream tea itself, but also to the use of memes to comment on the cross-border disparity over how to use the ingredients.

One of the most recognizable internet meme images, that of Batman slapping his ward Robin, has been adopted for this commentary. The panel image of Batman and Robin is a genuine piece of comic art, appearing in 'Imaginary Story', issue number 153 of DC Comics' *World's Finest* in 1965.[11] The story takes place in an alternative reality where Batman thinks that Superman and Superboy are responsible for the death of his father Thomas Wayne. The earliest known parody comes from 2008[12] and took hold so quickly that less than eighteen months later the first Batman Comic Meme Generator website was launched.

This meme has been employed as a social commentary on the Devon cream tea in an image created by devoncow graphic design, made available for purchase through the *thortful* greetings card website.[13] The card design 'Batman and Robin having a Devon cream tea' shows Robin speaking the interrupted phrase 'Jam on fir...' and being slapped by Batman who corrects him with 'No! Cream on first!!!!!'.

Other images and suggestions have been used to stimulate discussion on the subject online. In June 2018 the 'Devon Days' Twitter account posted an image of two scones, one with cream on first and the other jam, with the tweet text reading '#DevonDay is always a good time to debate the right and wrong way to enjoy a Devon Cream Tea—how can the cornish [*sic*] get things so wrong??'[14]. The image was annotated with the text 'Right Way (Devon)' and 'Wrong Way (Cornwall)' above the two scones.

Three months earlier, on 8 March 2018, the Cornish National Trust property of Lanhydrock House caused a social media backlash by advertising a Mother's Day afternoon tea at the property on their Facebook page, and inadvertently illustrating it with a photograph of a cream tea made the Devon way. Following a number of (mostly) tongue-in-cheek complaints in the comments on the post, the Trust corrected their error with a retraction worded in a similarly humorous style, noting that the member of staff concerned for the mistake had been 'reprimanded and marched back over the Tamar'. The whole incident was big enough news to be covered online by the national press.[15]

The internet is not the only home of folklore in modern times, of course. Discounting those practices which still continue today for which we can trace historic lineage, modern stories often emerge surrounding older superstitions. Freedom of Information Act disclosures to the county police force show that they still field emergency service calls with a professed supernatural theme. One caller from Plymouth in 2013 reported that a poltergeist had stolen nails from them,[16] while another stated that they thought that 'fairy type people' were stealing plants but that nobody other than the caller could see them.[17] In July of 2015 a caller in South Devon told the police that they were a vampire and were drinking their own blood.[18] Sometimes calls were from parties who were worried about another person. One logged from South Devon, a month after the vampire call, reported to the police concerns about their friend who was seeing ghosts of her dead mother,[19] and in June of 2016 a caller from the North and West Devon area said they were worried about a relative who stated that he was a ghost himself.[20]

The police take pains to point out on their disclosures that they do not normally attend an incident where paranormal activity is reported, unless there is concern for the welfare of the caller or another person, or unless the police believe an offence has been committed as part of the call.

Sometimes though, it is the police themselves who might be the witnesses, as we shall see in a moment.

Some folklore is naturally modern because the mythos itself only came into being in the last century. So, while people might have observed unusual lights in the sky many years ago, it is only since the adoption of the term 'flying saucer' by the press—following Kenneth Arnold's report of unusual objects seen while piloting a plane in the 1940s (now generally thought to be a misidentified flock of geese)—and the rise in popularity of the science fiction film genre that 'unidentified flying object' (UFO) is taken by default to mean 'spacecraft' rather than something actually unidentified.

In July of 2021, 36-year-old Matthew Evans saw a triangular formation of four lights from the window of his flat on the top floor of a building overlooking the seafront in Teignmouth. He described them as hovering for a period of ten seconds before flying off at some speed, but not moving in the way that an aircraft naturally would. Evans managed to take a couple of photographs on his mobile phone, which were subsequently published across the media online.[21]

It is worth noting that there is often a pattern whereby reports of UFOs are generally seen to increase after a major news event on the subject, or discussion at a governmental level. The month before the Teignmouth sighting, the Office of the Director of National Intelligence in the United States published a landmark unclassified report assessing sightings of airborne objects which could not be immediately identified.[22] This was of particular note because it did not emphatically rule out an extraterrestrial origin for all such cases, as governments and the military tend to do.

One of the most significant descriptions of a UFO was given by police officers Clifford Waycott and Roger Willey after they witnessed something unusual in the Devon skies between Holsworthy and Hatherleigh on 24 October 1967. Waycott described the object as 'a star-spangled cross radiating points of light from all angles. It first appeared to the left of us then went in an arc and dipped down and we thought it had landed. It seemed to be watching us.'[23]

The two police officers say that they pursued the light in their panda car, at speeds which hit ninety miles an hour at their maximum, for almost an hour. Then, fearing that nobody would believe what they had seen when they later filed a report, they stopped on finding a Land Rover parked in a layby. The driver, Chris Garner, was asleep in the vehicle and the two officers knocked on the window and woke the man, asking him to witness what they were seeing in the sky. Garner later corroborated the sighting.

As you would expect, with the main witnesses being members of the police force, the story was picked up and carried by not only regional but most national newspapers, along with an artist's impression of the cross of lights as they described it. Pressure was placed on the Ministry of Defence to explain the incident.

In a similar way to the 2021 example above, albeit on a more significant level, there was a heightened interest in UFOs at the time of this sighting. The time of year (just before Halloween) coupled with the ongoing political tensions of the time over the likelihood of being spied on by foreign powers such as the Soviet Union had brought the subject very much to the fore. In fact, there were 362 cases logged by the Ministry of Defence in that same year.[24]

This incident is valuable in demonstrating the effect the media can have on the shaping of stories, and subsequently on the way that folklore develops from them. In the twenty years since the 1947 sighting from Kenneth Arnold, the majority of UFO reports had described something akin to saucer-shaped objects. But now, suddenly, two seemingly credible witnesses were talking of something different—a flying cross. The effect of this was significant, and it led to many witnesses suddenly beginning to see objects of a similar shape. A retired wing commander from the Royal Air Force in Hampshire was one of the first.

Folklorist Dr David Clarke, who acted as spokesperson for the National Archives during the release of UFO-related documents by the Ministry of Defence, has examined the 1967 flying cross sighting and its aftermath in some detail, noting that the significance of the media coverage led to questions about the incident being asked in the House of Commons. Peter Mills, who was the Member of Parliament for Torrington at the time, wanted to know whether the object was one of the military's own aircraft or was something not able to

be identified. The reply from the Labour MP whose department was responsible for addressing questions on these matters was that most objects reported
over Devon had turned out to be aircraft, most lights seen were the planet
Venus and that a few reported sightings remained unidentified. Along with
weather balloons (the explanation given for the famous Roswell incident),
misidentified reports of the planet Venus and marsh gas have become stereotypical folkloric tropes to explain UFO sightings, to the extent that they are
often given as a sarcastic or satirical explanation for anything odd.

Later investigation by the Ministry of Defence, in fact, concluded that the
sighting made by the Devon police officers was an optical illusion caused by
Venus being particularly bright in the sky, and that the Hampshire flying cross
sighting which followed almost immediately after was the lights of an aircraft
over Boscombe Down airfield, coupled with military shells and flares from
night manoeuvres on the nearby Larkhill military range.

The role of print media in fuelling stories and hence helping with the
spread of modern folklore is still present, but it has been usurped to a certain
degree by television and, especially, social media—the latter allowing stories
to spread very quickly around the globe.

In the realm of television, the rise of 'paranormal' programming and, in
particular, that relating to ghosts has had a significant impact on modern
folklore. This takes one of two forms: in the first, documentary coverage,
with talking head interviews and dramatic reconstructions, tells of people's
allegedly real-life ghost encounters. In the second, camera crews follow
paranormal investigators or, more colloquially, 'ghost-hunters', as they search
for evidence in locations reputed to be haunted.

In 2001, London Weekend Television broadcast *Britain's Most Terrifying Ghost
Stories* on the ITV network, telling tales of real-life ghost encounters. In the
programme, a poltergeist case from Teignmouth was discussed by the woman
around whom the activities had centred—a 36-year-old nurse called Fiona
Hutchings. The haunting was said to have taken place in 'Hawthorn Cottage'
(it is not clear whether this is the real name of the house or a pseudonym)
between 1988 and 1993. Fiona's son had recently left home and she had
relocated from the moors to the cottage to be nearer to her mother. Starting
to renovate the property, Fiona felt that there was 'something strange' about
the atmosphere of the cottage.

After Fiona's mother passed away, Fiona met the resident of a neighbouring
property who began to tell her stories about Hawthorn Cottage. In a talking
head interview, Fiona tells us the neighbour had never passed the cottage
because she had been warned against it by her own mother, who had said that

there were 'all sorts of funny goings-on down there'.[25] The previous owner, she disclosed, had gone mad.

While gardening, Fiona dug up a number of dead cats. According to the interview she gave, these had been mutilated and buried in the directions of the cardinal points of the compass. The documentary makers' narrative takes pains to point out that the burying of sacrificed animals is often a part of black magic rituals. Following this, there were apparently more unexplained events in the cottage, including a string of electrical problems with appliances, and two fires.

One night, Fiona reports that she woke up and was unable to get out of bed. She believes that she saw a number of children in her bedroom, who she then realized were not real. After being unable to sleep at night for six months or more, Fiona called on the services of her friend Louise Barlow, who acted as a medium. Louise felt that 'rituals' had taken place on the land where the house was built. Because of this, she brought in a qualified exorcist from the liberal Catholic church in Exeter. He said that the children had been sacrificed as part of a ritual which Fiona 'would not want to know about'.[26]

After the exorcist's visit, the house appeared to become quiet. Fiona married a merchant seaman, Viv, who spent periods of time away, but there appeared to be no problems for some time. Then, more strange events began to take place, including Fiona finding her husband at the bottom of the stairs in the middle of the night with no idea of how he got there. And so, she once again called in her medium friend, who told her that the haunting had started again as a direct reaction to Fiona's life having become happier and more settled.

The documentary goes on to explain that Fiona learned of a local man who was said to be able to see ghosts and spirits, and who could help out in cases such as this. His name was John Parker. He worked as a bricklayer but was something of a modern-day equivalent to a local cunning man such as the 'Exeter White Witch' in times past (see Chapter Nine).

In 1993, John Parker visited the cottage and over a period of six hours he tells us that he battled the forces that were present there, which belonged to people who had been sacrificed for the cult to which they belonged. Eventually, he managed to send the spirits to 'the other side' and there were no further problems. Two years later, Hawthorn Cottage was repossessed by the bank.

The Teignmouth poltergeist case as described in the documentary is curious. It is presented on the programme in sensationalist detail, and yet there are no particular printed sources which refer to it, unlike hauntings such as those described in Chapter Seven. We would expect to find something in literature on the topic. The story entails much reference to black magic rituals and murdered children, and yet nothing in the historic record or local memory substantiates this.

It is certainly true that similar sacrifices have been made in the past, but in ancient or Roman times rather than more recently. It is more likely that these stories involve the 'Satanic Panic' of the 1980s, where ritual abuse relating to evil cults and black magic caused public consternation.[27] There are other such instances. Buckfastleigh Church, location of Squire Cabell's tomb, was destroyed by arson ascribed to 'satanists' or 'witches'. And cases of animal mutilation on the moors are often similarly attributed to 'satanic rituals': examples from Cox Tor on Dartmoor in 2006,[28] and a pony killing in 2015,[29] amongst many others.

Satanic ritual stories stem from a very old source, and circulate worldwide rather than being limited to the UK. Jeffrey Victor, writing on the subject in America not long after the Satanic Panic took hold there, notes that as far back as Roman times, there were stories claiming that Christians kidnapped Roman children for use in ritual sacrifice.[30] Victor's comments are of interest here because many of the tropes are hallmarks of the Teignmouth poltergeist case:

> The satanic cult rumor stories derive primarily from a very ancient legend that tells the story of children who are kidnapped and murdered by a secret conspiracy of evil strangers who use the children's blood and body parts in religious rituals ... Variations of the legend are commonly elaborated with symbols of mysterious evil: graveyard robberies and the mutilation of corpses, secret meetings of people engaged in secret rituals, strange incantations, strange symbols seen on walls, people clothed in black robes with black cats, making ritual animal sacrifices.[31]

Other elements of the Teignmouth case relate to aspects of folklore with old roots. Cats have been used as foundation sacrifices in older properties, and also to offer apotropaic protection against supernatural invasion.[32] But cats are also a popular domesticated animal and are often buried in the garden when they pass away. They may indeed look mutilated after having been in the ground for a long time. Fiona's reference to being unable to move after waking suggests the physiological phenomenon of paralysis during certain phases of sleep.

Unless the entire story has been fabricated, there can be little doubt that there was genuine concern from the main witnesses in the case. It is interesting to note that Fiona did not consider having the electrical problems investigated by a tradesperson, but rather called in a medium. This would suggest a pre-existing level of belief in the paranormal which might have influenced how the happenings were perceived. This is something often seen at work in the other type of paranormal television presentation—the ghost hunt.

There are many different ghost-hunting television programmes, but the pioneering show from the UK, and the one that spawned many of the overseas examples, is *Most Haunted*, produced by Antix Productions and first airing in 2002. This show, and witness perception in general, had a large part to play in an alleged haunting in a house in North Devon which my wife and I investigated as part of a group in the early 2000s.

The house was a private dwelling belonging to the mother of the young lad who invited us there, and for that reason the exact location remains off the record in terms of this discussion. The case was quite complex and after spending a little time there it became apparent to us that the witness was a fan of programmes like *Most Haunted*. He spoke of it on a number of occasions and we found that the way he conducted himself during investigations had many parallels with the methods of presenters and crew on such programmes.

In summary, although interesting phenomena were occurring in the house, it became very difficult to pin down exactly why. The case, essentially, became more of an investigation into the effects of witness psychology, rather than a more straightforward 'paranormal' investigation. We later discovered that after we had finished our part of the investigation, the witness invited a local medium in to look at the property. He later continued to see this medium and she subsequently started to teach him how to 'become a medium' himself.

What both of these Devon-based modern ghost experiences, moderated in different ways through the medium of television, show us is the legend-forming aspects of paranormal TV programming and the role this has in the production of modern folklore. Television not only conveys the views of individuals, but influences them too. The old idea of the 'most haunted building in Devon' as a tourist trap can also now be legitimized by the addition of 'as seen on television'.

All the examples in this final chapter serve to demonstrate that there is still plenty of folklore being generated in modern times. It is simply a case of recognizing that the term does not only define those things that we classify as old, and part of a superstitious past. We are a species that thrives on telling stories and those stories are disseminated in different ways in modern times. But their content is no less relevant.

Notes

Introduction

1. The letter, titled 'Folk-Lore', was dated 12 August and published under the pseudonym of Ambrose Merton in *The Athenaeum* 982 (22 August 1846): 862c–863a.
2. Dundes, A. (ed.), *The Study of Folklore* (Englewood Cliffs, NJ: Prentice-Hall, 1965): 2.
3. Bowring, J., 'Devonian Folk-Lore Illustrated', *Report and Transactions of the Devonshire Association* 2 (1867–68): 82.
4. https://hostingtribunal.com/blog/how-many-websites/, accessed 7 June 2021.
5. https://healthit.com.au/how-big-is-the-internet-and-how-do-we-measure-it/, accessed 7 June 2021.
6. Available at https://www.youtube.com/watch?v=PBDJ2UJpKt4, accessed 7 June 2021.
7. This is a Master of Arts course in Folklore Studies run at the University of Hertfordshire. It was presented for the first time in the 2019–20 academic year.

Chapter 1: Folklore Collection in Devon

1. Britannica, The Editors of Encyclopaedia, 'Kent's Cavern', *Encyclopedia Britannica*, 17 September 2013, https://www.britannica.com/place/Kents-Cavern, accessed 28 June 2021.
2. Cited in Forbes Julian, Hester, 'William Pengelly, FRS, FGS, Father of the Devonshire Association', *Report and Transactions of the Devonshire Association* 44 (1912): 188.
3. Harpley, Rev. W., 'A Short Account of the Origin of the Association', *Report and Transactions of the Devonshire Association* 44 (1912): 155.
4. Bray, A.E., *Autobiography of Anna Eliza Bray* (London: Chapman and Hall, 1884): 166.
5. The Royal Academy's catalogue record for the title (Record Number 13/2328) notes that the volume has 'Introduction and descriptions for Stothard's Monumental Effigies of Great Britain by Alfred John Kempe, 1832' and that 'the letterpress was supplied by his brother-in-law, Alfred John Kemp [*sic*]'. No mention is made of Anna Eliza Bray's involvement.
6. Bray, A.E., *Autobiography of Anna Eliza Bray* (London: Chapman and Hall, 1884): 192.
7. These two families feature in *Courtenay of Walreddon: A Romance of the West* (1844) and *Fitz of Fitz-ford* (1884) respectively. Bray acknowledged that the fictitious stories drew from truth.
8. The title was illustrated by Hablot Knight Browne, also known by the pen name 'Phiz', who had notably also illustrated works for Charles Dickens.

9. The archive, reference number GB 182 BRAY, consists of four boxes with a total of 444 individual items.

10. *Report and Transactions of the Devonshire Association* 11 (1879): 58.

11. In total, it took three days to deal with the sale of the books, resulting in the collection being split up between many purchasers.

12. *Report and Transactions of the Devonshire Association* 11 (1879): 58.

13. According to information compiled by book aggregation company Fantastic Fiction and regularly updated on their website: https://www.fantasticfiction.com/b/sabine-baring-gould/ accessed 27 December 2022.

14. Graebe, M., *As I Walked Out* (Oxford: Signal Books, 2017): xv.

15. The entry in Domesday in 1086 CE notes that the building on the site at the time was a royal manor, named as Lew House and owned by the Sheriff of Devon, though leased to a relative—Rogerius de Mole.

16. Information held in the University of Cambridge Alumni Database. This can be searched online via https://venn.lib.cam.ac.uk/ .

17. The songs featured in these volumes were collected by Baring-Gould and the Reverend Henry Fleetwood Sheppard, the latter providing musical arrangements.

18. Graebe, M., *As I Walked Out* (Oxford: Signal Books, 2017): xv.

19. Collection reference number 5203M contains Baring-Gould's personal copies of his folk song materials. There are many other collections with other papers relating to the family.

20. *Report and Transactions of the Devonshire Association* 26 (1894): 101.

21. Anonymous, *Report and Transactions of the Devonshire Association* 69 (1937): 33. Available at: https://devonassoc.org.uk/person/radford-emma-louisa/ accessed 27 December 2022.

22. Anonymous, *Report and Transactions of the Devonshire Association* 70 (1938): 24. Available at: https://devonassoc.org.uk/person/chope-richard-pearse/ accessed 27 December 2022.

23. http://www.torquaymuseum.org/explore/explore-our-collections/social-history, accessed 28 June 2021.

24. The current resident of the property described these residual remains to the author, but it was a previous modern resident who caused the damage to the wood panelling.

25. Blacker, C. and Davidson, H.E. (eds), *Women and Tradition* (United States: Carolina Academic Press, 2000): 248.

26. Davidson, H.E., 'Obituary: Theo Brown (1914–1993)', *Folklore* 104 (1993): 168.

27. Ibid.

28. http://devonandexeterinstitution.org, accessed 26 July 2021.

29. https://swheritage.org.uk/devon-archives/visit/local-studies-library/, accessed 26 July 2021.

Chapter 2: Stories from the Moors

1. Dartmoor National Park Authority Basic Factsheet. Available at https://www.dartmoor.gov.uk/learning/basic-factsheets, accessed 10 November 2021.

2. Anonymous, 'Countryfile Discovers Exmoor's Hope Bourne', *Devon Life*, March 2014. Available at https://www.greatbritishlife.co.uk/things-to-do/countryfile-discovers-exmoor-s-hope-bourne-7126948, accessed 24 August 2022.

3. For example, at Sinai Park House in Shobnall, East Staffordshire, a cook named Isabella Baxter was said to have become pregnant by one of the monks residing at the property when it was an abbey. When the truth became obvious, she was supposedly pushed down the stairs and killed. At Llanelly House in Llanelli a housemaid called Mira Turner also found herself pregnant, only this time she threw herself down the stairs after taking laudanum. Both events are said to have resulted in hauntings in the properties that continue to this day.

4. St Leger-Gordon, R.E., *The Witchcraft and Folklore of Dartmoor* (New York: Bell Publishing Company, 1972): 116.

5. Ibid.

6. http://www.dartmoor-crosses.org.uk/widecombe_churchyard.htm,   accessed   13 November 2021.

7. Widecombe and District Local History Group, *The History of Widecombe Fair* (Chudleigh: Orchard Publications, 2007): 30.

8. Baring-Gould, S. et al., *Songs of the West: Folk Songs of Devon and Cornwall: Collected from the Mouths of the People* (London: Methuen, 1890): 6.

9. Gray, T., *Uncle Tom Cobley and All* (Exeter: Mint Press, 2019): 138.

10. Widecombe and District Local History Group, *The History of Widecombe Fair* (Chudleigh: Orchard Publications, 2007): 1.

11. Graebe, M., *As I Walked Out* (Oxford: Signal Books, 2017): 121.

12. The English translation cited by *Collins Dictionary* (originally published in 1979 and now online at www.collinsdictionary.com) is 'Ghost Rider'. They class this translation as myth, aligning it with the broader mythology of the Wild Hunt.

13. Northall, G.F., *English Folk-Rhymes: A Collection of Traditional Verses Relating to Places and Persons, Customs, Superstitions, Etc* (London: Kegan Paul, Trench, Trübner and Co., 1892): 333.

14. Snell, F.J., *A Book of Exmoor* (London: Methuen, 1903): 50.

15. Bhanji, S., 'From Folklore to History: Some Notes on the Evidence Concerning the Doones', *The Devon Historian* 58 (1999): 25.

16. Accession number NDDMS 1991.1367.

17. Bhanji, S., 'From Folklore to History: Some Notes on the Evidence Concerning the Doones', *The Devon Historian* 58 (1999): 26.

18. For example, the pamphlet 'The Original Doones of Exmoor' by Ida M. Brown, which was essentially a reprint of an article from the *West Somerset Free Press* of 12 October 1901 (p. 7).

19. https://www.exmoor-nationalpark.gov.uk/Whats-Special/culture/literary-links/rd-blackmore, accessed 5 September 2022.

20. Kingsley, C., *Westward Ho!* (New York: Thomas Y. Crowell and Co., 1855): 229.

21. Gibson, E., *Brittania: Or a Chorographical Description of Great Britain and Ireland*, Volume 1 (London: Asonsham Churchill, 1722): 32.

22. Cox, T., *A Topographical, Ecclesiastical and Natural History of Devon* (London: E. Nutt, 1700): 273.

23. Milton, P., *The Discovery of Dartmoor* (Chichester: Phillimore and Co., 2006): 25.

24. Baring-Gould, S. *A Book of Dartmoor* (London: Methuen, 1907): 135.

25. Mills, A.D., *A Dictionary of English Place Names* (Oxford: Oxford University Press, 1991): 102.

26. Crossing, W., *Folk Rhymes of Devon; Notices of the Metrical Sayings Found in the Lore of the People* (Devon: J.G. Commin, 1911): 27.

27. https://drdavidclarke.co.uk/2017/03/30/dead-flows-the-don/, accessed 17 November 2021.

28. Coombs, M., 'Plymouth's Ancient Trackways', *Wisht Maen* 3 (1994): 11.

29. Gilbert, D., *The Parochial History of Cornwall* (London: J.B. Nichols and Son, 1838): 202.

30. Brown, T., *Devon Ghosts* (Norwich: Jarrold, 1982): 139.

31. Crossing, W., *Crossing's Guide to Dartmoor* (Newton Abbot: Peninsula Press, 1993 [1912]): 30.

32. Snell, F.J., *A Book of Exmoor* (London: Methuen, 1903): 50.

33. Ibid., 72.

34. Drury, S.M., 'English Love Divinations Using Plants: An Aspect', *Folklore* 97:2 (1986): 211.

35. Brown, T., 'Forty-Eighth Report on Folk-Lore', *Report and Transactions of the Devonshire Association* 83 (1951): 73.

36. Baring-Gould, Rev. S., *Strange Survivals* (London: Methuen, 1892): 5.

37. Norman, M., *Black Dog Folklore* (Cornwall: Troy Books, 2015): 25.

38. Brown, T., 'Seventy-Fourth Report on Folklore', *Report and Transactions of the Devonshire Association* 109 (1977): 211.

39. Spence, J., *Shetland Folk-Lore* (Lerwick: Johnson and Greig, 1899): 21.

Chapter 3: The Calendar Year

1. For a full definition of calendar customs, see Simpson, J. and Roud, S., *Oxford Dictionary of English Folklore* (Oxford: Oxford University Press, 2000): 44–45.

2. Author's definition. Written for online teaching materials at www.learnforpleasure.com, course HIST051.

3. Whitlock, R., *The Folklore of Devon* (London, B.T. Batsford, 1977): 135.

4. Johnson, B., 'Give Us Our Eleven Days', *Historic UK*. Available at https://www.historic-uk.com/HistoryUK/HistoryofBritain/Give-us-our-eleven-days/, accessed 22 November 2021.

5. Anonymous, *Jackson's Oxford Journal*, 15 September 1753.

6. Reed, S., *Wassailing* (Cornwall: Troy Books, 2013): 13.

7. Devon Folklife Register, *Folk Festivals and Traditions of Devon* (Exeter: Exeter City Museums Service, 1980): 7.

8. Whitlock, R., *The Folklore of Devon* (London: B.T. Batsford, 1977): 136.

9. Devon Folklife Register, *Folk Festivals and Traditions of Devon* (Exeter: Exeter City Museums Service, 1980): 8.

10. Amery, P.F.S. (ed.), *Devon Notes and Queries*, Volume 2 (Exeter: J.G. Commin, 1900): 113.

11. Chope, R.P., 'Thirty-Fifth Report on Devonshire Folk-Lore', *Report and Transactions of the Devonshire Association* 67 (1935): 140.

12. Simpson, J. and Roud, S., *Oxford Dictionary of English Folklore* (Oxford: Oxford University Press, 2000): 257.

13. Herrick, R., *Hesperides* (London & New York: G. Routledge and Sons, 1885): 222.

14. Chope, R.P., 'Thirty-Fifth Report on Devonshire Folk-Lore', *Report and Transactions of the Devonshire Association* 67 (1935): 141.

15. Doe, G., 'Seventh Report of the Committee on Devonshire Folk-Lore', *Report and Transactions of the Devonshire Association* 16 (1884): 122.

16. Chope, R.P., 'Devonshire Calendar Customs I: Movable Festivals', *Report and Transactions of the Devonshire Association* 68 (1936): 233.

17. Chambers, R., *The Book of Days* (London & Edinburgh: W&R Chambers, 1869): 255.

18. Bray, A.E., *A Description of the Part of Devonshire Bordering on the Tamar and the Tavy*, Volume 2 (London: J. Murray, 1836): 118–19.

19. Ibid., 119.

20. Various, *Devon and Cornwall Notes and Queries* 5:117 (1852): 77.

21. https://www.efdss.org/learning/resources/beginners-guides/48-british-folk-customs-from-plough-monday-to-hocktide/3373-shrove-tuesday, accessed 24 November 2021.

22. Chope, R.P., 'Devonshire Calendar Customs I: Movable Festivals', *Transactions of the Devonshire Association* 68 (1936): 237.

23. Lawton, C., 'Children "Tip Tip Toe" in Gittisham', *Midweek Herald*, 26 February 2016. Available at https://www.midweekherald.co.uk/news/20376129.children-tip-tip-toe-gittisham/, accessed 29 September 2022.

24. Chope, R.P., 'Devonshire Calendar Customs I: Movable Festivals', *Transactions of the Devonshire Association* 68 (1936): 234.

25. Ibid., 236.

26. Chanter, J.M., *Wanderings in North Devon* (Ilfracombe: Twiss and Son, 1887): 68.

27. Wunderli, M., 'Mothering Sunday', *British Newspaper Archive*, 26 March 2019. Available at https://blog.britishnewspaperarchive.co.uk/2017/03/26/mothering-sunday/, accessed 26 September 2022.

28. Hewett, S., *Nummits and Crummits: Devonshire Customs, Characteristics and Lolk-Lore* (London: T. Burleigh, 1900): 87.

29. http://www.cornishpasties.org.uk/henncock-pasties.htm, accessed 29 February 2022.

30. Cossins, J., *Reminiscences of Exeter Fifty Years Since* (Published by the author, 1877): 34.

31. https://www.bbc.co.uk/news/uk-england-devon-57986811, accessed 26 September 2022.

32. Anonymous, *The Random House College Dictionary* (New York: Random House, 1975): 993.

33. Hindley, C., *A History of the Cries of London: Ancient and Modern* (Cambridge: Cambridge University Press, 2011): 130.

34. Crossing, W., *Folk Rhymes of Devon* (Exeter: J.G. Commin, 1911): 142.

35. Norman, M., *Telling the Bees and Other Customs* (Gloucester: The History Press, 2020): 181.

36. Hewett, S., *Nummits and Crummits: Devonshire Customs, Characteristics and Folk-Lore* (London: T. Burleigh, 1900): 77.

37. Amery, P.F.S. (ed.), 'Twenty-First Report of the Committee on Devonshire Folk-Lore', *Report and Transactions of the Devonshire Association* 36 (1904): 97.

38. Chope, R.P., 'Devonshire Calendar Customs I: Movable Festivals', *Report and Transactions of the Devonshire Association* 68 (1936): 243–44.

39. Henderson, W., *Notes of the Folklore of the Northern Counties of England and the Borders* (London: Longmans, Green and Co., 1866): 63–64.

40. Simpson, J. and Roud, S., *Oxford Dictionary of English Folklore* (Oxford: Oxford University Press, 2000): 242.

41. Watkin, H.R., *A Short Description of Torre Abbey, Torquay, Devonshire* (Torquay: Fleet Printing Works, 1912): 11.

42. Chambers, R., *The Book of Days* (London & Edinburgh: W&R Chambers, 1869): 498.

43. The description comes from a Welsh-language poem titled 'I'r Fedwen' or 'The Birch' written by Gruffudd ab Adda. In a newer collection looking at medieval Welsh poems it was retitled 'The Maypole'. Clancy, J.P. (tr.), *Medieval Welsh Poems* (Dublin: Four Courts Press, 2003): 208–09.

44. An extract from the diary of Moretonhampstead resident Silvester Treleaven in 1801 reads: 'Cross-Tree, floored and seated round with a platform railed on each side, from the top of Mr. Hancock's Garden wall to the Tree, and a flight of steps in the Garden, for the Company to ascend, after passing the platform they enter under a grand arch formed with boughs—there is sufficient room for thirty persons to sit round and six couple to dance, besides the Orchestra. From the novelty of this rural apartment, it is expected much company will resort there during the summer.' Available on the website of the Moretonhampstead History Society at http://www.moretonhampstead.org.uk/gaz/dancingtree.ghtml, accessed 29 September 2022.

45. Blackmore, R.D., *Christowell: A Dartmoor Tale* (London: Sampson Low, Marston, Searle & Rivington, 1885): 100–10.

46. Simpson, J. and Roud, S., *Oxford Dictionary of English Folklore* (Oxford: Oxford University Press, 2000): 196–97.

47. Anonymous, *Aunt Judy's Magazine*, 1874, no. xcvii: 436.

48. King, R.J., 'First Report of Committee of Devonshire Folk-Lore', *Report and Transactions of the Devonshire Association* 8 (1876): 50–51.

49. Devon Folklife Register, *Folk Festivals and Traditions of Devon* (Exeter: Exeter City Museums Service, 1980): 19.

50. Chope, R.P., 'Devonshire Calendar Customs I: Movable Festivals', *Transactions of the Devonshire Association* 68 (1936): 249.

51. Cleaveland, E., *A Genealogical History of the Noble and Illustrious Family of Courtenay, Part 3* (Exeter: Edward Farley, 1735): 147.

52. Chope, R.P., 'Devonshire Calendar Customs I: Movable Festivals', *Transactions of the Devonshire Association* 68 (1936): 249.

53. Tugwell, G., *The North Devon Scenery Book* (London: Simpkin, Marshall and Co., 1863): 109–14.

54. Westcote, T., *A View of Devonshire in MDCXXX* (London: W. Roberts, 1845): 426.

55. Anonymous, *The Great Plum Pudding Contest Entry Form* (Torbay Libraries, 2016).

56. https://www.legendarydartmoor.co.uk/crazy_well.htm, accessed 29 November 2021.

57. King, R.J. (ed.), 'Second Report of the Committee on Devonshire Folk-Lore', *Report and Transactions of the Devonshire Association* 9 (1877): 90.

58. 'Volo non Valeo' (Gibbons, M.S.), *'We Donkeys' in Devon* (Exeter: Hamilton, Adams and Co., 1885): 10.

59. Owen, A.N., *History of a Devon Custom* (Published by the author, 2006): 3.

60. Chope, R.P., 'Thirty-Sixth Report on Devonshire Folk-Lore', *Report and Transactions of the Devonshire Association* 68 (1936): 97.

61. Tozer, E., *Devonshire and Other Original Poems; with Some Account of Ancient Customs, Superstitions and Traditions* (Exeter: Office of the Devon Weekly Times, 1873): 71.

62. Devon Folklife Register, *Folk Festivals and Traditions of Devon* (Exeter: Exeter City Museums Service, 1980): 5.

Chapter 4: Farming and the Weather

1. https://www.devon.gov.uk/environment/wildlife/habitats-and-species/farms, accessed 6 December 2021.
2. DEFRA, *DEFRA Statistics: Agricultural Facts. England Regional Profiles* (Department for Environment, Food and Rural Affairs, 2021): 35.
3. https://www.devonlive.com/news/devon-news/how-much-land-your-area-752168, accessed 6 December 2021.
4. DEFRA, *DEFRA Statistics: Agricultural Facts. England Regional Profiles* (Department for Environment, Food and Rural Affairs, 2021): 35.
5. https://www.devon.gov.uk/environment/wildlife/habitats-and-species/farms, accessed 6 December 2021.
6. King James Bible, Matthew 16: 2–3.
7. Bray, A.E., *A Description of the Part of Devonshire Bordering on the Tamar and the Tavy* (London: John Murray, 1836): 5–6.
8. Bowring, J., 'Devonian Folk-Lore Illustrated', *Report and Transactions of the Devonshire Association* 2 (1867–68): 81.
9. Ibid.
10. Doe, G. (ed.), 'Ninth Report of the Committee on Devonshire Folk-Lore', *Report and Transactions of the Devonshire Association* 18 (1886): 105.
11. Brown, T., 'Fifty-First Report on Folk-Lore', *Report and Transactions of the Devonshire Association* 86 (1954): 297.
12. https://www.metoffice.gov.uk/about-us/press-office/news/weather-and-climate/2017/do-cows-really-lie-down-when-its-about-to-rain, accessed 7 December 2021.
13. Hewett, S., *Nummits and Crummits: Devonshire Customs, Characteristics and Folk-Lore* (London: Thomas Burleigh, 1900): 118.
14. Amery, P.F.S. (ed.), 'Eleventh Report of the Committee on Devonshire Folk-Lore', *Report and Transactions of the Devonshire Association* 24 (1892): 51.
15. Doe, G. (ed.), 'Eighth Report of the Committee on Devonshire Folk-Lore', *Report and Transactions of the Devonshire Association* 17 (1885): 124.
16. Doe, G. (ed.), 'Fifth Report of the Committee on Devonshire Folk-Lore', *Report and Transactions of the Devonshire Association* 12 (1880): 113.
17. Chope, R.P. (ed.), 'Twenty-Seventh Report on Devonshire Folk-Lore', *Report and Transactions of the Devonshire Association* 57 (1925): 127.
18. Amery, P.F.S. (ed.), 'Twenty-Third Report of the Committee on Devonshire Folk-Lore', *Report and Transactions of the Devonshire Association* 38 (1906): 93.
19. Smith, J.B., 'Towards the Demystification of Lawrence Lazy', *Folklore* 107 (1996): 102.
20. Barnes, W., *A Glossary of the Dorset Dialect with a Grammar* (Dorchester & London: Case/Trubner, 1886): 77.
21. *Western Morning News*, 23 July 1925.
22. Amery, P.F.S. (ed.), 'Eleventh Report of the Committee on Devonshire Folk-Lore', *Report and Transactions of the Devonshire Association* 24 (1892): 51.
23. Chope, R.P. (ed.), 'Twenty-Seventh Report on Devonshire Folk-Lore', *Report and Transactions of the Devonshire Association* 57 (1925): 108.

24. Brown, T., 'Fifty-Eighth Report on Folklore', *Report and Transactions of the Devonshire Association* 93 (1961): 12.

25. Rose, H.J., 'The Folklore of the Geoponica', *Folklore* 44:1 (1933): 62.

26. Hewett, S., *Nummits and Crummits* (London: Thomas Burleigh, 1900): 116.

27. Ibid., 117.

28. Brown, T., 'Fifty-Sixth Report on Folklore', *Report and Transactions of the Devonshire Association* 91 (1959): 201.

29. *Western Morning News*, 17 June 1958.

30. Chope, R.P., 'Thirty-Fifth Report on Devonshire Folk-Lore', *Report and Transactions of the Devonshire Association* 67 (1935): 144.

31. King, R.J. (ed.), 'Second Report of the Committee on Devonshire Folk-Lore', *Report and Transactions of the Devonshire Association* 9 (1877): 90.

32. Rose, H.J., 'The Folklore of the Geoponica', *Folklore* 44:1 (1933): 69.

33. Vickery, R., *Garlands, Conkers and Mother-Die: British and Irish Plant-Lore* (London: Continuum, 2010): 4.

34. www.womenslandarmy.co.uk, accessed 13 December 2021.

35. King, R.J. (ed.), 'Second Report of the Committee on Devonshire Folk-Lore', *Report and Transactions of the Devonshire Association* 9 (1877): 101.

36. Elworthy, F.T., *Crying the Neck: A Devonshire Custom* (Plymouth: W. Brendon & Son, 1891): 2.

37. Robbins, K. et al., 'Agricultural Change and Farm Incomes in Devon: An Update', in *CRR Research Report No. 17* (Exeter: University of Exeter Centre for Rural Research, June 2006): 2.

38. Chope, R.P., 'Thirty-Second Report on Devonshire Folk-Lore', *Report and Transactions of the Devonshire Association* 64 (1932): 154.

39. https://www.almanac.com/content/setting-chicken-eggs-moons-sign, accessed 13 December 2021.

40. King, R.J. (ed.), 'Second Report of the Committee on Devonshire Folk-Lore', *Report and Transactions of the Devonshire Association* 9 (1877): 89–90.

41. DEFRA, *Agricultural Statistics—South West* (Department for Environment, Food and Rural Affairs, 2019): 2.

42. Baker, M., *Folklore and Customs of Rural England* (Newton Abbot: David and Charles, 1974): 45.

43. Ibid.

44. St Leger-Gordon, R.E., *The Witchcraft and Folklore of Dartmoor* (New York: Bell Publishing Company, 1972): 42.

45. Amery, P.F.S. (ed.), 'Twenty-Third Report of the Committee on Devonshire Folk-Lore', *Report and Transactions of the Devonshire Association* 38 (1906): 87.

46. Chope, R.P., 'Thirty-Third Report on Devonshire Folk-Lore', *Report and Transactions of the Devonshire Association* 65 (1933): 130.

47. Chope, R.P., 'Twenty-Seventh Report on Devonshire Folk-Lore', *Report and Transactions of the Devonshire Association* 57 (1925): 124.

48. Brown, T., 'Fifty-Sixth Report on Folklore', *Report and Transactions of the Devonshire Association* 91 (1959): 199.

49. Brown, T., 'Eighty-Third Report on Folklore', *Report and Transactions of the Devonshire Association* 118 (1986): 246.

Chapter 5: The Devil in Devon

1. White, E.D., 'Devil's Stones and Midnight Rites: Megaliths, Folklore, and Contemporary Pagan Witchcraft', *Folklore* 125:1 (2014): 60–79.
2. Harte, J., 'The Devil's Chapels: Fiends, Fear and Folklore at Prehistoric Sites', in J. Parker (ed.), *Written on Stone: The Cultural Reception of British Prehistoric Monuments* (Cambridge: Cambridge Scholars Publishing, 2009): 28.
3. Page, J.L.W., *An Exploration of Exmoor and the Hill Country of West Somerset: With Notes on Its Archaeology* (London: Seeley and Co., 1895): 91.
4. https://archaeology-travel.com/england/tarr-steps-exmoor/, accessed 22 September 2021.
5. https://www.legendarydartmoor.co.uk/devil_dart.htm, accessed 22 September 2021.
6. Kingsley, C., *Westward Ho!* (New York: Thomas Y. Crowell and Co., 1855): 201.
7. Prince, J., *The Worthies of Devon* (Plymouth: Rees and Curtis, 1810).
8. Harte, J., 'The Devil on Dartmoor', *Time and Mind: The Journal of Archaeology, Consciousness and Culture* 1:1 (2008).
9. https://visitdartmoor.co.uk/myths-and-legends, accessed 4 October 2021.
10. *Woolmer's Exeter and Plymouth Gazette*, 17 February 1855.
11. Ridout, B.V., 'The Devil's Footprints Revisited', *Report and Transactions of the Devonshire Association* 153 (2021): 291–306.
12. Coxhead, J.R.W., *The Devil in Devon: An Anthology of Folk Tales* (Brackness: West Country Handbooks, 1967): 32.
13. Anonymous, *A Pictorial and Descriptive Guide to Dartmoor* (London: Ward Lock and Co., 1937).
14. Whitlock, R., *The Folklore of Devon* (London: B.T. Batsford, 1977): 27.
15. Anonymous, 'High Church on Hill So Good They Named It Thrice', *Gloucestershire Echo*, 28 February 2019.
16. Gaydon, T., *My North Devon of Myth and Mystery* (Bideford: Badger Books, 1987): 42.
17. Hervey, Canon R., *The Place Where the Devil Died of the Cold* (Northlew: TS, revised 1944).
18. Brown, T., 'A Further Note on the "Stag Hunt" in Devon', *Folklore* 90:1 (1979): 18–21.
19. Baring-Gould, Rev. S., *Strange Survivals* (London: Methuen, 1905): 30.
20. Coxhead, J.R.W., *Devon Traditions and Fairy-Tales* (Exmouth: Raleigh Press, 1959): 34–35.
21. Baring-Gould, Rev. S., *Strange Survivals* (London: Methuen, 1905): 29.
22. It should also be acknowledged that the date of 'Devil Spit Day' can be ascribed to 10 October, now known as 'Old Michaelmas Day'. Prior to the 1752 calendar changes, this was the date on which many believed that blackberries were soiled by the Devil.

Chapter 6: Fairies in Devon

1. Grinsell, L.V., 'Some Aspects of the Folklore of Prehistoric Monuments', *Folklore* 48:3 (1937): 248.
2. Coxhead, J.R.W., *Devon Traditions and Fairy Tales* (Exmouth: Raleigh Press, 1959): 48.
3. Anonymous, *English Forests and Forest Trees: Historical, Legendary, and Descriptive* (London: Ingram, Cooke, and Company, 1853): 189.
4. Ibid., 190.

5. Harte, J., *Explore Fairy Traditions* (Nottingham: Explore Publishing, 2004): 74.

6. Chope, R.P., 'Thirty-Fourth Report on Devonshire Folk-Lore', *Report and Transactions of the Devonshire Association* 66 (1934): 78.

7. Milton, J., 'L'Allegro', in *Poems of Mr John Milton* (London: Humphrey Moseley, 1645): 34–35.

8. Anonymous, *English Forests and Forest Trees: Historical, Legendary, and Descriptive* (London: Ingram, Cooke, and Co., 1853): 188.

9. Amery, P.F.S. (ed.), 'Twenty-Second Report of the Committee on Devonshire Folk-Lore', *Report and Transactions of the Devonshire Association* 37 (1905): 113.

10. Chope, R.P., 'Thirty-Second Report on Devonshire Folk-Lore', *Report and Transactions of the Devonshire Association* 64 (1932): 159.

11. Venkataswami, M.N., 'Devonshire Folklore, Collected among the People near Exeter within the Last Five or Six Years. By Lady Rosalind Northcote', *Folklore* 11:2 (1900): 212.

12. There are no records of fairies with wings in terms of British folklore before the eighteenth century. For a full discussion of the development of the winged fairy, see Simon Young's chapter titled 'When Did Fairies Get Wings?', in Darryl Caterine and John W. Morehead (eds), *The Paranormal and Popular Culture: A Postmodern Religious Landscape* (London: Routledge, 2019).

13. Whitlock, R., *The Folklore of Devon* (London: B.T. Batsford, 1977): 28.

14. Anonymous, *English Forests and Forest Trees: Historical, Legendary, and Descriptive* (London: Ingram, Cooke, and Company, 1853): 188.

15. Tozer, E., *Devonshire and Other Original Poems with Some Account of Ancient Customs, Superstitions, and Traditions* (Exeter: Office of the Devon Weekly Times, 1873): 77.

16. Chope, R.P. (ed.), 'Twenty-Ninth Report on Devonshire Folk-Lore', *Transactions of the Devonshire Association* 60 (1928): 116–17.

17. Young, S. and Houlbrook, C. (eds), *Magical Folk: British and Irish Fairies 500 AD to the Present* (London: Gibson Square, 2018): 52.

18. Anecdote recorded in audio and sent to author as personal correspondence, 16 January 2021.

19. Bovet, R., *Pandaemonium, or, The Devil's Cloyster Being a Further Blow to Modern Sadduceism, Proving the Existence of Witches and Spirits, in a Discourse Deduced from the Fall of the Angels, the Propagation of Satan's Kingdom Before the Flood, the Idolatry of the Ages after Greatly Advancing Diabolical Confederacies, with an Account of the Lives and Transactions of Several Notorious Witches: Also, a Collection of Several Authentick Relations of Strange Apparitions of Dæmons and Spectres, and Fascinations of Witches, Never Before Printed* (London: J. Walthoe, 1684): 208.

20. Weber, H. et al., *Illustrations of Northern Antiquities* (Edinburgh: James Ballantyne and Co., 1814): 399.

21. Crossing, W., *Tales of the Dartmoor Pixies: Glimpses of Elfin Haunts and Antics* (London: Hood, 1890): 71–73.

22. Kirk, R. and Lang, A., *The Secret Common-Wealth and a Short Treatise of Charms and Spells* (London: David Nutt, 1893 [1691]): 6.

23. Menefee, S.P., 'A Cake in the Furrow', *Folklore* 91:2 (1980): 176.

24. Venkataswami, M.N., 'Devonshire Folklore, Collected among the People near Exeter within the Last Five or Six Years. By Lady Rosalind Northcote', *Folklore* 11:2 (1900): 212–19.

25. Hewett, S., *Nummits and Crummits: Devonshire Customs, Characteristics and Folk-Lore* (London: T. Burleigh, 1900): 38.

26. Wood, T., *True Thomas* (London: Jonathan Cape, 1936).

27. See, for example, the arrangement available at https://www.youtube.com/watch?v=YTutl5pkPPI, which also includes images of the musical notation.

28. https://www.tulipmania.art/folk-tale-from-devon-fairies-lulled-their-babies/, accessed 4 January 2022.

29. Crossing, W., *Tales of the Dartmoor Pixies: Glimpses of Elfin Haunts and Antics* (London: Hood, 1890): 2.

30. Baring-Gould, Rev. S., *A Book of Dartmoor* (London: Methuen, 1900): 221.

31. Ibid., 220.

32. https://www.heritagegateway.org.uk/gateway/Results_Single.aspx?uid=MDV9018&resourceID=104, accessed 11 January 2022.

33. Jones, M., *The History of Chudleigh in the County of Devon and the Surrounding Scenery, Seats, Families, etc.* (London: T.W. Grattan, 1852): 171.

34. Bray, A.E., *A Peep at the Pixies: Or, Legends of the West* (London: Grant and Griffith, 1854): 149.

35. Bezalel, M., 'The "Fairy Door" Phenomenon', *The Guardian*, 23 June 2006.

36. Young, S., 'Pixy-Led in Devon and the South-West', *Report and Transactions of the Devonshire Association* 148 (2016): 311.

37. Amery, P.F.S. (ed.), 'Eleventh Report of the Committee on Devonshire Folk-Lore', *Report and Transactions of the Devonshire Association* 24 (1892): 52.

38. Chope, R.P., 'Thirty-Fifth Report on Devonshire Folk-Lore', *Report and Transactions of the Devonshire Association* 67 (1935): 136.

39. Brown, T., 'Seventy-Eighth Report on Folklore', *Report and Transactions of the Devonshire Association* 113 (1981): 177.

40. Snell, F.J., *A Book of Exmoor* (London: Methuen, 1903): 252.

41. Ibid.

Chapter 7: Some Devon Hauntings

1. https://www.itraveluk.co.uk/maps/england/4533/devon/luffincott.html, accessed 11 October 2021 .

2. White, W., *History, Gazetteer & Directory of Devon* (Printed for the author, 1850): 786.

3. Personal correspondence to Theo Brown, recorded in Brown, T., 'Fifty-Seventh Report of Folklore', *Report and Transactions of the Devonshire Association* 92 (1960): 370. The original letter is now held in Theo Brown's archives at the Heritage Collections Library, University of Exeter.

4. Brown, T., 'Fifty-Seventh Report of Folklore', *Report and Transactions of the Devonshire Association* 92 (1960): 371.

5. Held in the archives of Theo Brown at the Heritage Collections Library, University of Exeter.

6. Brown, T., *Devon Ghosts* (Norwich: Jarrold, 1982): 89.

7. Young, F., *A History of Anglican Exorcism: Deliverance and Demonology in Church Ritual* (London: I.B. Tauris, 2018): 59.

8. Brown, T., *The Fate of the Dead: A Study in Folk Eschatology in the West Country after the Reformation* (London: The Folklore Society, 1979): 49.

9. Personal correspondence to Theo Brown. Held in the archives of Theo Brown at the Heritage Collections Library, University of Exeter.

10. Halliday, W.R., 'The Story of Sir Robert Chichester Together with a Note on the Rev. William Gimmingham', *Folklore* 65:2 (1954): 109–11. .

11. Ibid.

12. A summary of the history of the manor is available on the property's official website at https://chambercombemanor.org.uk/history/, accessed 5 October 2022.

13. Poole, K.B., *Ghosts of the Westcountry* (Peterborough: Jarrold Publishing, 1997): 47.

14. Warwick, C.H., *The Hidden Room: The Legend of Chambercombe Manor* (Published by the author, 1987).

15. https://johnhmoore.co.uk/hele/smugglers.htm, accessed 14 October 2021.

16. Watkin, H.R., *A Short Description of Torre Abbey, Torquay, Devonshire* (Torquay: Fleet Printing Works, 1912): 48.

17. https://ancientmonuments.uk/117332-st-michaels-chapel-chapel-hill-tormohun-ward#.Yz1hPnbMKUk, accessed 5 October 2022.

18. White, J.T., *The History of Torquay* (Torquay: 'Directory', 1878): 85.

19. Ibid.

20. Pike, J.R., *Torquay* (Torquay: Torbay Borough Council Printing Services, 1994): 5.

21. Mackenzie, D.A., *Wonder Tales from Scottish Myth and Legend* (London: Blackie and Son, 1917): 181.

22. https://www.visitsouthdevon.co.uk/things-to-do/ness-cove-beach-p242403, accessed 5 October 2022.

23. An account from one of the original explorers is archived via JiscMail at https://www.jiscmail.ac.uk/cgi-bin/webadmin?A2=mining-history;7135e7d9.02, accessed 5 October 2022.

24. Brown, T., *Devon Ghosts* (Peterborough: Jarrold Publishing, 1982): 135.

25. Savage, R., 'Shadow Land', *TES Magazine*, 7 January 2005.

26. Gray, C., 'Return to Albion', *Town and Country Magazine*. Available at https://www.powderham.co.uk/uploads/News/return_to_albion_article.pdf, accessed 17 October 21.

27. Brown, T., *Devon Ghosts* (Peterborough: Jarrold Publishing, 1982): 135.

28. McKenzie, R., *They Still Serve: A Complete Guide to the Military Ghosts of Britain* (Lulu.com, 2008): 52.

29. Fea, A., *Secret Chambers and Hiding Places: The Historic, Romantic and Legendary Stories and Traditions about Hiding-Holes, Secret Chambers &c* (London: S.H. Bousfield, 1901).

30. Brown, T., *Devon Ghosts* (Peterborough: Jarrold Publishing, 1982): 135–36.

31. Norman, M. and Norman, T., *Dark Folklore* (Gloucestershire: The History Press, 2021): 77.

32. Colton, Rev. C.C., *A Plain and Authentic Narrative of the Sampford Ghost* (Tiverton: T. Smith, 1810): 19.

33. Ibid., 20.

34. Quoted at http://www.sampevsoc.co.uk/the-sampford-peverell-ghost.html, accessed 21 October 2021.

35. Harding, Lt Col W., *The History of Tiverton*, Volume 1 (Tiverton: F. Boyce, 1845): 183.

36. Brown, T., *Devon Ghosts* (Peterborough: Jarrold Publishing, 1982): 56.

37. Baring-Gould, Rev. S., *Devonshire Characters and Strange Events* (London: John Lane The Bodley Head, 1908): 291.

38. Donne, John, *Devotions upon Emergent Occasions, Meditation XVII* (London: Pickering, 1840): 574.

39. References to the actual memoir appear to have been lost and this information is drawn from various retellings.

40. Cotton, R.W., 'The Oxenham Omen', *Report and Transactions of the Devonshire Association* 14 (1882): 221–46.

41. Ibid.

42. Norman, T., 'Histories and Mysteries: The White Bird of the Oxenhams', *The Moorlander*, 24 July–6 August 2020: 13.

43. Mills, A.D., *A Dictionary of English Place Names* (Oxford: Oxford University Press, 1991): 378.

44. Howell, J., *Epistolae Ho-Elianae: The Familiar Letters of James Howell, Historiographer Royal to Charles II* (London: D. Nutt, 1892): 309.

45. Pole, Sir W., *Collections towards a Description of the County of Devon* (London: J. Nichols, 1791).

46. Cotton, R.W., 'The Oxenham Omen', *Report and Transactions of the Devonshire Association* 14 (1882): 221–46.

Chapter 8: The Black Dog

1. A text version is available to view online through Project Gutenberg at https://www.gutenberg.org/cache/epub/657/pg657.html, accessed 5 October 2022.

2. Conan Doyle, Sir A., 'The Hound of the Baskervilles', *Strand Magazine* 23 (1902): 252.

3. Norman, M., *Black Dog Folklore* (Cornwall: Troy Books, 2015): 102.

4. Carr, J.D., *The Life of Sir Arthur Conan Doyle* (London: John Murray, 1949): 187.

5. Bray, A.E., *Traditions, Legends, Superstitions and Sketches of Devonshire* (London: John Murray, 1838): 320.

6. Norway, A.H., *Highways and Byways in Devon and Cornwall* (London: Macmillan and Co., 1911): 151.

7. https://www.gutenberg.org/cache/epub/657/pg657.html, accessed 5 October 2022.

8. Harte, J., 'The Devil on Dartmoor', *Time and Mind: The Journal of Archaeology Consciousness and Culture* 1:1 (2008): 84.

9. Straffon, C., 'Pagan Cornwall—Land of the Goddess', *Meyn Mamvro* (1993): 74.

10. Cabell Djabri, S., *The Story of the Sepulchre* (London: Shamrock Press, 1989): 2.

11. Baring-Gould, Rev. S., *Devon*, Little Guide Series (London: Methuen, 1907).

12. Cabell Djabri, S., *The Story of the Sepulchre* (London: Shamrock Press, 1989): 2.

13. Cabell Djabri, S., *The Story of the Sepulchre* (London: Shamrock Press, 1989): 7.

14. Ibid.

15. Campbell, M., *The Hound of the Baskervilles: Dartmoor or Herefordshire?* (New York: Magico Magazine, 1953).

16. St Leger-Gordon, R.E., *The Witchcraft and Folklore of Dartmoor* (New York: Bell Publishing Company, 1972): 51.

17. Norman, M., *Telling the Bees and Other Customs: The Folklore of Rural Craft* (Gloucestershire: The History Press, 2020): 159.

18. Brown, T., 'Eightieth Report on Folklore', *Report and Transactions of the Devonshire Association* 115 (1983): 174.

19. Crossing, W., *Folklore and Legends of Dartmoor* (Liverton: Forest Publishing, 1997): 50.

20. Personal correspondence held in the archives of Theo Brown, Heritage Collections, University of Exeter.

21. Ibid.

22. www.warrenhouseinn.co.uk/history.html, accessed 1 November 2021.

23. https://www.newscientist.com/article/2082809-the-three-hares-motif-is-an-ancient-mystery-for-our-times/, accessed 1 November 2011.

24. Sayer, S., *The Outline of Dartmoor's Story* (Exeter: Devon Books, 1987): 24.

25. Norman, M., *Black Dog Folklore* (Cornwall: Troy Books, 2015): 51.

26. Personal correspondence held in the archives of Theo Brown, Heritage Collections, University of Exeter.

27. Rudkin, E., 'The Black Dog', *Folklore* 49:2 (1938): 117.

28. Handwritten notes archived by the author in the Folklore Library and Archive.

Chapter 9: Witchcraft

1. Sample search carried out using the Google search engine on 10 October 2022 .

2. Callow, J., *The Last Witches of England* (London: Bloomsbury, 2022): 268–75.

3. Le Franc, M., *Le champion des dames*, 1451. Manuscript held at the Bibliothèque nationale de France and available at https://gallica.bnf.fr/ark:/12148/btv1b9059128w/f31.item.

4. De Blécourt, W., 'Witches on Screen', in O. Davies (ed.), *The Oxford Illustrated History of Witchcraft and Magic* (Oxford: Oxford University Press, 2017): 261.

5. Ibid.

6. *Western Morning News*, 18–19 January 1984.

7. St Leger-Gordon, R.E., *The Witchcraft and Folklore of Dartmoor* (New York: Bell Publishing Company, 1972): 133.

8. Northcote, Lady R., 'Devonshire Folklore', *Folklore* 11:2 (1900): 215.

9. Ibid.

10. Amery, P.F.S. (ed.), 'Twelfth Report of the Committee on Devonshire Folk-Lore', *Transactions of the Devonshire Association* 26 (1894): 84.

11. Chope, R.P. (ed.), 'Twenty-Seventh Report on Devonshire Folk-Lore', *Report and Transactions of the Devonshire Association* 57 (1925): 115.

12. Ibid.

13. Doe, G. (ed.), 'Fourth Report of the Committee on Devonshire Folk-Lore', *Report and Transactions of the Devonshire Association* 11 (1879): 105.

14. *Western Daily Mercury,* 28 January 1875.

15. *Western Times*, 28 April 1877.

16. *Honiton News*, 18 April 1975.

17. Venkataswami, M.N., 'Devonshire Folklore, Collected among the People near Exeter within the Last Five or Six Years. By Lady Rosalind Northcote', *Folklore* 11:2 (1900): 216.

18. Doe, G. (ed.), 'Fifth Report of the Committee on Devonshire Folk-Lore', *Report and Transactions of the Devonshire Association* 12 (1880): 104.

19. *The Times*, 8 November 1924.

20. *The Times*, 10 September 1930.

21. *Bideford Gazette*, 10 August 1926, republishing a letter originally in the newspaper in 1876.

22. Hewett, S., *Nummits and Crummits: Devonshire Customs, Characteristics, and Folk-Lore* (London: T. Burleigh, 1900): 74.

23. Venkataswami, M.N., 'Devonshire Folklore, Collected among the People near Exeter within the Last Five or Six Years. By Lady Rosalind Northcote', *Folklore* 11:2 (1900): 215.

24. Norman, M. and Norman, T., *Dark Folklore* (Gloucestershire: The History Press, 2021): 46.

25. Grzybowski, S. and Allen, E.A., 'History and Importance of Scrofula', *Lancet* 346 (1995): 1472–74.

26. Doe, G. (ed.), 'Fourth Report of the Committee on Devonshire Folk-Lore', *Report and Transactions of the Devonshire Association* 11 (1879): 104–05.

27. Gamlen, W.H., 'The Toad Stone', *Report and Transactions of the Devonshire Association* 6:1 (1873): 200.

28. Ibid., 201.

29. Norman, T., *Cards, Cocoa and Charms: Devon's Forgotten Witches* (Devon: Aamena Press, 2019): 18.

30. Amery, P.F.S. (ed.), 'Twenty-Fourth Report of the Committee on Devonshire Folk-Lore', *Report and Transactions of the Devonshire Association* 39 (1907): 105.

31. Amery, P.F.S. (ed.), 'Twelfth Report of the Committee on Devonshire Folk-Lore', *Report and Transactions of the Devonshire Association* 26 (1894): 85.

32. Doe, G. (ed.), 'Sixth Report of the Committee on Devonshire Folk-Lore', *Report and Transactions of the Devonshire Association* 15 (1883): 101.

33. Amery, P.F.S. (ed.), 'Seventeenth Report of the Committee on Devonshire Folk-Lore', *Report and Transactions of the Devonshire Association* 32 (1900): 92.

34. *Daily Mail*, 26 March 1906.

35. Chope, R.P. (ed.), 'Twenty-Ninth Report on Devonshire Folk-Lore', *Report and Transactions of the Devonshire Association* 60 (1928): 125.

36. Chope, R.P., *The Dialect of Hartland* (English Dialect Society, 1891): 16.

37. Brown, T., 'Forty-Eighth Report on Folk-Lore, *Report and Transactions of the Devonshire Association* 83 (1951): 75.

38. Brown, T., 'Forty-Ninth Report on Folk-Lore', *Report and Transactions of the Devonshire Association* 84 (1952): 297.

39. Pitt, S.J. et al., 'Antimicrobial Properties of Mucus from the Brown Garden Snail *Helix aspersa*', *British Journal of Biomedical Science* 72:4 (2015): 174–81.

40. Brown, T., 'Eighty-Fourth Report on Folklore', *Report and Transactions of the Devonshire Association* 119 (1987): 270.

Chapter 10: Modern Folklore

1. For a full account of Thoms and the development of the term 'folk-lore', see Roper, J., 'Thoms and the Unachieved "Folk-Lore of England"', *Folklore* 118 (2007): 203–16.

2. Simpson, J. and Roud, S., *Oxford Dictionary of English Folklore* (Oxford: Oxford University Press, 2003): 349.

3. Dundes, A., 'What is Folklore?', in Alan Dundes (ed.), *The Study of Folklore* (Englewood Cliffs: Prentice-Hall, 1965): 2.

4. Available at https://www.youtube.com/watch?v=PBDJ2UJpKt4.

5. https://www.facebook.com/groups/1041873339173017, accessed 8 November 2021.

6. https://www.facebook.com/groups/343826566790080, accessed 8 November 2021.

7. https://www.oxfordlearnersdictionaries.com/definition/english/meme, accessed 8 November 2021.

8. https://me.me/i/since-brexit-the-coca-cola-christmas-lorry-is-no-longer-4230880, accessed 8 November 2021.

9. http://news.bbc.co.uk/1/hi/england/devon/3407275.stm, accessed 8 November 2021.

10. Hagen, A., *Anglo-Saxon Food and Drink* (Ely: Anglo-Saxon Books, 2010): 51.

11. https://www.cbr.com/batman-slaps-robin-the-origin-of-the-panel/, accessed 8 November 2021.

12. https://knowyourmeme.com/memes/my-parents-are-dead-batman-slapping-robin, accessed 8 November 2021.

13. https://www.thortful.com/card/608299ded7a22a000192fffe, accessed 8 November 2021.

14. https://twitter.com/greatdevondays/status/1003551937479036928, accessed 8 November 2021.

15. https://www.dailymail.co.uk/news/article-5487929/Cornish-people-furious-ad-shows-scone-cream-jam.html, accessed 8 November 2021.

16. Freedom of Information Act Request No: 3831/15, Version Date: 14 August 2015.

17. Ibid.

18. Freedom of Information Act Request No: 3773/16, Version Date: 16 August 2016.

19. Ibid.

20. Ibid.

21. https://uk.news.yahoo.com/moment-student-large-ufo-devon-seafrontc-142649856.html, accessed 10 November 2021.

22. Anonymous, *Preliminary Assessment: Unidentified Aerial Phenomena* (Office of the Director of National Intelligence, June 2021).

23. Clarke, D., *How UFOs Conquered the World* (London: Aurum Press, 2015): 95.

24. Ibid., 97.

25. *Britain's Most Terrifying Ghost Stories*, London Weekend Television, 20 May 2001.

26. Ibid.

27. See, for example, Firbank, J., 'Children trapped by lure of the unknown', *North Wales Weekly News*, 24 March 1988. For the link from playing Dungeons and Dragons see, for instance, 'Vicar gets support for "danger game" worry', *Stapleford and Sandiacre News*, 18 October 1985. And 'Satan's children?', *Reading Evening Post*, 15 April 1991.

28. De Bruxelles, S., 'Sheep Are Mutilated "in Satanic Rituals"', *The Times*, 22 September 2006.

29. https://ph.news.yahoo.com/2013-07-26-pony-killed-satanic-ritual-devon-national-park.html, accessed 10 November 2021.

30. Victor, J., 'Satanic Cult Rumors as Contemporary Legend', *Western Folklore* 49:1 (1990): 60.

31. Ibid.

32. Hoggard, B., *Magical House Protection: The Archaeology of Counter-Witchcraft* (New York, Oxford: Berghahn Books, 2019): 45–54.

Bibliography

Amery, P.F.S. (ed.), *Devon Notes and Queries* (Exeter: J.G. Commin, 1900).

———— (ed.), 'Eleventh Report of the Committee on Devonshire Folk-Lore', *Report and Transactions of the Devonshire Association* 24 (1892): 49–54.

———— (ed.), 'Twelfth Report of the Committee on Devonshire Folk-Lore', *Report and Transactions of the Devonshire Association* 26 (1894): 79–85.

———— (ed.), 'Seventeenth Report of the Committee on Devonshire Folk-Lore', *Report and Transactions of the Devonshire Association* 32 (1900): 83–92.

———— (ed.), 'Twenty-First Report of the Committee on Devonshire Folk-Lore', *Report and Transactions of the Devonshire Association* 36 (1904): 94–100.

———— 'Twenty-Second Report of the Committee on Devonshire Folk-Lore', *Report and Transactions of the Devonshire Association* 37 (1905): 111–21.

———— (ed.), 'Twenty-Third Report of the Committee on Devonshire Folk-Lore', *Report and Transactions of the Devonshire Association* 38 (1906): 87–100.

———— (ed.), 'Twenty-Fourth Report of the Committee on Devonshire Folk-Lore', *Report and Transactions of the Devonshire Association* 39 (1907): 103–9.

Anonymous, *Aunt Judy's Magazine*, 1874, no. xcvii: 436.

———— *English Forests and Forest Trees: Historical, Legendary, and Descriptive* (London: Ingram, Cooke, and Co., 1853).

———— *The Great Plum Pudding Contest Entry Form* (Torbay Libraries, 2016).

———— 'High Church on Hill So Good They Named It Thrice', *Gloucestershire Echo*, 28 February 2019.

———— *Jackson's Oxford Journal*, 15 September 1753.

———— *A Pictorial and Descriptive Guide to Dartmoor* (London: Ward Lock & Co., 1937).

———— *Preliminary Assessment: Unidentified Aerial Phenomena* (Office of the Director of National Intelligence, June 2021).

———— *The Random House College Dictionary* (New York: Random House, 1975).

Baker, M., *Folklore and Customs of Rural England* (Newton Abbot: David and Charles, 1974).

Baring-Gould, Rev. S., *A Book of Dartmoor* (London: Methuen, 1900).

———— *The Book of Were-Wolves* (London: Smith, Elder and Co., 1865).

———— *A Book of the West* (London: Methuen, 1900).

———— *Devon*, Little Guide Series (London: Methuen, 1907).

———— *Devonshire Characters and Strange Events* (London: John Lane The Bodley Head, 1908).

———— *Strange Survivals* (London: Methuen, 1892).

Baring-Gould, Rev. S. and Fleetwood Sheppard, Rev. H., *Songs and Ballads of the West* (London: Methuen, 1892).

Baring-Gould, Rev. S. and Sharp, C.J., *English Folk Songs for Schools* (London: J. Curwen and Sons, 1920).

Baring-Gould, Rev. S. et al., 'The Exploration of Grimspound: First Report of the Dartmoor Exploration Committee', *Report and Transactions of the Devonshire Association* 26 (1894): 101–21.

Baring-Gould, Rev. S. et al., *Songs of the West: Folk Songs of Devon and Cornwall: Collected from the Mouths of the People* (London: Methuen, 1890).

Barnes, W., *A Glossary of the Dorset Dialect with a Grammar* (Dorchester & London: Case/Trubner, 1886).

Bezalel, M., 'The "Fairy Door" Phenomenon', *The Guardian*, 23 June 2006.

Bhanji, S., 'From Folklore to History: Some Notes on the Evidence Concerning the Doones', *The Devon Historian* 58 (1999): 25–31.

Bideford Gazette, 10 August 1926, republishing a letter originally in the newspaper in 1876.

Blacker, C. and Davidson, H.E. (eds), *Women and Tradition* (United States: Carolina Academic Press, 2000).

Blackmore, R.D., *Christowell: A Dartmoor Tale* (London: Sampson Low, Marston, Searle & Rivington, 1885).

Bovet, R., *Pandaemonium, or, The Devil's Cloyster Being a Further Blow to Modern Sadduceism, Proving the Existence of Witches and Spirits, in a Discourse Deduced from the Fall of the Angels, the Propagation of Satan's Kingdom Before the Flood, the Idolatry of the Ages after Greatly Advancing Diabolical Confederacies, with an Account of the Lives and Transactions of Several Notorious Witches: Also, a Collection of Several Authentick Relations of Strange Apparitions of Dæmons and Spectres, and Fascinations of Witches, Never Before Printed* (London: J. Walthoe, 1684).

Bowring, J., 'Devonian Folk-Lore Illustrated', *Report and Transactions of the Devonshire Association* 2 (1867–68): 70–85.

Bray, A.E., *Autobiography of Anna Eliza Bray* (London: Chapman and Hall, 1884).

———— *Courtenay of Walreddon: A Romance of the West* (London: Bentley, 1844), 3 volumes.

———— *A Description of the Part of Devonshire Bordering on the Tamar and the Tavy* (London: John Murray, 1836), 3 volumes.

———— *The Fate of the Dead: A Study in Folk-Eschatology in the West Country after the Reformation* (Ipswich: D.S. Brewer; Rowman and Littlefield, 1979).

———— *Fitz of Fitz-ford* (London: Chapman and Hall, 1884).

———— *A Peep at the Pixies* (London: Grant and Griffith, 1854).

Brown, T., 'A Further Note on the "Stag Hunt" in Devon', *Folklore* 90.1 (1979): 18–21.
———— *Devon Ghosts* (Norwich: Jarrold, 1982).
———— 'Forty-Eighth Report on Folk-Lore', *Report and Transactions of the Devonshire Association* 83 (1951): 73–78.
———— 'Forty-Ninth Report on Folk-Lore', *Report and Transactions of the Devonshire Association* 84 (1952): 296–301.
———— 'Fifty-First Report on Folk-Lore', *Report and Transactions of the Devonshire Association* 86 (1954): 295–301.
———— 'Fifty-Sixth Report on Folklore', *Report and Transactions of the Devonshire Association* 91 (1959): 198–203.
———— 'Fifty-Seventh Report of Folklore', *Report and Transactions of the Devonshire Association* 92 (1960): 368–73.
———— 'Fifty-Eighth Report on Folklore', *Report and Transactions of the Devonshire Association* 93 (1961): 112–15.
———— '74th report on Folklore', *Report and Transactions of the Devonshire Association* 109 (1977): 210–13.
———— '78th report on Folklore', *Report and Transactions of the Devonshire Association* 113 (1981): 177–81.
———— '80th report on Folklore', *Report and Transactions of the Devonshire Association* 115 (1983): 171–75.
———— '83rd report on Folklore', *Report and Transactions of the Devonshire Association* 118 (1986): 243–47.
———— '84th Report on Folklore', *Report and Transactions of the Devonshire Association* 119 (1987): 270–73.
———— *Tales of a Dartmoor Village* (Torquay: Devonshire Press, 1961).
Cabell Djabri, S., *The Story of the Sepulchre* (London: Shamrock Press, 1989).
Callow, J., *The Last Witches of England* (London: Bloomsbury, 2022).
Campbell, M., *The Hound of the Baskervilles: Dartmoor or Herefordshire?* (New York: Magico Magazine, 1953).
Carr, J.D., *The Life of Sir Arthur Conan Doyle* (London: John Murray, 1949).
Caterine, D. and Morehead, J.W. (eds), *The Paranormal and Popular Culture: A Postmodern Religious Landscape* (London: Routledge, 2019).
Chambers, R., *The Book of Days* (London & Edinburgh: W&R Chambers, 1869).
Chanter, J.M., *Wanderings in North Devon* (Ilfracombe: Twiss and Son, 1887).
Chope, R.P., 'Devonshire Calendar Customs I: Movable Festivals', *Report and Transactions of the Devonshire Association* 68 (1936): 233–59.
———— *The Dialect of Hartland* (London: The English Dialect Society, 1891).
———— (ed.), 'Twenty-Seventh Report on Devonshire Folk-Lore', *Report and Transactions of the Devonshire Association* 57 (1925): 107–31.
———— (ed.), 'Twenty-Ninth Report on Devonshire Folk-Lore', *Report and Transactions of the Devonshire Association* 60 (1928): 111–34.

———— 'Thirty-Second Report on Devonshire Folk-Lore', *Report and Transactions of the Devonshire Association* 64 (1932): 153–68.

———— 'Thirty-Third Report on Devonshire Folk-Lore', *Report and Transactions of the Devonshire Association* 65 (1933): 121–37.

———— 'Thirty-Fourth Report on Devonshire Folk-Lore', *Report and Transactions of the Devonshire Association* 66 (1934): 73–91.

———— 'Thirty-Fifth Report on Devonshire Folk-Lore', *Report and Transactions of the Devonshire Association* 67 (1935): 131–44.

———— 'Thirty-Sixth Report on Devonshire Folk-Lore', *Report and Transactions of the Devonshire Association* 68 (1936): 81–98.

Clancy, J.P. (tr.), *Medieval Welsh Poems* (Dublin: Four Courts Press, 2003).

Clarke, D., *How UFOs Conquered the World* (London: Aurum Press, 2015).

Cleaveland, E., *A Genealogical History of the Noble and Illustrious Family of Courtenay, Part 3* (Exeter: Edward Farley, 1735).

Colton, Rev. C.C., *A Plain and Authentic Narrative of the Sampford Ghost* (Tiverton: T. Smith, 1810).

Conan Doyle, Sir A., 'The Hound of the Baskervilles', *Strand Magazine* 23 (1902): 243–52.

Coombs, M., 'Plymouth's Ancient Trackways', *Wisht Maen* 3 (1994): 10–12.

Cossins, J., *Reminiscences of Exeter Fifty Years Since* (Published by the author, 1877).

Cotton, R.W., 'The Oxenham Omen', *Report and Transactions of the Devonshire Association* 14 (1882): 221–46.

Cox, T., *A Topographical, Ecclesiastical and Natural History of Devon* (London: E. Nutt, 1700).

Coxhead, J.R.W., *The Devil in Devon: An Anthology of Folk Tales* (Brackness: West Country Handbooks, 1967).

———— *Devon Traditions and Fairy-Tales* (Exmouth: Raleigh Press, 1959).

Crossing, W., *Crossing's Guide to Dartmoor* (Newton Abbot: Peninsula Press 1993 [1912]).

———— *Folk Rhymes of Devon; Notices of the Metrical Sayings Found in the Lore of the People* (Devon: J.G. Commin, 1911).

———— *Folklore and Legends of Dartmoor* (Liverton: Forest Publishing, 1997).

———— *Tales of the Dartmoor Pixies: Glimpses of Elfin Haunts and Antics* (London: Hood, 1890).

Daily Mail, 26 March 1906.

Davidson, H.E., 'Obituary: Theo Brown (1914–1993)', *Folklore* 104 (1993): 168–69.

De Blécourt, W., 'Witches on Screen', in O. Davies (ed.), *The Oxford Illustrated History of Witchcraft and Magic* (Oxford: Oxford University Press, 2017): 253–80.

De Bruxelles, S., 'Sheep are Mutilated "in Satanic Rituals"', *The Times*, 22 September 2006.

DEFRA, *Agricultural Statistics—South West* (Department for Environment, Food and Rural Affairs, 2019).

———— *DEFRA Statistics: Agricultural Facts. England Regional Profiles* (Department for Environment, Food and Rural Affairs, 2021).

Devon and Cornwall Notes and Queries 5 (1852): 117.

Devon Folklife Register, *Folk Festivals and Traditions of Devon* (Exeter: Exeter City Museums Service, 1980).

Doe, G. (ed.), 'Fourth Report of the Committee on Devonshire Folk-Lore', *Report and Transactions of the Devonshire Association* 11 (1879): 103–11.

———— (ed.), 'Fifth Report of the Committee on Devonshire Folk-Lore', *Report and Transactions of the Devonshire Association* 12 (1880): 99–113.

———— (ed.), 'Sixth Report of the Committee on Devonshire Folk-Lore', *Report and Transactions of the Devonshire Association* 15 (1883): 99–107.

———— 'Seventh Report of the Committee on Devonshire Folk-Lore', *Report and Transactions of the Devonshire Association* 16 (1884): 122–23.

———— (ed.), 'Eighth Report of the Committee on Devonshire Folk-Lore', *Report and Transactions of the Devonshire Association* 17 (1885): 118–26.

———— (ed.), 'Ninth Report of the Committee on Devonshire Folk-Lore', *Report and Transactions of the Devonshire Association* 18 (1886): 103–05.

Donne, J., *Devotions Upon Emergent Occasions, Meditation XVII* (London: Pickering, 1840).

Drury, S.M., 'English Love Divinations Using Plants: An Aspect', *Folklore* 97.2 (1986): 210–14.

Dundes, A. (ed.), *The Study of Folklore* (Englewood Cliffs, NJ: Prentice-Hall, 1965).

Forbes Julian, H., 'William Pengelly, FRS, FGS, Father of the Devonshire Association', *Report and Transactions of the Devonshire Association* 44 (1912): 157–91.

Eckett Fielden, M., *Dartmoor My Dartmoor and Other Poems* (Torquay: C.G. Jowitt, 1932).

Elworthy, F.T., *Crying the Neck: A Devonshire Custom* (Plymouth: W. Brendon & Son, 1891).

Exeter Gazette, 4 May 1900.

Fea, A., *Secret Chambers and Hiding Places: The Historic, Romantic and Legendary Stories and Traditions about Hiding-Holes, Secret Chambers &c* (London: S.H. Bousfield, 1901).

Gamlen, W.H., 'The Toad Stone', *Report and Transactions of the Devonshire Association* 6.1 (1873): 200–02.

Gaydon, T., *My North Devon of Myth and Mystery* (Bideford: Badger Books, 1987).

Gibson, E., *Brittania: Or a Chorographical Description of Great Britain and Ireland*, Volume 1 (London: Asonsham Churchill, 1722).

Gilbert, D., *The Parochial History of Cornwall* (London: J.B. Nichols and Son, 1838).

Graebe, M., *As I Walked Out* (Oxford: Signal Books, 2017).

Gray, C., 'Return to Albion', *Town and Country Magazine*. Available at https://www. powderham.co.uk/uploads/News/return_to_albion_article.pdf, accessed 17 October 21.

Gray, T., *Uncle Tom Cobley and All* (Exeter: Mint Press, 2019).

Grinsell, L.V., 'Some Aspects of the Folklore of Prehistoric Monuments', *Folklore* 48.3 (1937): 248.

Grzybowski, S. and Allen, E.A., 'History and Importance of Scrofula', *Lancet* 346 (1995): 1472–74.

Hagen, A., *Anglo-Saxon Food and Drink* (Ely: Anglo-Saxon Books, 2010).

Halliday, W.R., 'The Story of Sir Robert Chichester Together with a Note on the Rev. William Gimmingham', *Folklore* 65.2 (1954): 109–11.

Harding, Lt Col W., *The History of Tiverton*, Volume 1 (Tiverton: F. Boyce, 1845).

Harpley, Rev. W. (ed.), 'Obituary Notices', *Report and Transactions of the Devonshire Association* 11 (1879): 48–65.

———— 'A Short Account of the Origin of the Association', *Report and Transactions of the Devonshire Association* 44 (1912): 154–56.

Harte, J., 'The Devil on Dartmoor', *Time and Mind: The Journal of Archaeology, Consciousness and Culture* 1.1 (2008): 83–94.

———— 'The Devil's Chapels: Fiends, Fear and Folklore at Prehistoric Sites', in J. Parker (ed.), *Written on Stone: The Cultural Reception of British Prehistoric Monuments* (Cambridge: Cambridge Scholars Publishing, 2009): 23–35.

———— *Explore Fairy Traditions* (Nottingham: Explore Publishing, 2004).

Henderson, W., *Notes of the Folklore of the Northern Counties of England and the Borders* (London: Longmans, Green and Co., 1866).

Herrick, R., *Hesperides* (London & New York: G. Routledge and Sons, 1885).

Hervey, Canon R., *The Place Where the Devil Died of the Cold* (Northlew: TS, revised 1944).

Hewett, S., *Nummits and Crummits: Devonshire Customs, Characteristics and Folk-Lore* (London: T. Burleigh, 1900).

Hindley, C., *A History of the Cries of London: Ancient and Modern* (Cambridge: Cambridge University Press, 2011).

Honiton News, 18 April 1975.

Howell, J., *Epistolae Ho-Elianae: The Familiar Letters of James Howell, Historiographer Royal to Charles II* (London: D. Nutt, 1892).

Jones, M., *The History of Chudleigh in the County of Devon and the Surrounding Scenery, Seats, Families, etc* (London: T.W. Grattan, 1852).

King, R.J., 'First Report of Committee of Devonshire Folk-Lore', *Report and Transactions of the Devonshire Association* 8 (1876): 49–58.

———— (ed.), 'Second Report of the Committee on Devonshire Folk-Lore', *Report and Transactions of the Devonshire Association* 9 (1877): 88–102.

———— *The Forest of Dartmoor and Its Borders* (London: John Russell Smith, 1856).

Kingsley, C., *Westward Ho!* (New York: Thomas Y. Crowell and Co., 1855).

Kirk, R. and Lang, A., *The Secret Common-Wealth and A Short Treatise of Charms and Spells* (London: David Nutt, 1893 [1691]).

Le Franc, M., *Le champion des dames*, 1451. Manuscript held at the Bibliothèque nationale de France and available at https://gallica.bnf.fr/ark:/12148/btv1b9059128w/f31.item.

Mackenzie, D.A., *Wonder Tales from Scottish Myth and Legend* (London: Blackie and Son, 1917).

McKenzie, R., *They Still Serve: A Complete Guide to the Military Ghosts of Britain* (Lulu.com, 2008).

Menefee, S.P., 'A Cake in the Furrow', *Folklore* 91.2 (1980): 173–92.

Mills, A.D., *A Dictionary of English Place Names* (Oxford: Oxford University Press, 1991).

Milton, J., 'L'Allegro', in *Poems of Mr John Milton* (London: Humphrey Moseley, 1645).

Milton, P., *The Discovery of Dartmoor* (Chichester: Phillimore and Co., 2006).

Norman, M., *Black Dog Folklore* (Cornwall: Troy Books, 2015).

——— *Telling the Bees and Other Customs* (Gloucester: The History Press, 2020).

Norman, M. and Norman, T., *Dark Folklore* (Gloucestershire: The History Press, 2021).

Norman, T., *Cards, Cocoa and Charms: Devon's Forgotten Witches* (Devon: Aamena Press, 2019).

——— 'Histories and Mysteries: The White Bird of the Oxenhams', *The Moorlander*, 24 July–6 August 2020.

Norway, A.H., *Highways and Byways in Devon and Cornwall* (London: Macmillan and Co., 1911).

Owen, A.N., *History of a Devon Custom* (Published by the author, 2006).

Page, J.L.W., *An Exploration of Exmoor and the Hill Country of West Somerset: With Notes on Its Archaeology* (London: Seeley and Co., 1895).

Pike, J.R., *Torquay* (Torquay: Torbay Borough Council Printing Services, 1994).

Pole, Sir W., *Collections Towards a Description of the County of Devon* (London: J. Nichols, 1791).

Poole, K.B., *Ghosts of the Westcountry* (Peterborough: Jarrold Publishing, 1997).

Prince, J., *The Worthies of Devon* (Plymouth: Rees and Curtis, 1810).

Reed, S., *Wassailing* (Cornwall: Troy Books, 2013).

Ridout, B.V., 'The Devil's Footprints Revisited', *Report and Transactions of the Devonshire Association* 153 (2021): 291–306.

Robbins, K. et al., 'Agricultural Change and Farm Incomes in Devon: An Update', in *CRR Research Report No. 17* (Exeter: University of Exeter Centre for Rural Research, June 2006).

Roper, J., 'Thoms and the Unachieved "Folk-Lore of England"', *Folklore* 118 (2007): 203–16.

Rose, H.J., 'The Folklore of the Geoponica', *Folklore* 44.1 (1933): 57–90.

Rudkin, E., 'The Black Dog', *Folklore* 49.2 (1938): 111–31.

Savage, R., 'Shadow Land', *TES Magazine*, 7 January 2005.

Sayer, S., *The Outline of Dartmoor's Story* (Exeter: Devon Books, 1987).

Simpson, J. and Roud, S., *Oxford Dictionary of English Folklore* (Oxford: Oxford University Press, 2000).

Smith, J.B., 'Towards the Demystification of Lawrence Lazy', *Folklore* 107 (1996): 101–05.

Snell, F.J., *A Book of Exmoor* (London: Methuen, 1903).

Spence, J., *Shetland Folk-Lore* (Lerwick: Johnson and Greig, 1899).

St Leger-Gordon, R.E., *The Witchcraft and Folklore of Dartmoor* (New York: Bell Publishing Company, 1972).

Straffon, C., 'Pagan Cornwall—Land of the Goddess', *Meyn Mamvro* 22 (1993).

Thoms, W.J., 'Folk-Lore', *The Athanaeum* 982 (22 August 1846): 862c–863a.

The Times, 8 November 1924.

The Times, 10 September 1930.

Tozer, E., *Devonshire and Other Original Poems; with Some Account of Ancient Customs, Superstitions and Traditions* (Exeter: Office of the Devon Weekly Times, 1873).

Tugwell, G., *The North Devon Scenery Book* (London: Simpkin, Marshall and Co., 1863).

Venkataswami, M.N., 'Devonshire Folklore, Collected among the People near Exeter within the Last Five or Six Years. By Lady Rosalind Northcote', *Folklore* 11.2 (1900): 212–19.

Vickery, R., *Garlands, Conkers and Mother-Die: British and Irish Plant-Lore* (London: Continuum, 2010).

Victor, J., 'Satanic Cult Rumors as Contemporary Legend', *Western Folklore* 49.1 (1990): 51–81 (60).

'Volo non Valeo' (Gibbons, M.S.), *'We Donkeys' in Devon* (Exeter: Hamilton, Adams and Co., 1885).

Warwick, C.H., *The Hidden Room: The Legend of Chambercombe Manor* (Published by the author, 1987).

Watkin, H.R., *A Short Description of Torre Abbey, Torquay, Devonshire* (Torquay: Fleet Printing Works, 1912).

Weber, H. et al., *Illustrations of Northern Antiquities* (Edinburgh: James Ballantyne and Co., 1814).

Westcote, T., *A View of Devonshire in MDCXXX* (London: W. Roberts, 1845).

Western Daily Mercury, 28 January 1875.

Western Morning News, 23 July 1925.

Western Morning News, 17 June 1958.

Western Morning News, 18–19 January 1984.

Western Times, 28 April 1877.

White, E.D., 'Devil's Stones and Midnight Rites: Megaliths, Folklore, and Contemporary Pagan Witchcraft', *Folklore* 125.1 (2014): 60–79.

White, J.T., *The History of Torquay* (Torquay: 'Directory', 1878).

White, W., *History, Gazetteer & Directory of Devon* (Printed for the author, 1850).

Whitlock, R., *The Folklore of Devon* (London: B.T. Batsford, 1977).

Widecombe and District Local History Group, *The History of Widecombe Fair* (Chudleigh: Orchard Publications, 2007).

Wood, T., *True Thomas* (London: Jonathan Cape, 1936).

Woolmer's Exeter and Plymouth Gazette, 17 February 1855.

Young, F., *A History of Anglican Exorcism: Deliverance and Demonology in Church Ritual* (London: I.B. Tauris, 2018).

Young, S., 'Pixy-Led in Devon and the South-West', *Report and Transactions of the Devonshire Association* 148 (2016): 311–36.

Young, S. and Houlbrook, C. (eds), *Magical Folk: British and Irish Fairies 500 AD to the Present* (London: Gibson Square, 2018).

Websites

https://www.almanac.com/content/setting-chicken-eggs-moons-sign (accessed 13 December 2021).

https://ancientmonuments.uk/117332-st-michaels-chapel-chapel-hill-tormohun-ward#.Yz1hPnbMKUk (accessed 5 October 2022).

https://archaeology-travel.com/england/tarr-steps-exmoor/ (accessed 22 September 2021).

https://www.bbc.co.uk/news/uk-england-devon-57986811 (accessed 26 September 2022).

https://blog.britishnewspaperarchive.co.uk/2017/03/26/mothering-sunday/ (accessed 26 September 2022).

https://www.britannica.com/place/Kents-Cavern (accessed 28 June 2021).

https://www.cbr.com/batman-slaps-robin-the-origin-of-the-panel/ (accessed 8 November 2021).

https://chambercombemanor.org.uk/history/ (accessed 5 October 2022).

http://www.cornishpasties.org.uk/henncock-pasties.htm (accessed 26 September 2022).

https://www.dailymail.co.uk/news/article-5487929/Cornish-people-furious-ad-shows-scone-cream-jam.html (accessed 8 November 2021).

https://www.dartmoor.gov.uk/learning/basic-factsheets (accessed 10 November 2021).

http://www.dartmoor-crosses.org.uk/widecombe_churchyard.htm (accessed 13 November 2021).

https://www.devon.gov.uk/environment/wildlife/habitats-and-species/farms (accessed 6 December 2021).

http://devonandexeterinstitution.org (accessed 26 July 2021).

https://www.devonlive.com/news/devon-news/how-much-land-your-area-752168 (accessed 6 December 2021).

https://drdavidclarke.co.uk/2017/03/30/dead-flows-the-don/ (accessed 17 November 2021).

https://www.efdss.org/learning/resources/beginners-guides/48-british-folk-customs-from-plough-monday-to-hocktide/3373-shrove-tuesday (accessed 24 November 2021).

https://www.exmoor-nationalpark.gov.uk/Whats-Special/culture/literary-links/rd-blackmore (accessed 5 September 2022).

https://www.facebook.com/groups/1041873339173017 (accessed 8 November 2021).

https://www.facebook.com/groups/343826566790080 (accessed 8 November 2021).

https://www.fantasticfiction.com/b/sabine-baring-gould/ (accessed 8 August 2022).

https://www.greatbritishlife.co.uk/things-to-do/countryfile-discovers-exmoor-s-hope-bourne-7126948 (accessed 24 August 2022).

https://www.gutenberg.org/cache/epub/657/pg657.html (accessed 5 October 2022).

https://healthit.com.au/how-big-is-the-internet-and-how-do-we-measure-it/ (accessed 7 June 2021).

https://www.heritagegateway.org.uk/gateway/Results_Single.aspx?uid=MDV9018&resourceID=104 (accessed 11 January 2022).

https://www.historic-uk.com/HistoryUK/HistoryofBritain/Give-us-our-eleven-days/ (accessed 22 November 2021).

https://hostingtribunal.com/blog/how-many-websites/ (accessed 7 June 2021).

https://www.itraveluk.co.uk/maps/england/4533/devon/luffincott.html (accessed 11 October 2021).

https://www.jiscmail.ac.uk/cgi-bin/webadmin?A2=mining-history;7135e7d9.02 (accessed 5 October 2022).

https://johnhmoore.co.uk/hele/introduction.htm (accessed 14 October 2021).

https://knowyourmeme.com/memes/my-parents-are-dead-batman-slapping-robin (accessed 8 November 2021).

https://www.legendarydartmoor.co.uk/crazy_well.htm (accessed 29 November 2021).

https://www.legendarydartmoor.co.uk/devil_dart.htm (accessed 22 September 2021).

https://me.me/i/since-brexit-the-coca-cola-christmas-lorry-is-no-longer-4230880 (accessed 8 November 2021).

https://www.metoffice.gov.uk/about-us/press-office/news/weather-and-climate/2017/do-cows-really-lie-down-when-its-about-to-rain (accessed 7 December 2021).

https://www.midweekherald.co.uk/news/20376129.children-tip-tip-toe-gittisham/ (accessed 26 September 2022).

http://www.moretonhampstead.org.uk/gaz/dancingtree.ghtml (accessed 29 September 2022).

http://news.bbc.co.uk/1/hi/england/devon/3407275.stm (accessed 8 November 2021).

https://www.newscientist.com/article/2082809-the-three-hares-motif-is-an-ancient-mystery-for-our-times/ (accessed 1 November 2011).

https://www.oxfordlearnersdictionaries.com/definition/english/meme (accessed 8 November 2021).

https://ph.news.yahoo.com/2013-07-26-pony-killed-satanic-ritual-devon-national-park.html (accessed 10 November 2021).

https://www.powderham.co.uk/uploads/News/return_to_albion_article.pdf (accessed 17 October 2022).

https://www.royalacademy.org.uk/art-artists/book/the-monumental-effigies-of-great-britain-selected-from-our-cathedrals-and (accessed 8 August 2022).

http://www.sampevsoc.co.uk/the-sampford-peverell-ghost.html   (accessed   21 October 2021).

https://swheritage.org.uk/devon-archives/visit/local-studies-library/ (accessed 26 July 2021).

https://www.thortful.com/card/608299ded7a22a000192fffe (accessed 8 November 2021).

http://www.torquaymuseum.org/explore/explore-our-collections/social-history (accessed 28 June 2021).

https://www.tulipmania.art/folk-tale-from-devon-fairies-lulled-their-babies/ (accessed 4 January 2022).

https://twitter.com/greatdevondays/status/1003551937479036928   (accessed   8 November 2021).

https://uk.news.yahoo.com/moment-student-large-ufo-devon-seafrontc-142649856.html (accessed 10 November 2021).

https://venn.lib.cam.ac.uk/ (accessed 8 August 2022).

https://visitdartmoor.co.uk/myths-and-legends (accessed 4 October 2021).

https://www.visitsouthdevon.co.uk/things-to-do/ness-cove-beach-p242403 (accessed 5 October 2022).

www.warrenhouseinn.co.uk/history.html (accessed 1 November 2021).

www.womenslandarmy.co.uk (accessed 13 December 2021).

https://www.youtube.com/watch?v=PBDJ2UJpKt4 (accessed 7 June 2021).

https://www.youtube.com/watch?v=YTutl5pkPPI (accessed 3 October 2022).

Index

Affaland Moor, Devon 98
agriculture 38, 46, 58–9, 63–4, 67,
    70–71, 74–5, 182
Alwington, Devon 114
Anglo-Saxon Chronicle 146, 149
animals, supernatural 32–5
    see also Black Dogs
apples 40–42, 56, 60, 68, 70, 78,
    99–100
    see also cider; wassailing
archaeology 6, 11, 102, 115
Arnold, Kenneth 186, 187
Arthur (king) 96, 149
Arundel family 144–5
Ascension Day 53, 55–7
Ashburton, Devon 7, 60, 62, 151, 165
Ashford, Devon 98
astrology 76, 124
Axmouth, Devon 171

Badgeworthy (Badgery), Devon 26
balloons 90, 188
Bampfylde family 26
Banbury, Battle of (1469) 154
Baring-Gould, Edward 9
Baring-Gould, Sabine 9–11, 12, 22–3,
    28, 33–4, 52, 78, 98–9, 138,
    151, 158
Barle (river) 84
Barlow, Louise 189
Barnstaple, Devon 163
    Barnstaple and North Devon,
        Museum of 26
    fair 98
barrows 102

Baskerville, Harry 148
Bate, Charles Spence 6
Baxter, Isabella 194 n.3
BBC 21, 63, 155, 183
Becket, Thomas 152
Beer, Devon 134
bell-ringing 89–90, 95, 113, 116, 139
Belle Hole, Lincolnshire 34
Belstone, Devon 23, 56, 106
Bere Ferrers, Devon 7
Berry Pomeroy Castle, Devon 139–40
Berrynarbor, Devon 44
Biblicae, sortes 40
Bideford, Devon 12, 138
    Long Bridge 85–6
Bideford Witches 161, 163
Bigadon House, Devon 8
Bigg, L. Coutier 169
Bishops Nympton, Devon 74
Bishopsteignton, Devon 70, 171
Black Dogs 15, 34, 87, 93, 114, 135,
    138, 146–60
Blackdown Hills 110–11, 156
Blackmore, R.D. 24–7, 54
blacksmiths 26, 61, 167–8
Blagdon Hill, Somerset 111, 172
blight 99–100
Bohun, Margaret de 132
Bonfire Night 60, 95
Boobhill, Devon 174
Borley, Essex 122
Boscastle, Cornwall 159, 176
Boscombe Down, Wiltshire 188
Bourne, Hope 19, 20
Bovet, Richard 111

Bow, Devon 177
Bowring, John 3, 7
Bradworthy, Devon 170
Bratton Fleming, Devon 114, 125
Bray, Anna Eliza (née Kempe) 7–8,
        27–8, 37, 46, 65, 75, 78, 83, 105,
        115, 117–18, 120, 141, 148, 150
Bray, Edward Atkins 8, 83
Bridestowe, Devon 47, 56, 149, 177
Bridgerule, Devon 97–8
bridges 84–6
Broad Nymet, Devon 177
Bronescombe, Walter, bishop of
        Exeter 91
Brown, Dorothy 15
Brown, Theo 14–16, 23, 33, 81, 96–7,
        133, 157, 159
Browne, Thomas Warde 122–3
Bounds, Beating of the 56, 156
Buckfast, Devon 8, 142
Buckfastleigh, Devon 94, 149, 150, 152,
        155, 159, 190
Buckland, Devon 105, 108
Budleigh Salterton, Devon 178
Burnard, Robert 158
Butt, Mother 168

Cabell, Richard 149–52, 154–5,
        159, 190
Cadbury Castle, Devon 66
calendar customs 38–62, 95
Callcott, Maria 168
Cambridge, University of 10, 12, 124
Camden, William 28
Candlemas (2 February) 43–4, 45
candles 44, 69, 97–9
Capitana (Spanish ship) 129
Case, Sally 138
cats 67, 84, 93, 174, 189–90
        big 37
cattle 22, 32, 51, 67, 78–81, 154
        see also milking
caves 6, 28, 82, 114–15, 130–32, 158
Chagford, Devon 70, 110, 113, 169
Challacombe, Devon 114
Chambercombe, Devon 126, 128, 130
Chambers, Robert 45

Champernon family 126
changelings 119–20, 168
Chanter, John 25, 48
Chard, Somerset 111, 173
Charlbury, Devon 39
Charles II, king of England 25, 152
charmers 80–81, 116, 119, 162–3, 165,
        166, 169, 176–9
Chase, Beatrice (Olive Katherine Parr)
        19–21
Chaucer, Geoffrey 54
Chave, John 135, 138
Chestonford, Somerset 111
Chittlehampton, Devon 177
Chope, Richard Pearse 12, 45, 52, 178
Christmas 7, 43, 61–2, 68, 119, 182
        animals at 61
        Ashen Faggot, burning of 61–2
        Christmas Pudding 78
        Old Christmas (6 January) 40, 42, 61
Chudleigh, Devon 115
Chudleigh Knighton, Devon 178
Chulmleigh, Devon 60
Church Grims 34
churches 7, 9, 32–3, 36, 44, 48, 50,
        54, 56, 59–60, 92–5, 98–9, 116,
        122–3, 125, 127, 132, 134, 142,
        143, 150, 158, 166, 190
churchyards 22, 34, 93, 159, 167,
        169–70, 177
        earth from 152
cider 41–2, 58, 61, 77, 100, 106, 113,
        118, 119
Civil War, English 25, 27–8, 114, 152
Clarke, David 187
Clawton, Devon 123
Clinton, Lord 134
Clyst Honiton, Devon 166
Clyst St George, Devon 89
Cnut, king of England 142
coaches, phantom 98, 148–9
Cobley, Tom 21–3
cock-fighting 76–7, 96
coin scrambles 49, 73
coin trees 116
Colebrooke, Devon 22
Collier, William 23

Colton, Charles Caleb 136–7
Comb St Nicholas, Somerset 111
Combe Martin, Devon 50, 57
Conan Doyle, Arthur 138, 147–8, 155
    The Hound of the Baskervilles 138,
        146–8, 150–51, 153–6
Constantine VII, Byzantine emperor 71
Coo, Jan 29, 117
Corney, Thomas 52
Cornish, George 124
Cornwall 1, 6, 24, 31, 72, 93, 102, 121,
        159, 176, 180, 183–5
corpse roads 35
Courtenay, Hugh de 132
Courtenay family 8, 16, 132
Coventina 30
cows *see* cattle
Cox, Thomas 28
cream teas 182–5
Crediton, Devon 2, 9, 42–3, 119
Crewkerne, Somerset 116
Cromer, Norfolk 148, 151
Cromwell, Oliver 29, 114
crops, sowing of *see* sowing
Crosby, Lincolnshire 160
Crosse family 139
Crossing, William 30, 50, 111–12,
        114, 156
'Crying the Neck' 74–5
cunning-folk 19, 119, 162–6, 168, 171,
        173–4, 175–6, 189

daffodils 76
Dart, river 29–30
    crying of 30
Dartington Hall, Devon 116
Dartmoor 11, 14, 18–20, 23–4, 27, 29,
        32, 33, 43, 52, 65, 76–7, 78, 84,
        86–7, 91, 96, 102, 103, 107, 108,
        109, 110, 113, 114, 116, 148,
        149, 151, 154, 156, 157–8, 162,
        169, 178
    Birch Tor 92
    Branscombe's Loaf
    Cox Tor 190
    Cramber Tor 58
    Cranmere Pool 154

Crazywell Pool 30, 58
    Dartmeet 29
    Devil's Bridge 84
    Devil's Gully 85
    Dewerstone 86, 91, 150
    etymology of 29
    Flat Tor 29
    Fox Tor 148
    Heltor 96
    Hound Tor 156
    Merripit Hill 33
    Pixies' Church 116
    Prison 148
    Shaugh Bridge 109
    Whitehorse Hill 29
    Wistman's Wood 149–50
    Yar Tor 35
Dean Combe, Devon 152
Defence, Ministry of 187–8
Denmark 112
Derbyshire 82, 93, 160
Devil, the 2, 25, 52, 72, 74, 82–100,
        149–51, 176
    as seducer 97–9
    'devil's water' 31
    'Dewer' as alternative name for
        86–7, 91, 150
    footprints of 83, 87, 89–91
Devon and Exeter Institution 16
Devonport, Devon 90
Devonshire, earl of 133
Devonshire Association 3, 5, 6–7, 9,
        11, 12–13, 14, 15, 44, 66, 141,
        165, 177
dew 55, 176
dialect 12, 48, 65, 68, 69, 80, 102, 179,
        181, 182
diarrhoea, cures for 51
digital folklore 3–4, 84, 181–2, 184–5
divination 32–3, 40, 45, 57, 58–9, 60,
        61, 76, 124, 171
    see also astrology; *Biblicae, sortes*;
            molybdomancy; oomancy
Domesday Book 9, 132, 156, 193 n.15
Don, river (Yorkshire) 30
Doone family 24–7
Dorrington, Lincolnshire 94

Drake, Francis 129, 149
drownings 30–2
druids 75, 78, 82–3, 86, 87, 95, 121, 150
Ducking Day (2 May) 55
Dulverton, Devon 84
Dundes, Alan 1, 181
Dunhuang, China 158

East Anglia 147
East Budleigh, Devon 60
Easter 39, 45, 46, 48, 49–53, 57
    Lamb in the sun at 52
    sun dancing in the sky at 52
Edinburgh, Scotland 131
Edwards, Susannah 161
eggs *see* oomancy
elf-shot 115
Elford family 114–15
Elizabeth I, queen of England 27
Ellacombe, Henry Thomas 89–90
Evans, Matthew 186
Exeter, Devon 6, 9, 15, 16, 22, 49, 55,
    60, 67, 112, 119, 124, 167, 189
    Broadclyst 78
    Castle 161
    Cathedral 50
    St Thomas 162
    White Witch of 163, 164–5, 166,
        173, 189
Exford, Devon 26
Exmoor 18, 19, 20, 24–5, 26, 27, 32,
    34, 44, 72, 77, 84, 114
    Beast of 37
    Countisbury Hill 167
    Doone Valley 25
    Meshaw Wood 34
    Pinkworthy Pond 31–2
    Tarr Steps 84
Exmouth, Devon 69, 88, 176
exorcism 32, 122–5, 166, 177, 189

fairs 21–4, 39, 49, 53, 57, 60, 73,
    98, 104
    fairy 110–11
fairies 101–20
    appearance of 108–10
    culture of 110–13

dancing of 108–9, 110, 111, 113
    fairy midwife (folk tale) 104, 112,
        160, 174
    food of 110
    ploughman and the fairies (folk
        tale) 112
    see also pixies
Fairy Cross, Devon 114
fairy rings 32
Faggus, Tom 26, 28
farming *see* agriculture
Farquhar, Walter 140
Farway, Devon 56
Fens, the 147
Fenton, Edward 172
fetches (apparitions of living people) 58
Fielden, Marjory Eckett 14
Finns 35
first footing 43
First World War 74, 96
Fitz, John 148
Fitz family 8
folklore, definition of 1–4, 180
Folklore Society, The 4, 102, 160
folk songs 9, 10, 12, 21–4, 34, 40,
    42, 47
Forz, Isabella de, 8th countess of
    Devon 56
Fowell, Elizabeth 151
foxes 103–4
Francis, L.M. 177
Frost, Elizabeth 141
Fuller, Thomas 27–8

gambling 92–3, 105
Gammon, Mr 32
Garner, Chris 187
Gayer, Benjamin 154
Geoponica 70, 73
George Nympton, Devon 73
    Georgenympton Revel 73
ghost-hunting 188, 191
ghost-laying *see* exorcism
ghosts 23, 31, 121–45, 148–9, 150, 152,
    154, 155, 186, 188, 189
    animal 21, 33–4
    hoaxing 147

giants 30, 83
Gibbons, Maria Susannah ('Volo non Valeo') 60
Gibson, Edward 28
Giffard, Walter 133–4
Gilbert, Davies 31
Gimmingham, William 125
Gittisham, Devon 47, 55, 56
Glastonbury, Somerset 120
Glosen 34
Gloucester 94
Gloucestershire 54
goats 79, 91
Good Friday 50–51, 59, 174, 177
goodman's croft 72
Gorges family 126
Grandisson, John, bishop of Exeter 85
Great Torrington, Devon 67, 79
Gregorian Calendar 39
Grey, Jane 126
Grimspound, Devon 11, 158
Grinsell, Leslie 102
Gubbins family 27–9
guns 26, 40, 175
Gurney, Richard 85
Guy Fawkes 60

Hall, E.F. 178
Halloween (All Hallows) 46, 59–61, 108, 187
Hamilton, Margaret 162
Hanscott, Devon 95
Hardy, Thomas 25
hares 23, 91, 158, 174–5
Harpley, W. 6
Hartland, Devon 19, 51, 68
harvest 40, 41, 46, 59, 67, 71, 74–5, 77, 122
Hatherleigh, Devon 57–8, 68, 76, 187
hauntings see ghosts
hawthorn 80, 178
Hayne Park, Devon 73
hazelnuts 60
hearts, animal 166, 170, 174
Heathercombe, Devon 110
hedgehogs 80
Hel (goddess) 24

Hele beach, Devon 126, 128
Heliopolis, Egypt 99
hempseed 33, 45
Hemyock, Devon 156
Henley, Hannah 172–4
Henry I, king of England 183
Henry III, king of England 156
Henry VII, king of England 103
Henry VIII, king of England 129
hens, black 32
Hergest Court, Herefordshire 153–4
hermits 129–30
Herrick, Robert 43, 152
Highwaymen 26–7
Hine, Samuel George 55
hobby horses 24, 57
Hock-Tide 53
Hoke Day see Hock-Tide
Holne, Devon 78
Holsworthy, Devon 95, 122, 187
Honiton, Devon 56
    Hot Pennies Day 49
    fair 73
    St Michael's church 94
horses 21, 23–4, 26, 33, 34–5, 55, 67, 92, 97, 118, 120, 140, 148, 149, 150, 173, 174, 177
hot cross buns 50–51
Howard, Mary 148–9, 152, 154
Howell, James 142–3
Huddersfield, Yorkshire 12
Hughes, J.B. 52
Hunt, Robert 31
Hutchings, Fiona 188

Ilfracombe, Devon 48, 126–7
Ilsington, Devon 166
internet, the see digital folklore
Ipplepen, Devon 148
Ireland 43, 57, 118
Irish people 31, 160
iron 103, 124, 167, 169
    maiden nails 167

'Jack-in-the-Bush' 54
Jack o' th' Lantern see will o' the wisps
Jackson Knight, William Francis 15–16

Japan 41
'Jay's Grave' 20
Jeffreys, George 33
Jesuits 29
Johnson, Ursula 26
Jones, Mary 115
'Judas Steak' 81

Kempe, Alfred John 7–8
Kennedy, Peter 23
Kenton, Devon 167
Kidney Bean Day (6 May) 73
Killerton House, Devon 11
King, Humphry 141
King, Richard John 7–9, 86
Kingsbridge, Devon 41, 55
Kingskerswell, Devon 15, 147
Kingsley, Charles 27, 85
Kingsteignton, Devon 57
Kirk, Robert 112
Kissing Day (3 May) 55
Knowles, Thomas 152, 154

Lanhydrock, Cornwall 185
Larkhill, Wiltshire 188
Launceston, Cornwall 124
Laycock, Charles Hey 12–15
Leeds Castle, Kent 138
Lent 39, 46–8
Lent-crocking (Shroving) 47–8,
    50, 51
Leusdon, Devon 178
Lew Trenchard, Devon 9–10
Ley, John 34
Limbo 105
Lincolnshire 34, 94, 159
Littleham, Devon 88
Llanelli, Wales 194 n.3
Lloyd, Temperance 161
Loddiswell, Devon 55
London 9, 11, 18, 152
    Fleet Street 142
    St Andrew Undershaft 54
    Tower of London 50
Longworth, Oxfordshire 25
Lorna Doone (novel) 25–7
Luffincott, Devon 122–5, 163, 171

Lundy, isle of 68
Luppitt, Devon 166
Luscombe, William John 55
Lustleigh, Devon 93
Lydford, Devon 27–9, 33
    Lydford Gorge 28–9
Lympstone, Devon 88
Lynton, Devon 26, 93

magic 30, 55, 124–5, 154, 163,
    171, 177
    black 189–90
    fairy 118
    of protection 166–70
    see also charming; witchcraft
Man, Isle of 82
Manaton, Devon 20, 110, 156, 172
Mari Lwyd 24
marriage 7, 58, 60
Marshall, Edward 142
Marwood, Devon 98–9
Marwood Legend, the 98
Mary, Virgin 85
Maundy Thursday 49–50
May Day 53–5, 78
May Dolls 54
mayors, mock 53
maypoles 53–4
Meavy, Devon 79
mediums 189–91
megaliths 77, 83, 86, 93, 102, 121
Membury, Devon 172–3
memes 3, 182, 185
Midsummer 58–9, 76
milking 80
Milky Way 69
Mills, Anne 136
Mills, Peter 187
Milton, John 106
mines 23, 31, 34, 132, 157–8, 159
    tin-mining 31, 158
molybdomancy 40
Monkleigh, Devon 169
Monmouth, duke of 25
Moon, the 70–1, 76, 77, 109,
    136, 181
Morchard Bishop, Devon 93

Moretonhampstead, Devon 13–14, 37, 54, 96, 197 n.44
  Dancing Tree 54
Most Haunted (TV show) 191
Mothering Sunday 48–9
Mundy, Matthew 26
Murray, John 9, 86
mushrooms 106

Ness beach, Devon 131
New Year 39–43
Newall, Venetia 2
newspapers 15, 16, 19, 69, 72, 90, 117, 123, 137, 157, 167, 169, 170, 187
Newton St Cyres, Devon 135
Nonconformists 152
Norfolk 151
Norns 99
North Molton, Devon 26, 57
North Tawton, Devon 177
Northcote, Rosalind 108, 112, 163, 167, 171
Northlew, Devon 95–6, 97
Norway 112

O'Neill, Hugh, earl of Tyrone 57
Oakford, Devon 11
Oare, Devon 26–7
Oatway, Kate 126–7
Odin 150
Okehampton, Devon 47, 106, 153, 154, 159, 164
  Okehampton Beating 56
  Castle 148
omens 23, 133, 139, 140, 156
oomancy 76
Ordulf, earl of Devon 183
Osbourne, Otto 157, 159
Ottery St Mary 60–61
  flaming tar barrels at 60
overlooking 163–4, 165, 166–8, 170–71, 173, 175
Oxenham family 140–45, 147
Oxford 19, 124
  Bodleian Library 124, 141
  Exeter College 124

Merton College 12
University of 19, 124

paganism 39, 75, 95, 121
Paignton, Devon 57–8
Paignton Pudding *see* Paignton, Devon
Palgrave, Francis 168
pancakes 46–7
paranormal 2, 113, 126, 186, 188, 191
Parker, Franke 122–3, 125, 171
Parker, John 189
Parkham, Exeter 164
parsons, conjuring *see* exorcism
Pascombe, Devon 124
pasties 49
Peach, Samuel 22
Pen Glaz 24
Pengelly, William 6
Penzance, Cornwall 144
Perry, Charity 171
Peterborough, Cambridgeshire 149
pigs 33–5, 51, 70, 74, 103, 166, 171, 177
Pine-Coffin family 138–9
pins 57, 166–7, 168–9, 170, 174
Pittminster, Somerset 111
Pitt, William 140
pixies 20, 29, 101–110, 112–16, 130
  pixy-leading 117–19
  sacrifices to 78
  see also fairies
ploughing 74–5, 111–13, 174
Pliny the Elder 172
Plymouth, Devon 6, 10, 23, 27, 56, 168, 185
Pole, John 143
Pole, William 143
poltergeists 134–5, 138, 149, 185, 188, 189–90
Pomeroy family 139–40
Ponsworthy, Devon 108
pools, 'bottomless' 31
Portledge Manor, Devon 138–9
Postbridge, Devon 16, 33, 157
  Grey Wethers (stone circle) 77
portents 43, 133, 147
  ghosts as 138–45

poultry 75–7
Poundsgate, Devon 92
Powderham Castle, Devon 67, 132
Princetown, Devon 84, 118, 148
public houses 21–2, 37, 58, 76, 81, 82,
    97, 114, 118, 121, 132, 157–8
purgatory 24, 59–60

Radford, Cecily 11
Radford, Emma Louise 11–12
Radford, George Haynes 11
Radford, Ursula Mary 12
railways 15, 34, 58, 67, 86–7
rain 65–8
Read, Bobby 92
Reformation 59, 152
remedies, folk 64, 80, 164, 175–9
Reynolds, Jan 92
rice 32
Richards, Sam 34
Ring-in-the-Mire, Devon 56
river deities 30
robins 42–3
Robinson, Bertram Fletcher 148, 150,
    151, 155
Romania 99
Romans 54, 115, 134, 190
rooms, secret 126, 134
Rose Ash, Devon 174
Roswell Incident 188
Rowbrook, Devon 29
Rowle, Roger 28
Rowling, J.K. 106
Royal Academy 7
Rudall, John 124
Rudkin, Ethel 34, 94, 159

sacrifices 30, 93, 189
    foundation 33–4, 72, 99, 190
    to pixies 78–9
St Andrews, University of 15
St Dunstan's Day (19 May) 100
St Frankin's Days (Francimass) 99
St George, Alice de 134
St George's Day (23 April) 73
St Lawrence 68–9
St Mark's Eve (24 April) 59

St Marychurch, Devon 109
St Michel de Rupe, Devon 94
St Stephen's Day (26 December) 43
St Swithin's Day 68
St Valentine's Eve 32, 45–6
Sampford Peverell, Devon 136–7, 159
Satanic Panic 190
Sayer, Sylvia 158
Scandinavia 34, 149
Schimmelreiter 23
Scotland 30, 31, 82, 131
scrofula (King's Evil) 172
Scunthorpe, Lincolnshire 160
Second World War 73
Seoul, Korea 41
Septuagesima 45
Seymour family 139
Shaldon, Devon 131
Sharp, Cecil 10
Sharp, John 10
Shebbear, Devon 95–7
sheep 21, 77–9, 81, 173, 176–7, 178
    sheep-shearing 80
    sheep-stealing 27, 28, 154
Sheepstor, Devon 115
Sherwell, Devon 67, 76
Shetland 35
shipwrecks 126–7, 129–30
Shobnall, Staffordshire 194 n.3
shoes 45, 48, 91
Shrovetide 46–7
Sidbury, Devon 56
Sidmouth, Devon 124, 172
    Sidmouth Gap 68
Simonsbath, Devon 31
Smith, Jem 167
Smith, prebendary 9
smuggling 75, 120, 126, 128, 130, 131,
    134, 137–8, 147, 155
Snell, F.J. 25, 32, 120
Sokespitch family 106–107
Somerset 18, 66, 73, 110–11, 116,
    121, 156
soul cakes 59–60
souling 59
Sourton, Devon 91, 96
South Molton, Devon 76, 119

South Tawton, Devon 141–2
South Zeal, Devon 140, 141–2, 157
Southey, Robert 8, 148
sowing 44–5, 67, 71, 73, 87
Speed, John 129
Spiritualism 15
Spreyton, Devon 21–2, 149
Springheeled Jack 147
'stag hunts' 96
Starcross, Devon 88
Sticklepath, Devon 21
Sting-Nettle Day 55
stone circles see megaliths
Stoney Middleton, Derbyshire 160
Stothard, Charles Alfred 7
Stothard, Thomas 7
stray sod see pixy-leading
Stukeley, William 83
Suffolk, duke of 126
suicides 20, 32
sun dogs (parhelion) 69
Syms, John 152

Tamar, river 30, 185
Tamara (nymph) 30
Taunton, Somerset 111
Tavistock, Devon 8, 11, 35, 54, 65, 77,
      94, 104, 105, 114, 116, 120, 148,
      160, 183
Tavy (giant) 30
Taylor, Grace 10
Teign, river 86
Teignmouth, Devon 88, 186, 188–90
Thames, river 30
Thoms, William John 1, 3, 180–81
tin-mining see under mines
'Tinners' Rabbits' 23, 158
Tiverton, Devon 11, 48, 56, 73, 136
toads 170–72, 174, 177, 178
toadstones 178
Tongue, Ruth 156
Tooker, Joan 141
Topsham, Devon 88, 93, 106
Tor, Devon 54
Torquay, Devon 6, 14, 55, 60, 68, 130
    Kent's Cavern 6, 130
    St Michael's Chapel 129

Torre Abbey, Devon 53, 128–9, 130
Torridge, river 85
Torridge (giant) 30
Totnes, Devon 120
Tracy, William de 152
Treleaven, Silvester 197 n.44
Trembles, Mary 161
tunnels, secret 126, 128–32
Turner, Mira 194 n.3
Twelfth Night (5 January) 43
Twining, Alfred Hughes 55

UFOs 101, 186–8
Ugborough Beacon 68
Upton, Devon 54

vampires 32, 186
Vaughan, Black 153–4
Vaughan, Thomas 154
Vaughan family 154
Venton, Devon 19–20

Walrond family 134
Wardour Castle, Wiltshire 145
Warne, Elizabeth 33
wassailing 40–42, 68
Waycott, Clifford 186–7
Weare Giffard, Devon 133–4
weather-lore 58, 64–72
Wellacott, W.T. 170–71
well-dressing 57
wells, holy 57
West Country Studies Library 16–17
West Down, Devon 75
Westaway, Henry 23
Westcote, Thomas 57
White Bird of the Oxenhams
      141–5, 147
Whitlock, Ralph 2, 39, 40, 93,
      108–9, 120
Whitsun 53, 56–7
whooping cough 176–8
Widecombe-in-the-Moor 19, 93,
      105, 110
    St Pancras' church 92, 158
    fair 21–4
Wild Hunt 24, 86, 87, 146, 149–50

will o' the wisps 108
Willey, Roger 186
Williamson, Cecil 158–9, 176
Wiltshire 2, 145
wind lore 65, 66, 71, 113
Winkleigh, Devon 115, 132
wise women *see* cunning-folk
wishing wells 57
witchcraft 18, 73–4, 80, 111, 145, 156,
        158, 161–79
    modern 159
    scratching witches 167–8
    witch bottles 169–70, 174
    white witches *see* cunning-folk
women, folklore about 74–5, 76, 117

Wood, Thomas 113
Woodbury, Devon 88
Woodley, Robert 141
Woolacombe, Devon 152
Woolfardisworthy, Devon 91
wreckers 126
Wren Boys 43

yarrow 45
Yelverton, Devon 115
Yenworthy Farm, Devon 26
Yeoford, Devon 22, 109–10
Yorkshire 121

Zeal Monachorum 141–2

Ingram Content Group UK Ltd.
Milton Keynes UK
UKHW021445040523
421228UK00006B/18